The
Chicken
Sisters

Also by KJ Dell'Antonia

How to Be a Happier Parent

Reading with Babies, Toddlers & Twos
(with Susan Straub)

The
Chicken
Sisters

KJ Dell'Antonia

TWO
ROADS

First published in Great Britain in 2020 by Two Roads
An Imprint of John Murray Press
An Hachette UK company

This paperback edition published 2021

1

Published by arrangement with G.P. Putnam's Sons, an imprint
of Penguin Books, a division of Penguin Random House LLC.
First published in the United States in 2020.

A CIP catalogue record for this title is
available from the British Library

Paperback ISBN 978 1 529 35064 7
Trade Paperback ISBN 978 1 529 35062 3
eBook ISBN 978 1 529 35063 0

Typeset in Sentinel

Printed and bound in Great Britain by Clays Ltd, Elcograf S.p.A.

John Murray policy is to use papers that are natural, renewable
and recyclable products and made from wood grown in sustainable forests. The
logging and manufacturing processes are expected to conform to the
environmental regulations of the country of origin.

Two Roads
Carmelite House
50 Victoria Embankment
London EC4Y 0DZ

www.tworoadsbooks.com

✕

To my grandparents,
who took me to Chicken Annie's.

To my parents, who once
boldly took me to Chicken Mary's.

And to Rob, Sam, Lily, Rory, and Wyatt,
all of whom understand the importance of
good fried chicken—and enjoying it together.

✕

The
Chicken
Sisters

The hit TFC series *Food Wars* is back! And this time, it's personal. We're looking for rival restaurants with a deeper connection—married chefs, best friends with dueling taco trucks. If you're a restaurant owner or worker who shares a bond with the crew at a competing restaurant in your town, we want to hear from you.

It's a fantastic opportunity to showcase your food on TV, expose your brand to a national audience, and finally resolve, once and for all, who's the best at serving up your local specialty. *Food Wars* judges will vote on who provides the best dining experience, the best menu, and, of course, the most delicious, most authentic version of whatever it is you do, and it will all be shared live via social media and then on produced episodes of our show. The winner will be awarded $100,000 to invest in their business. Past victors have franchised and been offered lucrative product-branding opportunities.

To be considered for the show, both restaurants must be willing and enthusiastic about participating and must be available for up to five possibly nonconsecutive days of filming. Applicants should e-mail no more than 300 words describing the rivalry and relationship between your competing restaurants, along with some images that capture the scene. We need to locate our next competitors RIGHT AWAY, so drop us a line ASAP! Sabrinasky@thefoodchannel.com

×

[DRAFT]
To: Sabrinasky@thefoodchannel.com
From: Amanda.Pogociello@gmail.com
Subject: The Chicken Sisters (application for Food Wars)

In 1883, my great-great-great-grandmother Margaret (Mimi) and her sister, Frances (Frannie), answered an ad placed by Fred Harvey for "young women, 18–30 years of age, of good character, attractive and intelligent" to come west for a grand adventure—working in his "Harvey restaurants" along the railroad line. They lived in a dorm and wore a uniform. Harvey took good care of his girls, or at least, he kept them on a short leash, and my grandma Mimi resented it. She met a man who worked on the railroad, packed up Frannie, and followed him to Merinac, Kansas. They had a house right by the depot, so Mimi opened her own railroad restaurant, selling fried chicken, potatoes, and biscuits with Frannie. Before long they were making more money with chicken than Harvey was, and he didn't like it, but then he was crushed between two train cars and it didn't matter anymore. Meanwhile, Frannie and Mimi had a big fight; then Frannie got married and started her own place out by the mines. Thus, Chicken Mimi's and Chicken Frannie's were born, and so was their rivalry.

Mimi's daughter was also Mimi, and she ran Mimi's, followed by my great-grandmother, my grandmother, and now my mother. Frances preferred boys; she passed Frannie's down to her son Frank and then his son Frank and then his son Frank, and I married his son Frank. That would be Frank the 4th. And I know what you're thinking, but we share .0391 percent of our DNA or something and it's not gross, so quit it.

×

[DRAFT]
To: Sabrinasky@thefoodchannel.com
From: Amanda.Pogociello@gmail.com
Subject: The Chicken Sisters (application for Food Wars)

Chicken Mimi's fried chicken is pan-fried and people love it. Chicken Frannie's fried chicken is deep-fat-fried and people love it too. I am probably the only person in the world who knows how both are made, but I never make either. I hate chicken. I mean, I like chickens, but I don't like to eat them. I've been a vegetarian since I was 6. I grew up working the counter for my mother, who ran Mimi's, which was started by my great-great-great-grandmother. Now I hostess for my mother-in-law at Frannie's, which was started by my husband's great-great-grandmother. My dead husband. There should be a word for that, like ex-husband, that would be easier.

×

[DRAFT]
To: Sabrinasky@thefoodchannel.com
From: Amanda.Pogociello@gmail.com
Subject: The Chicken Sisters (application for Food Wars)

My name is Amanda Pogociello. I am a hostess at Chicken Frannie's, just outside Merinac, Kansas. Our rival, Chicken Mimi's, is right on Main Street. The restaurants were started by two sisters who hated each other in the late 1800s, one mostly for people on trains passing through and the other mostly for the men who worked in the coal mines. For over a hundred years families around here have been choosing one or the other. Loyalty gets passed down in families, even. Only newcomers eat at both, although not very many people actually sit down and eat at Mimi's anymore. They just get their chicken and go home.

The sisters' feud lasted until their deaths, and it's still going. Nobody from Frannie's is allowed into Mimi's, and vice versa. Chicken

Mimi's thinks Chicken Frannie's is pretentious and stuffy, because we have a fancy bar and a large menu of more than just fried chicken, and in the '80s we served quiche. Mimi's serves chicken, biscuits, fried potatoes, iceberg lettuce salad, and pie. That's it. It's not even a real restaurant. It's a chicken shack with tables. At Frannie's we think that's ridiculous. We think Mimi's needs to grow up and take things seriously, and definitely clean itself up. Mimi's thinks Frannie's could just let people seat themselves and relax.

×

[DRAFT]
To: Sabrinasky@thefoodchannel.com
From: Amanda.Pogociello@gmail.com
Subject: The Chicken Sisters (application for Food Wars)

Please pick us. We're dying out here.

×

[DRAFT]
To: Sabrinasky@thefoodchannel.com
From: Amanda.Pogociello@gmail.com
Subject: The Chicken Sisters (application for Food Wars)

Chicken Mimi's vs. Chicken Frannie's would be the best *Food Wars* ever. They're less than 3 miles apart, they both specialize in fried chicken, they were started by sisters who never spoke to each other again, and now they are run by my mother and my mother-in-law. My mother doesn't speak to my mother-in-law, either.

×

[SENT]
To: Sabrinasky@thefoodchannel.com
From: Amanda.Pogociello@gmail.com
Subject: The Chicken Sisters (application for Food Wars)

Chicken Mimi's vs. Chicken Frannie's would be the best *Food Wars* ever. They're less than 3 miles apart, they both specialize in fried chicken, they were started by sisters who never spoke to each other again, and now they are run by my mother and my mother-in-law. They are both super-excited to be on *Food Wars*. We all love the show and we have seen every episode.

I work at Frannie's but I know everyone at Mimi's too. People in town always argue about which chicken is best. It's a good way to start a conversation, by asking which you like. The restaurants are very different, Mimi's is pretty simple and BYOB while Frannie's has a bar. Some people go to Mimi's because they really love the pie but it's better to go to Frannie's if you have someone in your family who is a picky eater or vegetarian because they will be able to find something that isn't chicken. Chicken Frannie's has fried mozzarella and cheesecake.

We are pretty close to Kansas City, so it isn't too hard to get here. They say people used to come up just to try the different chicken, back when this area was booming. Everybody wants to do this and we really hope you pick us.

×

[REPLY]
To: Amanda.Pogociello@gmail.com
From: Sabrinasky@thefoodchannel.com
Subject: Re: The Chicken Sisters (application for Food Wars)

Dear Amanda,

The Chicken Sisters sound intriguing. We are wrapping up *Rib Wars* in Kansas City and would like to come meet you. If everything's as you say, we'll start filming immediately. How's Wednesday at 2?

Sabrina Skelly, Host, Producer, *Food Wars*
The Food Channel

AMANDA

It was one thing to put a message in a bottle and another thing entirely when that bottle came back to you from across the sea with a genie stuffed in next to the reply. She had to rub the bottle now, right? She'd cast the spell, wished the wish, and asked in prayer, and she had received. It would be different if she didn't believe. It wouldn't have worked if she didn't believe. But of course, she did believe. She believed with all her heart and soul that *Food Wars* had the power to change everything, and she was right.

Later, she wished she'd been a little more specific.

It had been fun, sending the e-mail. And honestly, she figured the result would be a few weeks of dreaming, of imagining how *Food Wars* could make everything better, followed by a letdown when they said no or just never replied. It was a lottery ticket, minus the dollar she couldn't afford to spend.

Now she was sitting in her car outside Walmart, idly scrolling, a new habit born of an unreasonable expectation that somewhere in her phone was something that would change her mood, when the reply appeared, a response beyond her wildest dreams that sent an actual, literal chill through her body. She turned her car back on, abandoning her planned shopping trip, and backed out of the parking spot she'd just pulled into, narrowly missing a beat-up Camry. Her foot shook on the gas pedal. Her whole leg was quivering. *This is it,* she thought. *From now on, everything will be different.* Different, and better.

Better. She kept repeating that to herself, and that conviction, *really this is going to make things better,* helped her squash down any doubts about her mother or about Frannie's or about what the hell Merinac was going to make of *Food Wars* and vice versa. It carried her past the two miles of corn and soybean fields between Walmart and Nancy's house and right through her mother-in-law's back door, bellowing her name. She stopped short when she saw Nancy, already in the kitchen and looking worried at Amanda's wild entrance.

"No, no, it's good, it's something good. *Food Wars,* you know, the show with the restaurants that compete—they want to come here! To do us, us and Mimi's. *Food Wars!*" She waited for Nancy's response, biting her lip, fists clutched, a euphoric and probably goofy smile on her face. Because, *Food Wars.* Here!

Nancy smiled back, but it was a confused smile, a little dubious. She did not look thrilled. Why did she not look thrilled? Amanda did not need doubts right now; she needed enthusiasm. She grabbed the older woman's hands and squeezed them tightly. "They're going to come here. And film us, and we will win a hundred thousand dollars, and everyone will know who we are and want to eat here, and Frannie's will be famous." She let go of Nancy's hands and let her feet do the little dance they wanted so much to do, waving her arms in the air and shaking her hips. "Here, they're coming here, they're really coming here! And we will be huge." She grinned. "Huge!"

Once, long ago, that had been the plan for Frannie's. Back then, the town had been bigger and the world felt smaller, and Daddy Frank—great-grandson of the original Frannie, and father to Amanda's husband, Frank—was a leading figure in Merinac's business scene, a restaurant owner and real estate magnate with big ideas. A Banquet chicken dinner in someone's freezer or the sight of a Tippin's potpie at Albertsons would send him into a lengthy monologue about his dream of sharing Frannie's with the entire country, or at least the shoppers at major midwestern grocery stores. They all dreamed big along with him, back when the Franks had been in charge of the business plan, Nancy a capable and steady first mate, and Amanda a mother first, a student second, and a Frannie's fill-in hostess and waitress only a distant third.

Now, six years after the car crash that killed both Franks and left Nancy and Amanda in charge, the restaurant did little more than break even. Every day brought more bills and more tax forms and, for Amanda at least, a giant, soul-sucking fear that the future held nothing but more of the same. She often thought that Frannie's could spiral around the drain and finally get pulled under and no one would even notice that she and Nancy had gone with it.

But *Food Wars* would change all that.

Amanda looked down at her mother-in-law's tiny, tense frame, at the burgundy hair that was due for a color, thinning, just a little, in a way that was hard to disguise. *Please don't let her start in on the risks and the worries and the things that could go wrong. Please let her see how much she needs this, how much we all need this.*

Suddenly Nancy rushed forward and hugged Amanda, hard. "*Food Wars?* Us? Frannie's? You did this? You got them to come here?"

One more wish, granted.

"I did. I did!" Amanda squeezed her mother-in-law back, dancing them both back and forth before they let go. "I wrote them, and they're coming. They loved what I told them about the chicken sisters, and the history and everything."

"We'll be on TV." Nancy grabbed a chair from around her kitchen table and sat down on it, hard. "TV. Like Mae—TV. Frannie's."

Mae. Oh hell. But even the thought of her sister wasn't enough to suck the glory out of this moment. "Television, yes, and they do a lot of live bits on the Internet. Social media." Amanda loved those. She followed all of TFC's social media accounts, but *Food Wars* was her favorite. Nancy, though, looked at her blankly. "Like, they record a little bit, and people can watch it on their phones or computers if they follow the show. It usually takes a while for the episodes to get on television, but they do a whole bunch of live stuff while they're recording, to get people excited about it. It's sort of a cross between a web show and a regular show."

Nancy brushed that aside, as though Amanda had said *Food Wars* would also be available for pandas to watch from the zoo, and rushed on. "Television! Do you have any idea what this could mean?"

Amanda, who thought she did, laughed, and Nancy got out of her chair and grabbed Amanda and hugged her again, then stood back, still clutching Amanda's shoulders. "We have to win," Nancy said. "I mean, of course we'll win. There's not even a comparison." Nancy paused, and her voice, which had been getting increasingly higher, dropped. "In fact . . ."

Amanda knew where she was headed, and this, unlike the mention of Mae, did suck a little air out of her bubble. Mimi's and Frannie's both served fried chicken, yes. And they had the same kind of name. And they had been started by sisters. But from there, the similarities—and any competition—ended. Frannie's was open all day, with an extensive menu. Mimi's offered only dinner: chicken, biscuits, French fries, and salad, and off-the-menu doughnuts on Saturday mornings for those in the know. And of course pie, but only when the spirit moved her mother to bake. It wasn't a real restaurant so much as an erratic takeout joint, supported by loyal customers willing to overlook the way the place had run down over the years.

There was no way Mimi's could compete. And very little chance Amanda's mother would want to.

Nancy gazed at Amanda, her expression serious. "Did you ask your mother about this?"

Amanda shook her head. "I didn't think they'd actually come." It was only in the past few years or so that she'd really been able to have a conversation with her mother at all. Ask her about a wild, crazy dream that could never happen? No way. Nancy sat back down, and Amanda joined her across the table, sighing. "I know. I know. She might not do it. But Mimi's could use more business. And she doesn't really even have to do anything differently from what she's doing. She just has to let them film her."

Nancy, who had known Barbara for thirty-five years, drummed her fingers on the table. "She's not going to win, that's clear enough, although the money could sway her. Mimi's always needs the money."

She didn't have to tell Amanda that. Mimi's need for money was in Amanda's bones. It seeped through her pores; it beat through her veins. Mimi's needed money, Barbara needed money, but whether her mother would accept the connection between *Food Wars* and her bank account was an open question. Barbara didn't see things like other people did, and certainly not like Nancy did. Amanda glanced around her mother-in-law's kitchen, at the clear counters, the sun streaming through the neatly curtained windows with barely any dust in the air to set alight. Amanda had loved this kitchen since she first set foot in it, although it felt more spare now, almost too clean, if that were possible. It was so unlike anything she'd ever known—and, she thought with a little regret, not much like her own kitchen, either.

Nancy leaned forward and gently snapped her fingers in front of Amanda's face. "Come back," she said. "This isn't going to go away if you do." Amanda smiled. It was a familiar joke between them. "She'll do it," Nancy said. "Why would she pass something like this up?"

Because it was Amanda asking, maybe? She put her chin in her hands and jiggled her leg under the table, silent.

"I know your mom can be tough." Nancy knew better than anyone just how tough Amanda found her mother. "But this is different. She has to see it. She will see it. And your aunt will love it."

That, at least, Nancy had right. Aunt Aida, who was actually Amanda's great-aunt, had once had a thriving career in movies and television, until she'd faded out and moved in with Barbara. No one would welcome the arrival of cameras more than Aida. "She won't be there, though. She hardly ever goes to the restaurant."

"Well, talk about her, then. And talk about all the business Mimi's will get." Nancy stood up. "Come on, then. Off you go. I'd go with you, but we both know that won't help."

Not hardly. And wait—she was doing this now? Amanda had been thinking later tonight. Or tomorrow morning. Or never—what if *Food Wars* just showed up? Wouldn't Barbara have to go along with it?

Her mother never went along with anything. Not for the first time, Amanda wished her mother was more like her mother-in-law. Reluctantly, she got up, then hesitated, her hand on her chair. "But what if she says no?"

Nancy smiled—the reassuring smile that had carried Amanda through a lot of years, ever since she'd married Frank and traded in her mess of a family life for Nancy's ordered world.

"You won't know until you ask," she said. "And she's going to say yes. This is going to be the thing you want that she wants too." She squeezed Amanda's arm. "They're coming Wednesday? As in, tomorrow?"

"That's what they said." Tomorrow. Well, talking to Barbara would be over by then, anyway. And once *Food Wars* showed up, Barbara would be *their* problem. Amanda straightened up and smiled back at Nancy, her excitement returning. The money, and just the business, and all the publicity—this could save them all.

Unless, of course, Barbara said no.

Nancy was right, Amanda thought as she left the table and the cozy kitchen. The faster she asked, the sooner she'd know.

×

Away from Nancy, Amanda's resolve faded almost immediately. When was the last time she'd been by Barbara's place, anyway? It had to have been months ago—she remembered walking there with Pickle after getting coffee last fall. The dog hadn't survived the winter. He had been her and Frank's first baby, picked out of a litter by two utterly unprepared newlyweds months before Gus was born. After Pickle died, things got even lonelier. Gus started thinking about college in earnest. His younger sister, Frankie, started shutting herself in her tiny bedroom. If Pickle were here, Amanda would feel better about tapping on her mother's door, knowing she'd at least have a sympathetic ear when she got back into the car.

Which was pretty pitiful when you thought about it.

So instead of thinking about it, Amanda turned into Mimi's parking lot, wheels spinning at the switch to gravel, and pulled up next to an unfamiliar pickup. *Must belong to the new fry cook.* Amanda felt a little curiosity mixed in with her nervousness. Her mother's dog, Patches, a fat black-and-white beast with a big head, hauled herself up from beside the stoop, barked once, then came forward to nudge Amanda's hand. Amanda rubbed her under the chin.

Barbara appeared in the screen door exactly as if the dog had summoned her, and with her, the scent of Mimi's, of frying and spice, a little musty, a little sharp, once the smell of Barbara coming home from work and then, later, Amanda's own hair after every shift. Frannie's smelled like cooking when they cooked, like cleaning when they cleaned, like fresh napkins and cooked vegetables. Mimi's only ever smelled like Mimi's.

"Amanda?" Barbara stepped out and stood for a moment, surveying her younger daughter. Amanda realized she should have prepared some sort of opener. Why was it always so hard to even say hello to her mother? She started forward, considering a hug, but Barbara leaned back into the kitchen. "Andy? Andy, come on out here. I want you to meet Amanda."

Okay, that would work. Barbara had never hired anyone to cook for her before, although she always had counter and dishwashing help. From what Amanda had heard around town, the guy was basically some sort of weird charity project for her mother— good-looking (Mary Laura, Frannie's bartender, had reported she "wouldn't kick him out of bed for eating crackers") but more than a little down on his luck, which was obvious, because otherwise, why would he be here?

Andy had to duck a little to step out of Mimi's kitchen back door. He was tall and broad, and he wore an apron over a T-shirt and standard-issue chef's clogs with shorts, which revealed pale but muscular legs, abundant tattoos (basically a Mary Laura prerequisite), and a lower-arms-only farmer's tan that had to have been years in the making.

"This is Amanda, huh?" He held out a hand, and his big, warm grip covered Amanda's smaller hand entirely. He held it an instant too long, looking at her face with curiosity. "The one who can't come inside?"

"The one who can't come inside, yes. Amanda, this is Andy."

Amanda didn't need any guy's hand lingering on hers, but she could see his appeal, especially given how few men there were in Merinac whom Amanda and Mary Laura hadn't known since kindergarten. She'd be willing to bet Andy could see his appeal too, and that he had a long history of making good use of it.

Did Barbara know she'd brought a fox into the henhouse, or maybe, given the lack of employed straight single men in Merinac, the other way around? Amanda couldn't tell. Her mother's interest had shifted from her protégé back to Amanda, and Amanda was glad of an excuse to turn her attention away from Andy's deep brown eyes and their appraising gaze.

"Well, you didn't come by to meet Andy," Barbara said, glancing back into the kitchen. The screen door had drifted open, and she reached out to shut it again, firmly. "Or to see me. So what's on your mind?"

Amanda ignored the jab and plunged in. "I was wondering if you guys—Mom, if you—if you would be in a restaurant competition with Frannie's. On TV. It's called *Food Wars,* and they want to come, you know, kind of see how we compare, judge the chicken. It would be fun, and it's good for everybody. It doesn't really matter who wins."

Andy, who was leaning against the building, smiling generally at them both, probably enjoying an unexpected break in the day's work, suddenly stood back up. "Oh man, I love *Food Wars.* They really want to come here? How did you do that?"

Amanda wasn't sure how to respond. She preferred to think she did not need Andy's help, and further, she hoped to downplay her own level of instigation, letting her mother assume that somehow, through the magic of the Internet, perhaps, or just magic in general, *Food Wars* had happened. She hesitated, feeling, as she always did, the presence of the building itself, no longer the comforting refuge it had been when she had painted the large Chicken Mimi's sign still prominently displayed beside the door. Like her mother, Chicken Mimi's resented Amanda's defection and always would, and yet there was still a link that made Amanda feel as if she had both betrayed them completely and somehow never been gone at all. Certainly that was what her sister thought. *You can't even leave right,* Mae scoffed, and it was true. Amanda hadn't even known she was leaving, and God knew she hadn't gotten far.

Okay, focus. Her mother had just hired Andy—wasn't that maybe a sign that she, too, was ready for some change? Amanda kept going. "There's a cash prize, of course. A hundred thousand dollars. For the best chicken." And a lot of other stuff, but if she made it sound like just the chicken, at least her mother could believe Mimi's had a shot. "I think a lot of people watch the show."

Barbara was staring at her, her mouth a little open, her face unreadable. She frowned a little. "So is this something you want to do, then, this *Food Wars*?"

What to say to that? Generally, the last thing Barbara wanted was to do anything Amanda wanted. But maybe Nancy was right; maybe this was the one thing they could all share. "I just thought we could all use, Frannie's, too, a little boost, something to get more people to try us out. It's just—you know there aren't as many people coming to town anymore, and this would help." If only she knew what her mother wanted to hear. She could hear herself babbling, but she just didn't seem to be able to stop.

"It would help the whole town. They just want to come film for a few hours, to start. Just get to know us, and that's probably it. Not a big deal, really. Except it might bring in business."

Barbara crossed her arms. "The trouble with you, Amanda, is that you never know what you want. Do you think this is a good idea, or don't you?" She turned to Andy. "It sounds ridiculous. You like it?"

Amanda held her breath. It might seem like Barbara wanted their opinion, but in Amanda's experience she never did. Andy should shrug, maybe, leave it up to her, let her decide. She tried to send him thought messages. *Tone it down, keep it light.*

Which is exactly what he did not do. "Are you kidding? I love it. And it's totally a big deal! It's awesome. Seriously, *Food Wars*? Here?" He looked at Barbara, who was still standing with her arms crossed, then back at Amanda, as if expecting her to share his enthusiasm. "So do they want to do a full thing, like all three competitions, or just the food taste-off?"

Had this guy not figured Barbara out at all? This was not the way to get her on board. Amanda backtracked frantically, trying to make it seem as if *Food Wars* still had to be earned, as if it was a challenge. "They just want to come check us out to start. Probably nothing will come of it. I mean, once they see this place . . ."

Her mother, who had been looking thoughtfully at Andy, swung her eyes back to Amanda, squaring her shoulders. *Too far,* damn it. Andy started to speak again—really, for a probable meth head with tattoo sleeves and as many piercings as he had, he was a strangely bubbly guy—and this time Amanda shot him a deadly glare. He needed to shut up, and he needed to do it now.

The expected explosion never came. Instead, Barbara took a

very visible deep breath, then looked from Amanda to Andy, as if weighing their relative merits. Her eyes narrowed as she asked the question Amanda had been praying would not come up. "What does Mae think of all this?"

"I don't know, Mom. I haven't asked her." And she wasn't planning to. She didn't need Mae's help with this one. In fact, she needed Mae to stay far away, which shouldn't be a problem.

Barbara turned to Andy. "I don't know if I've mentioned that my other daughter, Mae, has been doing something that sounds like this *Food Wars*. At least, it's a show on television. Reality television. *Sparkling*, I think it's called."

Andy's face lit up. "Wait, *Sparkling*? Your daughter is Mae Moore? Mae Moore who wrote the big clutter book?"

Barbara seemed pleased, but Amanda rolled her eyes. There was no way this project of her mother's, washed up for who knew what reason in the backwaters of Kansas and probably living in the trailer park east of town, knew who Mae was.

Andy grinned. "There's a girl who can declutter my underwear drawer anytime."

He had a real gift for the conversation stopper. Barbara looked at him strangely, and Amanda intensified her glare.

Andy caught himself immediately. "It's a quote! From a column, by this guy, he mostly writes about sports, but every year he does this whole holiday thing about hating the Williams-Sonoma catalog. And she was in it— Never mind." Andy's face was genuinely red, and against her better judgment Amanda found herself softening toward him. "It's probably not what he should have said either. Sorry. I didn't mean it like that."

He read. He hated the Williams-Sonoma catalog. He could tell, at least kind of, when he was being an asshole. Amanda was starting to get Mary Laura's crackers-in-bed call, but seriously, he liked Mae? Apparently, he couldn't see through a selfish, superficial fraud. At least that meant he couldn't possibly have actually watched *Sparkling.* Amanda had, and Mae was a disaster on it—stiff and fake and judgmental. One more reason Merinac was better off without her.

Barbara turned back to Amanda. "I think I'd like to know what Mae thinks," she said, and then, as if that wasn't enough: "Actually, I think I'd like to have Mae here, if I'm going to do this. After all, you'll be with Nancy. You're no help to me. I need Mae."

Amanda should have known; she absolutely should have known. Why had she not seen this coming? She expected the needling about her choosing Nancy over her own mother—that was an old refrain and one that hardly got to her anymore. But the rest—of course her mother would want to use this as bait to get Mae home.

But Mae wouldn't take it. There was no way. Mae hadn't been back in Merinac in six years, and she had *Sparkling,* as terrible as it was. The last thing Mae would want her picture-perfect life associated with was a dump of a chicken shack in the middle of Kansas, and especially one with Barbara's house looming out back—proof positive that Mae Moore was not who she said she was. *Sure, go ahead, ask Mae. But when Mae says no—*

"She's really busy, Mom. I don't think there's any way she could do this on such short notice. They're right in the middle of shooting their whole *Sparkling* season." Amanda knew that because Instagram. Because Facebook. Because Twitter. Because Mae made sure everybody knew it, just like everybody had to know about her perfect handsome husband and her beautiful apartment and her adorable flawless children. But that was okay, because it would hold Mae exactly where she was, which was as close as Amanda could stomach her. And Barbara had said, *If I'm going to do this.* She was more than halfway there, and even if Amanda couldn't imagine why, she would take it. "Andy will help you, though. And whoever else is working. I know they will."

Andy, beaming, conspicuously struggled to match her calm tone. "I think they'd be pretty enthusiastic," he said to Barbara. "I think they'd be disappointed if we—if you—said no." He laughed. "I know I would. I love *Food Wars*."

Barbara crossed her arms over her chest, and the smock she always wore atop her shapeless dress strained. "I'm still going to ask her, though," she said. "This is important, right? If we win, if our chicken is the best, you said we get a hundred thousand dollars?"

Well, yeah, but Mimi's wouldn't win. Amanda could see in Andy's face that he knew it, too. "We'll all get lots more business, too," Amanda said. "That's worth a lot."

"I'll ask Mae." Barbara turned to the screen door, which had swung open again, getting ready to go inside.

"But wait, Mom," Amanda said. "If she won't come, you'll do it anyway, right?"

Barbara paused, her hand on the door. "I don't know," she said. "Having Mae here would make it easier. It's nice to have a little family support." Dig, dig. But Amanda could let it go, if Barbara only said yes.

Andy went over to her. "We can do it," he said. "She's right, it will bring people in." He grinned. "It'll help you pay my salary."

The screen door again swung open, and this time Andy walked up the stoop and examined the latch. "I can't imagine why that keeps opening," he said. "I looked it over when we took the storm door off, and it's fine. It should hold."

Amanda met her mother's eyes. So there was at least one other thing about Mimi's that Barbara hadn't told Andy yet. Mimi's itself would have an opinion, and Mimi's would make that opinion known. The kids in town were always making jokes about Barbara's old house being haunted, especially around Halloween—and with its Victorian gables and worn gingerbread trim, it looked the part. But it was utilitarian Mimi's where, every so often, the Moores were pretty sure someone—probably Mimi herself, or that's what they liked to believe—lingered. It wasn't something they talked about much, even among themselves, and it was hard to imagine

Barbara mentioning it to Andy, who straightened up and shrugged. "Some breeze, I guess."

Amanda tried to take advantage of this moment of family solidarity and found herself, as silly as it seemed, trying to appeal to Mimi's as well. "Mimi's can stand on its own, Mom. You don't need Mae. You should just do things the way you always have."

Barbara blew out an impatient breath. "I don't need either of you, obviously." She glared at Amanda. "If I did, I'd be in big trouble. If Mae wants to come do this *Food Wars* thing, I'll do it. Otherwise, no. You're right. We should just keep doing things the way we always have."

This time, Barbara walked inside and spoke over her shoulder. "I'll call her tonight." She slammed the door behind her, and Amanda found herself left on the patio with Andy, who looked oddly cheerful.

"Damn it," she said, unable to help herself.

"She'll get over it," said Andy. "Do you think your sister will come?"

Amanda shook her head. "She hates it here," she said. Merinac had chafed at Mae since her sister turned fourteen and formulated, almost overnight, a plan for escape that she had always refused to believe Amanda didn't want to share. *Nobody ever did anything here*, she said. *Get out or die trying, unless you want to die here.* When Amanda, shyly, had confided in her sister that she was pregnant after her first semester at the local college, Mae had given her one shocked, terrible look and then marched out of the room, returning with the phone book. "We can take care of this," she'd said savagely. Stunned, Amanda had knocked the book out of her hands. Mae never believed that Amanda had wanted Gus, wanted the life she chose. Not then, not when Frankie had been born, not after Frank had died. Not ever, and Amanda both loved and hated her for it.

"That's okay," said Andy, leaning on one of the picnic tables. "She'll do it anyway. I mean, it would be cool if Mae came. I don't know your sister, but she obviously likes being on TV. And cleaning things. And I don't know if you know, but your mom's house is—"

Amanda had to laugh at that. "Oh, I know. Mae knows, too. It's always been that way."

Patches came back to Amanda and nudged her hand for petting again. Amanda rubbed the dog's soft head, still missing Pickle, and Andy came forward and knelt in front of Patches, rubbing under her chin. The dog instantly abandoned Amanda and dropped to the ground, rolling over and presenting an enormous belly to Andy for rubbing. *Traitor.*

But that charm could be useful. "You think Mom will do it even if Mae doesn't come?" She should know—she was Barbara's daughter, after all—but she had no clue. Who cared if this guy knew it? He probably wouldn't be around long anyway.

Andy looked up at Amanda. "Sure," he said. "It's too good to pass up. But you'll ask Mae, right?"

Oh, she'd ask. Andy just didn't need to know what she was asking for. All Mae really had to do was tell their mom it was a great idea—or better yet, say she was coming and then bail. Still, he was just a little too enthusiastic about even the possibility that Mae would appear.

"You wouldn't want Mae here," Amanda said. And really, he wouldn't. The thought was awful. "She's—she's too many cooks in anybody's kitchen." And she would think *Food Wars* was stupid and piddling, even while she took the whole thing over. That was Mae's specialty. She always made it look easy, and she always made you feel dumb for caring.

"I'd deal. Listen, try, okay? And I'll get your mom to sign on either way." He grinned, and it was a very appealing grin to conspire with. Amanda grinned back. Why not?

Barbara came to the door. "We need to get back to work," she called, and Andy rose easily, seemingly not at all bothered by the implied reproof in her words.

"Sure thing. Gotta be friendly with the competition, though, right?" He turned back toward Amanda. "I'll call you. I can get your number from your mom, okay?"

Amanda nodded. They probably should keep in touch—it made sense, and it would be much easier than talking to her mother.

And it would maybe even be kind of fun, if he was this excited about *Food Wars*. Even if he did think he'd like Mae. He'd learn, or rather, he wouldn't, because Mae would not be here.

Amanda took out her phone as she walked back to her car, typing as she went. Mae had to do this for her. She just had to.

And then it would all begin.

MAE

Mae Moore was wearing her fiercest boots.

It was May—never, despite the name, Mae's luckiest month—so strappy, expensive, high-heeled sandals might have been more appropriate for a meeting in the skyscraper that housed Glorious Home Television. But this was a big meeting. An important meeting, and possibly, as suggested by that worrying text from Lolly, not a good meeting. Which meant that Mae wanted both feet solidly on the ground and her thin skin well covered.

Standing in her Brooklyn closet, she'd chosen the tough-girl, ass-kicking, take-no-prisoners boots whose heels now hit the marble floors of the lobby with conviction as she flashed the ID card around her neck to Marcos and Jim at the security desk. Marcos pressed the button and waved her grandly through as he always did. They'd been here when she'd first walked into the building for her audition, wearing, she suddenly realized, these same boots. She hoped they weren't about to see her walk out the doors for the last time as well.

Mae quashed that feeling immediately. Things were going great. She and Lolly had bonded from their first shoot together, and she knew Lolly enjoyed having her on set. She was absolutely going to get the full co-hosting gig. Alone in the elevator (ignoring the camera), she struck the Wonder Woman pose that was supposed to fill your body with confidence. *This is going to be fine. No, great.* They were going to tell her that she'd rocked the five-show audition. Lolly, single and child-free, needed the vibe Mae brought to the lifestyle-redesign show. Mae, married with children, appealed to viewers scrambling to balance work and family and needing a neat, organized home to calm the chaos. Lolly filled closets. Mae cleaned them. And cleaning them, Mae knew, was exactly what most people craved in a consumer-crazy world. The success of her book had proved it.

So this was just going to be a good meeting. A renewal of her role for the rest of the season. A discussion of the immediate future, which included the next few episodes of *Sparkling*, and the slightly more distant future, which Mae thought should include a pilot episode for a show that was all Mae. She mentally ticked off the reasons why: Half a million followers across Instagram, Twitter, and Facebook. The book, *Less Is Moore*, named after her lifestyle philosophy. The contract for a second book, which she would absolutely figure out soon. The e-mail she sent out to more than twenty thousand subscribers every month. She was ready.

But the Wonder Woman pose and mental reminders of her successes never did quite enough to banish the out-of-place feeling Mae had every time she stepped out of the elevator at GHTV. The *Sparkling* set, which was staged each week in houses of ordinary, messy people with lives she was used to—that was one thing. But the enormous images of *Incredible Homes* that covered the walls, stills from the network's most popular show, were not places Mae Moore would ever belong, and the offices themselves, filled with women in clothes and shoes Mae could price instantly, no matter how foolish she thought them, made her feel as though she'd just got off the bus from Kansas.

Lolly was waiting for her as the elevator door opened. As she grabbed Mae's arm and pulled her into a practiced hug, she whispered in Mae's ear, "Okay, get ready. You're going to be fine, okay? This will all work out. Now, smile!"

Lolly couldn't have been less reassuring if she had tried. Now, without Mae getting to say so much as a word, Lolly swept her into a big conference room, with a long wall of windows looking out over Central Park and a long wall of interior windows allowing everyone who walked by to see who and what was happening on the network's main business stage. Smile-smile, kiss-kiss for Christine, their senior producer, in shoes identical to Lolly's. Smile-smile, kiss-kiss for Christine's boss, Meghan, in pumps of equal heel height but more gravitas, suggesting not so much that she took taxis everywhere but that she never, ever left this building. Smile-smile, kiss-kiss for the new social media director, for Meghan's assistant, and for Christine's junior producer, all glowing with confidence and sheer lip and cheek stain.

As she settled into her chair, trying to calm the nerves that Lolly's words had lit up, Mae's phone quacked loudly. No, seriously, she hadn't had the sense to put it on vibrate? Kicking herself, Mae grabbed for her phone in the pocket of the bag she'd set down next to her chair. As she fumbled with the mute switch, she read her sister's text:

FOOD WARS WANTS TO COME HERE. MOM NEEDS THIS. BUSINESS SUCKS, BUT SHE WON'T DO IT WITHOUT YOU. SHE'S GOING TO CALL YOU, CAN YOU JUST TELL HER YOU'LL COME AND THEN I'LL WORK IT OUT FROM HERE SO YOU DON'T HAVE TO? SERIOUSLY IT WILL BE GREAT FOR MOM. I JUST NEED YOU TO HELP ME GET HER THERE.

Shit, what? As much as she knew she needed to tune in to the women around her, Mae was fully distracted by Amanda's words. *Food Wars?* The competition show? Instantly, Mae could see how *Food Wars* would love the rivalry between Mimi's and Frannie's. And just as instantly, she could see what Amanda apparently was totally clueless about—that a reality show would steamroll their mother and rip the lid off every awful thing about Merinac, their house, their childhood, everything. She knew how this worked. Amanda, apparently, still believed in unicorns and thought this was a good idea. But Mae knew that about her sister, too. *Damn it, Amanda. Just stay in your own yard, will you?*

Christine was pouring water for Meghan. The new junior producer and Lolly were comparing shoes. Ordinarily, Mae would be regretting sitting down first, when clearly the protocol was more preening and socializing, but under the circumstances, she grabbed the chance to reply.

Hell no it would not be great, what are you thinking? Cameras in mom house fucking disaster. No way. Will deal with $$ later.

Not that her mom would let her send money. Not that she had much to spare, either. She could see the little dots indicating that Amanda was already replying, but Mae stuffed the phone, now totally silenced, back in its pocket. *Food Wars* on her home turf was not something she could think about right now, let alone whatever was going on with her mom.

In that tiny interval, the other women had all seated themselves, and Christine was now looking pointedly at Mae, who quickly put her empty hands on the table. The other woman gave a tiny shrug and looked away, and Mae felt dismissed, an inexperienced girl who did not know better than to text during an important meeting. She squared her shoulders, and Christine, no longer looking at Mae, addressed them all generally.

"*Sparkling,* as you know, is doing well. Very well, in terms of audience. And we did get some nice audience feedback on the five Mae episodes. Lolly, every woman on Instagram wants to be you, or at least have you come spark up their space, and, Mae, lots of them want you to come clean out their fridge."

Mae felt her smile tighten. She'd cleaned one refrigerator in one episode and then kicked herself for it for days. That wasn't who she was. She brought serenity and calm to the homes they redesigned, not just bleach wipes. But apparently once had been more than enough.

Christine went on. "We've been talking with our sponsors," she said, "and we're hearing mostly good things. Lolly, the message to you is mostly 'carry on,' and we've had a lot of interest in you doing actual advertising spots for products, in particular from Flowergram and Storage Store."

Lolly beamed and wiggled her shoulders. "I love Flowergram," she said. "I wish we could give every client, like, a biweekly delivery from them. Maybe they'd do, like, a branded *Sparkling* bouquet, one that really lasts."

"Oh, that's a great idea," said Meghan's assistant. "You could choose the flowers. A Lollygram!"

Lolly squealed. "I love it!"

Christine looked pleased, and Meghan nodded, and the assistant began tapping notes frantically into her phone. Mae boggled at the way that had flowed—a Lollygram was not an advertisement for *Sparkling*, as Christine had first suggested; it was an advertisement for Lolly—but that was the way things fell for Lolly. The assistant, Mae could tell, adored her. Everyone adored her. Flowergram would have a new spokesperson before it knew what had hit it. Why couldn't Mae do it like that?

"Mae," Christine said, "Flowergram has expressed some concerns to me about your Instagram."

Mae realized that she'd tilted her chair up on its front two legs— a nervous habit. The chair slammed down with emphasis, and Christine's eyebrows went up slightly again as she continued. "Apparently, you posted an image of a cabinet full of flower vases and a caption urging people to get rid of crap and clutter. Flowergram felt that you were denigrating its product."

Mae laughed. No one else did. "But wait," she said. "Old flower vases are, like, the definition of clutter. No one needs those. You need *one*. Maybe two. And not the ones that come with flowers." She turned to Lolly for support. "You need nice ones. You'd say that too, Lolly."

Christine answered. "But Lolly wouldn't put that on her Instagram. And she also wouldn't say, as you have said more than once while taping, that getting organized isn't about cute containers. The Storage Store *is* about cute containers. That didn't make them happy."

Lolly kicked Mae under the table and grinned. "I love cute containers," she said. "Mae loves cute containers too, don't you, Mae?"

Was this what Lolly had been talking about? She could handle this. "I love the Storage Store," she said. Of course she did. She would live in the Storage Store if she could. She just didn't think buying a bunch of containers was the first thing people should do. "Just edit it out if I say something that sounds like I don't," she suggested. Did they think she would mind? "Useful cute containers are great. Flatware dividers. I love those."

"Shelf separators," Lolly offered.

"Yes. And things that attach cords to the edges of desks."

"Tupperware that really stacks."

"Absolutely."

"Toothbrush holders."

"Ew, no. Those get gross. And if your toothbrush is on the counter it's collecting germs."

Christine waved a hand in between them. "It's not funny to the Storage Store," she said. "And if it's not funny to the Storage Store, it's not funny to me. Mae, your attitude toward the products of our sponsors is a real problem. It's not just containers. If you open a pantry, you're down on Nabisco. In a closet, it's H&M and disposable fashion. There's only so much we can do in postproduction. You never stop."

As Christine spoke, Mae felt a chill spread from the back of her neck forward. Without meaning to, she lifted her thumb to her mouth and bit the hangnail that was always there. When she caught it, she brought her hand down, quickly, ready to defend herself. Clutter was clutter. Nabisco was junk food. Disposable fashion wasn't good for anyone, not the people who made it or, in the long run, the overwhelmed people who bought it. But Christine wasn't done.

"I don't think you've fully understood who we are and what we do, Mae. We're not making little videos for our neighbors in Kansas. We're a national television program, funded by advertising and sponsorship, that needs to appeal to the customers of those businesses."

With the mention of Kansas, Mae's crossed leg went to the ground, the soles of both boots firmly on the floor. "I can understand that," she said, making purposeful eye contact. Had Christine mentioned Kansas deliberately? Was it a random insult, or one directed at Mae personally? "I hadn't thought of it that way. I can help people who have"—she chose her words carefully—"too much of certain things without bringing up the sponsors. I really can. It's not a problem—well, it is a problem—"

Meghan joined in. "It really is a problem."

There—someone got it! And not just someone—the boss. Perfect. Glad to have an ally, Mae rushed on. "It's a terrible problem. We really have way too much stuff, and when clothes and things are so cheap, it's hard for people to resist . . ."

Lolly kicked her under the table, hard. Looking at Meghan, Mae realized she'd made a mistake. That was not the problem she meant. Mae's chill came back, more strongly this time. She'd misread the most senior woman there, and there was no way to walk it back.

Meghan's face was serious. "That may be a problem for some families, Mae, but for us, unhappy sponsors are a much bigger problem. And many viewers feel that you are lecturing them. Your results are good, but you're very judgmental about the things that make people need us in the first place."

"I'm sorry. I can change that. I really can." Mae leaned forward. Couldn't they see she heard them? That this was something she could fix?

"We appreciate your willingness to try, Mae, we do. But for now we're going to continue the season without you. We may audition another co-host, or we may go forward with just Lolly. Or we might come back to you. But for now, we're not convinced you're right for this role, and we need to move forward without you. We'll be in touch." She picked up the folder she'd carried into the meeting and leaned over the table to shake Mae's hand. "We know you'll do some great things in the interval, and if this doesn't work out, that you'll make a big success without us, Mae. And we really appreciate all your hard work."

That's it? Apparently, it was. Everyone was getting up. Meghan was insisting on shaking her hand, as was Christine's new assistant, who looked like she was taking mental notes for when she got the chance to fire someone someday. Everyone filed out of the room, and Mae, holding her eyes wide open to keep tears from coming, turned away from Lolly and walked after them, willing Lolly to just let her go, but no. Of course not.

Lolly grabbed her and hugged her. "I'm so, so sorry! They made me totally promise not to tell you. But I knew you'd be okay! You're so strong. And you have so many ideas, Mae. You don't need *Sparkling.*"

Mae willed herself to speak without her voice cracking, trying to focus on the anger she felt instead of the mess of sorrow and fear. "I'll be fine," she said, and as she spoke, an idea flashed into her mind. The best idea. The perfect idea. "I'll be totally fine, you're right. In fact, I didn't say anything in there, and don't tell anyone yet, but I just got an invitation to lead a *Food Wars* feature."

Lolly looked surprised, and Mae rushed on. "It will just be a few episodes, but I'm pretty excited about it. I really can't share any details. Anyway, we'll keep in touch?"

"Of course," Lolly said, and based on the look of interest in her eyes, Mae thought that she just might mean it, for once. "I can't wait to hear about it."

"I'll text you updates. Remember, though, don't tell anyone yet." Lolly would, of course, and that was fine with Mae. She turned on one boot heel, hoping Lolly wouldn't follow. The elevator seemed to take forever to come, but when it did, it was blissfully empty. Mae didn't bother striking a Wonder Woman pose this time. She leaned into the corner, wiped her eyes with the back of her hand, and took her phone out of her bag. Apparently, she was going to Kansas.

×

By the time Jay got home from work, Mae was ready.

The apartment was spotless—sparkling, even. She'd booked tickets—taking two kids and a nanny to Kansas on a day's notice wasn't cheap, but she could write it off. She'd primed all her social media accounts with teasers. She was taking some time off from *Sparkling.* Exploring a new opportunity. She couldn't say more— but stay tuned! Her audience would be stoked. Now she just had to persuade Jay to see it her way.

Jessa, at her request, had taken the kids to the park and then to their favorite local diner for dinner. Mae used the time packing and stewing, both literally—making a lamb and tomato stew that Jay loved—and figuratively. Every scene she'd recorded at *Sparkling* had flowed! She and Lolly were great together—anyone could see that. And didn't the shopaholic Lolly need a foil? Or at least some- one to bring her down to earth?

In her own home, Mae had established sleek white perfection. Clear surfaces. Just the right things on every shelf. Unstuffed drawers that opened easily. Cabinets that held only what fit—useful, well-cared-for things that did their jobs and then went back where they belonged without jostling or juggling or pushing other things aside. The afternoon's cleaning binge had been unnecessary, really, but unless you kept on top of things, removing the excess and keep- ing just what you loved and what worked, everything piled up.

Just for the pleasure of it, she opened the drawer next to the stove, a deep drawer that moved quietly on slides she'd installed herself. There was the space for the Dutch oven, now in use on the stove. There was the spaghetti pot. There were the two saucepans. Those, plus the two frying pans that stood up in another cabinet, were both exactly what she needed and all she wanted.

Mae took a deep breath as she gazed down into the space, consciously dropping her shoulders from her ears. Who needed meditation when you had clean drawers? *Ooh, that was brilliant.* She grabbed her phone, took a quick picture of the drawer, then used an app to layer the words over the photo and share it to Instagram: *Who needs meditation when you have clean drawers? #cleanspace calmmind.* That was a Mae Moore mantra. Once she left her mother's house, she built her whole life around *clean space, calm mind,* and it worked.

But it was hard to stay calm when other people were so frustrating. Throughout that entire meeting, she'd wanted to shake Christine out of her ridiculous shoes. Mae had come home and composed an e-mail with all the things she hadn't been able to say—a gracious acceptance that of course they'd audition others, a list of all the reasons she was perfect for this job, and a promise to change in all the ways they needed her to change—and then she'd added that her hiatus from *Sparkling* was perfectly timed, because she'd been asked to do a few episodes of *Food Wars. Smoke that,* Christine. She had other opportunities, so *Sparkling* better snap her back up.

No need to mention that *Food Wars* had nothing to do with her and everything to do with her mother's chicken restaurant, which no one in New York even knew existed. Barbara would want as little camera time as possible, and that suited Mae, who was happy to be the face of Mimi's revival. She'd be on set, sharing with her five hundred thousand current followers and capturing *Food Wars* followers, which would make her even more attractive to *Sparkling* and her book publisher. Amanda's stupid idea was going to save her.

If the *Food Wars* episodes were popular enough, they could push Mae beyond *Sparkling* entirely. She could leap straight to a show of her own. One *Food Wars* restaurant had been given its own show—the one that made the crazy wedding cakes in Vegas. It could happen, and it was even more likely to happen to someone like Mae, who was already on the edge of viral. Gazing at the *Food Wars* website (and avoiding the headline story of the barbecue chef whose highly falsified culinary résumé had come to light during a recent taping), Mae had contemplated the crossover between home organization and food and come up with the perfect solution, and one that solved the dilemma of her next book as well. She could help people organize and simplify their kitchens, shopping lists, and family cooking habits. It was perfect: *Less Is Moore in the Kitchen.*

Mae was almost convinced that this was better than the *Sparkling* plan, except that *Sparkling* was a done deal, and this would require connecting a whole lot of dots. She had her foot in the door, though, and that was what mattered. She would make it happen, and once she had a television-size fan base, one that wanted her specifically, she'd be set.

She placed her laptop on the counter and started typing before she forgot any of her great ideas, but just as she'd started playing around with an actual pitch, she heard the clink of the gate outside their stoop. Quickly, she stowed her laptop away. This was not the day to be working when Jay came home.

The door swung open, and Jay burst in with his usual vigor, one arm behind his back. He hugged her with the other and produced, with a flourish, a bottle of champagne. "I'm so sorry," he said, and then, as he caught sight of the look on her face—Champagne? She knew he hated her job at *Sparkling,* but champagne?—quickly went on. "Not to celebrate. But my mom always says bubbles aren't just for when you're already feeling bubbly."

If Mae had hated Jay's mom before, she really hated her now. That was exactly the kind of empty pronouncement she would make, probably just before ignoring her grandchildren and leaving on a yearlong cruise around the world. Mae shrugged, and Jay leaned down and hugged her again around the bottle, his tall form making her feel even smaller than usual. "You'll come up with something great to do next. I know you will."

He meant this nicely, he really did, and it *was* sweet, especially after all the arguments they'd had over *Sparkling* in the first place. She hugged him back. She needed him to be on board with her plans, and while she knew that wasn't likely to be his first reaction, she also knew he could get there, if he just understood how perfectly this could all work out and what it could mean for her. That meant she needed to give him calm, collected Mae. Mae who knew what she was doing. Mae who took setbacks gracefully and was always moving upward.

"I already have an idea," she said. "But sit. Eat. Come on, I made us dinner."

Jay looked at the table set for two—nothing in front of the high chair and the booster seat. "Where are Madison and Ryder?"

"I sent them with Jessa to the diner, just for an hour."

"Which means you have a plan." He set down his workbag on the counter and started up the stairs as Mae picked up the bag to hang it in the hallway. "I'm changing first," he said. "I can't handle a plan in my work clothes."

When he came back, now in yoga pants, black hair mussed from where he'd pulled on his favorite 76ers T-shirt, he sat down and looked at the table appreciatively while Mae handed him his plate. "This is service," he said. "Very *Mad Men*."

Mae took a champagne glass from the shelf and began to pour as she had learned from watching him, glass tilted, but not too carefully, because those who were used to champagne handled it with a certain insouciance. Inside, she was calculating. Champagne meant an extra hundred calories, which meant she wouldn't eat the rice she had put on her plate to go with the stew, but she'd have to make it look like she did, because her avoidance of rice—and white bread, and pasta, and all of their many high-glycemic friends—annoyed Jay endlessly.

He took his glass, then held it out. "I know. We're not toasting. This sucks. But, Mae, it's also your chance. Our chance. You're always talking about seizing opportunities, and we could grab this one. Take my mom up on her plan, go to India, meet her family. Take a break from New York."

The fight. The same fight. How could he do this now? His plan, again—his ridiculous plan, born of, she had to admit, the worst deal he'd ever been staffed on, a merger between two monstrous restaurant chains based on the West Coast that had had him pulling constant all-nighters and taking the red-eye for months. His plan was for him to quit. *I just need to take some time,* he kept saying. *I can't even figure out what I want when it's like this.* A sabbatical, he kept calling it, but it wasn't, not the way he wanted to do it, with no strings from the firm and thus no promise that they'd bring him back, even though he kept insisting they would. It was throwing himself into the abyss, and he wanted to take her with him.

This wasn't fighting fair. He hadn't even given her a chance to tell him what she wanted before he dumped this on her. She got it. He hated the hours. She'd hated the hours, too, back when they were both starting out in consulting, but unlike Jay, she was used to starting at the bottom of the ladder. Hell, where she came from there hadn't even been a ladder. The consulting job they had once both had was a miracle for her, a major score, and she would have stuck it out, too, if they hadn't agreed she should be the one to quit when Ryder arrived and everything got, not twice as hard, but seemingly exponentially so. It was one thing to have a nanny—they still had a nanny, especially now that Mae had built up her new business and written the book—but for both of them to stay free to work eighteen-hour days meant two nannies, really, and then why even have kids in the first place? But if one of them wasn't going to stick with a steady paycheck and health insurance, they should never have—

But they had. Had kids, rented this place. They'd done it.

Now they were stuck. And Jay, Mae knew, truly felt stuck. If it weren't for her, if it weren't for the kids—had he ever even really had to do anything he didn't want to before? Ever had to stick with anything? Looking at her happy-go-lucky husband across the table, Mae wanted, as she so often had in the past year, to throw her glass at him. Oh, sure, he'd gotten through business school, the same one his dad had gone to before him. Mae now knew there were two ways to get through B-school, and the first might be her way, by memorizing every business case and going to every study session and doing every extra thing and just generally grinding the hell out of it, and the second was through charm and talk and the willingness to throw every idea out there with abandon and see what your classmates could make stick. The latter involved what Mae's friends called "the confidence of a mediocre white man," and although Jay wasn't white—his Indian heritage meant he didn't tick that box—confidence he had in spades.

Which was what made him think he could just walk away from a good job and find another one waiting when he was ready.

Fine, if this was the fight they were going to have now, she would have it.

"Do you think that would really be a break for me, a zillion-hour flight and then staying in a house with people we've never met, with your mother and a three-year-old and a six-year-old?" The kids barely knew Jay's mom. *He* barely knew his mom—his dad had raised him while his mom took Jay's sister in a complicated divorce-not-divorce Mae still didn't really understand, the kind of thing rich people apparently took for granted. Mae turned her own glass in her fingertips. She didn't really want champagne. She wanted a cold Diet Coke, not that they kept anything like that in the house.

"I'll be there too. And it's not like I'm suggesting we go camping in the Sahara. There will be help."

"Oh no, this isn't the camping part. That comes after." That was part two of Jay's lunacy. After the trip to India, they backpacked around Europe. Or rented an RV and drove across the US. It varied, but it was like the man who loathed all social media had been spending all his time following *#Airstreamlove* and *#havekidswill travel.* He'd be wanting a tiny house next.

"I can't even process this right now, Jay. I mean, I just got basically fired. I know that fits in with your dreams"—she refrained, barely, from saying *stupid dreams*—"but it wasn't in mine, okay?"

"We don't have to camp. I just—look, Mae, I know you. I'm sorry this happened. But it did, and now you're going to make choices because of it, and I want in on that." He picked up his fork, then set it down. "Don't you see? I'm just trying to buy us both some time."

"I don't want time," she said, unable to keep her voice from sounding sharp. "The *Sparkling* thing is—a setback. But it's just a small setback. I know you hate your job, Jay, but I don't. I don't want to tear everything up and start over."

"But I do."

His words hung between them for a moment—two children of single parents, two people who'd promised each other that whatever they did, they'd do it together, that their kids would never feel the way they had.

Jay looked down at his plate, took a bite, chewed. Mae bet he couldn't taste it. She couldn't even pretend to eat. "The lamb is good. I think the kids would like it, actually. I like the carrots." Mae could tell he was trying to take the weight away from what he had just said. It wasn't working. "Okay," he said, "your turn. You said you had a plan. Spill."

"I made enough to freeze," Mae said, "They'll get some." Her plan sounded absurd now, after the argument they were having, but she couldn't think of another way to present it. "The thing is," she said, "my plan would make things so easy for you. I know this last deal was rough, and you're about to get staffed on another one, so I'm taking the kids with me to visit my mother, and you'll get to just—be here. Bachelor it. Whenever you're not working, no us to worry about. I thought that would just take some of the pressure off, right? Give you room to hear yourself think."

"I can't hear myself think because I'm at work all the time," Jay said. "You don't want to go see my mom, but you're running off to see yours? Wait—back up. You haven't been to Kansas since Frank died. This isn't about me. Why would you— Tell me why you're going, Mae." He shoved another bite of stew in his mouth, angrily, chewing and watching her. Waiting.

This was it. Time to go big or go home. Jay hated *Sparkling* and all that went with it, from the hundreds of thousands of followers it brought to Mae's Instagram feed to the invitations that she and the kids do sponsored posts, the family photo shoots, the increased need for hours from Jessamyn, their nanny—hours that Mae's income covered but that he objected to just the same. With *Food Wars,* Mae could keep all that going, and she would need to, since at this point every time he left the apartment, she wondered if he would still have a job when he came back. But Jay was not likely to be enthused.

She forced a note of excitement into her voice, as though she expected him to welcome her news. "Well, I might not be doing *Sparkling* for a while, but my sister called, and *Food Wars* is doing a series of shows about my mom's restaurant, in Kansas. They need me to go home and help out."

Jay had picked up his glass while she spoke, sipping champagne, or pretending to. His eyebrows went straight up, and he let out a fast breath as he set down the glass, hard. His face was disbelieving, his tone flat. "They need you to go home and help with another reality show," he said. He didn't roll his eyes, but his look conveyed his disdain for the entire world Mae had become a part of.

"My mom really wants to do this," she said. *Damn it,* he should be excited. It was a miracle that she could get back into TV, and so quickly, and he should respect her willingness to jump on it. He'd loved this part of her once. Loved her drive at the consulting firm, her ideas for her own business and the way she had launched it when Ryder turned one, growing it fast into a book deal and influencer status and practically a mini-empire.

Now all he ever wanted was for her to pull back and slow down. She pushed on, trying to reach the old Jay somewhere in all of this disapproval. "And for me, Jay, it comes at just the right time! *Sparkling* will see how valuable I am, and if they don't, I can leverage this instead. You know how it is—it's always easier to get a job when you've got a job."

Jay glared at her, and she realized, too late, that her words probably sounded like yet another dig at his desire to take some time off "without boundaries." She rushed on. "And my sister hasn't done anything much since Frank died. She's just stuck there, doing the same thing every day. This is a chance to help her finally get out of that rut."

This time, Jay did roll his eyes. "Let me get this straight. You lost a TV show today, and your sister, who you haven't visited in at least six years, has gained one. So you're suddenly all revved to head home and be a part of it, and you're trying to convince me you're doing it for your sister and I should like it? That's bullshit." He pushed his plate away. "This is all bullshit, Mae. You've already said you'll go, haven't you? Already bought tickets. This isn't you even asking me if you can take the kids off to be another sideshow somewhere. It's you telling me. I bet you're packed already, aren't you? Tell me you're not packed."

Mae glanced toward the hall closet, where she'd tucked the suitcases, and felt her face get hot. "I did make plans, because we really have to go. This is a big chance for my mom and my sister—apparently business isn't too great—and it's a chance for me, and so what? I'm paying for it. I bought the tickets. I'm paying for Jessa to come with us. You don't even have to worry about it. You just get some kid-free time to do your own thing."

"You're going to Kansas. And you're taking the kids. To be on a reality show. And you didn't even wait to ask me?" Jay's voice was getting louder. "What if I'd worked late tonight? Would I just wake up in the morning and find a little note?" He shoved his chair away from the table and got up. "I hate this. I hate you not telling me things. I hate that now you're going to take the kids, and there will be posed airport pictures, and cute little traveling memes or whatever, and then you'll send them off with Jessa in some strange town while you try to get more fucking famous. You've got plenty of followers. When is it ever going to be enough?"

"I'm not just trying to get famous. This is how I sell more books, and get more work, and get paid, so I can pay the rent and the nanny and the private school tuition. This is the deal."

"You don't pay the rent and the nanny all by yourself, Mae. *We* pay the rent and the nanny. For *our* kids. And *we* have savings. Which I thought we could use, while we both take some time off to figure out where we're going, because *we* are lost."

"We're not lost. We have a great life here. You just don't see it."

"I don't see it because I'm never home to enjoy it."

"You will be. We just both have to push a little harder right now, and then things will get easier. That's the way it works. You work hard and you pay your dues and it pays off."

"Or you work hard and then you die. Maybe that's, like, the Kansas pioneer spirit. Maybe that's you. But some of us want time to make sure we really want what we're working for."

"And some of us know you don't always get another chance to go get it."

They stared at each other, the familiar stalemate reached, and Jay was the one who broke, looking away. That was it, and Mae knew it. She'd won. This time.

Actually she won every time.

Jay got up and walked to the trash to scrape off his plate, but when the trash can popped open, he stopped and reached in. Mae got cold inside. *Shit.* That was where she had put everything from her satisfying clear-out earlier in the day, and she hadn't covered up the things she was discarding with other trash, as she usually did. *Damn it!* She knew exactly what was coming. Jay stood up with a ratty stuffed chicken in his hand.

"You can't throw this away. Ryder loves this."

He did, but Mae hated it. The little stuffed chicken—a gift from her sister when Ryder was born—had grown gray and smelly and was beyond washing, and Mae had been able to slip it away from Ryder's bed for several nights running. With the trip, she figured he would forget about it, although she'd felt a tiny twinge of regret as she'd stuffed it into the trash can. It was just that it was so gross now, and there were so many stuffies. If she didn't get rid of them, they'd take over.

"He doesn't care about it. Not really," she said. It sounded weak, even to her. "It's so filthy, Jay. He's little. He'll like other things. It's just junk, anyway."

Jay turned on her. "You don't always get to decide what's junk, Mae. You don't get to pick and choose everything we have and everything we do and everywhere we go."

"I don't. Just—some things. And it's not the same."

Throwing away a toy was not the same as making all their life decisions—and how could she not make decisions right now, when everything Jay wanted to do felt so precarious? Couldn't he see that they wanted the same things, for the world to stay nice and safe and solid around Madison and Ryder and around themselves? She knew Jay had moved around a lot as a kid, and that at least once his dad had handed him a shoebox and told him that if it didn't fit in there, it couldn't come. But sometimes you had to get rid of things, even things you once loved, to make room for better things.

And sometimes you made mistakes. *Don't bring up the baseball glove. Don't bring up the baseball glove.*

She hadn't known the baseball glove was a perfectly worn-in classic Rawlings. Or that Jay had been hoping Madison or Ryder might use it someday. All she'd seen was that it was old. And kinda moldy. She honestly hadn't thought he would notice it was gone.

Sometimes you needed to make hard choices, and then just keep going. Apparently Mae was the only one here who knew how to do that.

She got up and started to clear the table. He could have the stuffed chicken if he wanted it. Let the battles continue. Was this how marriage worked? They just kept replaying this same scene? Wasn't there supposed to be some point where they got past it, where they did the right thing and moved on?

Maybe neither of them knew how.

"I'm going out to meet Jessa and get the kids," Jay said, and Mae shrugged, not looking at him as he left the kitchen.

Jay would get over it once she really had things sorted out. He'd get past this early midlife crisis he was having and just work all of his yoga and meditation and stuff into his job like a normal person. Maybe they'd even laugh about it, like they used to laugh at stuff like that.

And if not—Mae took a deep breath and turned on the water in the sink—she'd be ready for it. She was always ready.

The next morning, when she bent to buckle Ryder into the taxi to go to the airport, he was clutching the chicken tightly to his chest, looking so much like his father that it made Mae catch her breath with a combination of fear and love. "Daddy told me to take special care of my chicken," he said. "We gave it a new name, not just Chicken." He paused, then pronounced the name carefully. "Raw-lings. We called it Rawlings."

Damn.

AMANDA

On Wednesday afternoon, precisely at two, Sabrina Skelly and *Food Wars* showed up in Merinac, and Mae did not.

The minute the convertible came into view, van trundling along behind it, Amanda silenced her phone and shoved it deep into the recesses of her tote bag. Mae's absence was not her problem, and Andy's texts—at first conspiratorial, and now getting a little frantic as he apparently dealt with a Barbara who believed he could just postpone this whole thing—were a distraction she didn't need. This was the way she wanted it, anyway. Mae's sudden enthusiasm for *Food Wars* had been welcome and helpful; her insistence that she actually was coming to Merinac had not been. The less Mae, the better.

Amanda was ready. Frannie's was ready. Nancy was ready, or Amanda hoped she was. She was paler than Amanda had ever seen her and gripping Amanda's hand with sweaty force. It seemed entirely possible that her mother-in-law might faint, or burst, and that, at least, Amanda understood completely.

Worrying about Nancy was an excellent way to avoid worrying about herself. Amanda always drew chickens when she was upset— *those stupid chickens,* Mae called them, and Amanda's art teacher, along with every other teacher, agreed—and this year her sketchbook was full of them. She'd stayed up late last night, unable to stop, and the chickens that emerged from her pencil had fared poorly in front of the camera, tripping and rolling across the floor, molting all their feathers, unexpectedly laying an egg.

Amanda did not like cameras. In school pictures, she was the awkward tall girl hulking in the back and staring at the ground. She was not Mae, who starred in every school production. Amanda painted sets. She did not appear onstage. She'd thought, when she wrote that first e-mail to *Food Wars,* that maybe she could overcome that. She could be someone different. After all, she'd gained two children and a mother-in-law and lost a husband since those days—but she knew if Mae showed up, the old Amanda would reemerge.

But Mae wasn't here. The new Amanda, the one who made things happen in Merinac—made it a place Mae claimed to want to come home to, even—prepared a welcoming smile as Sabrina Skelly opened her car door and headed straight for her, arms outstretched, tiny self nearly running in spite of ridiculously high heels, her brown curls catching the sunlight.

"You must be Amanda! Oh, this is such a delight. We're just so glad to be here, and this"—she looked around, gesturing to the low buildings that made up Frannie's, the big sign, with its fifties-era lit-up outline of a chicken and an arrow pointing in, and the fields stretched out around it—"this is perfect. Just perfect."

Sabrina was right—it *was* perfect. This little northeastern corner of Kansas really gleamed in the spring, with a fresh light that everyone who lived here treasured before the heat of the summer kicked in, and a few rolling hills that took everyone expecting flat open spaces by surprise. Sabrina embraced Amanda, who returned it as best as she could, given that Nancy had not let go of her hand. "Amanda, really, it's just lovely to meet you finally."

Amanda, a little dumbstruck and very aware of her own lack of makeup and the unstyled waves of dull brown hair, which she cut herself at a boring and blunt shoulder length, settled for a straightforward response. "It's nice to meet you, too. This is my mother-in-law, Nancy, who runs Frannie's."

Nancy, too formally dressed in a silky blouse with a light

sweater over it, both in Frannie's maroon, hovered next to her. "I run it with Amanda," she said. "I couldn't do it without her." Behind Nancy pressed every member of Frannie's staff, all eager to be introduced and recognized, to have the sun of stardom shine on them for a moment. Sabrina waved over her crew, and there was a wild flurry of introductions and explanations before Sabrina clapped her hands. Clearly she wasn't just the star and nominal producer of *Food Wars*—this woman ran the show.

"My people! Get on with your jobs; get us settled. Frannie's people—let's get this party started! We brought cookies from McLain's in Kansas City, and let me tell you, they're divine." She ushered them inside and started pushing tables together, disrupting the existing precision arrangement, but after a moment even Nancy was dragging over a chair.

All around them, young men and women moved competently around, setting cameras in corners, opening curtains, carrying clipboards, and getting signatures. Amanda signed a release, as well as one for Gus and Frankie, leaning on the bar while watching someone set up a stepladder and begin wiring a camera onto a beam high above the dining room. Feeling as though Nancy's nerves were igniting hers, Amanda slid quietly around the table and into a seat opposite her just as Gus and Frankie came in. She reached out a hopeful hand to her daughter, inviting her to share the seat, but the gesture was met with a look of fourteen-year-old scorn as Frankie carefully took a chair next to her grandmother. Fine. Amanda found Nancy a far more comforting presence than her own mother as well, although she had tried so hard not to end up there with Frankie. It was just that lately, Frankie only wanted to talk when Amanda had nothing more to give, and when Amanda reached out, which was often, Frankie suddenly wasn't there as she had always been.

Gus, though, sat next to his mother and smiled, looking nearly at ease as he pulled over the bakery box. "Oh man," he said softly.

"Cup cookies from McLain's. Okay, *these* people know food." Amanda nudged him. *Shhh.*

Sabrina stood, gathering their attention even more intensely. "So, as I'm sure you know, I'm Sabrina Skelly, your gracious host, and also the producer of the show out here on the front lines. Everybody else gets the cushy jobs back at the office, but I get all the glory, so, you know, trade-offs." She smiled at them all widely, and of course they smiled back. They loved her. "You'll meet all the rest of the staff as we roll, but for now, let me set the scene for you and answer any questions. You probably all know the basic schedule. That is, if you've watched any *Food Wars*." Here she paused, as if she expected exactly the collective burst of laughter she got. Who hadn't watched *Food Wars*?

"Only every episode," called Mary Laura, who had rigged up a way to watch downloads on the TV that played constantly above her bar. Amanda wished, not for the first time, that she had Mary Laura's cool.

Sabrina smiled and went on. "Let me lay it out for you anyway. We've got people with cameras, and cameras that will stay in place. Those cameras will be running the whole time we're here, so don't think that if there's nobody with a camera following you, you're not on. We're pretty much able to take you live anytime, and we'll be putting little snippets up on social media, teasing the audience for the shows later." She said it all quickly, casually, as though it were the most normal thing in the world.

"Tonight we'll just film around the restaurant, informal, some background stuff. Tomorrow, Thursday, we'll do more of that but in a more organized way, capture whole meals, maybe follow one or two of you around for the night. You might do lunches, but we don't— we're strictly a dinnertime thing, gives the crew some time off. Then Friday we'll bring in our chef-judges for a visit and a meal, and first thing Saturday we'll do an official judging of just the chicken—a chicken-off. Then a little more filming Saturday night if we need it, then we announce the winners Sunday morning, and you can all go back to your lives."

Tomorrow? Friday? Amanda thought this was just a get-to-know-you visit, but apparently their appearance on *Food Wars* was a done deal. Sabrina must have noticed the surprise that rustled around the table.

"We're already here," she said, leaning in with a conspiratorial smile. "We're filming, and we start by assuming that we're going all the way with this. If things don't go well, we pull the plug, but it's rare that we can't make something happen. We can do this, people." She leaned back and beamed, her confidence lighting all their faces. "For right now, just get ready for a regular shift, and then a wild ride of a week."

There was laughter and some nudging of elbows. They wanted, every last one of them, to make this happen. The more talk there had been before the *Food Wars* crew arrived, the more Amanda had realized that the show touched a nerve in nearly everyone. If she saw herself, and Nancy, as doyennes of a televised chicken empire, their friends and staff saw themselves among the merry band of colleagues who would surround them, the scene-stealing side-kicks, the wry, knowledgeable besties. *Food Wars* would make them all real, and it all started now.

"I thought you'd want to split us all up and get us to talk about each other behind our backs," Mary Laura said.

"That comes later," a cameraman said with mock seriousness, helping himself to a cookie. Sabrina, who was somehow managing to fit right in, laughed along with him.

"It does look like that," she said, "but really we like to get everybody together at the beginning, just talking. I mean, of course we have a little fun with in-house rivalries, but it's the big competition we really focus on. We'll do the talk-to-the-camera stuff, but most of the time there are lots of people around, listening. So it's not like we're trying to corner anyone, or trick them. It comes out looking all secret, but it's really all open and friendly."

"Yep," said the cameraman, whom Sabrina introduced as Gordo, with his mouth full. "So, who here hates each other? Raise your hands." The staff giggled.

"We have a very friendly working relationship here," Nancy said stiffly. Her cookie sat untouched in front of her. "Everyone works together; everyone does everything that needs to be done."

"That's just what Amanda said in her e-mails," said Sabrina, and Amanda looked at her in surprise. Had she said that?

Sabrina went on. "That you guys were really a big family. Amanda's your daughter-in-law, right? Any other family members work here?"

"My grandson, Gus, washes dishes," Nancy said, smiling at Gus and putting an arm around Frankie. It was an unusually warm day for May, and Amanda could see a little sweat around Nancy's hairline and under her nose. "He's Franklin Augustus, actually. His sister, Frances—Frankie—is champing at the bit to join the family business, but Amanda thinks she's too young."

Actually, Frankie had repeatedly said, "Gross," to Amanda's suggestions that she join her brother for a shift or two, but that wasn't how Amanda had described it to Nancy, and it certainly wasn't how Frankie was playing it now.

"I'm going to bus tables this weekend," she said.

"That's perfect," Sabrina said. "But you two, Nancy, Amanda, how long have you been working together?"

"Oh," Nancy said, "ever since Amanda married my son, Frank."

Amanda noticed that the cameraman lifted his camera onto his shoulder and slid unobtrusively to a position in front of a window. *It's started,* she thought, and her stomach flipped over. This was exciting. It was supposed to be exciting. All the same, she wanted to warn Nancy and Frankie: they're recording! But she couldn't think of a way to do it without being obvious, so she settled for nudging Gus and nodding in the camera's direction.

Annoyingly, Gus patted her hand. "It will be okay, Mom," he whispered. "That's why they're here."

Nancy was still talking. "More than seventeen years ago now. Hard to believe."

"I can tell you get along beautifully," Sabrina said. "That's just amazing. Most mothers- and daughters-in-law we see working together, it can get a little tense."

"Oh no," Nancy said. "We don't have that problem." Now Amanda wished she had sat with Nancy, just so she could give her a hug. They didn't have that problem, as hard as it might be for outsiders to believe. Things between them just worked.

"And your husband and your son—they're both gone now?"

"For six years," replied Nancy. "They were killed in the same car accident, on the way to a Chiefs game. Amanda and I—we've always been close, and if anything, that brought us closer."

Amanda, needing to touch some member of her family, leaned on her son gently, and Gus put an arm around her. Okay, she was lucky. Nancy was being great—was great. And Sabrina was nice. This was going to be fine.

Sabrina turned to Amanda and smiled warmly. "But your mother runs Chicken Mimi's, right?" Somehow, the way she asked it, it didn't feel like a challenge, more like they were just laying the facts out. Of course people would have to know that.

Amanda took a breath, trying to find a way to explain. "She does," she said. "And I used to work there, too. And then—I married Frank."

Couldn't that be enough? Of course not. Sabrina was looking at her, waiting for more. "We fell in love. In high school. And then—" Oh, this was awkward. She fell silent, and Mary Laura leapt in instead.

"Of course we all knew Frank had a big crush on Amanda," she said. "It was like Romeo and Juliet, only with fried chicken." That got her a laugh and took the pressure off Amanda too, but Mary Laura never knew when to stop. "It was a little weird," she added cheerfully. "We thought they must be related, kinda, but I guess those relatives lived a really long time ago."

"Frank and Amanda were perfect together," Nancy said, giving her staffer a slight glare. "I was delighted when they began dating. Amanda was—is—a lovely girl."

Oh God. Amanda stared down at her cookie, willing them not to go any farther down this road. Nancy might have been delighted, or at least willing to pretend to be, but her mother and Mae had not been. Mae had been trying to drag Amanda down her own path, off to college, working her way through by doing every dirty but well-paid job imaginable, from cleaning crime scenes to exotic dancing. Mae had only laughed when Amanda started dating Frank (she'd pronounced it the "lamest rebellion ever"), but once they decided to get married, Mae's tolerance had been replaced by horror that Amanda planned to throw her life away on fried chicken and Frank, and she had said so, loudly and often, while offering to pay for the abortion she knew perfectly well Amanda never intended to have and demanding to know how the sister she'd seen to it was thoroughly educated in every aspect of birth control could possibly have gotten herself into this mess.

Her mother's reaction had been quieter but worse. She'd said hardly anything about the wedding, hardly anything about Frank, even, but then, she never said much. Everything that mattered in the Moore household went unspoken, and this turned out to be just another case where no one had told Amanda the rules Mae seemed to have been born knowing. Driving home after a short honeymoon in St. Louis, Amanda needed to pee desperately. In those days, there was no inn on Main Street, no coffee shop, no craft store. She told Frank to pull in at Mimi's.

"You sure?"

Amanda didn't even see why he was asking. Why would they not?

Barbara came out as the car stopped, and Amanda tried to rush around her. Peeing was far more urgent than a hug. But Barbara stepped in front of her and gently barred the way. "No."

"What do you mean, no?" Amanda could still remember her younger self's confusion.

"I mean no. You belong to Frannie's now, Amanda. You're a Pogociello. That means you stay out here on the porch."

Amanda had been shocked enough to stop in her tracks. "You can't mean that."

"It's not me, Amanda. You know the way this works. You've always known. Did you really think you could have both?" She must have been able to tell from Amanda's expression that that was exactly what Amanda had thought. "If you're part of Frannie's, you can't come into Mimi's." She steered her daughter away from the door, but Amanda tried again to push past her. "Mom! I just have to go to the bathroom. Come on, this is ridiculous."

Barbara didn't move, and after a stunned moment, Amanda turned away. Barbara stood in the doorway, watching, while Amanda got back into Frank's car.

"We could run into the hardware store, probably," Frank muttered.

Amanda sat down heavily in the seat, her legs still out the door, staring back at Mimi's. "She wouldn't let me in," she said.

"Well, no," he said. "Of course she wouldn't." He looked at her, and she realized that she had disappointed him somehow. He stared down at the steering wheel. "You thought she would?"

Without another word, Frank drove them to his parents' house, where Amanda rushed to the bathroom, and he sat in the car for a while before he came inside. She knew now, although she had not been able to see it then, that realizing she didn't understand the consequences of their marriage made Frank doubt her from the very beginning. She had taken the story he'd been imagining, of her giving up everything for him, and turned it into a tale of supreme youthful cluelessness.

She had never told him so, but she would have married him anyway. At nineteen, she'd craved everything he offered: love, security, faith, a predictable future. But who the hell knew what they really wanted at nineteen? At least she had dumb-lucked herself into something pretty good, she thought, looking around at the cozy crowd of friends and family, at Nancy, calmer now and beaming at her across the table. Her sister and her mother were her history. This was her present.

"Romeo and Juliet," said Sabrina, smiling at her. "It sounds like a wonderful romance. And now you're part of this." She gestured around her, and Amanda nodded.

"This is my family now," she said, thinking of Frank but speaking to Nancy, "and I wouldn't trade it for anything."

There was a small collective "awww," and everyone smiled at an embarrassed Amanda until Sabrina broke things up with a shift in her tone and body language that made it clear that she had been playing to the camera before.

"We do want to set up somewhere for those offstage interviews," she said. "Amanda, is there an office or something? It's better for the sound if it's in a small room, if there is one. We can even clean out a closet."

×

"Perfect," Sabrina said as she looked around the tiny windowless office Amanda shared with Nancy. She hopped up on the desk Amanda used for payroll and the occasional late-night drawing session and sat, her perfect legs dangling. "Amanda, honey, grab that chair and take a seat." She turned to the cameraman. "Gordo, want to get set up? Use Amanda for target practice, see how the lighting is, et cetera?"

Amanda pulled the old armchair out of the corner into the spot Gordo indicated and settled into it while he fussed about her, first setting up his tripod and a camera, then pulling lights from a big bag and moving them around, then going back to peer at his screen. She tried to relax. He was just setting up, after all. There was nothing to worry about. She leaned back and crossed her legs, watching him move around the room, and tried to think of something to say that didn't sound totally dorky.

She failed. "I can't believe you picked us." She couldn't, either. Couldn't believe that she was here, in their office, hanging out with Sabrina Skelly. "You must get so many e-mails. We're so excited—I mean, it's just so cool that you're here."

"You'd probably be surprised how few we get," Sabrina said. "Most people don't have the balls to actually go after what they want. They talk about it, and they think about it, but they don't often make it happen."

Amanda touched her hair, pleased. It was pretty rare for anyone to tell her she had balls, even indirectly.

"So that's really your son out there? You must have been a baby when you had him. You can't be more than thirty now." Sabrina's tone was casual, even if the question felt a little sudden. Gordo was still fussing around with lights and cords, paying them little attention. She must just be used to asking personal questions—and most people asked this eventually. Might as well get it out of the way.

"I'm thirty-five, actually." Thirty-five with a baby face, although at least they'd finally stopped carding her at liquor stores a few years ago. "I was nineteen when Gus was born."

Sabrina looked thoughtfully at her. "Oops?"

Amanda laughed. "Not really." She hated it when people assumed that. No, she hadn't exactly planned to get pregnant, but she hadn't had better plans, either, and Frank had loved the idea of starting a family young. That was another thing Mae had never understood—that not everybody needed to control everything. Sometimes you rolled with what came. But she didn't want Sabrina to think she was some sort of hayseed, or even that she had been at eighteen. "Start young, and you end up like me—two great kids who can mostly take care of themselves, and you're not too old to enjoy it."

"Exactly! You can do anything now, right? What's the plan? More Frannie's? Your mother-in-law seems great."

"Oh, she really is," Amanda said, and then stopped. More Frannie's was the plan, as far as she'd made one. But that sounded so—in Mae's old word—lame. She couldn't really tell the glamorous Sabrina that she just wanted things back the way they had always been. She was happy to talk about Nancy, though. "She loves us—all of us, I mean, everybody who works here. She always wanted a big family, but she just had Frank, so we're all kind of her family."

Amanda remembered Nancy's joy when Frankie was on the way, her hope that Amanda and Frank would go on to have many more; she'd confided that Frank being an only child was not at all what she'd planned. But this was a little too close to Nancy's heart, here. "What about you, do you have kids?" Thanks to *Wikipedia,* she knew the answer, but it seemed weird to admit it.

"God no. This is scarcely the lifestyle for it, and I'm not really cut out for looking after other people. Except my crew, right, Gordo?" Gordo, making adjustments to a tripod in the corner, grunted. He was creating an extraordinarily elaborate setup, with a phone on a small tripod hanging beneath the bigger camera and lights everywhere that he began to turn off and on. Sabrina turned back to Amanda. "So you guys will win this thing, then settle in and make Frannie's great? Spend the rest of your life here, bring the kids into the business?"

From her tone, Amanda didn't think Sabrina was impressed. "Well..."

"Well? That sounds a little hesitant. Is there maybe more to Amanda Pogociello than fried chicken and the wide-open spaces of the prairie? My parents run a car dealership, and I like cars, but ..."

Amanda laughed. "Of course there's more. I love Frannie's, and I love what I do here, so that really is the plan. But I do other things—" Should she tell Sabrina this? The other woman had moved closer, her face warm and interested. And it was just a hobby, really, not something that would ever get in the way of Frannie's. "I like to draw." That sounded so small, *I like to draw,* and now Amanda felt like she was being disloyal to the thing that filled so much of her free time—sometimes encroaching on time that wasn't technically free—to the huge canvases that she painted on over and over because she couldn't afford new ones, to the sketchbooks that served as her diaries, even to the chicken characters that had taken on a life of their own this past year. Those were easiest to describe. "I make these—comic books, I guess you'd call them. Graphic comic books. Not funny, mostly. About chickens."

"Really?" Sabrina looked interested, and Amanda smiled back at her, glad that they were connecting. "That's so cool. Is that what you were going to school for?"

Amanda laughed. "No, I was going to do something practical. Like accounting." "Going to school" was a grandiose phrase for her efforts anyway. She had drifted into classes at the local college just like she drifted into everything else. It was only later, when the kids were little, after their school and her work and dinner and baths and bedtime, with Frank grading papers in the living room, that she'd tried to get a little more serious, always "making a mess" of the kitchen table.

Which led to the late-night arguments about whether they could move to Kansas City—just for a little while, a year or two— where she could take classes, maybe get her own art degree and teach, too. She had even applied to transfer the few credits she had to the college of art and design in Kansas City. She could have commuted, probably. Frank would have come around, would have seen that she could still make their life with the kids and Frannie's work.

They would have figured it out. They would have. Or if they hadn't—but no, they would have. But once he was gone, she never responded to the letter inviting her to remain on the wait list and send more of her work, to apply again the next year. Too much, too hard.

"I'm not that good," she said. "It's just something I do on the side."

Sabrina smiled sympathetically. "When you get tired of chicken— I mean, do you get tired of chicken?"

Amanda laughed. She couldn't help it. When she wanted to throw her Frannie's uniform across the room, more like. When the smell, the grease, the way the soles of her work shoes always felt just a little slippery no matter what she did, surrounded her and wouldn't let her go. But she didn't need to say all that. "I guess," she said. "It can get a little—the same, all the time. Which is what's so great about your job. For you, it's always something new."

Sabrina looked at her without speaking for a moment, then laughed herself. "I guess so. It's funny you draw chickens, though. Can I see them? Did you draw any of the chickens on the specials menu? Do you have any sketchbooks with you right now?" She looked searchingly at Amanda. It wasn't really a question—and of course she was right. Amanda always had her current sketchbook with her, and this one was chock-full of chickens. Her eyes went to the coatrack, where her bag was hanging, and Sabrina sprang up. "Come on, you have to show me. I love it. Don't get up. Tell me where. This one?"

Wait, really? Did she really want to show Sabrina her chickens? Sabrina might laugh—people were supposed to laugh, at least at some of it, but there was laughing and there was laughing. Too quickly, Sabrina had her hands on Amanda's big tote, and she swung around, extending it to Amanda.

"In here?"

"No," she said, "I don't think I have anything." She took the bag, trying not to snatch, and held it tightly in her lap.

Sabrina let it go and took up her place on the desk again. "Later, maybe?"

"If I can find anything," Amanda said, still clutching her bag. "My bag is a mess. My whole house is a mess." A mess where her art supplies were the one thing she could always put her hands on, but Amanda's willingness to share had cooled off.

Sabrina smiled cheerfully. "Oh, mine too. I'm a total slob. It's the worst. My family is always on me to clean up my act."

Amanda jumped on the change of subject, even if this wasn't one of her favorites either. But at least everybody felt like they were kind of messy. Except Mae, of course. "You have no idea. Nancy's always telling me I should clean up a little at a time and stay after it, but it just doesn't work, I get home so late and I'm wiped."

"My mom keeps threatening to go clean out my apartment herself," said Sabrina. "I'm like, Mom, just stay out of it. I'm happy this way."

That was far from Amanda's problem, but she did have one family member she'd match up against Sabrina's mom every time.

"My sister hasn't been here in ages, but if she saw my house, she'd be all over me. Supposedly she's coming to help Mom with Mimi's, though I'm not convinced she'll show up. If she saw my kitchen now, she'd freak."

Sabrina smiled. "Maybe we can keep her off your back. I didn't know you had a sister coming—that's perfect. Sisters started Frannie's and Mimi's, and now sisters running Frannie's and Mimi's."

"She doesn't exactly run it." Amanda rolled her eyes. "I mean, she hasn't been in the place in six years."

"We can stretch a little," Sabrina said. "We like to tell a good story. So she's coming back after being gone for a while? How's that going to work? What's she been doing?"

"I don't think it *is* going to work," Amanda said, happy to share her frustration. "My mom has always run Mimi's on her own, but now she has this new cook she brought in, and she's trying to drag Mae home—I don't know what she's thinking. They fight, when Mae's here, even though when she's not here, my mom is always talking about her. They're a lot alike, except Mae is this obsessively neat and organized person and my mom is—" She stopped.

Her mom wasn't something she wanted to talk about.

Sabrina looked interested. "Wait, is your sister Mae Moore? Who wrote *Less Is Moore*?" She paused, then laughed. "Oh man. That would be tough."

Damn it, she knew who Mae was. Did everybody? But at least that made it easy to explain. "Exactly. And it sucks, you know? She literally wrote the book on being perfect, but in real life, she's not so—I mean, she does do all that stuff, throw everything away, put everything back, keep it all clear—but she's not so . . . fun about it. She's more pissed."

Sabrina again hopped down from her perch on the desk. "I know Mae," she said casually. "It will be great to see her again."

She *knew* Mae? Actually knew her? And Mae might be on her way here, to help with Mimi's— Was that fair? Sabrina must have noticed how shocked Amanda looked, because the diminutive host leaned down and gave Amanda, who was still seated, a one-armed hug.

"It's okay! We met a long time ago is all, and I see her around. TV is a small world. It doesn't matter." She plopped onto the floor next to Amanda's chair. "It's not like we're friends. She seems like she might be hard to be friends with. I've got an older sister who's like that, and we don't get along at all."

Amanda sank down farther into the chair and stretched her legs out. Sabrina had that right—and maybe it wasn't so bad that she knew Mae if Sabrina and Amanda had so much in common.

"In the book she just sounds so nice and together, and she kind of is, but—" How to explain Mae? It was harder than it sounded. "She's, like, messy inside. I mean, she probably wouldn't want me to say that, but it's true."

Sabrina nodded. "Isn't everybody? My sister hates for people to know that about her too. I'm supposed to be the messy one."

It was nice to talk to someone who really got it. "She knows how everybody should live their lives, just like she knows how everybody should keep everything clean," Amanda said. "It was okay when we were little. But now, we hardly ever talk, and when we do, it's like she doesn't know I grew up."

When they were little—Mae was Amanda's rock, back then. Amanda had been easily eight or nine before she realized that in most families, it was the mom who made lunches, who got out clothes for the next day or made sure you did your homework. Barbara did none of those things, but Mae did, so well that Amanda had never felt the lack. It was just that Mae never stopped doing them.

Sabrina was gazing up into her face, smiling encouragingly. "I bet she has ideas about your job, right? Mine's always saying how I could do better for myself. Every job I get, she puts down."

Amanda wondered what Sabrina's sister could do that she thought was so much better than *Food Wars,* but at least she understood the attitude. "That's exactly it! And it's not like she's perfect. Everybody here knows it, too. She used to smoke, and she got good grades but she always kind of annoyed the teachers. She always acted like she knew better than anyone else. And then she went to college in Dallas, and then New York, and it just got worse."

"That's the first time I met her," said Sabrina. "We had a dancing gig together, when we were both first getting started."

Amanda looked at her, surprised. Really? Maybe that was what Sabrina's sister was giving her a hard time about. At least that made some sense. "Seriously? You knew her at"—oh gosh, what would be the right way to say it?—"that place in Dallas? The, uh, gentlemen's club?"

"The what?"

Maybe that wasn't the way people said it. Especially if they worked there. "Um, the exotic dance place? The Yellow Rose, or something like that?"

Sabrina stared at Amanda for a second, then hooted. "Wait! No. Seriously? Mae worked as a stripper? No." She leaned on the desk and laughed, a huge laugh that told Amanda that her earlier laughs had been nothing but polite, a laugh that left her wiping her eyes as she turned to Gordo. "I met her at MTV, we were both in a video, and then we auditioned to be VJs. Not"—she laughed again—"the Yellow Rose of Texas. Oh man, that's unbelievable. Seriously? Gordo, did you hear that? Tell me you're dying here."

Gordo stepped out and stretched, and Amanda suddenly realized he'd been behind the camera for some time, not twitching the lights or setting the scene. "I'm dying," he said, plainly sarcastic.

"Oh shit, you don't know her." Sabrina wiped her eyes again. "Well, maybe you will. If she comes, and now, oh man, I really hope she comes. And then you'll see. Oh, that's a total crack-up. Mae Moore, a stripper? Well, you've fired the first salvo in the *Food Wars* big-time, Amanda. Family-Friendly Frannie's versus—what—Hot-Mama Mimi's?" She laughed again, but for Amanda, this was suddenly not very funny.

"Wait, you weren't recording that, were you?" she asked. They would have said they were filming, right? They would have asked her questions about Frannie's and chicken. "You can't use that. That wasn't about chicken or anything. I thought we were just talking."

Sabrina smiled, her face still full of laughter. "Your first on-camera interview," she said. "I could tell you might be nervous, so I eased you into it."

Wait, really? She'd said a thousand things she would not have said if she'd realized they were taping. Or probably not, anyway. About Mae, yeah, but also about getting tired of chicken, and

Frannie's, and— What had she said, anyway? *Shit.* "Wait—I didn't—I mean, especially about Mae. She was putting herself through college, we literally didn't have any money—and I wouldn't want Nancy to hear that I get tired of chicken, because I don't, not really."

She could have cried. This was awful. How were they going to win and get people here if they heard her saying stuff like that about Frannie's? And Mae—everybody knew, but she might be mad, and Amanda didn't need that. If Mae even showed.

Gordo, still fiddling with the camera, spoke. "The stripper thing is probably too much, to start off with," he said.

Sabrina sighed. "I know," she said, and then she looked at Amanda. "Oh honey, don't worry. He's right. It's just funny to me because I know her. You didn't say anything else bad. That part about her being messy inside—that's very perceptive. If she comes and you're competing, that might be nice to work in. Other than that, it's all just B roll."

If she comes, and you're competing— Somehow, in all the e-mailing and the flurry of back-and-forth texting, it had never occurred to her that she would be competing with Mae. She couldn't compete with Mae. No one could, but least of all Amanda. Every nerve she'd managed to set aside as she and Sabrina talked was back, and then some.

Sabrina seemed to know what she was thinking. "It's okay," she said. "You're going to be great, and this is going to be a fabulous *Food Wars*. It's totally different from what Mae's used to. She'll be her, and you'll be you, and you'll be wonderful and relatable and the audience will love you. This is what we do—we show them who you really are. And we make a fun rivalry for the audience. It's no big deal."

Amanda wanted to believe her. And if Gordo said they'd leave the part about the Yellow Rose out—of course they would. Still, she wished she hadn't said it. She didn't say anything else now, and Sabrina smiled and patted her leg.

"It really is okay," she said. "Now I'm going to talk to your mother-in-law, and we'll start off the night here, and then I'm going to go over to Mimi's and see just how right you are." She got up and, before Amanda could stand too, bent over her, so close Amanda could smell her perfume, a faintly citrusy floral, a little cloying. Her smooth hands lifted Amanda's hair off her neck, and Sabrina held the thick brown mass up speculatively, with a look back at Gordo. "But first, I was wondering. How would you feel about cutting your hair?"

MAE

When Mae boarded the first flight out of LaGuardia, she'd looked exactly as she meant to when she arrived in Merinac. She was smartly but simply and practically dressed in a hot pink V-neck T-shirt tucked into a full khaki skirt and paired with a cloth belt she wouldn't have to take off for security: classic, nontrendy clothes that would work as well when they landed in Joplin to get the rental car as they did stepping into the cab in Brooklyn, a moment that she had, of course, documented and Instagrammed. She had all the markers of a hometown girl made good, including two appealing and generally well-behaved children, copies of her book to share if anyone was interested, and a great answer to anyone asking "So, what have you been up to?"

Her plan—to bring a little Brooklyn to *Food Wars* and Chicken Mimi's—was rock solid. Her followers loved fresh local foods. They valued authenticity and originality. They wanted to spend more time with family. She knew all this because profiling your target market was Social Media Brand Building 101. They might like the Chicken Mimi's part of her history. She didn't know why she hadn't thought of it before.

Well, she did, actually. There were very good reasons for keeping this particular piece of the past in the past, but if she couldn't do that, she could at least make sure it was worth it. But after two delayed flights, including a three-hour wait on the boiling-hot tarmac in Chicago and an additional two hours in the rental car with two cranky kids, she felt rumpled and exhausted, more like a dishrag than a returning heroine. Jessa had politely invoked their agreement that she have the evening off, so Mae dropped her at the hotel on the outskirts of town before heading toward Mimi's. The kids dozed in the back seat, which Mae knew she would regret when bedtime came, but she couldn't bring herself to rouse them.

There was a moment every time Mae made the drive into Merinac, when she knew she was almost home. She'd taken this same highway home from Dallas and SMU all through college, and then, later, from the airport in Joplin. And every time, when she saw the exit, it sank in: *Here we go again.*

Here we go with *that girl of Barbara's has always been trouble* and *thinks she's too good for this town.* Here we go with people who thought they had her pegged when she was in grade school and hadn't rethought it (or anything else) since. Mae had armor she wore in this town, and she didn't even think of it as a metaphor.

Once past the truck stop, every turn meant something. The exit, past the QuikTrip. The shortcut to the dam, the stoplight at the intersection by the high school, the turn-off for Kenneth's house, the new road that had replaced the dirt cut-through to the strip mall with the Albertsons. As she turned down Main Street toward Mimi's, Ryder started to stir.

"I go potty," Ryder said.

"No problem, sweetie. We're almost there."

"No, I go potty now, now, Mommy, now—"

"One minute." They were turning into Mimi's. "One minute, really, less, I'm parking."

"Now!" Ryder was squirming, trying to get to his own seat belt while Madison leaned over from her booster seat and pushed his hands away. "Now, now, now," he roared, and then, "Oh."

"Ryder!" Madison screamed. "Ryder, that stinks! Ryder, eww."

Plane travel had not agreed with Ryder. Mae acted fast, without exactly knowing what she planned to do next, slamming the car into park and undoing her own seat belt as she opened her door, "It's okay, Ryder. Hold still. Ryder! No!"

Ryder had put a hand under his bottom and pulled it out, obviously wet and dark, then slid from the seat, frantic, and wiped it on the back of the driver's seat.

"Mommy! I'm dirty, get it off, get it off, Mommy!"

As she tried to pull him from the rental car while touching him as little as possible, he plunged his hand into her hair, trying to hang on. She swung him around into her body to get his hand away and found the front of her skirt and the bottom of her shirt in nearly as bad shape as everything Ryder was wearing. "Ryder! No! Hold still!" She put him down, fast, on his feet.

"I'm dirty! Mommy, clean me. I need new pants, Mommy. New pants. Not these pants. I don't like these pants."

"He's going to need a new car seat, too," Madison said sadly.

Or something. Damn. She had clothes—with her one clean hand, she carefully lifted the smaller of their two suitcases out of the hatchback—but she couldn't clean this up without water, and lots of it. This was how she'd be making her return entrance to Mimi's, then. Covered in shit and with a kid in even worse shape, and another kid hopping along helpfully narrating the whole thing.

"Mommy! How will we clean the car, Mommy? Will Grandma help? I'm going to tell Grandma Ryder pooped in the car." Slowly, because Mae couldn't put a hand on Madison and move her along, they made their way around the back of the restaurant, skirting the patio area and walking around behind the fence that separated it from the parking lot. Even with her attention on the kids, Mae could see that things looked worse than she had expected. A lot worse. The grass hadn't been mowed, and clearly more than one patron had chosen to dump trash back here rather than in the trash cans on the side of the patio. Her optimism about this whole plan was disappearing fast. At least the door to the kitchen was propped open.

She gestured to Madison to stay behind her and leaned her head into the door, carefully holding both of Ryder's hands so that he wouldn't touch anything.

"Mom?"

The guy at the fryer was easily six three, as tall as Jay but with twice his bulk. He wore a black T-shirt, shorts with a white apron tied around his waist, and Mario Batali–style orange clogs. There was no sign of her mother. Instead, clearly framed by the pass-through window into the serving area, she saw the last person she wanted to see at this moment: Sabrina Skelly, *Food Wars* host. The convertible and the fancy van in the crowded parking lot suddenly made sense; how had she not realized they would beat her here? She'd turned back toward her car when Madison started to push past her.

"I want fries!" Mae hip-checked her daughter, still not wanting to touch her, and Madison fell to the floor dramatically, howling. "That hurt! Fries!" she said. "You said fries and chicken and I want fries and chicken and where is Grandma?"

Her shouts caught the attention of the cook, who started across the kitchen before cursing and turning back to the fryer, pulling out the chicken, plating it quickly, and grabbing two of the paper orders off the row in front of him.

Another woman Mae didn't recognize leaned into the pass-through window from behind the counter. Sabrina had disappeared from view. "Can I help you?" the woman asked, but the man spoke over her, sliding the plated chicken through the window as he did.

"Door's on the other side," he said over his shoulder. "This is the kitchen. Go around."

"I know this is the kitchen," snapped Mae. "I know where the door is, too. I'm looking for my mother—Barbara. Barbara!" she repeated loudly, knowing it was hard to hear over the fryer but suspecting the man was ignoring her anyway. Who the hell did he think he was—and who was he, anyway? "My mother! Barbara! Is she here?" Mae cast a frantic look toward the door that separated the kitchen from the dining room. Had Sabrina heard her?

"You must be Mae, then," the cook said, turning fully around. His expression was hard to read, but Mae thought he looked amused. "Finally. Your mom stuck around a long time waiting for you before she went home." He put out a hand. "Andy."

Damn him, he had been messing with her. He knew who she was. And Barbara went home? What the hell? Before Mae could react, Sabrina Skelly appeared in the door that connected the kitchen to the counter area, her face a perfect expression of delight and excitement, trailed by the inevitable camera. "Mae! Mae Moore!" She rushed forward, clearly ready to embrace Mae, and Mae frantically backed away from them both, holding up her hands.

"I really can't," she said. She pointed at her son, and she could see from Sabrina's face that the smell was telling its tale.

Andy turned to Sabrina and her camera, grinning cheerfully. "Kid shit his pants," he said, and Sabrina cast the dismayed look of the childless at Ryder while Mae nodded, cursing the choice to leave Jessa at the Travelodge. She would have paid any amount of money to hand Ryder off and greet Sabrina gracefully, setting a professional tone for the next few days.

"We just need to clean up a little," Mae said. The camera turned to her, and she lowered her hands and tried to look as if this were just a little incident, instead of the full-blown stinker that was painfully obvious to everyone present. Ryder, though, had other plans. "We got to clean off the POOP," he declared, and started to march himself into the kitchen.

Mae gave in and picked him up, holding him almost as though there was nothing wrong. "You got it," she said, smiling pleasantly at the camera. She should laugh; she knew she should. Just another mom dealing with the mess. But Mae Moore didn't do mess, and the probably forced-looking smile was all she could manage. "Y'all excuse us, okay?" *Oh God. Y'all?* What was she doing? She had to get away.

Andy pointed to Madison. "She better wait out here," he said. "The office is small."

"I know it's small," Mae started, her frustration with him and with the whole situation creeping into her voice again, and she thought she saw him grin. "Come on, Madison." Anything to get away from Sabrina and the camera.

"Suit yourself, then," he said. "Or I've got French fries." He shook a few onto a plate and held them out to Madison, who looked up at her mother. Too annoyed to be grateful for the favor, she shrugged.

"Go ahead, honey," she said. "Ryder and I will be a while."

"I want fries!"

"I'll save you some, Rydie," said Madison, looking questioningly at Andy, who nodded. "You go with Mommy."

Sabrina knelt down to Madison, and Mae had to let whatever exchange was going to happen, happen. Even Sabrina—and Mae had known her and known of her for years, and she wouldn't put much past her—wouldn't mess too much with a six-year-old without her parents around. Especially with the camera there, Mae couldn't hold off on changing a minute longer. They did look like good French fries, she noticed. When she'd last worked in the kitchen, they'd been frozen, but those looked freshly cut. Barbara hadn't mentioned hiring a cook, which was so unlike her that Mae could hardly wrap her head around it, but at least the guy seemed to have persuaded Barbara to make some changes.

Fifteen disgusting minutes later, Mae was ready for her *Food Wars* debut. In the kitchen another man, a smaller one, was teaching Madison to spray the dishes and slide them through the commercial dishwasher while Sabrina and her camera looked on, cooing admiration and encouragement. "Thank you, Zeus," Madison said. "Mommy, look!"

Mae must have looked surprised, because the woman—young, pretty, cheerful—who was doing the serving behind the counter heard her, laughed, and introduced herself. Angelique, she said, and the dishwasher was Zeus. "He's really Jesús," she said, pronouncing it the Spanish way, "but the first cook he worked with called him Zeus, and it stuck."

With a promise that his own French fries were coming, Mae set Ryder up at a picnic table just outside the restaurant door with a coloring sheet, where Mae and Amanda had spent their childhood summers, close to their mother but out of the way. Angelique produced cups of crayons, the cups slightly squished to fit through the slats of the picnic table, just as they always had, and Mae touched the table gently. Same table, exactly. Same smell of crayons in the waxy cup. Possibly even some of the same crayons.

But Sabrina's presence left no time for nostalgia, even if Mae wanted to feel it. She came over quickly, trailed by Madison and the camera, and leaned over the coloring page as one of her young minions pushed a clipboard at Mae. "Your sister drew that, right, Mae?"

Sabrina knew who Mae was and that she was coming, too, then—and knew her history with Amanda and who knew what else. They were just going to jump right into things. Mae signed the release quickly, not reading it—they were all the same—then looked into the camera. "She did," Mae said, carefully choosing her words. "Amanda's always been a good artist." She wasn't expecting to talk about Amanda so soon, without a chance to see her sister first. What would Amanda have said about Mae? Had Sabrina talked to Barbara yet? Not for the first time, Mae cursed both the delay and her mother's and sister's unwillingness to strategize by text. They could keep the "war" focused on the chicken if everybody would just be smart about it, and they could be. They'd been a team once, she and Amanda, and, yeah, they'd had some rough years, but now was the time to put all that in the past and focus. Damn it, if only she knew what Amanda or Barbara had *said*.

"It's funny that you still use that drawing, though," Sabrina said.

Mae could feel Sabrina pushing slightly, laying her bait. She smiled internally—she was not that easy, and Sabrina ought to know it. "Not really. She painted the sign outside, too." Amanda's chickens belonged at Mimi's. It was hard to imagine one at Frannie's, although maybe she drew them there, too. Mae looked again at the familiar chicken. Of course. Frannie's probably had an Amanda-designed coloring page too. She'd just never thought of it before, and she had that feeling you get when you see a friend you'd thought of as unchanging suddenly living a new life. It took her a moment to tune back in to Sabrina.

"Let's talk about you, though. This is a real homecoming for you, right?"

Mae glanced around. They were going to do this here? Out behind the kitchen, before she had even seen her mother or spent any time in the restaurant? Mae tried to avoid looking around at the space that would be the backdrop for her first appearance in front of all these potential fans and followers, and turned her attention to Sabrina, keeping her shoulders open and addressing the camera trained on them both. "It is. I'm really excited to come home and do some work on the place."

"Work?"

"Well, spruce it up a little." She gestured to the nicer of the two weedy strips along the patio, hoping the camera would avoid the other, which featured cracked pots and dead plants, with nothing growing but a fork planted tines down in the dirt. Time to take the focus off their surroundings. "And I've been thinking about the menu," she said, picking one up and hoping the camera would focus in. "It's simple, but maybe it's a little too simple."

Behind her, Andy deposited plates of chicken, biscuits, salad, and fries in front of Madison and Ryder, looking up as he did. "How so?"

The camera swiveled, and Sabrina stepped back while Mae kicked herself. This wasn't a conversation she meant to have with this guy, and certainly not now, on camera, when they'd just met. But then, he must be the one who persuaded her mother to up their game on the fries. Andy repeated his question, his tone challenging, but maybe interested as well. "How is it too simple?"

"I love what we serve, of course, Andy." She reached down and took a fry from Ryder's plate. He protested, but she ignored him, biting it appreciatively. "These are excellent." Andy waited. Not flattered, then, judging from the look on his face. Who did he think he was, the guardian of Mimi's? "But the menu's been the same for a long time." *And I have been around for longer than you, dude.* "I just thought it was something we could talk about—looking into some healthy, organic options. Maybe"—she glanced around, then focused on a little wooden bowl of simple iceberg salad—"mix some kale in with the lettuce. Something like that. We don't need to talk about it now, of course."

"Why not now?"

"Well, because my mother's not here. It's her call. I'm just thinking out loud." She smiled, gracious and reasonable.

But Andy wasn't buying it. He crossed his arms over his chest. "I know she wanted you here because you've done this whole reality thing before." He gestured to the cameras. "But Barbara and I are pretty much on the same page in the kitchen, and that's the same page Mimi's always been on. We serve what we serve, and it's all the best of its kind. We leave the messing around with mozzarella sticks to Frannie's."

Great. Clearly Andy saw her as some kind of threat, and one who knew nothing about Mimi's and its business besides. This was ridiculous. She hadn't really even been thinking about the menu, although there were things they could do—it would be nice to have a healthier option, for example. She'd just wanted to get the attention off her "homecoming." Without meaning to, she crossed her own arms. "Not mozzarella sticks. And really, we should wait for my mother."

"Sounds fine," he said, turning away. "You know she'll agree with me."

Sabrina, still smiling brightly, stepped back up, and Mae glanced around her for a way to end this conversation before it began again. She leaned over and grabbed Ryder's only remaining piece of chicken and bit into it enthusiastically. "That's good, isn't it?"

Ryder's howls caused both Sabrina and her cameraperson to step away, and once they'd engaged with a customer, asking about the evening's food, Mae slid a piece of chicken from Madison's plate to Ryder's, knowing her daughter cared far more about the fries. "I'm sorry, buddy. I was hungry. I should have asked, right?"

Ryder sniffled and nodded.

The chicken was good, at least. Even better than she remembered, and she took more of Madison's generous serving. She had eaten next to nothing all day, and it had been years since she'd eaten a French fry, let alone fried chicken. Good fried chicken was remarkably hard to come by in New York, but this—tender, with just enough crust-only bits protruding, skin peeling easily away from the meat—this was *good*. The fries were thin and still hot, some with crunch, some with bite, lightly sprinkled with the salt blend they'd always used. The biscuits were fresh and flaky, and the salad's iceberg lettuce was dressed with Mimi's trademark sweet oil dressing—a closely guarded (but really very simple, and once very common) recipe. Delicious, all of it, if technically speaking a nutritional catastrophe.

Jay would like this, she thought absently. *If he'd like anything to do with her right now.* And if she were to bring Jay anywhere near this place, which she would not. Of all the things Jay was never going to taste, this chicken topped the list. This was a guy who thought the twenty-eight-dollar fried chicken plate at Blue Ribbon had a little touch of slumming it, especially when eaten at one A.M. after a night in the bars of the Lower East Side. She'd known from their first date that Jay would never get Mimi's.

They'd attended a wedding once, of a college friend of his, in St. Louis. It had been a very nice wedding, actually, but Jay, the only nonwhite person in attendance, had been forthright in his East Coast condemnation of the entire city, the entire state, the entire region. Mae had joined in at the time, agreeing that she didn't much miss "the suburbs of Kansas City," where she had long since relocated Merinac when relating her precollege history, and internally renewing a vow of her own: Jay would never, ever set foot in her hometown. A few years wouldn't have erased the small-mindedness that had always kept people here from dreaming big or doing anything with their lives. She was lucky. She got out. Jay didn't ever need to know just how far she had come.

He would like the chicken, though. And the biscuits. And the whole history of the place, if he could just see past the *Wizard of Oz* jokes. Jay worked with restaurants, damn it. It was his consulting specialty, and he might be sick of consulting, but he never got sick of restaurants and food and eating out. He should see that *Food Wars* was going to be great not just for her but for Mimi's as well. Of course, he didn't know about Mimi's so he couldn't care about Mimi's. Lately he didn't care about anything she cared about that wasn't obviously kid related.

She looked at Madison and Ryder, sated with fries, now eating the salad with their fingers, as she and Amanda once had. Amanda's kids would have eaten their salads at Frannie's, with forks, most likely. Another weird thought. Back here, in this familiar space, the more distant past had way more power over her memory than anything that might have changed since then—had changed since then. Amanda's kids should have belonged at Mimi's, but they didn't. Her kids hadn't grown up here, but here they were, and they had never met their cousins, not once. Mostly, Mae managed not to think much, if at all, about how things were with her and Amanda. It was just—background. Something that would work itself out in time, that didn't affect her here and now and therefore did not have to be worried about. Mae didn't borrow trouble, and she didn't have any trouble letting the past stay in the past.

Her marriage would be one more thing she'd have to deal with later. For the moment, clearly the best thing to do was to write tonight off, from a filming point of view, and regroup tomorrow.

×

As the night rolled to a close and Andy, Angelique, and Zeus began the shutdown routine, Mae made her excuses and carried an exhausted Ryder back to the rental car, with Madison trailing behind. Armed with a roll of paper towels and some spray cleaner, she laid a garbage bag over the now-disgusting car seat and kept the windows down. She buckled the kids in over complaints about the smell and turned on a video, sitting in the driver's seat until they both fell asleep, waving to Sabrina as she and her convertible pulled away, sending a quick text to Jay.

Getting the kids to sleep, can't talk, all ok there?

She'd finally got a sympathetic reply from him at about hour three of the flight fiasco (albeit one tinged with *it's not like this wasn't your idea*). He'd even wished her luck, which she chose to interpret as for her entire endeavor, not just her travels.

She gazed down at the screen, wondering if he'd answer. He was just as attached to his phone as she was, for all his big talk about disengaging and getting away from the cacophony. Sure enough, there he was.

Kinda late isn't it?

It's an hour earlier here. And they napped.

Oh.

Go okay?

Yes! A little messy but I made it work.

Talk once they're asleep?

She considered. Did she want to actually talk to Jay? She'd conveniently left out that she was getting the kids to sleep in the car; she still had to carry them into the motel—thank God for first-floor rooms! And she wasn't even going back to the motel just yet. She started up the car, one eye on the kids still asleep in the back seat—Madison shifted, but her eyes didn't open—and drove the few hundred feet into the driveway of the house, where she could comfortably leave the kids but still keep a close eye on them.

Mae's plan was to go find her mother, but as she parked, she saw a car pull into the Mimi's parking lot—and a figure that was unmistakably Amanda walking toward the back door of Mimi's.

Thank goodness—they'd finally get to hash out a plan. With a quick glance at the kids—they'd be okay, she never had to go out of sight—Mae got out, ready to call to her sister. But something made her stop and watch, as Andy came out and greeted Amanda with more pleasure than Mae would have expected, given the quality of her own earlier welcome. A lot more pleasure. He came all the way out of the kitchen, and the screen door banged behind him. She could hear his "Hey," but not Amanda's response, although she heard her laugh, then laugh again. She looked different somehow, too. She couldn't be taller, but there was something slender and sleek about her silhouette—her hair. She had cut her hair. And as Mae watched, Amanda put a hand up to the back of her neck, and then Andy reached out to touch her sister's head.

Wait a minute. Amanda was flirting! That was totally flirting. Now she could hear her sister: "The day was great—filming was fun. How did it go for you guys?" And then, Mae swore, a giggle. A giggle like a twelve-year-old. *Jeez.* Mae hesitated. She had plans, and she wanted Amanda's help, but her sister wouldn't be happy if Mae walked in on her now, and Mae had things to say that were best not said in front of Andy. This was ridiculous. Could Amanda seriously not find any guys not already within the Merinac fried chicken web? In spite of everything, Mae had been somehow expecting to get the old, pre-Frannie's version of Amanda back. But if Amanda would just walk up and start flirting with this dude, then she really had changed, and not just with a haircut.

Shit. Jay. She looked at her phone, where his suggestion that they talk still dangled. No. She really couldn't talk to Jay tonight.

> Sorry, had to settle Ryder. Sharing a room, don't want to wake them, am wiped.
>
> Tomorrow?

She tucked the phone in her pocket, not waiting for a response, then headed toward the house, which was set farther back from the street than Mimi's. Amanda could wait. All night, in the back of her mind, Mae had been stewing over her mother. How could Barbara leave before she got there? Her mother wasn't one to leave anything to do with Mimi's up to anyone else, and Barbara had been skeptical about *Food Wars* when they spoke, so Mae doubted she'd just let them film without her without a good reason. It must have made sense to her mother somehow, but Mae was damned if she could see how. Not that she always got what Barbara thought was important. But this was weird—and not in the usual way.

Curious, but not exactly worried, Mae stepped up to the door. The lights were off, and the house quiet, but Barbara always kept the front of the house dark when the restaurant was open, to discourage people from heading this way, so that meant nothing. Mae lifted her hand and, mindful that Amanda and Andy could possibly hear her, gave a soft but sharp rap on the door. Mae waited, but there was no answer. She knocked again, still cautiously. She wanted to see her mom tonight, especially given her unexpected disappearance from Mimi's. But her great-aunt Aida, who lived with Barbara, was almost certainly asleep by now, and Mae didn't want to wake her. There would be plenty of time tomorrow for Aunt Aida. Suddenly from within, she heard a low, growling bark.

Patches. Her mother's dog. She'd never met the mutt and wondered now—did Patches' presence suggest that Barbara was home, or not? Mae had no clue, but the low bark settled one thing: she wasn't opening the door. Mae didn't know much about dogs, and she didn't want to. Patches, she knew from pictures, was not a small dog and didn't look friendly. Mae had no desire to find out if she would instinctively recognize family.

She wasn't setting foot in the house anyway. If Barbara was home, they'd talk in the garden, or walk out behind the house. Mae had decided a long time ago that Mimi's was fine, but she was never going in her mother's house again.

There was no reason Mae could imagine that her mother wouldn't open the door to her. Either she hadn't heard the knock or she wasn't home. But where would she go? It was nearly ten o'clock. The only thing open was the Dillons, and even that would close in half an hour. More likely Barbara was simply not answering the

door. It had always been her cardinal rule: don't open the door
to anyone; don't let anyone into this house. The succession of
older family who lived with them—long ago, her great-grandmother
Mimi and her great-great-aunt Mary Cat and now presumably
Aida—followed it too: no outsiders in the house.

Mae only broke the rule once—although once had been enough
to change everything, at least for her. Barbara had taken Mary Cat
to gloat over an old friend who, at eighty-nine and a full decade
younger than Mary Cat, had fallen and broken a hip. Mae, six, and
Amanda, almost five, promised they would not touch the stove.
They would not wander off. They would stay in the house with their
coloring books on the cleared-off part of the counter and they would
not use glue, and they were proudly living up to their new responsi-
bilities when the doorbell rang.

The doorbell never rang. Once, maybe twice ever, and her
mother had opened it and stepped out and come back in quickly,
shaking her head. *Mormons,* she'd said. Mae figured she could do
the same, and hesitantly opened the door. She had no idea what a
Mormon was, but when Mae saw the tall man standing there, he
was so unlike her mental image of a Mormon (which looked something like a Munchkin) that she forgot to step outside and shut
the door but instead just stood there.

The tall man knelt down in front of her and put out a hand.
Mae took a step back, almost into the house. "Mae?" he asked, and
she nodded and took his hand. It was dry and hot and rough on the
edges, and he shook her hand hard.

"Do you know I'm your father, Mae?"

She shook her head vigorously. She did not know this. She was
not sure she believed this. Of course she had often asked Barbara
why she and Amanda did not have a father. "Because he's a fool," her
mother would snap. "A fool and a weakling. Some people you're just
better off without." And the old ladies, Mary Cat and old Mimi, her
sister, would agree, if they were around. This man did not seem like

a weakling—he was big and tall and a little scary—and just as suddenly as he'd knelt to take her hand, he stood up, dropping it and staring past her into the house. He said a word she did not know, and she could tell by his face that he was surprised, and not in a happy way. Too late, she went to close the door behind her, but he leaned over her and held it open.

"My God," he said, and pushed harder on the door. "Frank, look at this." Out on the sidewalk Mae saw a man she recognized. He owned Frannie's, she thought. And he had a big car, a big red car with no top that he drove everywhere all summer long, and a little boy who was in Amanda's kindergarten who rode in back and always got ice cream. That man came and looked in behind the first man, who was pushing on the door and trying to get past her.

The door didn't open any farther—Mae could have told him that. There were boxes behind it, and a big piece of countertop leaning on them. Sitting on top was a doll Mae didn't like, with arms and legs and a face made of ladies' hose stuffed with something and tied with thread to create fingers and a nose, chin, and toes, wearing a feathered hat. There was tons more, too, but that was mostly what kept the door from opening.

She tried to block his way, but he pushed past her, and when she turned to try to get in front of him she saw that Amanda had finished coloring and was trying to push her barstool back and climb down.

"Manda, wait," she called.

"I'm coming," said Amanda, and shoved herself back as hard as she could. The barstool tipped backward and Amanda shrieked, but instead of hitting the ground, the stool was caught by the box stacked on the end table behind it, and Amanda rolled off over the box, over the arm of the sofa, off the sofa, and onto the floor. The man had pushed Mae aside and tried to rush to Amanda, but he tripped and nearly fell on her instead, and Amanda began to scream.

"It's okay!" the man shouted above Amanda, reaching for her. "Are you okay? Where does it hurt?"

Amanda rolled onto her back and kicked up, catching the man sharply under the chin so that he screamed too, a sort of strangled *argh* sound as he collapsed onto the sofa. Amanda, surprised by the success of her move, paused in her screaming, but the room didn't quiet, because Barbara, still young then, still thin, still angry, slammed the open front door into the stack of boxes again.

"Gary?"

Her face was pale, and as the other man, the convertible man, tried to come in behind her, Barbara elbowed him in the gut.

"You get out of here, Frank Pogociello. I know your daddy sent you, but you've got no right to be in here, no right. This house is not for sale." Mae could tell her mother was mad. Madder than she'd ever seen her, maybe, and seeing this, she ran around the fallen man, grabbed Amanda, and stood in front of her little sister like a shield.

Barbara didn't scream at the man in the house. Her voice got real low, real quiet. "Gary Logan, you get out. You get out right now, before I have to figure out what I'm going to do if you don't."

"I just want to talk to you. I want to see the girls."

"You don't just show up here trying to talk and see. You don't just show up anywhere. Right now, I want you to get out. If that's all you want, if you just want to talk, then you call me, and then we'll see. You don't go sneaking in here without me."

The man stood up. "I thought you were here," he said. "Hear that, Frank? She wasn't here, and this child opened the door right up for us. Couple of strangers."

"Oh, I was here," Barbara said. She was talking fast now, right over him. "I was here. I was out back, and I heard you come sneaking in."

The man edged past Barbara, squeezing through the boxes, and looked out the front door. "That car wasn't here before," he said. Mary Cat was coming slowly up the walk.

"It was." Barbara crossed her arms. "I don't care if you didn't see it."

He looked back at Mae. "She wasn't here, was she, Mae?" he asked.

Mae was a fast thinker, and she knew her mother. If Barbara lied, she would lie. She crossed her own arms. "She was." Mae heard Amanda get up behind her. Amanda was a truth teller, every time; she could not be made to see that sometimes it was better that grown-ups and other people not know everything. Mae knew what she had to do. She bent her leg and kicked backward, hard as she could, and felt her foot make contact. Amanda screamed again and fell over, holding her arms wrapped around her stomach and rolling from side to side, and Mae turned around and made her fiercest face at her sister, hoping she would understand so Mae would not have to kick her again. Their eyes met, and Amanda shut her mouth up firm and lay still.

"I was in the back," Barbara said. "Gardening." Now that she was between the man and the girls, she started walking toward him, willing him out the door.

Mary Cat stood aside as if to let him by. She seemed to know who he was. "Gary," she said. "I take it you were just leaving?"

The man ignored her and turned back to Barbara. "This place is a shithole," he said. "It's— What is all this?"

Barbara Moore's house might have been a mess, but she herself was not. She brushed off the front of her blouse casually, as if to suggest that no speck of dirt would last anywhere near her, and said firmly, "We have just inherited a few things, and I have not yet unpacked. But you will not be here long enough for it to bother you."

Gary Logan kicked the stack of boxes nearest him, and the doll perched on top fell over. "That was your mother's," he said. "She died five years ago, Barb. Seriously, what is all this crap?" He turned to look down the hallway, and Barbara seized this opportunity to take him by both shoulders and march him out the door, following and slamming it behind them. The windows that would have shown Mae what happened next were covered, but she could hear her mother shouting.

Amanda sat up. "Is he gone?"

"I don't think so."

"You kicked me. And she wasn't here. You know it."

"I know."

"She lied. You lied."

Mae shrugged. She knew that, too, and while she didn't know why she'd lied, she knew she'd been right to do it. When they heard Barbara coming back inside, the girls rushed back to the counter and resumed coloring, heads down.

"Who let him in?" Barbara's voice was low and fierce.

Mae kept her eyes on her coloring book. "I— Amanda fell off the stool. I opened the door and Amanda fell off the stool and he came in." Mae knew that Amanda wouldn't say anything now, even if she'd seen something different. She wouldn't lie, but sometimes she could keep her mouth shut.

"I told you not to open that door. I told you, while I'm gone, don't you open that door to anybody. Not anybody, no matter what they say."

Mae thought she just wasn't supposed to let anybody in, but she didn't argue. Barbara turned and walked back out the door. She spoke over her shoulder as Mary Cat took a glass from the sink, rinsed it out, and opened the refrigerator, ignoring them all.

"Get your shoes. Get in the car."

Mae and Amanda, confused, didn't move.

"I'm not leaving you here again. Now!"

They drove straight to the big house where her mother's best friend lived, and Barbara went in, leaving them in the car. After a while, Barbara and Patti came out and they all drove home together; Patti held the girls' hands as they followed their mother into the house. Mae got her sister a coloring book, but Amanda didn't open it, just held it tight. Instead, they watched as Barbara and Patti, and then more grown-ups, filled boxes and bags and carried them out, then came in and did it again and again. Amanda's head rested heavy on Mae's shoulder before falling into her lap, and Mae laid her own head down on her sister, just for a minute, while she tried to figure out what was going on.

When she woke, the room was so empty that she didn't recognize it. There was the sofa, the big chair beside it, and in front of them both a glass-topped table Mae barely remembered, with two magazines carefully stacked on it next to an empty ashtray. There was a round rug over the worn carpet, and a set of glass shelves against the wall holding nothing but the television and two bookends shaped like monkeys with their hands over their mouths or eyes. The whole thing gleamed, from the mirrored silvery supports to the sparkling clear shelves.

It was the most beautiful thing Mae had ever seen. Mae got up and walked over to the shelves, putting her head under and staring up through the glass. It was so clear she could see straight up, and she lay down in the center of the room and spread her arms and legs wide, making a snow angel in the rug, then rolled all the way to one side, then the other, basking in the space to move. She had never even known how much she wanted this until now.

Did the rest of the house look this way? She heard voices in the kitchen and followed them, walking quietly with tiny steps through the neat room.

Patti was standing on a chair, wiping out a cabinet. Her mother stood beneath her, a *Smurfs* glass in each hand, ready to hand them up. The kitchen was as clean as the living room. Mae wanted to eat at that clean counter, drink from that *Smurfs* glass, stay in this kitchen forever.

"Can I have some cereal?"

Her mother turned, and one of the glasses—the best one, the one with Smurfette—slipped from her hand and shattered. Her mother stared down at the mess, and Mae froze as Barbara lifted the other glass above her head and dropped it. Glass flew even farther.

"Barbara . . ." Patti climbed carefully down from the chair. She had on shoes. Barbara was in her stocking feet and Mae, barefoot. "Don't move, Mae, honey. Not one step."

Amanda, also barefoot, appeared in the door, and Patti picked her up and swung her up on a counter, then lifted Mae up next to her. "I'll get a broom."

Barbara didn't move her feet, but she put her hands on her hips and looked right at Mae.

"You let a world of trouble in here last night," she said. "Gary Logan wants nothing but money, and that friend of his, that Frank Pogociello, he'll steal this house right out from under us if he can. We can't give them any excuse to go snooping around, you hear me? If they think I can't manage, and bring in social, they'll take you two away. Is that what you want? Is it? Because that's what you did, when you let him in."

Patti ran back in without the broom.

"They don't know, Barbara. Stop."

Mae stared at her mother, trying to understand. Barbara walked right through the glass and put her hand under Mae's chin, talking straight into her face. "Now it's clean, and it will stay that way, but if you tell anyone it wasn't, or that I left you alone here, that gives them a way in, do you see? People think a woman alone can't do anything, and just because we don't have money, because I need to work and I can't be spending all my time making it pretty around here, they think they can run right over me and get what they want, and what they want is to get us out of here, pave this place over, turn it into a parking lot or something. And we are not going to let that happen."

Mae nodded, and Patti said, "Barbara. You're scaring her. It's okay. It's going to be okay."

"I told you what Mary Cat said," said Barbara. "If they make that mortgage due—"

"They won't. There's no reason to."

"They could take it all away, Patti. And we—the girls and me—"

Mae *was* scared. Who would take what away? What had she done?

"It's okay, Mae," said Patti, but Mae didn't believe her. She didn't believe anyone but her mother, and her mother did not look okay.

Mae crawled over the counter and off on the other side, away from the broken glass.

She picked up the broom and took the dustpan in her other hand. "I can make it pretty, Mama," she offered. "While you work."

It took years for Mae to realize that she could not keep that promise no matter how hard she tried. Her father had never returned, at least as far as she knew. "Dead of his drinking, and good riddance," her mother said a few years later, when she asked, and Mae couldn't find the energy to care. Frank Pogociello came around a few more times, knocking, and even left papers taped to the door, which were the only things Mae ever saw her mother manage to throw away.

The house, though, reverted to its previous state within a matter of months. Twice more, Barbara's friends, and later Mae and Amanda, took the house all the way back down to the bones, and twice more it returned to chaos. Entropy happened fast on Barbara's watch, and as Mae stood outside the house now, she understood that it had been a long time since anyone had tried to stop it. She had no intention of trying. Her only involvement with her mother's house on this trip would be to prevent *Food Wars* from coming anywhere near the place.

From somewhere behind her she heard a car door slam, and she took off at a run, thinking it was Madison or Ryder. But when she reached the edge of the house, she saw taillights turning out of the parking lot. Amanda and Andy, then, leaving, faster than she would have expected. She'd have to find Amanda in the morning. Barbara too. Damn.

It was late, but Mae felt restless. Time to make things happen. She yanked out her phone and texted her sister as she walked. Didn't want to interrupt you and Andy. Slick moves, chick. Meet me after your school drop-off. We need to make a plan.

The back door of Mimi's hung open, and as she reached in to shut it, she felt the gloom wrap around her in a way that it had not when Andy, Angelique, and Zeus were bustling around. The whole place spoke to Mae of decay and despair, and always had, in spite of the bright yellow paint. The first Mimi had started it not out of a burning desire to share her family chicken recipe but out of desperation when money first got tight, and it never loosened up. In the picture that had always hung on the wall she looked pinched and worried, and she was no happier in a later picture with the two daughters who would become Mary Cat and Mary Margaret, the second Mimi, the old ladies of Mae's childhood.

Enough Mimis, enough memories. Mae spun around, away from the picture, waving her arms to stir things up as she went. Clearly it was time for bed. It was a warm night, but Mae felt a familiar chill as she walked out the front door and let it shut behind her. There was a shitload of ghosts in here, and most of them weren't even dead.

AMANDA

Amanda woke up to the sound of Frankie in her closet.

Her head was pounding. She'd slept poorly, which was typical, and her last memories were of a dream with Frank in it, dark hair freshly trimmed and wearing the khaki pants and button-down he wore to teach, frying chicken at Mimi's and telling her to go back to Frannie's, never once turning so that she could just see his face. What she wanted was Pickle, whose heavily panting presence was the lullaby that kept her sleeping. But Pickle was gone, and Amanda still wasn't used to it.

Yesterday had not ended well, and everything she'd gone to sleep trying not to think about was still there today. Mae showing up in Merinac after Amanda had convinced herself that she wouldn't, and then sending that text, summoning Amanda to the royal presence. Where the hell had Mae been that she'd been spying on Amanda without Amanda seeing her? What business was it of hers? Sabrina, who had been so nice but still left Amanda feeling a little like everyone felt sorry for her, and then the stupid impromptu haircut, which had attracted far too much attention last night at Frannie's. Her kids and Nancy all said it looked good, but they were probably just trying to be nice. She put a hand to her hair, which felt shorn on the sides, and pulled angrily at the springy curls that at least remained on top. How fast could this grow back? She'd have to find a baseball cap. There was probably one in the closet. With Frankie.

"What do you want in there? At least let me find it for you." Frankie in her tiny walk-in closet was a shortcut to catastrophe;

she had no respect for Amanda's system, with the handful of things she actually wore in the front on the right, winter clothes jammed into the front left, and the piles of things she needed to sort and maybe give away pushed up carefully under the older hanging stuff in back.

"I'm not looking for me," Frankie said, and turned to dump an armful of hangers and unfolded items onto Amanda's bed. Amanda winced. System destroyed, plus now all of this would be on the floor next to her bed for the next month or more.

"We have to figure out what you're wearing today." Frankie riffled through her choices. "This does not look good on you anymore; you need to either get a waist or get rid of it. This isn't bad, but the pattern will look awful on a screen. This"—she threw a three-quarter-sleeve T-shirt with a crisscrossed neck in a bright blue at her mother—"this is pretty good. It's a good color for you. Do you have any clean jeans that are decent?" She pulled out a pair from her pile. "There is really no way you can still wear these. Why don't you go through here and get rid of the stuff you don't want?"

Honestly, she sounded like Mae, and it had never been more horrifying. "I like those jeans," Amanda protested.

"They make you look like you're wearing a sack on each leg." Frankie walked around to the side of Amanda's bed and looked down at the pile of clothes on the floor. "Wear the ones you had on yesterday; they're not awful. With sandals."

"I'm not wearing sandals to work! And I can't wear any of that, anyway. I'm wearing the Frannie's shirt, and so are you."

"You can wear this for the first part," Frankie said. "Make it look like you've just come to work from the rest of your great life. And if there's a part where you talk to the camera, you can ask to change. The Frannie's shirt makes you look like you've been sick for a week. Your hair is awesome, at least. You can't mess that up."

Frankie disappeared in the direction of breakfast and the school bus, where she would no doubt bask in the reflected glory of the first day's *Food Wars* filming, whereas Amanda, who had not very much enjoyed being told that she was shapeless and pale, got up slowly, avoiding the mirror on the closet door, which told her that Frankie was right. At least Frankie was being nice about it, even if she did remind Amanda of a slightly more docile version of her sister. Frankie didn't know yet that Mae would be here for *Food Wars,* and Amanda was avoiding telling her. Frankie had written about her largely unknown aunt for a school essay ("write about someone you admire"), and her teacher had scrawled, *How nice that you have a successful family member to look up to,* across the top.

Bitch.

Amanda felt nothing but dread for the day ahead. She did her chicken and garden chores quickly, feeding the birds, checking their water, dropping the watermelon rinds they loved without taking time to hold one out and laugh at the way they pecked their way right through the red and white and down to the green. The longer she thought about the things she had said to Sabrina yesterday, the dumber they seemed, and apparently she had looked so pitifully out of style while doing it that Sabrina had been moved to make her over, producing her own hair and makeup artist to do so. Both she and Gordo had pronounced the result "fantastic," but it was so far removed from any haircut Amanda had ever had, or even any haircut that anyone—any woman, at least—in Merinac would choose, that she took no pleasure at all in her arguably improved appearance.

And then, when all she'd intended to do was go to Mimi's and find Mae to try to figure out why Mae had gone from *hell no* to *of course I'll come* in ten minutes flat and then followed that up by actually coming, instead of backing out like she totally should have, Amanda found Andy instead. Andy liked the haircut. Andy had demanded to "pet the fresh fuzz" where her hair was shortest, on the back of her neck, and the feeling of his hand running up and down the shorn hairs had sent little shivers up and down parts of her that she hadn't let shiver in a long time. He'd known it, too, damn it; she knew he did. But he had been nice about it. He'd stepped back instead of forward, and she'd been grateful, and if she'd also been a little disappointed, he never needed to know that. The guy was a player. He had to be. And he was way out of her league.

Following directions, even while wishing she had the balls to just ignore Mae and get on with her own life—her own great life, per Frankie—Amanda hauled her bright-blue-shirt-wearing self to the Mimi's parking lot.

Mae, looking quite cheerful, probably because her hair was still long and dark and shiny and normal-looking, was seated on the opened back of a rental hatchback with all the windows down when Amanda pulled up. From a distance, it looked as though the little car was crawling with kids; up close she saw it was only Mae's two, the boy trying to pull himself up through the sunroof, the girl pretending to drive.

"Nice playground," she said by way of greeting. Mae hopped up to embrace her, and Amanda returned the hug with less enthusiasm. Mae looked exactly the same. Oh, Mae would probably say she looked different. The jeans, the sleek hair, the way the arms of her shirt folded up perfectly, the thick-soled white sneakers in a brand Amanda didn't recognize—she looked expensive now. She even smelled expensive, like sharp honeysuckle, aggressively clean.

But she was still Mae, with that expression that said she was ready for action, and why hadn't Amanda done whatever it is she would do yet?

And there were her kids. Kids Amanda had never met, although she'd talked to them, sort of, on FaceTime as they ran around ignoring her the way kids did any face on the screen that wasn't animated and speaking in that hellish educational TV voice. They were ignoring her now, too, still caught up in all the car had to offer. Mae followed her gaze, then shrugged.

"It's a novelty to a New York kid. Anything for a few minutes' peace."

Amanda could remember feeling that way, but for her it came with a shot of longing. When her kids were that little, she'd been exactly what everyone wanted, Frank, Gus, Frankie, all craving her presence, all touching her, all the time, and just like Mae, she'd wished it away. If she'd known how quickly it would end, would it have mattered? The phrase *I was beautiful then* drifted through her mind, and she was embarrassed to realize, after a moment, that it wasn't a fragment of poetry but a line from the musical *Cats*.

Mae was going on and on about Amanda's hair. "Seriously, it's so fresh. You should have done this years ago! It's so—I mean, you just look so fab, and young, and cute, and with your height—I wish I could carry that off. I'd just look like I got a mom cut, I know I would. And it's going to be so easy!"

Great. That translated to, *You look like an old lady who will need to get her hair set every week, and I would never, ever do that.* Amanda should have found that baseball cap. "I think I hate it," she said.

"No, it's lit. Really. It's cool even for New York, because it's so artsy and unique. And you don't even have any gray yet, do you? I have to cover mine every six weeks already."

Amanda shook her head about the gray hair—there, one advantage to being younger—but she was still stuck on the double-edged sword of "unique." Unique good, or unique weird? "Not yet," she said, and then, finally, the kids rolled out of the car, one after the other, and stopped short at the sight of her. Mae scooped up Ryder, who lifted the stuffed toy he held clutched in his hand to his mouth before Mae gently pushed it away.

It was the chicken she'd sent him when he was born. Amanda was surprised—and delighted. She wouldn't have thought her sister would care about that at all. She smiled and touched the chicken's dirty wing, gently. "Hi, Ryder," she said.

Ryder buried his face and the chicken in Mae's shoulder, but Amanda didn't give up. "I sent you that chicken," she said softly.

"When you were a little baby. I'm glad he's so loved. What's his name?"

Ryder said something she didn't understand, and Madison reached up and held his foot. "It used to be Chicken but now it's Rawlings," she said. "Daddy named it. Rydie still calls it Chicken, though."

Mae set Ryder down and crouched behind both children. "Give your aunt Amanda a hug, then," she said. Madison hesitated, and Ryder backed into Mae as Amanda held up her hands and took a step back.

"No way," she said. "I haven't earned a hug yet, right, guys? I can't hug you. I just met you." She crossed her arms and made a pouty face, and Madison giggled. "No hugs for you. Maybe later." Mae met Amanda's eyes with a look that said she'd noticed Amanda's implied critique but was ignoring it, and then her attention was caught by someone coming down the sidewalk, a girl Amanda didn't recognize, carrying two cups from Patrick's.

Mae stood up and waved. "There she is," Mae said. "The lattes at that new place, 1908 something, are to die for. Jessa brought me one, and I already sent her for a second. I should have had her grab you one, too. Have you been? Main Street is so different. You never told me someone reopened the five-and-dime, and it's totally cute now. Or about the craft store. Or the bookstore. They had my book in the window!"

"Of course I've been to Patrick's," Amanda said. No one called it the 1908 Standard, no matter what it said on the sign. "They have the best coffee in town. Plus, that's part of Kenneth's place. His bed-and-breakfast, the one they've been renovating for years. You're on Facebook, Mae; you have to know this stuff. Patrick is Kenneth's husband, and they came back a while ago and redid the old inn, and there is no way you could have missed it. They put up pictures every day for months."

Mae looked down for a second, then straight at Amanda. "I

haven't spoken to Kenneth since we graduated, except at your wedding," she said. "I'm not Facebook friends with anyone from Merinac except you."

Amanda was shocked. "But that's the whole point of Facebook. To keep up with people. You're on Facebook *all the time*. What the hell are you doing? And Kenneth was your best friend. I know you dropped everyone when you went to college, but Kenneth? Plus his place is gorgeous. I can't believe you aren't staying there."

"I'm close enough to Mom's house as it is," Mae said. "Look, Kenneth went and did his thing. I did mine. And now I'm back, and I will say hi and drink his husband's unbelievable coffee, and what really matters, especially if he owns a business on Main, is *Food Wars*. *Food Wars* is going to fucking save this town." She turned away from Amanda as the coffee carrier rushed up.

"Sorry that took so long, Mae; there was a line," she said.

"That's totally okay. Jessa, my sister, Amanda. Amanda, this is Jessa, our nanny."

Amanda stuck out her hand. *Nanny?* Mae brought a nanny? To Merinac? Her sister truly had lost touch, and not just with Kenneth, which Amanda still couldn't believe. Bringing a nanny was an asshole move, and her comment about *Food Wars* saving this town raised every one of Amanda's hackles, even if she had thought much the same thing. Merinac was actually doing fine, thanks for asking, with more new people and businesses than there had been in years—case in point, the coffee Mae loved so much. "Nice to meet you," Amanda said to the girl, but Jessa's attention had already turned to the kids, who were greeting her with a lot more enthusiasm than they had shown Amanda, possibly because she also produced juice boxes from the bag over her shoulder as she handed Mae her coffee.

"Guys," she said, "I found a swing set. And a slide! Let's go!" She quickly turned back and took Amanda's hand. "Nice to meet you, too," she said as she picked up Ryder and held out a hand to

Madison. "We're off, then," Jessa said to Mae, and Mae waved. No fuss, no hugs, and the kids were heading down the street.

"Bye," Amanda called after them, and Madison turned. In that over-the-shoulder glance, Amanda could see that she looked just like Mae.

"Bye, Aunt Amanda," Madison called, then tugged at Ryder. "Say bye, Ryder."

Bossy, too.

Ryder waved his chicken at Amanda, and she felt a small crush of affection for him rush through her. "Bye," he called. The obedient younger. For now.

"They're so cute," she said to Mae, who had already turned away. "We could have taken them with us. I mean, your *nanny*? You brought a nanny?"

"Please, Amanda, everybody in Brooklyn has a nanny. You didn't think I was going to come out here and try to do *Food Wars* while juggling a six-year-old and a three-year-old, did you?"

Three references to New York in less than as many minutes, true to Mae form. Also true to form was the annoyance Amanda felt after a few minutes of her sister's company, an experience she could usually end by hanging up the phone. Once past the hair, Mae hadn't asked a thing about Amanda, or her kids. She'd managed to combine insult and condescension in nearly every sentence, and now she was brushing off her own kids as if they were just another inconvenient bump on the golden Mae road. Why not have them at Mimi's? Of course, in *New York*, things were different. "We grew up at Mimi's," she said. She couldn't remember a single babysitter, not ever. Only the great-aunts, and Mae, always in charge, always there.

Mae rolled her eyes. "And I am sure Mom would have been more than happy to get us out of her hair sometimes. Plus, she had Grandma Mimi and Mary Cat. My kids don't know anyone here, they're not going to hang out with a stranger, and they don't need to be in every scene of *Food Wars*. I know how this works. One wrong move, and next thing you know, they've made your kid look like a spoiled brat, or you like a monster."

"Great, now you'll look like someone who leaves her kids with someone else all the time. Gus and Frankie were at Frannie's every day, and they're fine." Amanda was happy to needle Mae about this one. There wasn't much she'd done before her sister, let alone done better—but at least she'd been able to raise her kids without hired help, even as a single mom.

"You have no idea what this is going to be like, Amanda. It's not just getting filmed while you do your usual stuff. It's being able to do the scenes they want over and over, which kids don't get—plus you have to watch out for what they're trying to make happen. Did you read the release you signed? They can do anything they want with any footage they get, so you have to be sure they don't get anything you don't want out there."

Amanda thought of the interview she hadn't realized she was doing. But Sabrina had basically said they wouldn't use it. "I'm sure Sabrina isn't like that," she said.

Mae laughed. "Everybody's like that. But if we're smart, we can manage the story they tell." She handed Amanda a sheet of paper. "Here," she said, "I made some talking points. Just, good things we can say about each other, right? I've got some too. Just so it's clear we're all besties, right?" Amanda glanced down at the page as Mae slammed the back of the car shut. *Shared history. All family. Keep the challenges in the kitchen.* Mae must have clicked the lock button on her key fob, because the car gave a light honk, which made Amanda snicker silently as she shoved the paper in her bag. Nobody locked their cars in Merinac. Mae had no idea where she was any more.

"Come on, walk with me. We have to figure this out." Mae headed toward the little wooded area that stretched behind Mimi's and the house, and Amanda reluctantly fell in beside her. The story didn't need managing, and she didn't need Mae's help.

"We don't need to figure anything out, Mae. *Food Wars* wants a rivalry, and we have that. All we have to do is what we usually do. I don't even know why you're here, to be honest."

"Because Mom wants me here." Mae gave Amanda a smug look. "And she's not doing this without me, so if you want to do it at all, you're stuck with me."

For a nickel, Amanda would just end the whole thing right now. "Maybe I don't want to do it anymore," she said. But she did, and Mae, who knew it, turned and bounced off toward the trees without even so much as looking behind her. How could Mae always be so certain that she had everything under control, that other people would fall in with her plans? It was even more annoying when she was right.

"Listen," Mae was saying, and Amanda had to hurry to catch up so that she could hear her. "I get it. Frannie's is big and Mimi's is little, and you expect to win, and you probably will. And you need me to help Mom keep Mimi's in the running, and I will. But we want to keep them out of Mom's house, right? And out of our family lives. We don't want them poking around, asking your kids how they feel about their dad's death, stuff like that. If we hand them the story, they're not looking for a story. So we're, like, three very independent women who need our own things, but we respect each other. Like sports. We keep the competition on the field; off the field, we're fine." She glanced up at Amanda, possibly to see how her sister was taking this rewriting of history.

Amanda kept pace with Mae on the familiar walk down to the railroad tracks, long out of use, and then to the river, entering into the conversation in spite of herself. "Have you run this brilliant plan by Mom yet? She'll love respecting me as an independent businesswoman."

Mae let that go. "They'll focus on you and me if we let them," she said. "And we can pull it off, Amanda. We're adults. We can be—cordial. No, warm. And I was thinking—"

Amanda, who was uncomfortably aware that she had already

blown this plan of Mae's out of the water, tuned in at that phrase. "I was thinking," from Mae meant that something mattered enough to her that she was at least trying to present it in a way that was palatable to the other person. It meant that somewhere in her plans, Mae had run across something she couldn't just make happen on her own. Amanda eyed her sister cautiously. Mae went on without looking at her.

"I was just thinking that while I'm here, maybe I could help organize your kitchen. That could be, like, a friendly scene we do together. They'd love that."

What the fuck? "Hell no, Mae, you're not messing with my kitchen. You haven't been in my kitchen in six years! What makes you think it needs organizing? My kitchen is fine." It was, too. Or if it wasn't, it was how Amanda wanted it. She wasn't Barbara. Her mess was just a mess; she could clean it up in an hour if she wanted to, and the last thing she needed was Mae's help. If Amanda had her way, Mae wouldn't even come near the little house—and especially not with her own agenda. "Why would they even want that? The personal stuff is not what they're after, Mae. Haven't you watched? They just film in the restaurants."

Mae whacked her on the arm. "Haven't *you* watched? What about the one where the guy is adopted, and he just wants his dad to be proud of him making the cheesesteaks, and the dad has never said it and then he does and they both cry at the end? Or the one where the husband and wife fight over where they get the lobster and it turns out that it's her ex's boat?"

Amanda had seen the cheesesteak one, yes, but she thought that stuff just happened. If you did enough *Food Wars,* probably some people were bound to have emotional things going on. And it was a nice story, at least. "Right, but they're not *looking* for it. And they want their viewers to, like, feel good."

"Good that their wife isn't maybe still sleeping with her ex, yeah. I think that couple got a divorce."

Why did Mae have to act like she knew so much more about everything than Amanda? She might have been on TV a few times, but *Food Wars* was different, and this was Merinac, not New York. "There's nothing like that going on here. You're making this too big a deal, Mae."

"You don't think they'd be happy to run with you flirting with Andy? Because I guarantee they would. And, seriously, Amanda? One chicken guy wasn't enough?"

Amanda's face got hot. She'd forgotten that Mae had seen her last night. And she wasn't flirting, anyway. Andy wasn't even her type. She didn't have a type. She had a fourteen-year-old and a seventeen-year-old. "I wasn't flirting. I was looking for you. And where were you, anyway?"

"Walking back from Mom's, and I didn't want to interrupt you. But maybe I should have, if you can't figure out for yourself that the guy's a real dead end."

She didn't say, *Another dead end,* but Amanda knew she was thinking it.

"Goddamn it, Mae," she began, intending to respond to that slap about Frank. Amanda wasn't interested in Andy at all, she'd tell Mae that, and that it was pointless trying to do anything with Mimi's besides just make it through the weekend. But before Amanda could even decide how her sentence would end, they came to the bend in the path where the railroad track grading ended and you made your way down to the water. The big cottonwood that grew on the bank should be looming over them, its upright trunk just coming into view, the tree they'd climbed as kids, sat under, carved their names into.

Instead, they saw a ripped stump. The tree itself lay across the bank and out into the water, a fallen giant, limbs stretched up to the sky.

"Oh no." Amanda put her hands over her mouth and stopped.

Mae, in front of her, put a hand down on the bank to help herself down the steep slope. "Our tree! It's—how long has it been down?"

Amanda shook her head. "I don't know. Mom didn't tell me—I don't know if she knew." She felt more upset than she should have. The tree was old, and cottonwoods came down all the time; Amanda and Mae knew that better than most. It was one of the reasons people didn't plant them in their yards anymore. But this had been *their* cottonwood. Her cottonwood. She had drawn it a hundred times, leaned on it, measured her height by its limbs. Somehow she'd thought it would last forever. From the look on Mae's face, her sister must have felt the same way. Amanda made her way down next to Mae. The way the tree had fallen had erased the names they'd once carved into it, and the stump, while jagged, looked worn. She should have known something was wrong while they walked—the shade was gone, leaving the familiar path fully exposed. "It must have been a while ago. You'd think she'd have heard it, though."

Mae had turned her back on the tree, and on Amanda, and was staring out at the river. "Trees fall," she said. "If there wasn't anyone here to hear it, maybe it didn't make a noise."

Amanda knew her sister was just trying to lighten the mood, but the comment set something off inside her. "Of course it did," she said, and to her surprise, she was crying. "Of course it made a fucking noise, Mae. It was a big tree. It fell. It made just as big a noise as you can imagine."

Mae started to turn, probably to tell Amanda that she was only kidding, but Amanda had had enough of Mae's jokes, and of Mae, and of everything. She turned around without saying another word to her sister, hitched up the tote bag that was slipping off her shoulder, and left. She didn't need Mae's help, or her sympathy, or her plan.

She needed to go home.

MAE

Amanda was such a drama queen. Mae followed her up the slope, well aware that her sister wouldn't stop until she got wherever she was going, and that wherever that was didn't involve Mae. It was a tree, and, yeah, it was sad, but it was ancient history. Things changed, just like they'd changed between her and Amanda. Mae had hoped, with a shared mission, that they could at least slip back into their old ways a little. Weren't they on the same side? Of course, that's not the way *Food Wars* would see it, but in reality. The Merinac side, the make-this-a-huge-success side. Why wouldn't her sister even listen to her? It would be so much better for everyone if they worked together behind the scenes, at least a little, but no. Amanda had to be stubborn.

Mae squared her shoulders as she walked through the back-yard, avoiding even so much as a glance at the house. She'd heard the door slam just before she came up the ridge, and now she could just see her mother disappearing in front of Mimi's. On to the rest of the day. Step one: chase Barbara down. Mae sped up slightly. Step two: figure out how far Barbara would let her go in getting Mimi's increasingly more camera-ready before each *Food Wars* appearance. Sadly, *burn it down and start over* was not a practical option, but *scrape the counter area and the patio back to walls and concrete* was, and Mae intended to persuade Barbara to let that happen.

Mimi's wasn't going to win in a head-to-head beauty pageant with Frannie's, and everybody knew it. But it could appeal to a certain subset of viewers—the ones who valued simplicity and authenticity over variety and constant change, who would prefer one classic, beloved, well-made handbag over a collection of cheap knockoffs.

The ones like Mae, in other words, and the ones who would do two things: follow Mae, giving her increased visibility and setting her up for the next stage of her career, and, if they were at all local, come check out what Mae intended to bill as "fried chicken like your great-great-grandparents loved." That would bring in a fresh influx of customers, all ready to see Mimi's in a new light. Win-win, even in the face of an ultimate *Food Wars* loss.

Because while Barbara might have been adamantly declaring that Mimi's was in fine financial shape, all around her Mae could see the same old signs of penny-pinching—except, of course, for the bizarre advent of Andy. Which brought her mind back to her mother's disappearance last night, also bizarre. Step one and a half: figure out whether there was a reason Barbara was acting so strangely, or whether this was just one of those Barbara things. That might be step three, actually, because if they were going to get anything about Mimi's improved before the *Food Wars* crew showed up again, they didn't have much time.

Mae, now out on the sidewalk just past Mimi's, could see her mother disappearing into the Inn. She set out after Barbara, not quite at top walking speed because the coffee shop was extremely likely to also contain Kenneth. Reunions weren't on Mae's agenda, as much as she wanted to hear the story—Kenneth had wanted out of town even worse than she had, and she couldn't imagine why he'd trade pulling all-nighters at a start-up in San Francisco for pulling shots of espresso in Merinac. Later, though. Could she just pretend she already knew the whole thing? Her mother's dog, sprawled on the sidewalk next to the Inn's door, looked up but didn't move as Mae grasped the handle and pulled it firmly open. Bells jingled, heads turned. Fine. She was a New Yorker now, a TV personality, a little bit famous. She put a little cock in her walk. She could handle this.

Her mother's back was to her, but the man behind the counter, who was not Kenneth, looked up immediately. "Mae Moore," he said with evident pleasure, and set down the cup he was holding, as if to come out and greet her.

Barbara leaned forward and tapped on the counter. "Patrick Lehavy," she said without turning around, "you finish my coffee before you do one more thing."

Patrick, still smiling widely, picked the cup back up and began carefully topping it with frothed milk, looking up at Mae as he did so. "Welcome," he said. "Kenneth has been assuring me you'd turn up sooner or later. Said you couldn't hold out against the best coffee in town."

"It is that," Barbara agreed. "Make Mae one—she'll be needing it." Her tone was casual, as though she and Mae ran into each other here every day of the week, but she turned and smiled at Mae, leaning back against the counter. Her hair, in two gray braids, hung over her shoulders; she wore, as she always did, a full floral apron over shapeless polyester pants and a high school sweatshirt—baseball, because it was spring. She looked exactly as she always had, and Mae felt an enormous loosening inside of her, an untying of knots she had not known were tied, as she walked straight into her mother's outstretched arms.

As they stepped apart, with Mae hanging on for just a half second longer than Barbara, Patrick handed Barbara a thick mug, filled not quite to the brim. "I think, if I am not mistaken, that I have already made Mae at least one coffee," he said. "Am I wrong in thinking that the young woman who's already been in here twice this morning works for you?"

Of course. Nothing went without comment in Merinac. Not your coffee, not your groceries, not your decision to try running or subscribe to *The New Yorker,* which had once made Kenneth a topic of discussion all over town. It was a little ironic, then, that it was Kenneth's husband who was heading up this morning's gossip brigade, but as much as it pushed Mae's old Merinac buttons, she held in the snippy response that rose to her lips and smiled back instead.

"Yes," she said, mindful of Amanda's reaction to the word "nanny." "I brought someone to help me with the kids."

To her surprise, her mother and Patrick nodded. "Probably smart," Barbara said as she picked up her mug carefully, using both hands, and turned away. Greeting over, then, and it was time for Mae to fall into line beside her mother. This coffee shop, with its two gay proprietors and its lattes, should have felt like Mae territory, but it was Barbara who was at home here. Barbara's affections were unpredictable and, once set, unchangeable, and she did not care what other people thought. It was why she always clicked with Jay on her rare visits to New York, where she refused to make the slightest alteration in her appearance to fit in with her surroundings. They shared that rebel quality.

You just couldn't ever be sure if she might choose today to rebel against you. Still, even with the nagging worry in the back of Mae's mind about how Kenneth would greet her, even with the coffee grapevine in full swing, finding Barbara in this atmosphere made Mae feel like things might be going her way.

Patrick didn't leave her in doubt about Kenneth for very long. "You can wait for that third latte," he said. "I'm getting Kenneth. I know, I know, you guys have lost touch. We're fixing that. Right now." He disappeared into one of the two doors behind the counter, this one clearly leading to the lobby of the bed-and-breakfast. "I'll be back," he called over his shoulder. "I know you won't go anywhere without your coffee."

"He seems like a nice guy," Mae said to her mother as she followed her to a pair of armchairs. The guy she would have wanted for Kenneth, once she had realized, almost before she had been old enough to have the thought, that Kenneth was not for her.

"He is. Good to have Kenneth back in town, too." Her mother

pointed to the chair across from hers, which she took a little stiffly. "Sit. He'll be a minute. Kenneth's father has been sick. Alzheimer's. You know all this?"

Mae shook her head. She didn't need to pretend with Barbara, who never wondered why other people did things.

"Well, he's helping his mom, and he sees a lot of his sister and her family, too. Nice."

Mae's sense of connection disappeared. She knew where this was going. For so long, her mother had supported her choices, but lately Barbara had begun to ask just how long Mae intended to stay in New York—as though the city were temporary, a brief extension of college. It rankled. "Mom," she started, and Barbara held up her hand.

"Just stop," she said. "It wasn't about you. That's what he's doing, is all. You're here to help with these *Food Wars* people, and that will be good, because I didn't even realize when I called how much they would be into every little thing, and it's hard to keep the kitchen going with them underfoot and asking questions. Nancy's got Amanda to take care of all that. So you deal with them for me, and I'll be happy."

Great. Now Mae, who admittedly wasn't here wholly out of the goodness of her heart, felt guilty. Trust her mother to put a pin straight into Mae's weak spot, and get in a shot at Amanda besides. Never mind that there were excellent reasons that neither of Barbara's daughters were coming around for Sunday dinner every week. She parried. "Where were you last night, then, if it's hard to keep going with them around? You left Andy kind of underwater. I mean, I did turn up, but I had the kids. I wasn't much help."

"So you met Andy," her mother said. "He's an excellent cook. I've been really happy to have him. Food's just as good as it always was."

Mae didn't say anything to that. The food was just as good as it had always been, the chicken so exactly the same that it had almost made her cry, the fries better. Andy was a good cook. An asshole, but a good cook. That had not been her question. "Right, but where were you?"

Barbara looked up toward the back an instant before Patrick returned, Kenneth trailing behind him. She might have heard them coming, but Mae suspected that her mother, always a private person, was intentionally avoiding what should have been an easy question. There wasn't time to push her on it, though. Mae braced herself for Kenneth's approach. As much as she didn't want to admit it, Amanda's reserved greeting had shaken her, and Barbara wasn't much better. It wasn't that she'd expected a parade, exactly. But neither was she quite prepared to be treated as though she'd either never been gone or never been here in the first place. She didn't know what to expect from Kenneth, but she knew she didn't deserve much.

But both men were smiling, welcoming. Patrick seemed delighted to be engineering the reunion, and Kenneth, coming up with his arm around his husband's shoulders, was clearly enjoying the other man's excitement.

"Mae," Kenneth said, and reached down and pulled her out of her chair as though no time had passed at all. "Mae-my-Mae, how very, very nice to see you."

Mae hugged him, too, as hard as she had her mother. This was a Kenneth she had never known, at ease with himself and his surroundings. A Kenneth who, she could see at a glance, could afford to let the years he and Mae had gone without talking be water under the bridge, even though it had been he who had tried, a few times, to reach out and she who had ignored him, unable to allow any piece of Merinac to intrude into her new life.

"You too," she said, looking into his eyes and meaning it. When Kenneth walked into the room, something inside Mae clicked into place, and standing between him and Barbara, meeting Patrick— she was home, and the only thing missing was Jay, reaching out to shake Kenneth's and Patrick's hands, matching Kenneth's smile.

Kenneth might be enjoying himself, but with the thought of Jay, Mae felt her confidence ebbing away. She let go of Kenneth's arms, noting his expensively, intentionally crumpled linen green gingham shirt. Eyeing the room, she observed that the Inn had been renovated with no expense spared—and no bank would have bet on this, which meant the money came from somewhere else. Mae had a sudden suspicion that it wouldn't take more than a single Google search to tell her exactly how Kenneth had spent the last decade and a half, or where his newfound ease and wealth came from. She was ashamed not to have done it already. She should have known about the Inn, about Kenneth, and if she hadn't been so determined to keep Merinac and everything that came with it in the past that she had swiped away its every possible appearance in her present, she would have.

"We have hours of catching up to do," said Kenneth, "but I know your mother, and her patience for a trip down memory lane is limited. Plus, you guys have a big day ahead. So let's just pretend we already know everything and get on with it, shall we?"

"Facebook has ruined reunions," said Patrick sadly. "I, for one, want to hear both of you tell each other your entire life stories since high school. But"—he glanced at Barbara—"you're right. Not now. So, what can we do to help make your *Food Wars* a success, ladies? Besides fuel you with superb coffee, which you will be sure to tell the camera came from the 1908 Standard?"

"I do want to trade stories. I'm actually not that great at Facebook—I only use it professionally. I'm totally behind." She smiled, she hoped with regretful charm, and went on. She took the flyer she'd printed this morning at the motel out of her LESS IS MOORE tote bag with a cautious glance at Barbara. Her mother liked to have Mae's help, but one wrong word and she was likely to begin to see that help as bossy or, worse, back talk, and that would be the end of it. But her mother had always liked Kenneth and clearly liked Patrick. If they bought in, she might, too.

Mae spoke carefully. "We might have a few things to do before the cameras show up. Maybe—straighten up a little?" A quick glance at Barbara showed a neutral face. "And I thought we might offer a special tonight. You guys could help share it, maybe, let people know?"

Kenneth picked up on the dance Mae was doing as if they'd been planning ways to work around Barbara just yesterday. "Of course. Mimi's looks great, its fabulous classic self, but there's always something you can do for a camera. And a special is a great idea. What do you have?"

"Chicken, of course," said Mae. "Salad, fries. But with a slice of pie." This was where it got dicey. Putting the pie on the special was a risk—there wasn't always pie, especially if her mother was feeling pissed off at the world, but Mae figured even Barbara would pull out all the stops for *Food Wars*.

"Perfect," Patrick said, looking at Barbara, who smiled back at him, flooding Mae with relief. Pie it was, then. "Best pies in the world. We'll share it like crazy."

Mae smiled. "Sweet," she said. All she wanted was their help getting Barbara on board, but she would take the rest. "Every little bit helps."

Patrick looked at her sharply, and Mae realized he had caught the implied slight. His eyebrows went up. "Every little bit." He laughed. "Show her, Kenneth."

Kenneth took out his phone (the latest, with no case, in the manner of the person for whom replacing a phone or a cracked screen was nothing) and opened Facebook. "We've been sharing *Food Wars* like mad," he said. "Of course, we put an Inn spin on it." Mae took the phone and scrolled down—it was a Merinac Main Street page, and she could see it was popular from the astonishing display of likes. The last posts were about supporting *Food Wars*, and one included a lengthy discussion about what a successful series could do for the entire town. Kenneth saw her reading it.

"That's nothing compared to the conversation on the Listserv," he said, and took the phone back. "And of course we covered Twitter and Instagram, too. We're huge on Instagram. I think you'll probably have a lot of out-of-towners trying to get in tonight as well as the locals. Frannie's, too. We told anyone who can't get in to bring their takeout here. I warned Andy last week, and Amanda, too, to be ready for a rush."

Kenneth held out the phone again, this time open to an Instagram post with 14,903 likes. "It's going to be a gorgeous weekend, too. We should get some road trippers."

"I'm putting your special up now," Patrick said, taking a picture of the flyer arranged on the coffee bar with a fork and knife beside it. "Especially if you amplify"—he gave her a look, and she knew he was fully aware that she didn't follow them—"you should have more of a crowd than you can handle."

Mae, who had assumed her hometown would have essentially no social media presence, now felt like a fool. The posts were well designed, each a thing of graphic beauty, and she suddenly remembered that Kenneth and Amanda had had art in common, although Kenneth took a much more practical approach when he picked web design. She was busted, and she knew it.

"Didn't think we had it in us, did you?" said Kenneth, and his eyes were kind. "It's okay. You've been gone a while. I'll come find you later, after the thing tonight. We'll catch up then."

"That would be great," Mae said, meaning it. "For now—coffee? Please, Patrick? I'm following you right now. I'll make up for lost time." He smirked, but it was a friendly smirk, and Mae felt like she was getting off easier than she deserved. "And maybe a couple of those muffins? We'll take some to the kids. They're just at the playground."

Patrick returned to his station behind the espresso machine while Kenneth loaded a bag with chocolate chip mini-muffins. As he handed Mae her mocha, Patrick looked over at Barbara, who was heading for the door, leaving her empty cup on the table. "Want me to make some pies to send over tonight?"

Mae jolted to a stop. This had been going so well—what was Patrick doing? Horrified, Mae waited for her mother's explosive response to the suggestion that she would need outside pies, but Barbara instead looked thoughtful. "You get started this morning," she said. "More blueberry, I think. And strawberry rhubarb. I'll check in on you later."

Patrick seemed unperturbed by this opaque response. "Sounds good," he said.

Mae, carrying her coffee and the muffins, followed her mother out onto the sidewalk. The fat dog stood up, too, nudging at Barbara's hand with her square black-and-white head.

"He's going to make you pies?" Honestly, if things got any weirder, she was going to have whiplash from all the mental double takes. She ran a few steps to catch up with Barbara, being careful not to spill her coffee.

Barbara rubbed the dog's head. "A little after they moved up here, when they were redoing the place, Patrick asked if I could teach him to bake pies like mine, so I did. He's very good at it now."

Mae tried to imagine Barbara and Patrick, side by side, matching rolling pins in their hands. Mae and Amanda were customers of their mother's pies, just as dependent on her whims as anyone else. Mae dreamed about her mother's chocolate cream, Amanda loved apple, they would both take a slice of lemon meringue, but Mae hardly dared to request a flavor, let alone a baking lesson. Pies were Barbara's department, and she accepted no help.

Well, damn. Maybe Patrick would teach her. If nothing else, it would make a hell of an Instagram post. Which reminded her—she stopped to point her camera phone down into the white bakery bag. The muffins inside glowed, lit by the bright sunlight. *Breakfast in my hometown,* she typed with a practiced thumb, *#yum*. She used her keyboard shortcut to add one of her strings of set *Food*

Wars hashtags: *#FoodWars #hometowngirl #midwesteats #food trip #bestfriedchicken #worththecalories.*

"Good, then," she said, ready to move on, her mind halfway to Mimi's already. What if they started outside? Replant the planters, power wash the patio, her mother couldn't mind any of that, and then Mae would carefully, delicately approach the counter and the rest. "We'll have even more pies tonight. Sounds like we're going to need them." She reshared Patrick's clever Facebook post of the pie special, text over what must have been an image of pies on the Inn's counter, then took a muffin for herself. All this talk of pie was making her hungry.

"We'll see." Her mother stopped, still out of sight of the park, and sat down heavily on the bench outside the craft store, which had not yet opened for the day. The dog sat too, then flopped down as though her bulk was just too much to hold up. Barbara looked at Mae, her friendly expression replaced by one of cautious interest.

"Now, before we go any further, tell me exactly what you have planned, because I know there's something." Unexpectedly, Mae heard an echo of Jay in her mother's words, with the same resignation, and it annoyed her. She made good plans. People just needed to give them a chance instead of getting so caught up in doing things their way.

"It's only minor details," she protested. "We can just get started. And I know you want to see the kids." Her mother was not a small-children person, but still.

"Mmm-hmm," said Barbara. "I saw them at Christmas, in New York, where they were far more interested in presents and their babysitter than me. Today they will be more excited by the muffins, which is fine. Saturday I'll fry them doughnuts and be the greatest thing ever for about ten minutes. Now, let's hear it." She patted the bench beside her. "I've had my coffee. I'm as ready as I'll ever be."

AMANDA

Ordinarily, Amanda hated going home to her empty house while the kids were at school. If she wasn't working the lunch shift, she went anywhere else: Patrick and Kenneth's, Nancy's, Walmart. She volunteered, becoming the de facto art teacher for the elementary school, where the teacher provided by the district (who also taught at the middle and high schools) could only get there once a week. She took her sketchbooks and sat on benches and at picnic tables when the weather was warm. Anything to avoid the mess, which never reached Barbara level but still made her feel defeated inside. And the silence. Mostly the silence.

But after seeing Mae, she couldn't go anywhere but home. The tears that had overwhelmed her when she saw their fallen tree were threatening to become an all-day affair, and she needed the privacy of her tiny house to pull herself back from the sense that it wasn't just the tree that was being torn from its roots.

Mae was so totally not cleaning her fucking kitchen. The last time Amanda saw Mae was here, in her little kitchen, two days after Frank's funeral. Mae was already packed, already heading home, basically gone, but she stopped in for one last assault on Amanda's entire life. Sitting at the kitchen table, organizing sympathy cards into neat rows, asking—no, demanding—to know what Amanda's plan was now. "Action is the best cure for anxiety," Mae declared, hopping up to straighten Amanda's counters. In her mind, Amanda, in a burst of fury, had swept everything, cards, blender, toaster, coffee cups, off every surface, raging at her sister that this wasn't anxiety, it was horror, it was a shit show, it was the impossible meeting the unbearable and crashing into the unthinkable and Mae had no idea, none . . .

In reality she'd done no such thing. She'd sat and stared down at the linoleum and muttered something, wanting Mae to leave or at least to stop acting like Amanda's grief was some sort of offense against Mae herself.

Mae had knelt in front of her, pregnant belly dangling, and grabbed both of Amanda's hands. "Come to New York," she said. "We'll find a place out of the city, where we can afford it, you and me and Jay, with the kids, find you work, get you back into school—help you start again. I know this is terrible, but you'll get through it. You just need a plan."

Amanda shook her head. Frankie, then barely eight, wandered into the kitchen, and Mae reached out and pulled her over. "Frankie, you want to come live with Auntie Mae, right? And Mommy?"

Frankie, still a little bashful, leaned into Amanda and didn't say anything. Amanda held her daughter close, pressing the little head into her own chest and glaring at Mae. "You don't just do that," she said. "Just—no. Don't ask the kids stuff like that. We can't— We're fine, Mae. Fine without you."

Mae didn't get what it was like to be her. She never had, and she never would. Amanda's kitchen was fine. She was fine. Amanda dropped her tote bag on the floor, and Mae's talking points slid out. *We're close but we have our own lives!* Amanda snatched the paper off the floor and crumpled it up, quickly, then pushed it deep into the trash.

There. She'd cleaned.

She cleared a space on the table, dumping the breakfast dishes in the sink with the plates from last night's pizza, and turned her back on the kitchen, on the boxes and the curled, ripped tabs from past frozen dinners, on the bottles waiting to be rinsed and recycled, on

Pickle's bowls, still under the counter, on everything that wasn't right with her world. She sat down with her latest sketchbook, mashing it open angrily on the table. She felt better the minute she had the pencil in her hand, and a chicken chased by a tornado began to take shape on the page, rough and running for a coop that was obviously in the path of the wind.

You don't grow up in a small town as "the kid who can draw" without ending up with requests, and as a result, one variety of Amanda's chickens—she thought of them as the friendly biddies—was scattered all over town. She drew these plump chickens with simple, clear lines, drinking coffee, grocery shopping, and knitting, and traded them for local services, happy to see her biddies take up residence on her families' menus and on various store posters.

The rest lived only in her notebook, and those chickens came in every color, shape, and size, including, even especially, the nasty nellies. The ugly chickens, the scrawny, the wild top-knotted, the molting: their stories all lived in here. To begin with, they'd been just single drawings; then they'd grown into panels, still on a single page. Now, just this year, they'd grown again, into a story that transcended a single page, that required her to go back, again and again, trying to map a journey that she hadn't planned on, creating and re-creating panels and characters and dialogue until she was almost, but not quite, frustrated enough with herself to quit.

She knew enough to understand that the process of telling a visual story could be easier with a little training. All the college mailings arriving for Gus reminded her that there were places where people learned to do this stuff. It probably was easier for someone with real talent, like Bill Henderson, legendary as Merinac High's most successful graduate, twenty years before her time. He'd taken his comics of a boy and a penguin and turned them into beloved icons—and then retired and become a total recluse after his success. But he'd gone to art school. She'd checked, damn it. And every time she saw classes in things like illustration and narrative design she had to face it: if she'd finished school she probably wouldn't be flailing around quite this much.

She shaded in more of the tornado, a little fiercely, then turned back a few pages and let herself be pulled into the world of Carleen, the least popular chicken in her high school, pecked down by plumper hens and scorned by cocky roosters.

Carleen's story wasn't hers. Amanda had been quite well liked in high school—mostly because she stayed resolutely in the middle of the road, dressing like everyone else, doing the things everyone else did. Amanda had made those choices thanks to Mae, who had already made all the mistakes. Unlike Mae, Amanda did exactly what was expected of her and not anything more. She was a good girl.

Carleen was not a good girl. She was the dark chicken of her small town, pulling the other chicks in with her schemes and plans when they were young, then finding herself alone as a teenage chicken with a lot to prove and only her mysterious telekinetic powers, powers the others in the flock didn't share, to do it with. Carleen had been thoroughly rejected and cruelly humiliated by her peers, and would continue to be until she allowed the forces within her to burst free—at prom, of course, in homage to *Carrie,* one of Amanda's favorite books—and annihilate the chickens around her in a rampage of oil and flames.

Carleen, Amanda thought, would end her prom night with a fried chicken dinner.

Amanda stayed deep in her notebook for as long as she could, until she looked up at the clock and had to rush wildly to pick up Frankie and Gus for the night's filming as promised, leaving her work spread out across the table to clean up later. She arrived at Frannie's with a funny sense of carrying along a mood that wasn't entirely hers: Carleen, crushed to the point of drastic action and ready to rumble.

She, Amanda, was feeling better. Her greeting from Sabrina reassured her that Mae was entirely off base in her assessment of *Food Wars* and its plans. If Sabrina had secret designs she would never be so warm and welcoming. Amanda might have spouted off at the mouth a little in her first interview, but she herself had no secrets, and she hadn't said anything that wasn't true, anyway. The relief made her bouncy, and Carleen's determination was giving her confidence. With an unusual, pleasant sense of being fully in control of the situation, she hung up her bag, then joined Nancy and Sabrina at the bar to go over table assignments.

"These tables are the ones where we've got the spacing just right for the camera," Sabrina said. "Can you split that section up, just for tonight, so we can see two of your team in action? And I'll help Amanda seat it, so we get a variety of customers. No sending in ringers to talk the place up on my watch!" She laughed, but Nancy looked horrified, whether at the idea of splitting the front section or cheating, Amanda didn't know.

Amanda could see that Nancy was concentrating on trying to even out the table assignments, and thus the tips, so she agreed with Sabrina on her mother-in-law's behalf.

"Great." Sabrina made a mark on the pad she was carrying. "Now, are you guys doing anything specific for tonight? A *Food Wars* deal, an appetizer or a drink special?"

Amanda thought of the Mimi's special, dinner plus pie, which she'd seen all over Instagram. They could do so much more than that, but she didn't want to imitate Mae in any way, either. She drummed her fingers on the table, thinking, while Nancy got up to take the new table map to the hostess stand. "Not a dessert special. Mae's doing that. And if it's food it has to be chicken, and those are already our best deals . . ." Trust Mae to have already taken the easiest idea. What could Frannie's do that Mimi's couldn't?

She had it. "Drink specials," she said. "Alcohol and virgin, too. Like, a *Food Wars* theme."

Sabrina looked thoughtful. "Not bad," she said. "But what about something a little more competitive? Mae was saying last night that she wanted to bring a little Brooklyn to Mimi's. You could kind of play up that you don't need to change anything. I mean, I know she's your sister, but it's all in good fun, right?"

Amanda felt a wicked urge rise in her. "We'll give the drinks local names. Sex on the Prairie. The Missouri Mule." She saw Mary Laura walk in and called to her. "We're renaming your cocktail menu tonight, ML. It's the anti–New York drinking fest."

"Ooh," said Mary Laura. "The MOhito, like Missouri MO. The Soured on the City."

"Long Way from Long Island Ice Tea," said Amanda. "Or here's one just for Mae—the Not-So-Sparkling wine. Because we don't need making over."

Sabrina ripped a sheet of paper off her pad with a grand gesture and handed it to Mary Laura. "Your menu for tonight, then," she declared. This was perfect, except that Mae might never even hear about it. After the morning, Amanda wanted to rub Mae's nose in the distance between Mimi's and Frannie's—and between Mae's idea about what people wanted and the way things really were around here.

"How can we make sure everybody knows?" she said. "People around here would come in just for the drinks, but all we can do is put it up on the sign outside."

Sabrina gestured with her phone. "Put it out there," she said. "Facebook, Twitter, Instagram. Get it on all your accounts now and set it to keep going all day."

Amanda shook her head. "We don't do that," she said. Amanda loved Instagram, but she was more of a follower than a poster, and Nancy had long been adamant that it wasn't Frannie's style. *We don't need to advertise,* she'd said, quoting Daddy Frank, even when they clearly did.

Sabrina sighed. "You're going to have to start," she said. "But for now—get those guys at the coffee shop to do it. The 1908 Standard. They're probably one of the biggest accounts in the state."

Amanda picked up her phone, then hesitated. Kenneth was fundamentally loyal—and he'd been sharing Mae's special all over the place, even if she had been dissing him for years. But didn't he want *Food Wars* to succeed for the town, not just Mae?

Sabrina, irritated, took the phone from her hand. "You can even put it on their Facebook page yourself," she said. She started arranging bottles and glasses into a cluster on the bar and handed Amanda the chalkboard they always used for drink specials. "Write up a couple and make them beautiful," she said. She opened Amanda's camera app and looked through it, then started carrying the bottles to a table closer to a window.

Amanda started to letter quickly. *Frannie's Proud Flyover Country Drink Specials,* she wrote across the top, then listed their genius drinks. She sketched in a cocktail and handed it over, and Sabrina propped it up behind her improvised photo studio.

"There," she said after a minute, handing the phone back. "I put it on their page. Ask them to spread it, and send them the Instagram shots and some tweets." Amanda took the phone, trying not to reveal her confusion, and as Sabrina walked away, Mary Laura slid the phone from her hands again.

"I'll do it," she said. "I'll tell them it's me."

Amanda smiled at her, relieved. "I mean, tell them it's me, too. It's all of us."

From then on, the night sped up. There were no more one-on-one chats with Sabrina, only a few awkward moments in front of the microphone to offer a cheerful take on how the night was going, which was great. Given how many people there were at Frannie's, there couldn't be many at Mimi's. She'd had a hard time holding on to their usual corner table for the Aarons, who came in every Thursday with their three boys after baseball. Sabrina wanted to give it to a big, noisy crew who must have come over from the local college, but Amanda held firm and slipped her loyal customers past the crowd in the bar, where they were making it abundantly clear that they loved the drink specials—and, Amanda knew, would order another round while they were waiting.

It felt like everyone in town was there. She saw Morty Rountree, famed for never wearing a shirt on his tractor between April and October, but wearing one now and braying cheerfully into the camera with his arm around his wife. "I don't want her to cook every night," he was declaring. "We like to get over here once every couple weeks or so, have the chicken." Morty was a big presence, his wife more retiring and turning as best as she could away from the camera, but the affection between them was, as always, visible.

Frankie showed signs of wanting to follow the camera, but the rest of the staff were making sure she put in a full night's work, and more than once Amanda saw Gus save her when she set off from clearing a table with far too heavy a tray. She'd learn—and judging from the crash Amanda heard from the serving station at one point, she was learning the hard way, like they all did. She wanted to rush back to help with the mess and make sure they got all the glass, but things were too busy out front. Instead, she found herself pointing the district's new art teacher toward the bar and promising him the shortest wait she could manage.

"Oh man, I told you to come in, didn't I? I didn't know it would be like this—we'll get you guys in as fast as we can." She smiled at him, then peeped at the sleeping baby strapped to his chest.

"That's okay," his wife said. "We don't care. This is fun. Not exactly what we expected when we left St. Louis."

"Tell Mary Laura drinks are on us," she said. "See you next week?" Last Tuesday, his weekly day at the elementary school, she'd been volunteering and wild with excitement. By Tuesday next this would all be over, but there wasn't even time to think about that now.

Frannie's party atmosphere kept flowing even when, leaving a few cameras behind, Sabrina slipped out, presumably to go do the same thing at Mimi's. As the tables cleared out, Mary Laura started passing around samples of her concoctions, and Amanda, who liked her drinks sweet and embarrassing, grabbed the excuse to order a Long Way from Long Island Iced Tea to top off her Sex on the Prairie. By the time she noticed that Mary Laura had commandeered the letter sign outside (*Happy with Your Messy Life? Fight the* Food War *with a Not-So-Sparkling Wine*) she was utterly sold on the idea of the drink specials. It was brilliant. She felt brilliant. Even the text from Kenneth she found on her phone once she finally retrieved it from Mary Laura—a little snarky, but a good idea—didn't dampen her mood.

The staff gathered around the bar as the various cleaning tasks wrapped up, playing to the camera as they postmortemed the night. Amanda felt a surge of love for them all. These were her friends. These guys were awesome. She never wanted to leave them. Gwennie had had multiple tables with toddlers and had taught one to say, "I love Fwannie's best." Mary Laura reported that the Soured on the City was going to be a permanent addition to the cocktail menu. Frankie's feet hurt, casualties of the cool-but-flat Converse sneakers, and Gus offered to carry her to the car as the *Food Wars* crew started to fold up, shut down, and grab their own drinks.

Amanda really wasn't ready to go home. Tomorrow, once the professional chefs showed up, things would probably be far more tense. This was the fun part, but she, as always, was heading home with the kids. Reluctantly, she got up to follow Gus out, but Sabrina, back from Mimi's and still going strong, stopped her. "Gus can drive, right?"

Amanda nodded.

"Let me take you home, then. Stay and debrief. I want to hear everything."

It was a tempting idea, and Gus seconded it, hefting his sister into a better piggyback position on his back while she shrieked.

"We'll just go home, Mom. You stay. It's okay. Frankie needs her beauty sleep," he said. That earned him a swat on the head from Frankie as he hauled her out, leaving Amanda behind.

Sabrina was describing the night at Mimi's. "They ran out of all the pie except banana, and someone offered your aunt Aida a hundred dollars to make her a chocolate cream to take home, and she gave her this look and said, 'Young woman, I do not bake the pies. I present them.' I just love her—she's perfect. And your town is really coming out for this. I had to stop that one big guy from talking to the camera at both places." She grinned. "I showed Mae your drink specials. She said they didn't have anything to do with anything, but Andy and your mom laughed."

Nancy, coming in with fresh bar towels, raised her eyebrows, and then a look of understanding rolled over her face. "Oh," she said. "I get it now. I was kind of wondering why all the New York stuff. You were trying to get at Mae." She shook her head at Amanda. "It's not about Mae, Amanda. It's about Mimi's and Frannie's."

"I know," said Amanda. "It was just a joke." She could feel her high slipping. But it was a joke. And clearly everyone had loved the drink specials—Mary Laura's beer pitcher tip jar with its COWS HATE BEING TIPPED, BUT BARTENDERS DON'T sign was stuffed to overflowing.

"I get it," said Nancy. "Just don't take it too far. We don't need"— she cast an unexpected glance at Sabrina—"any family drama."

Damn it, now Nancy was managing to sound like Mae. Amanda stared down at her drink, and her mother-in-law handed Mary Laura the bar towels. Mary Laura set them on the bar and offered Nancy a glass.

"To a Frannie's victory," Mary Laura said, toasting cheerfully— hoping, Amanda suspected, to break up the mood. Nancy toasted, then slid her glass, still mostly full, back to Mary Laura. "One to hand wash, then," she said, "so we don't start the day tomorrow with any dirties. I trust you'll all clean up after yourselves. I'm going to bed. Amanda, honey, are you sure you don't want me to run you home?"

After a glance at Sabrina, Amanda shook her head. Nancy was clearly going to pour cold water on her with a lecture about keeping things professional, but Amanda thought the little dig at Mae was funny and clever and well within the bounds of making *Food Wars* fun without "drama." "I'll get a ride," she said.

Nancy, still looking dubious, headed for the parking lot.

Sitting at the bar while Sabrina quizzed Mary Laura about her love life, off camera, Amanda felt deflated. Why couldn't Nancy just enjoy this? She ought to know Amanda could poke her sister a little without it turning into a big deal, and it wasn't like Mae hadn't said plenty about Frank and Frannie's over the years. Amanda shoved the thought of her arguably explosive revelation about Mae's stripper past firmly out of her head. Frannie's would win, it would all be over, and there would be no drama.

Amanda sighed and tuned back in to the conversation around her to find Mary Laura and Sabrina both looking at her quizzically.

"What's up?" Mary Laura asked, "Did we not have an excellent time tonight? Are we still not having an excellent time?"

"Nothing. We did. We still are." She pushed her glass toward Mary Laura, who filled it before gesturing toward Sabrina with the shaker.

Sabrina covered her glass and shook her head, and with a flourish, Mary Laura emptied the rest into Amanda's glass. "Excellent," Sabrina said. "What we need now is somewhere to continue the party, and someone to continue it with."

Mary Laura laughed. "There's nowhere to go around here," she said. "Pull up a stool. We're the only game in town, and normally we'd have closed an hour ago."

Nowhere to go, and nobody to go with. Amanda sighed again. "As usual, I'll be heading home to my buddy Ben and my buddy Jerry." She took too big a sip of her drink, and then, for good measure, another. She was not driving.

"How about your buddy Andy?" Sabrina smiled and lifted her

eyebrows suggestively. "He was asking about you tonight. Check your phone. Bet he texted you."

Amanda dug in her bag, under the Frannie's shirt she had already changed out of. Her phone was off, as per Nancy's rules for Frannie's staff and the *Food Wars* filming suggestions. She powered it on: a long pause, then, yes, a notification. A text, from a number she knew was Andy's even though she had not yet given it a name.

Hey, bet you were great tonight.

As she read it, the telltale dots appeared. He was typing. Amanda felt a little surge of the same feeling that had lit her up last night when he brushed his hand up the back of her neck. He was typing. Right now. To her.

I'm still cleaning up. Almost done. If there were anywhere to go I'd ask you if you wanted to get a drink.

Sabrina was looking over her shoulder, and she read the last part out loud. "Come on, tell him you will. Tell him to come here."

Mary Laura shook her head. "I cannot be a party to this," she said, and then laughed at the look on Amanda's face. "Kidding! Honestly, I promised my boyfriend I'd come home after we close, and I already haven't. I think he has champagne. He thinks this *Food Wars* thing is really cool. But you know Andy can't come here."

"There has to be somewhere," Sabrina said, and both Amanda and Mary Laura shook their heads.

"Nope," Amanda said. "This is why teenagers here hang out in the QuikTrip parking lot. There truly isn't anywhere to go unless you drive a pretty long ways."

Sabrina hopped off her barstool. "Well, I left my notepad with all my stuff on it for tomorrow at Mimi's anyway. So I have to go there. And there's a parking lot there, too. You can channel your inner teenager. Tell him you'll bring him a beer."

Mary Laura took two Schlafly Summer Lagers from the fridge behind the bar and set them on the counter. "There. You're all set."

Amanda put her phone in her pocket. She knew she was getting bulldozed, but it was really just a little fun distraction—even if Mae and her mother would think it was a terrible idea. It was just the parking lot, it wasn't like she was going in, and they were just texting. In fact, she wasn't even doing that. She was just—going along for the ride. "I'm not telling him anything," she said. She didn't have to make a fool of herself. "No way. If he's there, great. Otherwise, I've got two beers."

MAE

Mae hoped to clean out Mimi's to prepare for the second night's filming, but she expected her mother to fight the removal of each and every bedraggled paper napkin. Instead, once the reunion with Madison and Ryder was over (a much warmer reunion than Barbara's dry attitude had led Mae to fear; instead, she had found herself worrying over her mother's willingness to take Ryder down the slide, which she had managed with surprising dexterity), Mae was standing in the tiny Mimi's dining area, watching this strange woman—because this could not be her mother—direct Andy to pull everything out from behind the counter before Mae even had a chance to get a good look at what was there. They had fresh paint, they had a power washer, and they had a mission.

"Just drag it all out," Barbara commanded. "I'll look at what's worth keeping while you start painting." She knelt and began prying open a can of paint, and Mae, who was carefully taking the pictures off the walls, ran to stop her.

"No, Mom, not yet. We need to wipe everything down, tape off the windows. You don't just paint over the dust."

Barbara shrugged. "I thought we were in a hurry here," she said, but she put down the paint and straightened up. "Fine. You do it your way, then."

Mae considered this statement. Was Barbara about to pull back? She had this sense of balancing on a fine wire, unsure of what lay beneath. So far, Barbara had wholeheartedly and without hesitation bought into Mae's vision for a quick overhaul. *Yes* to painting the walls and counter front, *yes* to carrying everything out of the tiny dining area and deep cleaning it, *yes* even to dumping the assortment of mismatched paper goods her mother collected.

When Mae suggested they start by sprucing up the patio, Barbara called her friend Patti, now working in the Home and Garden department at Walmart, and asked her to take care of them; now Patti was out there, dropping fresh soil all over the place. Aida, after a warm hug for Mae, was supervising, pointing vigorously with her crutch, avoiding any actual work by gesturing dramatically to her broken foot, which she made look like a stylish accessory.

"We'll talk later, *polpetta*," she said, and hearing her great-aunt call her little meatball—like Grandma Mimi and Mary Cat once did—made Mae blink and look away. Aida reached out to her all the time, actually, asking her about her book, about *Sparkling*, offering advice from her own TV career that was mostly wildly off base but occasionally on point. She even texted, and Mae suspected her great-aunt had bought the phone purely to communicate with her. Why hadn't Mae taken the time to answer more often? She would, from now on.

For now, though, Aida's enthusiastic presence, along with Barbara's strange mood of cooperation, were far more difficult to manage than Mae's original plan, which involved something like sending her mother on an errand and then doing everything herself, quietly and without all this input from the peanut gallery. Having more than one cook in the kitchen was every bit as problematic as the proverb said.

But this cleanup was clearly not going to be a solo act. Andy reappeared, followed by Zeus. "How about we paint, and you ladies sort through all the stuff outside?"

Mae glanced at Barbara and saw that her momentary mutinous look was fading. Andy painting was probably the best use of time—if Andy would paint right. She held up the rags and the roll of painter's tape. "You'll use these, okay?" She didn't care if she offended Andy.

Andy took the tape from her hand. "Well, I was planning to just slop paint all over the windows and paint over the dead fly on the sill, but if you insist."

Mae, already running out of patience, glared at him and held on to her side of the tape roll. "Seriously. The details matter. I want this job done right the first time."

"He'll do it right, Mae," snapped Barbara, and Andy, with a smirk, pulled the tape from Mae's hand, then relented. "I really will," he said, too softly for Barbara to hear. "You help your mom sort through stuff, okay?"

When they got outside, though, Barbara didn't seem to want to go through the things they'd pulled out. She left Mae to it, wandering around instead, helping Patti for a moment, putting her head back into Mimi's to ask Andy a question, then coming back before wandering off again, often with Aida trailing after her. That was fine, if a little odd. It gave Mae a chance to fill a trash bag with paper plates intended for a child's birthday party—technically usable but completely unappealing—but it also made her nervous. Could her mother not just settle down, or go somewhere else? Maybe Mae could send her for more coffee, although coffee seemed to be the last thing Barbara needed.

Finally, her mother came and stood next to her for more than an instant, holding the dog-shaped plastic bank the Humane Society provided for gathering contributions. "Do you really think we can win?" she asked softly.

Oh no. No, Mae did not think they could win. She hadn't even been considering winning. Frannie's was bigger. It had a full menu, not just five uniformly unhealthy items plus doughnuts on Saturday mornings. It had a bar and a full staff. It was open for regular hours and everything was always available, unlike Mimi's, where hours and pie choices were subject to Barbara's whim. Mimi's had appeal, yes—in Brooklyn it might win a cult following—but here, in the land where Applebee's ruled, Frannie's was the Goliath and Mae was short on slingshots. Mae would make Mimi's look its best, show off what she could do on live camera, and boost her own brand. She did think it would help Mimi's, but winning? No.

"I don't know, Mom," she said carefully. If wanting to win was behind Barbara's mostly cooperative spirit, Mae didn't want to tear that down, but neither did she want to set her mother up for a fall. "I didn't know you were worried about winning."

"Of course I want to win, Mae. Why else would we do this? That's a hundred thousand dollars. I'm not just helping the Pogociellos take that home on a silver platter. They don't need that money, never have. And we do, Mae." Barbara looked at Mae intently. "We do."

"Just being on *Food Wars* will bring more people to Mimi's, Mom. It's basically a win even to be asked."

"That's not the kind of win I'm talking about, Mae. All this cleaning, painting—this is going to get us a real shot, right? Our food is better; everyone knows it. Theirs is—half of it is frozen. I see that big Sysco truck there all the time. And now Mimi's will look like it should. So we should win."

Case closed, apparently. Mae hesitated. Could they win? Last night, looking around, she had spotted families she knew had been eating Mimi's chicken for generations making the effort to come out for *Food Wars*. Her mother's high school baseball sweatshirt had, she knew, been given to her by a grateful team: Barbara had donated the food for a fund-raiser again this year, and not just because baseball was Gus's sport, and Gus was hands down her favorite family member. She did the same for every team, every year. Frannie's was more polished. But Mimi's was special, if Mae could just help the judges see it. And if Frannie's really served frozen food to the judges, they wouldn't like that one bit.

Still. She wanted to muster up some honest hope for her mother, but it wasn't happening. "I don't know, Mom," she finally said. "I'm here, and I'm going to do everything I can, okay?"

Barbara didn't look satisfied, and Mae realized she had sounded weak, at best. "Seriously," she said, straightening her shoulders. She forced a smile, then saw Patti, behind Barbara, holding up what was truly a beautiful pot of flowers, with Aida standing by, smiling proudly as though it was all her doing.

The sun was shining, there wasn't a cloud in the sky, and somehow Patti, a Michelangelo hidden in a big-box store, had managed to create a masterpiece out of the humblest of materials. It was a tiny thing, but Mae felt her smile becoming real. If nothing else, it was kind of fun that Barbara was so into this. They'd get Mimi's cleaned up, and then they'd see.

"It's just the beginning, Mae," called Patti. "Wait until I get started along the fence."

"It looks awesome," Mae said. And it did. "We're going to give it our best, Mom, and that's what matters, right?"

"What matters is winning, Mae," Barbara said, but at least she was smiling now, too.

"Then could you quit fidgeting around and do something?" Mae rummaged through her supplies. "Here," she said. "Go start scraping the fence."

There was only so much even Mae could achieve in a day, but by the time the Mimi's makeover team was trading high fives and heading off for well-earned showers before *Food Wars*—and the night's customers—showed up, they had made a visible difference. Some projects, like the peeling paint around the entrance, Mae just abandoned for now, planning to set an alarm for the crack of dawn and tackle them before anyone else was up in the morning. As for the rest, they had come a surprisingly long way since last night, and as she made her way back to Mimi's, ready for the night ahead, Mae felt deeply satisfied. She realized with a start that she hadn't posted the progress anywhere—no before-and-afters, no Instagrams of the new coming in and the old going out, no selfie with a carefully soiled gardening glove and a pot of blooming flowers. How had she missed so many opportunities? She had been so deep in the work, and so sure of her every next move, that she'd never stopped to check in with the rest of the world.

Damn, she'd meant to promote every aspect of this. She'd have to try to catch up. She went inside and arranged sharp piles of simple white plates and napkins on the freshly painted red counter—dry, thank goodness, but only just—and took a shot from the top down, then another from the side. As she was kneeling beside the counter so that she could see how the shot would look with the top of the phone level with the top of the stack of plates, Andy's voice startled her.

"What are you doing? Paper plate glamour shots?"

Sheepish, but not willing to abandon the angle, which was much better than the others, Mae took her picture, then slid everything back into place under the counter. "Social media," she said. "You know, encouraging people to come out. I should have been doing it all day."

Andy laughed. "Kenneth and Patrick have been blasting about this nonstop. We're going to have more than we can handle tonight," he said. "Hope you brought your A game."

He'd been getting in little digs about her long absence all day, but somehow it didn't bother her. With a pleasant sense of confidence, Mae took her place next to him in front of the big stove, where they had agreed she would start the night. He'd been prepping for an hour, but still, she ran her own accustomed check on every burner, the knobs as familiar as her own hands. It had been a long time since she had run the kitchen at Mimi's, but frying chicken, for her, was like riding a bicycle. She was totally at home in this kitchen, just as the women in her family had always been. Signs of them were everywhere, from the cast-iron pans seasoned from long use to Mimi's original recipe, burned into her brain but still framed and hung on the wall behind the prep counter. She had this.

"Oh, I'm always at the top of my game," she said cheerfully. "Clean living, that's what does it."

Andy gave her a sharp look. Mae, who had her suspicions about how an obviously smart and extremely well-trained chef had ended up at her mother's chicken shack, met his gaze squarely. She'd been aware since she arrived that he thought she was a lightweight, and while she didn't care much—it was always easy to manage someone who'd underestimated you—she had no intention of letting him push her around tonight. "Plus, you've got my back, right?" She smiled. "We both want to knock it out of the park."

Just as Mae finished speaking, Barbara, dressed in fresh slacks and a short-sleeve blouse and looking bare without her usual covering smock, walked in. "Knock it out of the park," Barbara echoed, too loudly. Mae and Andy gaped at her. "What?" Barbara asked. "That's the point, right? Whatever it takes." Barbara took her apron down from the wall and wrapped it around herself, murmuring. "Whatever it takes," she repeated softly.

Andy's eyes met Mae's again, this time sharing their surprise at Barbara's oddly phrased vehemence, but there wasn't time to talk about it. Customers were arriving; Angelique was beginning to call orders into the pass-through. The night had begun.

Mae had carefully mapped out the evening to give herself the most camera time. When Sabrina arrived, about an hour later, it was Mae who explained the kitchen, the frying process, the ways it had changed over the years. Leaving Andy at the stove, she led the camera behind the counter and then out front, talking about the pictures and the history, giving Barbara just the lead-ins she needed to contribute but helping her to keep off center stage.

The place was packed with locals as well as out-of-towners, but Mae, who had learned something from her encounter with Kenneth, was—after half an hour on Facebook—ready.

"Great to see you again," she said warmly to one old classmate, not thrown off by the change in gender. Heck, Merinac's apparent acceptance of the shift from Jeff to Julia gave her hope for humanity.

"You look just the same," she squealed to another, ignoring gray hair and two decades of sun damage, especially as Crystal Kennedy, who now taught the Catholic Sunday school she, Amanda, and Mae had all attended, embraced Julia enthusiastically before ordering three of the night's special, all with chocolate cream pie. Kenneth and Patrick came by, and with Kenneth leaning on the counter, picking at the plate of drumsticks Barbara made just for him, it was as if she'd never left Merinac at all. She still belonged in this town.

×

The night was a triumph, even after Sabrina shifted her attention back to Frannie's. Mae, freed from the need to perform, took over from Andy and started catching her mother's orders and sliding the plates through the pass. As she watched each batch of chicken or French fries, waiting for the split-second shift in color and scent that told her when to flip them or shake the basket, she lost track of time completely, hearing only her mother's voice as she called the orders and moving with the rhythm demanded by the craft, surrounded by the familiar sounds and the savory smells of Mimi's kitchen in action. It only needed Amanda on the other side of the window alongside Barbara to make it complete, and as she shook the oil off the last pieces of the night, Mae realized she was happy.

"Right back at home?" Andy asked. She hadn't even realized he was still in the kitchen. Mae took the towel from the string of her apron and wiped her face before she answered.

"I was doing this when you were still getting stuffed into your locker in middle school," she said. "This was my culinary education right here."

"Well, I doubt you can clarify a broth, but this you can do." He held out a full plate. "I'm the last customer of the night. Want some?" Mae grabbed her own plate, and he shook a share of chicken and fries onto it. "Your mom asked me to tell you to meet her out back. I'll finish cleaning up."

Not bothering to take off her apron, Mae carried her plate across the parking lot and around to the back door of mother's house. She tapped on the window over the sink, trying not to see the dirty dishes or anything else, and Barbara, carrying a piece of chocolate cream pie, opened the sliding glass door and stepped out. She lowered herself onto the step next to Mae and set down the pie, and Mae picked it up and took a quick bite, making sure to get layers of cream and chocolate and graham cracker crust all stacked on her fork, before going back to the chicken and French fries. She'd forgotten how hungry cooking made a person, and now she was going to forget everything her trainer back in Brooklyn said about empty calories. She was hungry, and she was going to *eat*.

The door opened again, and Aida, who had spent the evening asking customers how they were doing in a regal tone and then ignoring their answers, especially if they wanted napkins, stuck a chair through the opening. Barbara pushed herself up to get it; then Aida herself came carefully out, carrying two more pieces of Patrick's pie. She handed one to Barbara and then seated herself, back upright, on the chair.

"It went magnificently," Aida declared. "I have not enjoyed a night at Mimi's that much since—since never, actually. I think that young woman was very pleased with me. She promised to add some scenes from some of my earlier guest appearances. I suggested *Bonanza*."

Mae, who would have much preferred her aunt highlight

another moment of her career, such as the brief stint on *Golden Girls,* which Aida preferred not to discuss, rolled her eyes at her mom, but the night had gone so well that a little touch of corn pone was not going to turn them into *Duck Dynasty.*

"It did go well," said Barbara, sitting back down. "I really do think that was thanks to you, Mae."

Mae, her mouth full of French fries, nodded. There was no point in being modest. Knowing everything about both how Mimi's worked and what Sabrina was likely to do or want next meant Mae could basically orchestrate the evening like a rock star. Almost immediately, the cameras had begun to follow Mae instead of the other way around, and knowing they were there—that she was on and making a connection that would eventually be shared with millions of viewers—felt like writing a term paper on Adderall. She had been tight, focused, on fire, and, as she'd promised Andy, at the top of her game. She'd bet anything Amanda had been a flaky mess at Frannie's. With Mae on Team Mimi's, maybe they had a shot.

"It would have been very distracting, Sabrina following me around asking me questions. Because we didn't really need you to do anything, you could just kind of be an extra person to talk to her," Barbara said. "Maybe I should have thought of that before I dragged you all the way here. Maybe Patti could have done it."

"Really, Mom?" Mae was outraged. It wasn't just being an extra person. It was everything Mae brought with her. It was being Mae. "Patti wouldn't have known half what I know. Sabrina would not have paid any attention to her."

"She did work for me once, a long time ago," Barbara said, "Before you were born." *You don't know everything,* Barbara's smile said.

Mae, brought down a considerable notch, put down the plate of chicken bones and took her pie. "Patrick's pies are so *good,*" she said. "Not as good as yours, of course"—this in answer to Barbara's sidelong look—"but you're obviously a good teacher. You could do

Mimi's pie classes," she said, getting a little excited. "That would be another reason to come out here from Kansas City. People would love it."

Barbara didn't respond, and Mae took another bite. This had to be the fattiest meal she had eaten since college, and she knew other people would be thinking the same thing. Classes were a good idea, but to really build Mimi's—assuming her mother wanted to—it was going to be tough to get people to come back again and again without addressing the health factor. "We really should add, like, just one healthy thing to the menu," Mae said.

"We have salad," Barbara said, in a tone that suggested it was the end of any discussion.

"Iceberg lettuce is not healthy, Mom. It's basically water. I'm thinking something affirmatively good for you, like, *Yeah I'm eating fried chicken but I also ate this, so I'm good.* Like kale. What if we offered one version of the salad with kale in it? It would still be the same salad."

"No kale," said Barbara. "That's ridiculous. Nobody comes to Mimi's for kale. Raw kale stops you up, too. It's terrible stuff."

"My mother forced us to eat it as kids," Aida said. "It grew so easy. It was always gritty, though. And stringy. Oh, I hated that stuff. I can't believe people eat it now."

Sometimes people had to hear an idea a whole lot of times before they came around to it. Mae let their objections go for now. She was on a roll, starting to see what Mimi's could be. People liked it; they really did. They weren't just looking for another Olive Garden. Crystal, Julia, Morty Rountree, all the people she had recognized, and way more that she had not—it just felt like people really got how important and cool it was to eat real food. Food with a history.

"People love the salad dressing," she said. "And the chicken is so good. Andy says he called Caswell's to up our usual order of fresh chicken for tomorrow—but do you know if they're organic? Sabrina was asking, and I told her I thought it was, basically, because of course it should be. If it is, we should highlight that on the menu." It would be cool to put up a sign or something—chickens born and raised right here in Merinac. Amanda could draw— Well, no, Amanda probably wouldn't. But just the sign would be cool. She started to say so, then realized that her mother, beside her, had stiffened and was glaring at her.

Barbara put down her pie on the porch beside her and spoke firmly. "I do not know if the chicken is organic, Mae, but I assume it's not, since he isn't charging me an extra arm and leg for smaller pieces. It's just chicken, from Caswell's, same as ever."

That was fine; it didn't really matter. Mae nodded. "They're at least free-range, right? People love knowing that. The Caswells have been doing this for as long as Mimi's has been around. We can share the story behind the food, that it's fresh and locally sourced." She smiled reassuringly at her mother. The organic label itself really didn't matter. "That's all anybody in New York ever talks about right now, where the food comes from and stuff."

Barbara was not soothed. Everything that had been easy between Mae and her mother seemed to disappear in an instant. "People do not come to Mimi's for organic food and kale, Mae," said Barbara, raising her voice. "We've been serving Caswell's chicken and lettuce salad since before you were born, and we will keep serving it long after you go back to Brooklyn, since you're so set on that. You're here to help me win this, not to turn Mimi's into—into—some fancy New York place."

Barbara's lack of an example at the end made her want to giggle, but Mae knew her mother was serious—and that her mother had seriously misunderstood. Mae just wanted to tell customers what Mimi's already was, not make it something different, or at least, not very different. But before Mae could defend herself, she heard footsteps coming around the side of the house. She leapt to her feet, and Barbara struggled up next to her.

"Hello?" The voice was Sabrina's, and without any need to

consult, the Moore women swung into action. Aida, leaving her chair, held the door for Barbara, who rushed inside to turn off the lights. Mae rushed toward the corner and nearly collided with Sabrina just as the lights went off, leaving her grabbing the other woman's arm in the dark.

"Oh, hey!" Mae tried for a casual tone. "My mom just went to bed. Um, come on, I was just about to go get my car. I'll walk you back." The path was uneven, but the light from Mimi's kitchen windows was just enough to show Sabrina where she was going—and not enough, as long as her mother didn't turn any inside lights on, to reveal anything unusual about the house.

"Oh, I thought I would catch you guys," said Sabrina, turning around and heading for the parking lot. She didn't seem to have noticed anything. "That's why I came back. You should be celebrating. That went great."

"I know," said Mae, delighted. "It was fun. More fun than *Sparkling*, really."

"Well, you practically had this stage all to yourself," said Sabrina, with a wicked smile that Mae took to be a dig at Lolly, her scene-stealing *Sparkling* co-host, until Sabrina went on. "Amanda told me you've always liked having the whole town's eyes on you, and then some."

Mae, walking beside Sabrina in the near darkness, faltered. "What?" Sabrina's tone had shifted from congratulatory to teasing, even a little aggressive, and Mae wasn't sure why. But then again, she could guess. She had known some mocking of her small-town roots was coming the minute she agreed to come back to Kansas, and she tried to respond lightly, ready for the inevitable Dorothy joke or white-trash reference. "Oh, I know. So classic, small-town theater geek. I even had the lead in *Our Town*, did she say? I'm a walking cliché."

This time, Sabrina laughed. "That wasn't exactly what she said, but that totally makes it better." She snorted. Mae could tell she was genuinely laughing, not just playing her *Food Wars* host part, and suddenly Mae knew exactly what was coming, even as part of her mind was arguing that, no, it was impossible, Amanda would never have gone there.

Sabrina, still giggling a little, went on. "No, she was talking about the stripping. In college. I almost didn't believe her, but she convinced me." As she spoke, they stepped into a circle of light from the only streetlight off the Mimi's parking lot, and Mae would have sworn she'd timed it so that she could see Mae's reaction to her words.

But Mae was frozen. Frozen with anger and frustration and just a tiny bit of fear, because why the hell would Amanda do this to her when she knew—she must know—that even though Mae was totally cool with her past choices, this was not one she advertised, and not one she'd told Jay about, either.

Fuck her. Fuck her sister.

Fuck. Sabrina was still there, smiling cheerfully. Well, fuck her, too. No response was actually the perfect response. She wasn't ashamed of what she did, not one bit. She had decided a long time ago that there was no point regretting something you'd already done. Choices only move in one direction. Anyway, she hadn't been used by all those men; she had used them. Their worn and folded bills had added up to enough to finance her road to B-school, and she was proud of her resourcefulness—but that didn't mean she had to make it easy to drag this out there, even if Jay probably wouldn't care. She'd sounded him out about it, long ago, thought about telling him. It just never came up; that was all.

His family would care. Big-time. Not that she herself cared about that, but still. She forced herself to keep walking, out of that little circle of light, and Sabrina kept pace with her, eyes still on Mae's face. If she didn't say anything, Sabrina had—what? Probably nothing.

She would just ignore it. See what Sabrina did with that. Mae pushed a breath out through her nose, knowing her lips were pressed together and her expression probably wasn't the calm, neutral face she was reaching for, then tilted her head and spoke. "I have to get back to the kids," she said. "I'm just going to grab my bag—I left it in the kitchen."

"You do that," said Sabrina. She still seemed amused, and now she glanced toward the kitchen. "I'll just wait here. These heels are killing me."

Mae hurried up the walk. *Damn, damn, damn.* Would Sabrina use whatever Amanda had said? Was it on tape? Would they have to prove it before they thought they could run it? Because Jay—that was so not the way she'd want this to come out for him. Or his family. Or Lolly, or *Sparkling,* good God—

She had her hand nearly on the screen door before she heard it—Andy's voice, a low rumble, then a woman's laugh. Automatically, she kept going, opening the door as the owner of the laugh clicked into place in her head, so that she saw Amanda at the exact instant that she realized she knew exactly who and what she was about to see.

Amanda.

Amanda, in Mimi's.

Amanda, her double-crossing sister, in Mimi's, her butt up on the counter, her legs wrapped around Andy's waist, her hands buried in the hair at the back of his neck, Andy pressing his body into hers.

Goddamn it! All of the fury Mae already felt toward Amanda, all the words she'd just held back in the parking lot, boiled up and out. She slammed the screen door into the wall, shouting, "You do not come in here! Andy! You know she doesn't come in here!"

Amanda and Andy jerked apart, Andy leaping a foot back and then sticking out a hand to steady Amanda, who nearly fell off the counter.

"Mae! Oh God, I'm sorry, I'm sorry, I just—we just—I—"

"Get out!"

Mae ran to Amanda, wildly shaking her hands at her. "Do you even know what you're doing?" She turned to Andy. "A hundred years, right? More. A hundred years since we let anybody from Frannie's in here. What were you thinking?" This wasn't about Amanda's betrayal, not anymore. No. This was Amanda trying to destroy everything. With difficulty, she refrained from kicking her sister, who was scrambling to pick her flip-flops up off the ground. "Can you even imagine what Mom would say? What she would do? Get out! Just get out!" Amanda stumbled, then scrambled for the door. Mae chased after her. "Out!"

To Mae, it was as if the lights were flashing and thunder crashing, even if those reactions came from her heart and mind. Amanda could see them too; Mae knew she could. The screen door had flown open and a gust of wind rushed from the pass-through toward the door, pushing them, although the night had been still. Mimi's might not speak to Andy, but it was howling at the two Moore girls.

Amanda had only been inside Mimi's once since marrying Frank and taking up her work at Frannie's. It had been the day after his funeral, when she had come quietly in and sat and watched Mae helping Barbara prep, and they hadn't said anything. The air had gone out of the kitchen and things became very quiet, just the three of them, until Barbara took an apron from the hook on the wall and held it out to Amanda.

Amanda shook her head.

Barbara held the apron out again, and again Amanda shook her head.

And Barbara, as if possessed, started shaking the apron at Amanda, saying nothing, flicking it at her, flapping until Amanda fled her stool, urging her toward the door.

"I thought you were coming back to us," Barbara said, staring straight ahead. "If you're not, go home. You've got another family now."

Amanda struggled with the door, which finally burst open, then ran, slamming it behind her, never once looking at Mae. Barbara resumed her work as if nothing had happened.

As if Amanda had never been there at all.

At the time, Mae felt like her mother took the whole thing with Amanda and Frannie's more than a little too far. She had tried to go after Amanda but known instantly by the look on Barbara's face that it would be the wrong move, that staying, then trying to bring them together later, would have a better chance at working.

It hadn't. Amanda hadn't wanted her, either. And seeing Amanda, here, now—Barbara was right. Amanda had chosen. And now she needed to live with that choice and leave Mimi's alone.

But Andy did not seem inclined to follow the rules.

"What the hell are you doing?" He put a hand on Mae, who knocked it away—what, did he think she was actually going to punch her sister? She might have wanted to, but they weren't twelve. She kept her hands on her hips, very aware that Sabrina had just appeared in the doorway, phone in her hand. Although her stance was casual, Mae was dead certain she was filming.

Sabrina smiled as though nothing was happening. "Amanda, you found Andy—great! But I guess I thought you didn't usually go into Mimi's?"

Mae had to admire the lure Sabrina tossed out there. As angry as she still was—and she was; she was shaking all over—she mentally willed her sister to show a little sense for a change. Say anything at all, and Sabrina would have some interesting footage. But if they kept quiet—she pressed her lips together and tried to give both Andy and Amanda an intense look. *Just shut up,* she thought. *She's setting us up. Just shut up and go. Don't give it to her.* Well played by Sabrina, yes. And Mae owed her sister one, and Amanda was going to get it. But it was still possible to keep a little family dignity, if only Amanda and Andy would play this cool.

They did not.

"I asked her in," Andy snapped.

"No, she's right, I shouldn't have come in," said Amanda, wildly looking around, smoothing the long hair she no longer had, then hopping on one foot to put her second flip-flop back on. "I knew it, I'm sorry. I'll just go now." She wasn't meeting Andy's eyes, or Mae's, and she couldn't seem to stop talking. "I should get home anyway, I don't know why I came in, just dumb, I guess, I didn't really have a reason..."

We all know your reason, thought Mae. Now that she could see Sabrina's machine working, it was far easier to tuck away her anger over Amanda's betrayal and follow her own script, not Sabrina's. Fine, she had a scene. But let it be a scene of Mae calmly handling an unwanted intrusion, not losing it. She shifted her tone, hoping that Sabrina's phone hadn't caught her earlier. "It's no big deal, Amanda," she said, ignoring the looks on Amanda's and Andy's faces. "You said hi, and, yeah, you can just head out." *Just basically say nothing,* she told herself. "Here's your bag." She picked up Amanda's tote bag from the floor where it had fallen. Her phone had spilled out, along with her Frannie's shirt from earlier.

"I see you changed before you came," Mae said, holding one strap of the bag as Amanda reached out and took the other. Their eyes met. She wanted Amanda to know that she knew what Amanda had done—and that there would be payback. "Guess you probably weren't planning to strip down here." Mae held the bag for just an instant too long, knowing her face was away from the camera, and she dropped everything fake and friendly from her face while keeping her voice light. Let the viewers hear her containing her anger, but Amanda was going to see it loud and clear. "Have a nice night."

She saw understanding in Amanda's eyes before she turned away, hearing rather than seeing her sister slip out the door.

Amanda, it seemed, was going to break every rule. She didn't respect the rules, or the past, or, clearly, Mae and Barbara. Or even

Andy, who was still gazing after her sister, actually looking hurt, the fool. Jerk though he might be, he could probably have any single woman in this town through sheer lack of competition, and he actually had a thing for Amanda?

He'd regret it. Because if Amanda wasn't going to play by the rules, Mae wasn't either. Plan A had been making Mimi's look good while Frannie's took the crown, but Plan B was even better: Mimi's triumphs, and Frannie's looks like the Olive Garden wannabe that it had turned itself into. She'd highlight the authenticity that was Mimi's, the way nothing ever changed because it didn't need to and the hell with the kale salad. She'd use everything she had to make this story go her way, and she could do it, too. She knew how this worked, and Amanda didn't have a clue.

Her mother was right. Mimi's could win this thing. Mimi's was just what everyone wanted now: local, fresh, homemade, real. She could have people coming from three states away to taste their perfectly crafted limited menu and weeping when they found out Mimi's was out of pie.

Mae was going to run Frannie's right into the ground, and Amanda with it.

Sabrina seemed to be waiting for something. Her phone was still out, but she hadn't said anything. Just as Andy's puppy-dog look was starting to change into one of confusion, Amanda appeared outside the screen door, and as Sabrina turned, Mae could see that she had her phone camera focused exactly there.

"Hey," Amanda said. She wobbled a little, and Mae could see, if she hadn't guessed before, that her sister wasn't just being stupid; she was very, very drunk. "I, um, Gus took my car. And I probably shouldn't drive anyway. Can somebody take me home?"

Amanda's eyes were on Andy, but Sabrina, who probably had her reasons, rushed forward. "Oh, of course," she said, slipping her phone into the back pocket of her perfect white jeans. "Let's go."

Amanda was such a softball. Taking down Frannie's—and her sister— was going to be almost too easy. If Mae had to, she'd ride out the stripping thing just fine, because that was exactly who she was—she did what she needed to do to get what she wanted.

She had ahold of herself now, too. She knew what she was doing. Mae picked up her own bag but waited a beat before following the other women, choosing her words carefully. Andy needed to be put in his place, too. Now.

"Amanda never could stay away from the guys in the kitchen," she said to Andy's back, and continued over her shoulder as she walked out the door. "Guess you're joining the club."

She left without giving him a chance to answer.

×

Mae slipped out of her motel room early the next morning with a welcome sense of being ready to shake things up. By the time Kenneth and Patrick opened for coffee, she was going to have earned it. After all, Mimi's needed a fresh look, and that old sign of Amanda's was worn, chipped, and dated. It wasn't as if Amanda even cared about Mimi's anymore. She probably didn't even want them to use that chicken she had painted now that she was with Frannie's, and if she did, well, she should have acted like it. Mae didn't feel bad about painting over it. Not one bit.

It was still dark when she started, but Mae had set up her supplies for this last night. She could work by the porch light until the sun came up. Rolling the paint over the sign, pressing down hard, felt good. She was erasing yesterday. Today would be great.

Her worried mood of the night before had mostly passed, leaving her invigorated. She could do this. She could keep the attention of *Food Wars* where it belonged, on the food, and if not, she'd serve up Amanda and Andy on a silver platter. She herself would give up nothing, and really there was nothing to give. The dancing gig was a nonstarter, and Sabrina clearly knew it. There wasn't a whisper of it anywhere on any social media channels. It wasn't even worth saving up for later, not if she wasn't going to react anyway.

Jay she would deal with when she got home. Their whispered conversation last night had been unsatisfying—her trying not to wake Madison and Ryder, him trying to—what? Convey his boredom? She had wanted to share her plans for defeating Frannie's, but it was too hard to explain where she was and what was happening, especially when he wasn't even bothering to pretend to be interested.

When she'd met Jay in business school, Merinac was so far behind her that it was second nature to let him assume as everyone else did that the "suburb of Kansas City" where she had grown up was basically the equivalent of Long Island. By the time it was clear he was sticking around, it was too hard to clear it up, and Mae only partially wanted to. She was just another student by then. Everybody had a (well-paying) summer internship. Everybody had student debt—not Jay, it turned out, but most people. It was fun, becoming someone who was accustomed to buying her clothes new and putting down her credit card for big group meals split sixteen ways (and trying not to mentally calculate who had had more to eat or drink because clearly that was not the way it was done). And Jay liked that version of Mae. Loved that she could roll with courtside seats at a 76ers game or the tasting menu at Vetri Cucina as easily as downing beers at a dive bar. Was excited by her ambition and delighted by the opportunity to show her all the new things fulfilling those ambitions meant she could do and buy and be.

She pressed a little harder with her paint roller. All she had been hoping for last night was to feel the tiniest connection with that old Jay. The one who would think the Yellow Rose of Texas was funny. She'd tried to turn the conversation to him, ask how work was going, but he had given her nothing. Couldn't he at least try? Try to find what he'd once liked about his job? Try to find what he'd once liked about her?

It had been like he didn't want to talk. Not to her, anyway.

This was not confidence inspiring. But the shiny fresh paint was. And so was remembering last night's final text, from Kenneth:

Breakfast? Tell all?

Be ready with coffee. I'll be there when you open.

See you at o dark-thirty.

That at least was something to look forward to.

Kenneth was waiting for her behind the counter, cup in hand, ready to brew.

"You always were my dream man, Kenneth, and now you've achieved true perfection," she said.

"Taken, so very taken," he replied. "Which is obvious. You, on the other hand, much less obvious. You wear a ring, it is true, but you do not exude the beatific joy of the beloved that shines from my very soul. So let us go there immediately, since you bring it up. Why has your better half never, to my certain knowledge and you can be sure I have checked, graced our fair town?"

Nobody got her like Kenneth. Mae stood there, waiting for her coffee, and didn't offer the flippant answer that would have been easiest. This was why friends sucked. There you were, keeping things safely tucked away in their own spaces, and somebody like Kenneth came along and just pulled everything out, kind of the way Mae used to when she was hired to organize a closet.

That wasn't really a good comparison. *Out of sight, out of mind* was a bad idea for clothes but not for problems, which sometimes really did go away if you just avoided them for long enough.

Kenneth, carrying two cups, walked around the coffee bar and set them both on a table. His foam made a perfect heart; hers, a floating question mark.

"Screw you," she said, without rancor, and sat down, dumped in three packets of sugar, and ruthlessly stirred away. "I am happily married."

She was, too. For now. "Why would you home in on that, anyway?" she asked. "I've done a zillion other things since we graduated, and you just want to know who I'm shagging?"

"Everything else about you is wide open. I can find out what you had for breakfast a week ago last Tuesday in three different places. But your delightful-looking husband, other than the occasional photo op, remains shrouded in mystery. Although I do note that holding hands with him, in some parts of this state, might in fact earn you more than a few sideways glances. Is that why he stayed home?"

"God no. That really doesn't—I bet it doesn't happen any more for us than it does for you. Less, even. He's American. Yeah, his family is from India, so maybe once in a while somebody says something, but mostly no."

Kenneth waited, perfect eyebrows raised. Mae licked her spoon. It was true—Jay's brown skin (and Madison's and Ryder's, for that matter) wasn't the norm in Merinac, but neither was it entirely out of the ordinary. The crowd at Mimi's last night had been much more diverse than the one she went to high school with. And Jay was also a tall, good-looking rich kid who carried an air of privilege everywhere he went. She knew he felt his differences—it was one of the things they shared, especially at the very WASPy consulting firm, a feeling of being an outsider—but she wasn't going to pretend to Kenneth that Jay's background had anything to do with his absence.

"Jay just wouldn't get Merinac," she finally said. "Plus, he kind of thinks it's Kansas City."

Kenneth hooted, and Mae smiled a little. It was funny. She'd worked so hard to hide the differences between the way she was raised and the way Jay was raised, and she'd been so successful.

But it also wasn't funny. Because if she'd been less successful, if Jay and his family had seen through the cracks to the total void where Mae's supposedly solid middle-class background was supposed to be, maybe she wouldn't be stuck trying to convince someone who had never really worked for anything that you didn't give up everything you'd worked for. But that would mean no Madison, no Ryder...

Mae might really need to fall back on that no-regrets policy.

"Kansas City." Kenneth laughed. "Well, maybe if you brought him straight to the Inn. Blindfolded. Seriously, Mae?"

She shrugged. "We swore we were never coming back, right?"

Kenneth took a sip of his latte. "You also swore you were never getting married," he said. "I would very much like to see the guy who talked you down a road this Moore sister swore she'd avoid."

"Yeah, well..." She couldn't help it—she looked down at her coffee, even knowing Kenneth would read into her avoiding his eyes what only he could. "Maybe I was wrong. Maybe not every Moore woman gets left." And maybe she was right. The rest of the sentence lay right there on the table between them, and after a minute, Mae slipped over it, knowing Kenneth had heard what she had not said. "Come on, how about you? How'd you drag the love of your life to the hairy armpit of the universe?"

"Armpits are cozy," Kenneth said. "Not nearly so bad as we once thought. Where did we think we wanted to be, anyway? The nipple? The cheek? It seems like a great metaphor, but it really falls down when you try to extend it."

Mae smiled. She'd forgotten what it was like to be with someone who knew not just the public side of you but all the crap you'd have preferred to hide and still was okay with it.

Kenneth knew she was waiting for more, so he sipped his own coffee and stared into the distance, making a big show of contemplating, before he relented. "My dad has Alzheimer's. Your mom probably told you." Mae nodded. "It's hard for my mom and my sister. And it sucks for him; he knows it's happening. For years we just—I could send money, you know, no problem. All the money they needed. Home help, that kind of thing. But you can't—" He put down his coffee, looked straight at Mae. "Some stuff you can't hire. You can't pay somebody to care like you care. If you're not here, you're not here. You're not really there for someone if you're jetting in and out. You gotta be coming for dinner and picking up groceries."

Mae nodded. Kenneth had been lucky with his parents. He'd had a hard time in high school, but not at home. Never at home. And his parents had been there for Mae, too, when she'd let them, which hadn't been often. His mom had let Mae use their washer-dryer as if it was her own, and as if needing to borrow something like that was as normal as asking for a cup of sugar, while Kenneth's dad used to carry her laundry basket out to her beat-up car. It was hard to imagine his dad not remembering all that, and she could see why he would want to be here, but the whole picture still didn't add up.

"Right, but you're not just here for—the time being. For whatever happens. You guys are *here* here. All in." She gestured around. "This is not a California design lab. It's not even a Kansas design lab. It's a bed-and-breakfast and it's in Merinac and I don't get it. It's not what you worked for, right? Is it what Patrick wanted? Are you going to do something else, later?" She knew, now, that Kenneth had been the most sought-after branding and interface creator in San Francisco, still talked about and with plenty of opportunity to go back to. For him to be here, brewing coffee on Main Street, was just a waste.

Kenneth shook his head. "No, it's not for Patrick. Not just for Patrick. Look, we did Silicon Valley. We moved fast; we broke things. It was kind of great, and I kind of loved it, and I kind of didn't. I'm good here."

"For now, sure. But this isn't what you wanted. Or what your mom wanted for you, either. Or your dad." She watched Kenneth's face carefully, not wanting to go too far, but he just sat there, seeming totally at ease. "This is just not where you were supposed to end up."

He stuck a finger in his latte, pulling out some foam to lick off, then jutting out his lower lip in a very familiar gesture that meant he was reluctant to disagree, but he was going to do it anyway.

"I was different there," he said. "I'm different here, too, but here I'm different from other people. There I was different from me."

"Profound," said Mae in a voice that meant she thought he was just blowing air out of his ass, and Kenneth stood, grabbing her now-empty cup.

"You know what I mean," he said. "There's just something about being in a place where what matters most is right in front of you. And look—here you are. If you didn't care about this place, if you didn't see something worth saving in Mimi's, in something that's been around longer than either of us, you'd just let it go." He gave her a quick glance. "Honestly, I figured you probably would."

Mae flushed. There it was, all he was going to say, probably, about the way she had left not just Merinac but him. And now he was giving her too much credit, damn him. Saving Mimi's was not why she was here. She started to say something, but what would she say? Instead, she followed him to the counter, where he set their dishes in a tub, then glanced at his watch, a solid, fat anachronism of a thing. "This place is going to be jammed in a few minutes. I'll let Patrick take over, walk you back to Mimi's, maybe say hi to your mom."

Mae accepted this in silence, smiling at Patrick as he came out from the back room, relieved when he didn't press for conversation. As they left the Inn she looked sideways at Kenneth. She'd done her morning's work with satisfaction, but the thought of watching other people take its measure didn't feel as good as she thought it would, and especially not now. "You're going to be surprised," she said.

"By what?"

"I painted Mimi's."

Kenneth stopped short, then picked up his pace. "No way. That place hasn't been painted in— Oh no, Mae. You didn't." As Mimi's came into view, Kenneth gasped. "You painted over Amanda's sign!" He looked like she'd destroyed an icon of their childhood, and maybe she had. "And it looks like crap! Mae, you didn't even do a good job. It's bleeding through."

He was right. When she'd left it this morning, the sun hadn't been fully up, and the wet paint had erased all traces of the painted chicken underneath it. Now, though, the original painting appeared in shadow form. Kenneth picked up the can of paint she'd used. "This paint is never going to cover that, Mae. You'll need something oil-based, and it won't dry fast enough. And why would you do it anyway? Amanda's sign was great. Everyone loved it."

It did look awful. Half-done at best and shoddy at worst. Seeing what she had done through Kenneth's eyes—and seeing that she hadn't even done it right—made Mae feel defensive. She took the bucket of paint from him angrily, as though it were his fault it hadn't worked. "I can't just put another coat on it?"

"It won't look any better. It's just not the right kind of paint, Mae. Why didn't you ask someone?"

Because anyone she'd asked would have said not to paint over the sign, of course. Kenneth didn't know how much Amanda deserved to be erased from the face of Mimi's at this point. Nobody did. Mae could try to explain, maybe—but no one else would get why this made sense.

Had seemed to make sense.

And now it looked awful. She didn't want Amanda's sign. Amanda's sign didn't belong there anymore. But how could she have

messed things up so badly? Tears came to her eyes. "I just didn't."
She felt like a belligerent teenager with no way to excuse her bad
behavior. "It's done now, though. And you're right; it looks like crap.
What am I going to do?"

"Okay," he said, taking in a deep breath and looking at the ugly
wall. "I have an idea. Wait here." Seeing her face, he smiled a little.
"This was stupid, Mae. But I think we can make it better."

He turned, heading toward the Inn, and Mae sat on the bench in
front of Mimi's. The sign wasn't all she was upset about. Mimi's had
been around longer than they had, yes. So had Merinac. But if you'd
outgrown something, there was no point in pretending otherwise,
right? Maybe Kenneth wanted to tie himself to this place again.
Good for Kenneth. But for Mae—wasn't it enough that she was here
now? Kenneth had his whole family to come back to—and he'd done
what he set out to do when he left. She had a backstabbing sister and
a mother who would never really change, a house she'd never enter
again, and a whole lot more to lose. He'd understand, if he gave it
more thought than he gave his annoying latte art.

She flicked her phone awake. Silence from Jay, which did not
make her feel better. Instead of words, she sent him a picture of the
kids playing in the car from yesterday, knowing he would assume it
was from this morning, and then started the ritual of checking social. *Food Wars* was tagging her on Instagram and retweeting her.
If only she'd done more yesterday. Even as it was, she had more than
a thousand new followers—way more than she had ever had in a
single day, even with *Sparkling.* She snapped and shared an image
of the flowers in front of the freshly painted Mimi's (on the side of
the building that looked good) before Kenneth returned. She was
getting things done.

Kenneth was pushing a dolly with a big white signboard on it,
made of four two-by-fours bolted together, with hooks at the top. On
the side facing Mae, it read COMING SOON.

Kenneth set down the dolly, then walked the sign around on its corners until it was leaning up against the bench. He gestured to Mae, and the two of them lifted it up.

"I don't get it," Mae said. "I mean, yeah, it would cover it—"

"Hush." They set down the sign again, leaning it on the wall, blank side out. Kenneth pulled a Sharpie out of his pocket. He stepped back from the sign, then, with concentration, stepped forward and started drawing. In less time than Mae would have thought possible, he'd outlined "Mimi's" in a big, fat cursive, and, underneath, in smaller block letters, "since." He looked back at Mae.

"Eighteen eighty-six."

He finished by outlining the date. "I'll paint this in and hang it," he said. "You get out of here before you make it worse."

Mae stared at the sign he'd made. She loved it. It captured everything she wanted to about Mimi's—the simplicity, the history. Even if they were misunderstanding each other a little, at least—unlike Andy, and sure as hell unlike Amanda—Kenneth really did have her back. *Screw Amanda, anyway.* This sign was going to be much better. "Oh, but wait," she said, pointing. "That second eight is uneven. The first one is more straight."

Kenneth sighed. "*Wabi-sabi,* Mae. It's the beauty of the flaw that makes it perfect."

She looked at him for a minute, then at the lettering. "Yeah, but you made a mistake. You started to write a six and then you changed it."

"It's all in how you look at it. Go away. I'm doing you a favor here."

AMANDA

Gus was hovering, and it was making Amanda crazy. For the second morning in a row, she had woken up to a head full of recrimination and regret, only this time, the hangover wasn't metaphorical. The coffee she was trying to make wasn't just coffee. It was medicinal. But at every turn, Gus seemed to be there, between her and the drawer with the coffee scoop, in front of the trash can when she needed to dump yesterday's filter.

Normally, Amanda's seventeen-year-old was the most independent person imaginable. He dealt with his own homework and test prep and friends and getting rides wherever he needed to go. On school days he got ready for school and got on the bus (he was saving for a car for senior year), sometimes barely exchanging a word with Amanda, who was not at her best in the morning. Frankie was much the same, a side effect, probably, of growing up with a single parent who often worked a late shift. Amanda tried to at least be up in the morning before they went to school, but she usually wasn't much help.

This morning, though, Gus was different. He leaned against the counter, watching her while she watched the coffee, waiting for enough to drip down into the pot to fill her mug. He was right behind her as she went to the fridge for the milk. He sat down across from her at the table and fidgeted with his Pop-Tart, when usually he'd have eaten it in two bites while running out the door.

Amanda, who usually drank that first cup of coffee while staring into space and letting her household rush around her, finally set her cup down a little too hard, looked at her son, and said, "What?"

Gus, who was already looking back at her, shrugged and looked down at his Pop-Tart instead. "Nothing. I just thought I'd sit down this morning. For a change."

Amanda said nothing to that, just lifted her eyebrows slightly. She could hear Frankie banging around in her bedroom, and part of her hoped her daughter would stay put until Gus brought himself to say whatever was on his mind, while another part—the slightly hungover, precoffee part—hoped for a speedy interruption. She wanted Gus to tell her when he had something on his mind. She totally did. Just maybe not today.

Gus broke off a piece of crust and played with it, then glanced up at her and back at his plate. "I read your book," he said.

For a minute, Amanda didn't know what he was talking about. "My book?"

Gus gestured to the table. "Your—the comic. About Carleen. It was on the table last night."

Right. She'd come home after an uncomfortable car ride with Sabrina, who thought the whole scene with Mae and Andy was just funny, and cleaned up the sketchbook and pencils she had left behind earlier in the day, but of course Gus would have been home first.

Gus rushed on. "And it's good, Mom. I mean, really good. Your story—I loved it. When Carleen lays the egg in gym class, and all the other chickens are laughing—it's amazing. The drawings, the way you have them say just enough—it's so cool. You should show it to someone."

Now it was Amanda's turn to stare down at the table. Gus's praise made her even more uncomfortable than his lingering had. She shrugged. "It's not really my story. It's Stephen King. You know, *Carrie*."

"I know, but the way you did it—it's just really cool, Mom. I think you could, like, sell it. I really do."

Amanda wanted to crawl away. How could she have left her stuff where Gus could find it? And praise like that . . . well, he was probably just being nice. But even if he was just trying to be nice, that was pretty amazing in itself. Teenagers weren't supposed to be nice to their moms. She tried to smile, although she could feel that it was more of an awkward grimace. "Thanks, Gus. I appreciate that."

"I mean it, Mom. I'm not just saying it." Her kid knew her well. "If I didn't think it was cool, I wouldn't say anything. I know it's kind of private. Maybe I shouldn't have looked. But it's really awesome, Mom. Seriously."

Frankie burst out of her room, rushing for the door. "The bus, Gus," she called, backpack straps hitting the chair as she sped past. "Come on!"

Gus got up, grabbing his own backpack, and reached for his plate.

"I'll get it," Amanda said, thankful for the interruption. She went in for the rest of the Pop-Tart, but Gus beat her to it.

"Think about it, Mom," he said, following Frankie as he spoke over his shoulder. "I mean it."

Sweet. Her son was sweet. But Amanda hoped he never brought it up again. Tender, possibly a little condescending encouragement from Gus was not what she needed at this moment. What she needed was more and better coffee—not this sludge she had made, which was now cold. And not a Pop-Tart, either. It was going to take something far more decadent and delicious to drown out the thoughts that kept spinning around in her aching head, especially now that the kitchen was empty. If it hadn't been for Mary Laura and the constant topping off of her Sour in the City, or whatever it was, maybe she wouldn't have gone to Mimi's. And if she hadn't gone to Mimi's, Andy wouldn't have come to the door, which just swung open, she swore. It was like her feet just carried her in.

And then he was so—kind. About *Food Wars*. He got it. "I was nervous," he said, and then she could admit it—she was too.

"All those cameras."

He patted the counter, and she hopped up on it while he hung the last of the pans, and then when he leaned next to her, talking, it was a little like being in a car, not looking at each other.

"What made you ask them to come?" He smiled, glancing at her. "If you don't like cameras."

"I didn't think so much about the cameras," she said, and it sounded a little ridiculous. "I mean, when you watch on TV, you don't see the cameras."

Andy laughed, and after a minute, she did too. He wasn't making fun of her. She could tell. "You just see the people, and they come to life, you know? And it feels so—intense. Like they're really doing big things."

"I think that is the cameras," he said, and there it was, the second time tonight someone made her think about what happened when all of this was over.

"Maybe the cameras leave some of that behind," she said, and then, because she didn't want to talk about that anymore: "or at least I'll still have my stupid haircut."

"I like the stupid haircut," he said, and then he touched the back of her neck again, and it had been so long since anyone looked at her that way, or touched her that way, and something just felt right, there in Mimi's, exactly where nothing had felt right for a long, long time.

And if he hadn't touched the back of her neck again . . .

That would be such a good memory if it weren't for Mae and everything that came next. And if it didn't make her feel so sick inside, like she had betrayed everyone she loved, and if she didn't know how little she deserved to have any man return her interest, since she'd already proved with Frank, back when they were fighting so hard over the life she had wanted so badly, that she didn't know her own mind or heart. And if the whole idea of running away from Mae, and Andy, in front of Sabrina didn't make her feel like erasing herself from the entire planet.

She needed coffee from Patrick, who would be blessedly unaware of her humiliation at Mae's hands. And one of his glorious, lightly glazed brown butter scones.

Which was a great plan, except that before she could get the coffee, before she could even park at the Inn, she had to drive by Mimi's, and while she was driving by Mimi's, she saw that the work of erasing her from the planet had already begun.

Her chicken sign, the one she had painted freehand at fifteen and that had been there, gently peeling, ever since, was gone. The little building was freshly painted in the same old barn red, and someone—Kenneth!—was painting the word "Mimi's" on a new sign, a white one, leaning against the bench in front.

Amanda wanted to be somewhere else. Now. She would gun the car and drive right out of here and never come back. No, she would swerve right into the building and drive right through it.

Instead, without realizing it, she had taken her foot off the gas. As the car slowed down, Kenneth looked up, and then she did speed up, pressing down the pedal until the sluggish little car shot forward. She kept going past the Inn, where she would never stop again, past Main Street and toward Frannie's. She drove angrily, jerking the car around the turns, her thoughts churning. That must have been Mae's doing, although her mom and Andy had to know about it.

And that was what Mae meant, last night, when she gave Amanda that last look, the one that so clearly said, *I'll get you for this.*

The sign had been there for so long. It was just the Mimi's sign now; no one ever even thought about who drew it. And it was one of her first best chickens, a chicken Amanda loved. She had been thinking of Mimi when she drew her, and it had come out in the bird, a certain spirit of determination. It was the first time she'd really been able to see the personality she was imagining come out in a drawing, and it had sent her in pursuit of more chickens to draw. And now the original, the matriarch, was gone.

That chicken was a piece of Amanda, and her sister just wiped it away, just like that.

Damn Mae, with her whole bossy *you're supposed to stay out of Mimi's* and her *Ooh, let's have kale and organic chicken like we're in Brooklyn* thing that Sabrina had described on the way home last night, trying to make Amanda laugh. And she *had* laughed, because Merinac wasn't a kale town, and Mae would never be able to get that much organic chicken around here even if she tried. Nobody could spend that kind of money on getting certified, with the ridiculous hoops you had to go through, all set up by the big companies so none of the little farms could manage it. Mae had better not even ask John Calvin Caswell about organic chicken. She'd just piss him off. He'd taken over for his dad almost fifteen years ago, when his parents left for Florida, but his family had been supplying chicken to both Frannie's and Mimi's for long before that. The chickens were happy, healthy, and fat right up until the day when they suddenly weren't. Any suggestion that organic was somehow better would just piss him off.

It would really piss him off.

And when John Calvin was pissed off—Amanda had a sudden memory of him in school, standing frozen and angry when Tom Parker, who had gone to school with them all since they were three but who turned into a real jerk once he made the football team, sniffed the air around John Calvin and declared that suddenly, everything smelled like chicken shit. John Calvin just stood there, staring at Tom while Tom and his friends laughed, making a big deal of holding their noses. And while nobody saw who'd keyed Tom's Trans Am on both sides in the school parking lot before the end of the day, everybody could guess.

Amanda pulled into the Frannie's lot without caffeine but with an idea. A brilliant idea. Sabrina, holding a coffee, damn her, was just getting out of her little convertible. Amanda didn't even bother to park, just pulled next to Sabrina and rolled down the passenger window.

"Hey," she said. "Want to see something funny?"

Sabrina cocked her head to one side, then slipped into the passenger seat. "Where are we going?"

"You'll see. Well, first to Starbucks. Then you'll see."

MAE

Mae swung Barbara's old truck onto the gravel of Mimi's parking lot and hit the brakes. She was out almost before she slammed it into park, running across the lot, calling frantically for Barbara.

"Mom! Mom!" Her mother appeared in the doorway of Mimi's, followed by Andy, Madison, and Ryder. Ryder ran to Mae, and she picked him up, but her attention was on her mother. "John Calvin won't sell me his chicken." Had refused to talk to her, actually. Had come to the door, shaken his head at her, closed it, and walked away. Mae was still shaking with fury. Who just locked the door in someone's face, especially someone they'd known since they were kids? And then let her stand out there banging and calling?

They had a deal, a long-standing deal, that on Fridays and Wednesdays Mimi's picked up fresh chicken if they needed it. Today's order was supposed to be bigger than usual, and Mae had gone to pick it up so she could see the Caswell place again. The chicken might not be organic, but it was fresh and free-range and local, raised by the same family in the same way for generations, and that was a great story to tell.

Her mother took off her cooking apron and handed it to Andy. "I knew I should have gone over there. What the hell did you say, Mae?"

Mae glanced at Madison, who was looking deeply interested, and Barbara gave her a look that said "hell" didn't count as swearing. Mae was too upset to argue. "Nothing! He wouldn't even let me in the door. I swear, Mom, I never got close enough to talk to anyone. I wasn't even taking pictures. I wasn't doing anything." She had thought about taking pictures, but it was dicey, live chickens in this context. People got upset.

"Come on." Her mother walked over to the driver's side of the truck, followed by Madison. "We're going back over there."

"He's not going to talk to me, Mom. I tried."

"He doesn't have to talk to you. He has to talk to me. How could you screw this up? What do you imagine we're going to do now, run over to Whole Foods?"

"I didn't screw it up!" Mae put her hand on the truck's hood, still hot, and watched Madison contemplate a vehicle with no back seat at all, let alone no car seats. Mae looked at Andy, feeling desperate.

"Can we leave them with you? Jessa should be here any minute."

"I want to go too!" Madison opened the driver's-side door. "Grandma, tell her I can go."

Barbara started to slide out, and Mae knew instantly that she was planning to put Madison in the middle of the truck's bench seat. Not happening. She swung Ryder down off her hip, getting some air to avoid his objections. Andy looked unsure, Madison rebellious. If there was going to be swearing, the kid wanted to be there.

Time for the big guns.

"The iPad's in my bag," she said to Madison. "If you'll sit at the picnic table and wait for Jessa, you can watch a show with Ryder." She lowered her voice. "You can pick," she whispered. Ryder wouldn't care, he'd be thrilled by the unexpected appearance of any show, but Madison would.

Madison crossed her arms and looked at the truck, then at her mother, considering. Mae applied the final bribe. "There's Goldfish."

"Real Goldfish? Not the healthy things?"

Madison had been on to her since forever. Mae nodded. "Real

Goldfish." Ryder reached up, pulling down at her neck as she bent over Madison and knocking her off-balance. Barbara honked, and Mae shot up into the air and glared at her mother.

"Mae! Now. Get them in the car or leave them, but do it fast."

Madison took pity on her mother. "Goldfish," she said to her brother. "In Mommy's bag."

Ryder took off toward Mimi's without a backward glance. "They better be cheddar," Madison said.

"Parmesan," Mae said. She always bought Parmesan unless Madison was with her. She didn't know why. They seemed less—orange.

"Bring cheddar next time," Madison said as she followed her brother, sounding exactly like Clemenza telling Rocco to leave the gun, take the cannoli.

Barbara was backing up, honking again, and Mae ran for the truck. When did she turn into the minion of a couple of godfathers? She grabbed the passenger door and climbed inside, feeling about ten years old. Her mother was never going to believe she hadn't made this happen somehow. And what *were* they going to do? She couldn't even imagine where they would get the chicken they needed besides Caswell's. They were fucked; they were totally fucked.

She stared out the window as the fields rolled by, some green with tiny soybeans, some the shade of new wheat, one with little rows of corn, just up above the dirt. She really hadn't had a chance to say anything to John Calvin, let alone offend him. She'd just been driving along the familiar roads, thinking that Jay would love this, seeing where the actual food came from. Caswell's chicken would fit right into his new one-holistic-life philosophy. No lines between work and life. She wondered how the kids would take the connection between the birds scratching around in the dirt and the ones on the plate. She herself had never known anything different. Grandma Mimi even had chickens, for a while, when she and Amanda were little, for eggs. Amanda still did.

Her mother pulled up into Caswell's driveway and got out of the truck without saying a word. Mae watched her walk around to the back door, just as Mae had done earlier, disappearing into the space between the house and the old barn, a couple of dogs sniffing around her feet. Past the barn, as far as Mae could see, were the corrugated steel buildings that housed the actual chickens, each with wide doors opened out into separate yards. It wasn't some sort of idyllic farm scene, with multicolored hens pecking through the grass, but the yards were big and clean and the place used practical, healthy methods to raise birds on this scale. More than once, growing up, there had been rumors that the Caswells would sell out to Tyson, but it had never happened. Surely now, with people more interested in where their food came from, things were easier. They probably did, Mae realized with shock, sell to Whole Foods.

Barbara, looking extremely angry, stalked back around the building, followed by John Calvin in his Carhartts. John Calvin walked toward the big freezer trailer that was parked farther back into the drive, and Barbara got back into the truck and slammed it into gear.

"What? What are we doing?" Mae asked.

Barbara swung the truck around and backed up to where John Calvin was lifting the big latch on the side door. "Come on," she said.

John Calvin handed Barbara a box. "Grab the next one," she said to Mae, who was processing. Frozen chicken. John Calvin was giving them frozen chicken.

He stepped down from the trailer, which was plugged into a generator behind the shed. "I got pretty mad," he said, over the noise. "Our chicken's good enough chicken for anybody, and your sister said you didn't think so anymore."

Mae took the box, putting her hands in the openings on the slightly waxy sides as John Calvin released it. Amanda said—

"But your mom says your sister had it wrong," he said. "If that's so, I'm sorry."

He turned and went back into the trailer, not waiting for a reply. Mae hurried after her mother, carrying the box, which was so cold against her stomach that it hurt.

"Amanda did this," she said angrily when she caught up.

Barbara shrugged. "Just put the box in the truck," she said.

"But—"

Barbara turned back and glared at Mae. "Amanda doesn't matter right now. Just put the box in the truck."

Mae slid the box onto the open back of the pickup and went for another. With effort, she stifled her urge to shake the placid man in front of her, who was calmly handing her boxes as though he hadn't just destroyed all of their plans.

Twelve more boxes, and Barbara slammed the gate up.

"Goddamn it, John Calvin, we're going to have a hell of a time defrosting these."

"I believe it." He stood looking after them as they got into the cab. "You take care, now," he called. "Good luck tonight."

The minute the doors slammed, Mae burst into speech. "What the hell happened? What are we going to do with frozen chicken?"

Her mother turned the key and backed out of the driveway. Mae could tell by the set of her face that she, too, was angry, but Barbara didn't answer her until they were down the drive and out on the road.

"Amanda went over there this morning and told him you were planning to switch over to organic chicken, and so he sold her our order."

"But that's crazy. I'm not—I didn't—"

"You must have said something to somebody. Stuff like that gets around, Mae. You can't just mouth off here."

"I didn't! I didn't say anything to anybody but you and Aida. And that's not even what I meant! I just wanted to know if it *was* organic! It doesn't even matter—this is better than organic."

Mae knew things got around here; her mother didn't have to

teach her that. She grew up here. And for John Calvin to believe she would mess with a deal between their families that was four generations old was absurd, no matter what Amanda had said. Amanda had gone too far. Way too far. She wasn't going after Mae anymore but Barbara, and a whole night's receipts, and she knew good and well that their mother couldn't afford that.

"I swear I didn't say anything to anyone, Mom. I didn't. This was all Amanda."

"I don't know what happened or who said what, but that's what he thinks, and this is what we've got, and we're going to have to deal with it."

Barbara sat rigidly behind the wheel, turning carefully at the four-way stop, and even as angry as she was, Mae couldn't avoid the fact that her wild-woman mother, known for flying down the back roads with a cigarette dangling out the window, had turned into a very cautious driver. She was getting older, and Mae didn't want to think about what that meant—except that it made what Amanda had done even worse. This was playing dirty. She and Nancy both. And Mae hadn't even done anything. Not anything that would really hurt Frannie's, anyway.

Not yet.

×

Safely defrosting whole frozen chicken meant a water bath, and not a warm-water bath, which might work faster, but an ice-water bath. The water and ice had to be changed at precise intervals and precise temperatures. They bought twenty-four white five-gallon buckets and bags upon bags of ice, filled the buckets at the hose, and began throwing the chickens in. The chickens had been prepared for sale, essentially shrink-wrapped, and for a while, they kept them in the plastic, moving them from bath to bath, and dumping the water baths out as the ice melted, but once they were able, they hacked the chicken into fryer pieces and then sealed the pieces into bags and kept going. You couldn't wear gloves for that work. Only hands could press the chicken breastbone in just the right spot to crack it for the scissors; only fingers could scoop the bloody ice out of the neck and the folds of the skin.

It was miserable, and it had to be done. If they couldn't defrost the chickens in time, they couldn't open tonight. The chefs would come and find—nothing. *Food Wars* was over.

Andy sulked at Mae for the first hour, sharing Barbara's conviction that she was to blame for this, then cracked a few dark jokes as the whole thing grew more and more ridiculous. Barbara worked in stoic silence, and Mae spent the entire time conducting an imaginary conversation with Amanda that started with *How could you?* and then listed all of her sister's sins against their mother and Mimi's. *You're here all the time. You can see her. She's obviously getting older. You may be pissed at me, but do you want to ruin her? This place raised you, and you want to burn it to the ground?*

She mentally reviewed everything she'd said since she showed up in Merinac. She'd done nothing to John Calvin, said nothing about the farm except to her mother, and that hadn't been bad, even. She'd been thinking of the farm as part of the Mimi's story, not something to be excised from it. Because the Mimi's story was killer. The longer she thought about it, the better it got. Mimi's was a piece of authentic American history, and the original Mimi a heroine, an early feminist. Frannie's was a copycat, run by men for most of its years and now so far from its origins that it was unrecognizable, with its long menus and the frozen foods truck parking out back once a week. Cheesecake, biscuits, French fries . . . who knew what else they just yanked out of a bag or box and threw into the oven or onto the plate? Would Nancy and Amanda bother to defrost all this chicken, or would they just say the hell with it and steer customers toward meatloaf and burgers?

You don't even get what Mimi's is all about, or what it means to carry on a tradition, she silently told her sister. Mae might have left, but she hadn't forgotten what was important.

Or how to get along in this town. Mae plunged her hands angrily into another chicken. Mae was doing just fine here, at least temporarily. John Calvin and Amanda aside, nobody around here seemed to resent her for leaving or for her sudden return.

In fact, nobody seemed to resent Mae for much of anything. Not for the kinds of things her fellow New Yorkers seemed to resent other humans for just as a matter of standard practice—being in line for coffee, for example, or having children who didn't walk in a straight line on the sidewalk. And not for other things, either. Living with Jay had felt like such a minefield lately. She had almost felt as though she needed to hide her work, to write her blog posts when he wasn't looking, remove the evidence of the little scenes she staged for Instagram and Facebook and smuggle herself off to record *Sparkling* behind his back. At *Sparkling,* things hadn't been much better. As much as she hadn't wanted to admit it, Lolly and the women around her hadn't been listening to Mae's ideas for weeks. Again and again, she had found herself organizing a room or a cabinet that didn't end up in the final shoot.

The result, she was realizing, had been that she had gone home angry or frustrated. Maybe she hadn't been a whole lot of fun for Jay, either. Or the kids, who seemed to be loving Merinac. She'd sent them with Jessa down to a shallow wading spot on the river today. That would have been a much more pleasant way to get her hands wet. But no. She was here with the chicken baths, and they weren't even close to done.

Her mother leaned on the counter beside the sink, where they were soaking some of the bags that were closest to defrosted, and closed her eyes. It was physical work, the moving of the chickens and the dumping of the water, and Barbara had not spared herself any of it. And even though she couldn't figure out how, Mae knew that on some level, her mother and Andy were right: this was some-how her fault.

"You need a break, Mom." She put a hand on her mother's broad back. "Why don't you go back to the house for a while?"

"I didn't sleep well," Barbara said. "It's nothing."

"I didn't say there was anything wrong. Just that you could probably use a break. Go check on Aunt Aida. Make sure she's getting glamorous for tonight."

Andy, carrying a bucket of chicken pieces, came into the kitchen. "You guys are slowing down," he said, and Mae glared at him. To her surprise, he seemed to catch on immediately. "Which is fine," he said, looking at Barbara. "We're closer to done than it looks, and I just called Zeus to come a little early. We'll be on to normal prep in about an hour. If Mae helps, we'll catch up long before the cameras arrive."

Barbara untied her apron and hung it on its hook. "If we're that close, I will take a break," she said. "Mae, don't forget to leave yourself a little time to clean up. You're a mess."

Without looking back, she left the kitchen, and Andy laughed. "She won't thank us for telling her she looks tired," he said.

"No," agreed Mae. "She hates to be told what to do, too."

"Runs in the family, I'm guessing," he said. "Sometimes I feel like your Mimi doesn't even want me looking at her recipe. I swear the frame falls off the wall whenever I come near it. I had to hang it back up this morning."

"I wouldn't think you needed a recipe by now."

"I just like to check my proportions every now and then, imbibe a little of the spirit of the original cook. Even if she might not have liked me much."

"I don't think she was big on men."

"We're really not all alike." He finished shifting the chicken from the bucket to the sink and paused, a serious look on his face. "Hey, have you noticed anything odd about your mother?"

Mae froze, then quickly turned so Andy couldn't see her expression. She had, and she didn't want to talk about it. Barbara seemed flatter, somehow, and when she wasn't flat, she was obsessing about this win, and about money, in a way Mae had never seen. Yesterday, with the exception of her willingness to clean up Mimi's, she had been even more Barbara-like than usual, and Mae had felt reassured, only to watch her mother fade away as the day wore on. Today she'd disappeared even more quickly. This chicken job had not been fun, but it seemed to have taken a lot out of Barbara. And yesterday, after work, Barbara had been much quieter than usual, even with Ryder and Madison. But Andy didn't need to know any of that.

"She seems great," Mae said. "Glad to see us, working as hard as ever."

Andy shrugged. "She gets tired earlier than she did when I first got here. She leaves more things to me—of course, that was the idea, but I get the sense she's not what you'd call a delegator." He gave Mae a hard look and lowered his voice. "And the mess. I keep having to take bags out, stuff she's left here that we can't work around. It's not just the house anymore."

Oh no, Mae thought. He knew. He had to know—of course he would. How could he not? She looked down at the ground, then spoke before she could catch her words and hold them back—because the Moores never, ever talked about this with outsiders.

"We can't let anyone see the house," she said. "Or know that's an issue. It's just—it would mess things up, right?"

Andy looked at her thoughtfully. "Most people around here know," he said. "But, yeah, I can see why you wouldn't want it on TV." He laughed, and Mae glared at him again, then relaxed. He was right, after all. No harm in that.

"I don't," she said.

"She won't let you..." Andy made some vague gestures with his hands that Mae took to mean cleaning up, and she laughed.

"Not hardly," she said. "It's like you said. She's not much of a delegator." It was a relief to trust him, even this much. "I think she needs to take it easier. You're right. And maybe—there's you, and if we win *Food Wars,* you could do so much, right? Like, this could be a real cult destination." Andy nodded, and Mae was relieved to move the conversation on.

"You're thinking we could win now? Really?"

"I am. Look, Mimi's is special. You know it is. And you're special." Butter him up a little—plus, he really did have a feel for the simplicity of the kitchen. "You could really impress those chefs tonight with the way you want to get just these few things perfectly right. And then people would come. They'd take road trips for your chicken. Nobody's going to take a road trip for a frozen mozzarella stick."

Andy gazed at her thoughtfully, and Mae had a feeling her compliments hadn't moved him much. She wondered if he saw this as his opportunity to move on to bigger and better things. Maybe not. Merinac, she was starting to see, wasn't actually a bad place for someone with some history to start over.

"Maybe if you wanted to, Mom would let you play with some lunch service, or adding something special to the doughnuts Saturday morning." There had to be some room in this for him. "And I was even thinking she could give pie-making classes. Or, well, Patrick would. And people would come. Especially with the Inn here, and the lakes—this kind of thing can really work now, you know?"

Andy seemed to be catching a little of her fire. "Like that pie place in Iowa," he said. "Or the one the woman from that home makeover show started down south."

He did get it. Mae nodded. "Exactly."

Andy looked around, then sighed. "We just have to win first," he said. "And I gotta tell you, I don't know if we can do it. And this chicken's not going to be as good—"

"The chicken will be fine," said Mae. Oh God, he was just a temperamental chef at heart. "Seriously. Anybody can have to start with frozen chicken once in a while. Probably most places do. It's not like we're plating a bunch of fried chicken tenders we just warmed up, or defrosting stuff and calling it ours." She grinned. "Not like some restaurants I know."

Which was really the point. She'd felt it, a minute ago, when she said the words "frozen mozzarella stick." A little shift in her mind, almost a click, and then Mae knew exactly what she could do to derail Amanda and set Mimi's up to be America's sweetheart chicken shack. And it probably wouldn't take more than two words in Sabrina's ear. After she cleaned herself up, of course. And after they finally finished all this chicken.

AMANDA

Frannie's was packed. Utterly, totally packed. Word that tonight was the night the celebrity chefs would come had spread. Every seat was taken, the bar was full to standing, and in the little entry and waiting area people were packed in on the benches. There was even a couple standing squashed in behind the Lions Club candy machines. Outside, they'd set up more benches—Amanda and Gus had even loaded a wagon wheel and a wooden wheelbarrow planted with annuals into Mary Laura's old truck and brought them over for atmosphere—and a big orange cooler of water with paper-cone cups for people waiting in the hot sun. Amanda fielded a few takeout orders, but most people wanted to come in, enjoy the air conditioning, and have their delicious meal served with a flourish on a classic divided-oval off-white diner plate.

They wanted to be a part of it.

Between the crowd and the cameras, the waitstaff should have been in a panic, but Amanda had to give full credit to Nancy. She never let them break a sweat. She was everywhere, telling them they were doing great, that a little spill or slosh wouldn't matter, that everyone was having a fantastic time and to just keep it up. Except Amanda. Amanda she was ignoring.

The first chef to arrive at Frannie's was Simon Rideaux, famed as much for his hard-drinking, straight-talking approach to food as for his series of bestselling cookbooks. He came in without Sabrina, who had said she would return later with the other chefs, and striding ahead of his *Food Wars* handlers. The crowd parted for him as best they could, and Amanda, who had been prepared and essentially pushed into place by one of Sabrina's minions, showed him to his table.

"I never eat alone," he declared. "You will sit down with me, then. Take a load off. Someone else can seat people for a while. You'll be forgiven, I guarantee it."

Amanda cast a frantic look around, but there was no one to rescue her. The producer behind the camera gestured for her to sit. Oh, this was not going to help with Nancy. She had not found the discovery of a dozen boxes of chicken originally meant for Mimi's in her walk-in funny, and she had made it clear to Amanda through whispers and glares that she was disappointed in her. She didn't know yet that Sabrina had filmed Amanda doing it, but she would soon enough. The wave of self-righteous glee that had led Amanda to invite Sabrina along to help rub Mae's face in her failures had vanished, replaced by a miserable cocktail of regret, guilt, and remorse.

Rideaux refused the menu a nervous Gwennie was extending to him. "Bring me the specialty of the house, of course. Fried chicken and whatever you serve with it, however it's most popular. And this lady will have the same."

Amanda looked at him in horror. "No, no. I can't do that. I already ate, anyway. Really." The only thing worse than sitting while everyone else worked would be to have the cooks plate food for her—food they knew she wouldn't eat. At the rate things were going, Nancy would probably spit in it. *You're letting down Frannie's, playing like that. Letting down the whole town.*

Rideaux seemed to take pity on his victim. "Fine, fine, bring her a drink, then. You surely know what she likes. And bring me a bourbon and be ready with another. Now." He settled back into his chair and looked around, taking in everything from the glimpse of the pool table that was visible through the door into the bar to the Tiffany-style lamps that hung above every table. "I grew up in a town like this one. In Indiana. Never wanted anything as much as I wanted out of that place. But you. You're still here. Do you love it? Are you happy? Satisfied?"

There were two cameras around the table, one stationary, the other with an operator who pointed it at her face as he asked the question. Amanda didn't love anything at this moment, and she felt stripped bare by the question. *Turn it back on him,* said a small, helpful voice in her head that sounded suspiciously like her sister. *You don't owe everybody a little piece of yourself.*

"Why is that everyone's first question?" she asked. "This is where I live. Why wouldn't I be happy? Why would I want to leave?"

"Because it's very small. Because there are two restaurants and they both serve fried chicken. Because you must know everyone and have solved every mystery about their sad little Hobby Lobby lives a long time ago."

"I love Merinac," said Amanda, stung. No wonder he made her think of Mae. When it came to their hometown, he sounded just like her.

"Perhaps. But what do you do, when you have eaten all the chicken you can eat, and slept with all the men?"

You kick asshole outsiders in the balls, Amanda thought, unable to hide her surprise at the bald question. She would have loved to maintain a cool exterior, as Mae surely would have, but she knew she had turned beet red. Rideaux beamed. Was he expecting an answer? Flirting in some weird way? He stretched his arms wide and leaned back in his chair, smiling directly into the camera.

"I think it's a question worth considering for anyone who considers at all," Rideaux opined grandly. "Did I choose to stay, or did I just stay? Some people, they wake up, they're sixty, they're still here, and it's either all they ever wanted, or they kill themselves. Or maybe fried chicken is your life. Is fried chicken your life, Miss Amanda Frannie's?"

He was drunk, she realized. Drunk, and quite possibly pretty much always that way, so she could stop worrying that he was some sort of soothsayer.

"Of course," she said agreeably. "And look, your fried chicken is right here." Mercifully, Gwennie was here with the food, and Amanda didn't give a damn what was polite or what *Food Wars* wanted; she wasn't sitting here any longer. She stood. "I'm afraid I have to be getting back to work now."

He surveyed the plate in front of him with interest, but as Amanda started to walk away he reached up and touched her arm, then beckoned her down. Reluctantly, an eye on the camera, she bent slightly, letting him whisper his alcohol-scented advice in her ear. "You can love a town and still leave it, you know," he said. "You think you have all the time in the world. But you don't."

How good were those microphones? She gritted her teeth. "I hope you enjoy your chicken." *Asshole, asshole, asshole.* He didn't know anything. Just enough to tar everyone with his own brush and try to make trouble.

What Amanda needed was a few minutes to catch her breath, and to pour Rideaux's words back into whatever bottle he'd magicked them out of. Instead, everywhere Amanda went, someone was on her with a camera. Check on Gus at the dishwasher? Camera. Give Frankie a hand with a tray, just to be with her for a minute? Camera. Slip into the office for a quick break? There was Gordo with his bright lights and that damn chair she hadn't meant to sit in again. "Is it always this busy on the weekend?"

How did she want to answer that? "Friday is pretty much always our busiest night," she said. Not like this, true, but wouldn't it be better if they looked as if they were used to these crowds? "I think everyone's having a great time. And the kitchen is killing it." Truly, they were, and the diners were eating the evidence of her morning. It was probably a good thing they had so much chicken.

Which made her think of her mom and Andy. It couldn't be this busy over there. They did have chicken; that she knew. Unable to stand the fear that she might have genuinely ruined her mother's ability to open tonight, Amanda had asked Mary Laura to text Angelique. Everything was fine, apparently; by the time Angelique got to work everything was basically normal, except for Patrick frantically bringing down all his pies.

"Something about your mom not having time to bake," Mary Laura said with a wink, and Nancy, walking past them, stopped.

"It's not funny," she said. "You think about your mother, Amanda. You know what coping with all that frozen chicken must have been like. And to know you would do that to her—to think *we* would do that to her—is that what you want? We can win without—without that kind of"—she stopped, then spat out the word as though it cost her something—"crap, Amanda. That kind of *crap.*"

Without giving Amanda a chance to defend herself, Nancy stalked off in the direction of the kitchen. Mary Laura had turned to a customer, and Amanda leaned on the bar for a minute, the crowd pressing behind her. Mae deserved it. Painting over Amanda's sign wasn't even about *Food Wars;* it was just plain mean. And Barbara—the image of her mother and Andy cheering Mae on while she erased Amanda's favorite chicken was a humiliating scene playing on constant repeat in her brain. Maybe it had never been a good sign in the first place. Maybe Sabrina, who didn't know it was her sign, had suggested that it go. Barbara was always telling her drawing was a waste of time, that she should do something more productive with herself. She had probably been wanting to cover it up for a long time. Probably meant to do it sooner.

The last thing Amanda wanted was to be roped into the arrival of the next two chefs, a husband-and-wife team who almost never seemed to agree on anything, but it was obvious from the moment Sabrina arrived with them that she wanted their visit to mirror Rideaux's in every respect. Amanda would greet them, Amanda would seat them, Amanda would, damn it, sit right down and chat, but she had had it with chatting. "Would you like to see a menu, or should we just bring the chicken?"

"Bring the chicken, please," said James Melville without looking at her. He was turning to take in the entire restaurant, even rising from his chair to look toward the kitchen.

"And also the menu," said his wife and partner, Cary Catlin. Gwennie brought a menu, and Cary Catlin took a pair of glasses from where they were nested in her abundant brown hair and opened the folder, running a finger down each column. At the bottom of the first page she looked up at Gwennie. "I just wanted to see the menu, not order from it," she said, gesturing her away. "Bring the chicken, of course."

"The meatloaf is also very good," offered Amanda.

"If I ate anything but what we're supposed to eat at these stops I'd be as big as a house. Just the chicken is fine."

Gwennie rushed off, and Cary Catlin leaned over and snapped her fingers at her husband. "Pay attention." She turned to Amanda. "Okay, let's have a look at this menu. Mozzarella sticks. Frozen?"

Amanda was taken aback. Of course the mozz was frozen; people expected it to look like the little sticks you get everywhere. But why were they asking? "Yes," she said cautiously.

"Stuffed mushrooms? Crab cakes? Frozen?"

Amanda nodded. The chef was running a finger down the other side of the menu, possibly preparing more questions. *Jeez, could she get some help here?* Amanda looked around and saw Nancy heading their way, but bearing menus, and with two regular customers following her. Maybe Nancy would stop. The Russells knew where they were going. She tried to give her mother-in-law a desperate look.

"Amanda," Cary Catlin said, "I understand the famous Frannie's biscuits are frozen?"

No. They were on shaky ground with this one, and she knew

from the smug look on her inquisitor's face that Catlin knew it. Making the biscuits by hand required three additional cook shifts weekly, and the switch to frozen biscuits meant a substantial savings, but they'd been quiet about it, because the biscuits were, like the chicken, at the heart of Frannie's. They were practically house made—the company they ordered from used nothing artificial, and even when they had made their own at Frannie's, they'd frozen them before baking, everyone did, even Mimi's, probably—but there was no getting around it; the biscuits did come frozen. Could she say anything other than yes?

"Yes, but—" She tilted her chin up and tried to sound very matter-of-fact. "Yes. Fried chicken is our absolute specialty, so it's made fresh here, from locally sourced chicken." Just don't mention the biscuits again. *Chicken.* "We bone it ourselves for the tenders. And we use Frannie's original recipe for the seasoning—it's over a hundred years old, her recipe. We've never changed it. It's always exactly the way she made it, and then her son, and then his son."

She could feel her voice rising as she went on about the chicken, and she smiled at Nancy, who had paused in answer to her look, and the chefs'. That was a good answer.

Nancy didn't look happy; in fact, she looked horrified, but what else could Amanda have said? "We just keep frying up the same perfect chicken."

Nancy turned away, probably not wanting to risk anyone bringing the conversation back around to the biscuits, but Tony Russell, following Nancy as she led the way to his usual table, stopped, leaning on his cane, and listened to Amanda.

"Never changed it? I'd have sworn you switched the chicken up some, few years back. It hasn't tasted the same for a while now, to me."

Gus was still giving the Russells' table a last wipe, and they were all caught there, trapped in a conversation most of them didn't want to be having, cameras on. Tony's wife, behind him, rolled her eyes. "You let Amanda be, Tony. You've been saying that about everything for years. Nothing ever tastes the same to you."

"No, this is different. I've been eating here since I was a kid, and it's just never been the same. Not since Frank went. Must have changed the recipe."

Nancy, in front of them both, didn't turn around, but spoke over her shoulder. "There is no recipe, Tony. But it's the same old chicken. There was even a jar of seasoning Frank mixed himself, for a while."

Gus looked up, his sudden movement catching Amanda's eye. "But—" He started to speak, then went back to wiping the table with a glance at the camera. "Never mind," he said softly. She hadn't realized he was so nervous.

No one else seemed to have noticed Gus's interruption. "We just all miss them," said Tony's wife, giving him a gentle push. "Nothing's the same."

"I still say it's different," said Tony, although he walked on. "Never used to have all these cameras here, either."

This time, his wife laughed outright. "I'd have kept him home if I could, Nancy."

Nancy, now at their table and holding out a chair, did smile at that. "Not on a Friday night. Never. We'd have had to come see where you two were."

Amanda suddenly realized this was her chance. "Let me get your drinks, Tony," she said, and jumped out of her seat, nodding to James and Cary. "Gotta take good care of our regulars." She rushed off, avoiding any further questions about what was and wasn't frozen, although they'd pretty much covered it except for the desserts. It was hard for a small place to have a big menu without some help, and people expected at least a little variety. Buying the biscuits also meant they could serve them generously, in a basket on the table, instead of parceling them out with the chicken. It had been a good business decision, but maybe it made bad television.

Why did they even care? She'd watched three full seasons of

Food Wars and never seen them ask this, and of course some of the restaurants were putting frozen stuff on the plate. Handling all your own vegetables just didn't make economic sense, and no one more than a few miles from the ocean was serving up fresh shrimp and seafood. So why suddenly give Frannie's, and her, a hard time about it? It wasn't like they were serving frozen fried chicken.

Now Amanda was determined to evade the cameras, or at least offer them little of interest. She started moving fast and constantly. If she wasn't seating people, she was carrying bar orders or busing tables. It helped that Frannie's was so busy. Everyone needed an extra hand. Maybe she should have talked up the biscuit bakery, played up how they were helping another small business. But the desserts and the other stuff didn't do that. Damn it, did they have to get absolutely everything right?

Or she could have lied. They used to make the biscuits, and they could again. She could have talked about how all restaurants needed the support of their suppliers. Or avoided the first question. Or insisted they talk to Nancy. Or faked her own sudden death from choking on an ice cube.

By the time the place finally cleared out, she was exhausted. Everyone around her was limp, quiet, the celebratory mood of the night before replaced by a sort of anticlimactic silence. All that was left, filming-wise, was the chicken tasting tomorrow and then the big announcement.

Amanda wanted to talk to Nancy, to make things right, to apologize for the biscuits and maybe the chicken and anything she could think of to get Nancy on her side again, but Nancy was avoiding her, and with Sabrina and her team still in the restaurant, it felt impossible to just grab her and insist that they talk. Instead, Amanda, running her sweeper furiously over the patterned carpet, was caught by Sabrina, sitting on a table, somehow managing to arrange her short dress to perfectly show enough leg to be sexy but not sleazy, high heels dangling from her fingers.

"Frozen biscuits, huh?" she said with a frown. "They kinda nailed you with that one."

Irritated, Amanda pushed the sweeper toward the host, who laughed and lifted her feet higher so that Amanda could get under the table. "Everybody uses frozen stuff," she said. "Why were they making such a big deal out of it?"

"Because Mae did. She made sure they tasted Mimi's biscuits, with the fresh local honey. Said they were just as much part of the tradition as the chicken."

Amanda could not remember Mae ever saying one single thing about Mimi's biscuits, which were just the same as anybody made. And she didn't remember any special honey, either. "There's no such thing as a special biscuit recipe. I mean, some people make them better than others, but basically there's only a couple of ways to do it."

"That's not what Mae said. And she made sure Cary and James knew yours were frozen, too."

"They freeze theirs! They make them once a week and freeze them. That's what we used to do, too. They actually bake better that way. This is ridiculous."

"Well, Cary Catlin loved that every one of the three things Mimi's serves besides chicken was totally homemade, and then that the pies were, too. She kept saying how brilliant it was to specialize. She asked your mother what happened when they ran out, and your mom said, 'We close,' and Cary laughed like crazy. Called it brilliant."

Frankie, who was wielding the second sweeper while Gus lifted chairs up onto tables, stopped, with a worried look on her face. "Does that mean we're going to lose, Mom?"

"But Frannie's makes a whole lot more than four or five things," Gus said angrily. "We might not make everything from scratch, but we actually make way more than Mimi's does—the meatloaf, the mashed potatoes, the gravy, the coleslaw, all the chicken, the wings, the steak with mushrooms, soup when we have it—it takes three cooks. That's not fair."

Sabrina shrugged, her perfect slim shoulders in their perfectly styled wrap dress irritating Amanda as much as her words. "Not everybody plays *Food Wars* fair. A hundred thousand dollars is a lot of money. Your aunt wants to win; that's all."

"Well, we want to win, too," Frankie said.

Sabrina chuckled. "She told them to be sure to ask you, too, Amanda. Said you couldn't tell a lie to save your life."

"I don't need to lie about that," Amanda said hotly, even though she'd been partially wishing she had all night. "Making biscuits the way we do is absolutely the right call for us right now. Mae's just being a—a jerk." She could have lied if she had wanted to. Or thought of it fast enough. She listened as Gus went on and on to Sabrina about the costs that went into the kitchen, and why frozen food made good sense. He knew more about it than Amanda did, surprisingly, and Frankie, too, was passionate in her defense of everything Frannie's did. Was this how Amanda was supposed to feel? Because what she felt, mostly, was exhausted beyond caring, and like maybe Frannie's was better off without her.

"I get it, Gus, but what can I do? The chefs are the judges," Sabrina said. "Right now, Mae's looking good to them. She's the queen of all things honest and homemade, even if it's not really any better. And you should have seen her kids. It was like they were made for the camera. She set herself up really well for tomorrow. She's the golden girl."

In her mind, Amanda snarled.

"Well, that will change when they compare our chicken," said Gus, as Nancy appeared in the doorway of the kitchen, looked out at them, then shut the door again, probably at the sight of Sabrina. They were on the same page there at least. Amanda was sick of the host at this point too. "I'm going to see if Grandma needs a hand getting ready tomorrow. Even if I can't come in to the taping." He paused and looked questioningly at Sabrina, who shook her head.

"Just your mom and Nancy for this one. You can be in on the win reveal."

"Okay." He lifted up a last chair and nodded to himself. "It's going to be great."

Sabrina slid off the table and picked up Amanda's phone from where it sat up on the frame between the booths. "Don't forget this," she called to Gus, as she flipped it over, screen up. "Oops—not yours. Your mom's. And you have a message." She raised her eyebrows suggestively and tossed the phone to Amanda, but Gus shot his arm in. "Pogociello for the interception," he said, and glanced down at the screen before quickly looking up and extending it to Amanda. "Oh—sorry," he muttered.

Amanda barely stopped herself from snatching the phone away. Nancy, still scolding her, or ready to make up? No—Andy.

Sorry about last night. Hope things went ok tonight. We were busy. Maybe I can buy you a drink?

Amanda looked at her son, walking toward the kitchen. Had he read the message? He had to have seen it was there, probably whom it was from, but if he hadn't really read it, just glanced at it—from the shape of his shoulders and the speed of his walk, she had a bad feeling. There had been no one after Frank—could be no one, really. She and Frank—that was her love story, and if things had been a little rough at what had turned out to be the end, Gus never needed to know it. Where would they be, if Frank hadn't died? She wanted to think she would have come to her senses, realized what she had the way she did now, but she had been so frustrated, felt so trapped.

A little like she felt now, but she wasn't screwing this up again.

Food Wars was her shot, and nothing—certainly not some guy who thought he could help destroy a part of her history and still have her jump when he called—was going to get in her way. She wanted to run after Gus, grab him, promise that she never had loved anyone but his dad and never would. But if he hadn't read the text after all, she'd just be making things worse.

She looked down at her phone and imagined typing *No, you can't buy me a DRINK. Not now, not ever, not for a whole lot of reasons.*

"Yeah, I don't need to answer that," she said loudly, making sure Gus could hear, just in case. Suddenly she was intensely aware of Sabrina's and Frankie's interested faces. The *Food Wars* host wasn't just a friendly girlfriend, and she didn't care about kids. She might prefer that Amanda do or say something just because it would make better TV, but nothing kept Amanda more sober, in every sense of the word, than Gus and Frankie. She might have slipped a little last night, but not again—and especially not with somebody who thought she was desperate enough not to care that he was helping Mae ruin her work with one hand and texting her with the other. "I'll deal with it later," she said, and shoved the phone into her pocket untouched. Or never. Never sounded good.

Gus walked into the kitchen, and Amanda wanted to follow him, but she couldn't leave Frankie with Sabrina and didn't want Sabrina in there, anyway. Silently, she finished the floor, then redid the parts Frankie had missed when her daughter went to put their things in the car.

Followed by Sabrina, she stuck her head into the kitchen, holding the swinging door with one hand. Gus and Nancy were huddled over something on the counter, Nancy's arm around Gus's shoulders, and they turned quickly as the door opened.

"You ready, Gus?"

Gus looked at his grandmother, who nodded. She was smiling and looking lighter than Amanda would have imagined possible after the night they had had, and Amanda, conscious of Sabrina, who was looking in over her shoulder, ventured the fewest words she thought might cover it. "I'm sorry," she said. "About tonight."

"That's okay," said Nancy briskly, pushing Gus gently toward them but not leaving the counter herself. "You go with your mom, Gus. I'll take it from here. See you in the morning."

Gus turned, and he and Nancy exchanged a huge smile that Amanda would have given a lot to be part of. *That's okay* didn't go nearly far enough, but as Amanda stood there and Gus slipped past, Nancy turned away, cutting off further conversation. After lingering for a minute in case she changed her mind, Amanda followed Gus out.

At home, Gus and Frankie quickly slid off in the direction of their rooms. Although Amanda could still hear them through the thin walls, particularly Gus, who was playing music, she was alone, which was exactly what she wanted, though she felt terrible once she got it.

Food Wars should have been a slam dunk for Frannie's, a win to pay off bills and steady the ship and be able to go on exactly as they always had. Instead—

She tossed her tote bag onto the table and missed, so that the bag slid to the floor, contents spilling everywhere, sketchbook open, pages bent. Amanda picked it up and began to smooth out her drawings. She could sit down, it wasn't that late, but as she looked down at the chickens, the young hens who were mocking Carleen seemed to be mocking Amanda, too. What the hell was she doing wasting her time on this? This would never amount to anything, and neither would Amanda, or Frannie's, apparently.

She tossed the book across the kitchen onto the counter, then shook the pencils and erasers out of the bottom of the bag, which they perpetually turned gray, and shoved the lot into the back of the junk drawer. It was all just junk, anyway. That was exactly where it belonged.

MAE

This was like waiting for exam results. Or worse, auditioning to be host of a show like, say, *Sparkling*.

Mae stood in between Andy and Barbara in front of the longest table the largely unused dining room at the Inn had to offer, with Andy carefully holding an enormous platter of Mimi's chicken. Next to them, in another clump, were Amanda and Nancy with an equally ridiculous serving for the three people in front of them. Amanda's son, Gus, was slipping out after a high five with Nancy, which gave Mae a small pang—would her kids ever feel that close to any of their grandparents?

No use worrying about that now. Cameras were set up at every angle around the room. Up until that moment, Sabrina had pulled off the illusion that *Food Wars* was something of a shoestring production, just her and her team, but with them all gathered in one place and accompanied by their trucks and tables and assistants, it was suddenly clear that this was truly a massive endeavor, and that every moment that had led them to these final scenes wouldn't just be tossed out into the world as a quick Instagram story, but produced and shaped into fast-paced entertainment for the waiting masses.

Sparkling was amateur hour compared to this, and as a makeup artist stepped away from Cary Catlin and rushed over to adjust Sabrina's hair, Mae was conscious that she'd done her own makeup with Madison and Ryder watching curiously, demanding to know why she was coloring on her face, and Jay talking to them all through FaceTime, trying to distract the kids while Jessa got a solo break at breakfast and politely wishing Mae luck, although she doubted his heart was in that one. Not that he would want her to screw up on TV, necessarily— Oh hell, she'd given up on figuring out what Jay wanted. He was all over the place at this point. He missed her, sure, or he said he did, but did he really miss *her*? Nobody ever seemed normal over FaceTime, but Jay seemed especially antsy. When Mae took the little screen back as the kids drifted away, he looked her in the eyes, and then oh so quickly looked away. "I'll talk to you later, okay?" he said, and as badly timed as it was, she couldn't help herself.

"Why? Is something wrong?"

"No, just, I'll talk to you later. Why wouldn't I talk to you later?"

"I don't know," Mae said, wishing she could reach through the screen. "You just seem weird." And had, the whole time she was gone. Of course they had fought. And of course he didn't like *Food Wars*. But none of that was new. This sense of distance was.

And he hadn't argued; that was the thing. "Just go do the show, Mae. And I'll see you—I mean, I'll talk to you later. Everything's fine."

He hung up then, and if he'd planned to throw her off-balance, he'd succeeded. But she couldn't think about Jay right now. She tugged at her shirt, making sure it wasn't blousing too much over her skirt, and fished in her pocket for more lipstick. She looked like a rube; she just knew it.

She glanced over at Amanda, expecting to see the same doubts running across her face, but the sister who never wore makeup looked almost as good as the professionals.

Mae had expected to feel at ease—after all, she had done this before, and she'd certainly faced less appealing audiences under different circumstances—but instead, she felt as if she were shrinking. She felt fine in Mimi's—she was killing it in Mimi's. Planning with Andy, seamlessly trading shifts at the fryer, stepping out to greet everyone from her old chorus teacher to the guy who'd pumped gas at the Texaco throughout her whole childhood, she'd felt dropped right back into place but even more so, combining what she had learned about business and showmanship with what she had always known about running Mimi's. But that confidence seemed to have come with a trade-off—here, she had become a supplicant.

The surroundings were right, but she was in the wrong place, in between a visibly nervous Andy and her mother, who had dressed for the occasion in her usual slacks and blouse covered with her usual smock. Mae, with an increasingly forced smile on her face, felt her inner churning speed up. What was she doing behind a platter of fried chicken on national television? This had been a terrible, stupid idea, one that would mark her as "not one of us" forevermore in the eyes of everyone who mattered—to her career, to her whole life.

How had she forgotten the cardinal rule of the makeover/ remodel reality television genre—that you never want to be the one who needs help? She'd been fooled by the different format, but now here she was, the yokel in a roomful of pros. Jay had been right. This wasn't going to help her career; it was going to destroy it.

At this auspicious moment in her thought process, the lights came on and Simon Rideaux addressed her.

"So, Mae, tell us what you have for us today."

Mae stepped forward, feeling as if she ought to curtsy, and gave Andy what she hoped was an imperceptible tug; he set the platter in front of the three chefs.

"This is Mimi's fried chicken, Chef. We use the same seasoning recipe Mimi used when she started Mimi's in 1886 as a whistlestop. Passengers on the train used to get off and buy her chicken and biscuits in a box lunch. Hers was so good that conductors would tell the passengers they liked best to skip the earlier stops and wait for Mimi's."

Now it was Andy's turn. "We cook the chicken pretty much

exactly like Mimi would have, in big cast-iron skillets, with a few concessions to modern taste."

As expected, that caught the chefs' attention. "What have you changed, then?" James Melville asked, his expression suggesting that truly authentic cooks at a truly authentic legacy restaurant would have altered nothing.

"Well, Mimi probably would have used pure lard, which is impractical today, although we do use a blend. And it's likely she would never have changed the oil at all, just replenished it."

Argue with that, James Melville, Mae thought. She'd watched hours of this guy to figure out what they could say that wouldn't set him off on a "but real chefs do it this way" tirade, and what had felt like even more hours convincing Andy that he couldn't just wing it.

Andy went on. "We start our oil up fresh every Saturday, and we do keep up one tradition we think sets the oil up right—we do a batch of doughnuts in it first thing Saturday morning."

"That sounds delicious," said Cary Catlin. "Are those on the menu?"

"Nope," said Andy, sounding, just as they'd planned, very casual. "We just sell them to whoever stops by until we run out."

Mae would bet Cary Catlin hadn't eaten a doughnut in years, but she could see the plan working: Cary was trying to figure out how she could get a doughnut. And she couldn't. *No doughnuts for you,* Mae chanted in her head.

"Today's went fast," Mae said, feeling more confident now. In fact, they'd eaten most of the doughnuts themselves. "It's pretty much the same with the chicken, and definitely with the pies, although of course those are on the menu," she added. "We just serve what we serve, until we run out, just like Mimi used to. Legend has it that once, a customer who didn't get any pulled out a six-shooter and offered to duel somebody for his box. And that means you ought to get here early, people."

In New York, people clamored for anything that was limited.

Mae was betting it would work here, too. Win or lose, she thought anyone close enough who saw this episode would want to come try the chicken worth dueling for.

Rideaux turned to Amanda next. "And what do you have for us?"

Mae listened to her sister go on. *Frannie's fried chicken, original recipe, coal miners, blah blah.* But mostly she focused on Amanda's haircut. It looked good. Mae's hair would not look good like that: she was too short, her neck not long and elegant. But the short cut made Amanda's blue eyes look huge and her cheekbones sharp. Mae noticed that Andy was staring at her sister too, the dope. Amanda, at least, hadn't so much as looked his way.

Now they were tasting the chicken. Traditionally, the chef-judges refrained from commenting on the food in front of the contestants, and they didn't today, either, although they did taste it—and looked at it, and compared it, nudging one another and murmuring among themselves as one held a piece of Mimi's chicken up and broke off a crispy golden piece of skin and another bit loudly into a Frannie's drumstick. It was hard to see whose chicken they were eating more of, though Mae subtly craned her neck to try.

Although they'd been told to remain at their posts, Barbara went and sat at a table off in the corner; when Mae looked again, her mother was gone, presumably back home to Patches, who was apparently "a little under the weather." Mae and Andy stood awkwardly by, as did Nancy and Amanda. Sabrina, noticing, beckoned. "There's a lot of chicken," she said. "Try some. You probably never eat each other's chicken."

Amanda, of course, hung back—had she really managed to hide the fact that she didn't eat chicken? Nancy took a leg from the Mimi's plate and then stood, holding it and not eating, looking like someone who hates cake trying to be a good sport at a children's birthday party.

Mae stepped toward the platter. Frannie's chicken had long

been forbidden fruit. She'd always wanted to try it. She nodded to Andy, and they both took a piece. She held hers over a napkin and took a bite.

It was pretty good, really. Maybe less crispy than Mimi's. Not as flavorful, of course; this was chicken that came with a frozen biscuit and a side of "just slap it on the plate and get on with it," but it was okay. She'd eat it. She watched as the judges huddled over the chicken, an assistant offering them paper and pencils. Sabrina gestured to a cameraperson to come in close over that scene, then stopped to confer with Rideaux and the assistant as the chefs waited, Cary Catlin turning over the chicken on the Mimi's platter while her husband gazed, apparently bored, into the distance.

Andy took one bite of his wing, and then, his eyes growing large, another, before he dropped his piece into his napkin and grabbed Mae's arm. "Wait," he said, looking confused. "Wait. Do you taste that?"

Mae detached his greasy hand from her sleeve and hissed at him. "Don't react to their chicken. They're filming us."

"But this is so weird," Andy said. "Don't you taste it?"

"We'll talk about this outside," Mae said, glancing at Sabrina, who was turning back toward them. "Just stop."

Sabrina came back, the camera following, and gestured broadly. "We'll ask the restaurateurs to go, so the chefs can start evaluating," she said. "No listening at the door!"

Mae, with a firm glance at Andy, began to walk out, taking another bite of her chicken as she went. She didn't taste anything weird at all.

Andy, though, could barely contain himself. Ignoring the cameras and Mae's glare, he stepped forward, right in front of the judges, took two more pieces of Frannie's chicken, and wrapped them in a napkin to take with him. Sabrina watched him, her curiosity apparent, then turned away as one of the assistants touched her arm.

A blast of unseasonable early-summer heat met them as Andy shouldered the Inn door open. Once they were outside, Amanda and Nancy immediately headed for the Inn's parking lot, but Andy grabbed Mae's arm again and pulled her out onto the sidewalk.

"Did you taste their chicken?"

"It just tastes like fried chicken to me," Mae said. "Maybe not as good as ours, but it's just chicken. Sabrina totally noticed you making a big deal out of it, too."

"Not as good as ours? It's exactly as good as ours. It *is* ours. It's the same. You can't taste that? They fry it differently—it's deep-fried, not batch-fried—but other than that, it's the same. It's exactly the same chicken."

Even in the hot sun, a tingle ran over Mae's skin as she took that in. "The same? How could it be the same? Andy, that's ridiculous."

"No, seriously, it's the same. Mae, I tried every fried chicken in the state getting ready for this job. I played with the heat of the oil, the oil blend, everything but the seasoning, to get Mimi's chicken just right, and I asked every chef who would talk to me to tell me what they did and why. I know you think you know fried chicken, but you only know Mimi's fried chicken. I know fried chicken—and this *is* Mimi's fried chicken."

"But how could it be? Did you eat from the wrong platter? Or maybe they got switched?"

"No, it's theirs. It's fried differently. It's the seasoning that's the same. And the thing is, Mae, it wasn't the same before. I ate there before I took the job with your mother. A handful of times. And the chicken wasn't like this. It wasn't even always the same from one day to the next. Once I swear it had dill in it. I mean, it was always cooked the same, but the seasoning wasn't the same."

They stood there, on asphalt so hot Mae could feel it through her shoes, staring at the chicken leg in Andy's hand. Mae felt pieces falling into place in her mind, and at the same time a rising sense of anger and disbelief. "She took the recipe," Mae said. "Or probably she took a picture of it. It was down on the counter when Amanda was in the kitchen. I remember you putting it back up the next day and saying something about Mimi hiding things from you."

Andy shook his head. "No way."

"It's the only way. She hasn't been inside Mimi's since the day after Frank's funeral, and she sure as hell didn't take it then and wait all this time to use it. We told you: my mother doesn't let Amanda into Mimi's. You knew it, too. Until you let your dick overrule your brain."

Andy turned red. "It wasn't like that."

Mae was furious, mostly with Amanda, but Andy was here in front of her, and without him, this never would have happened. "It *was* like that. It was absolutely like that. It was a stupid guy letting a smart woman use him." *Smart woman* was not a phrase she had expected to use about Amanda, who had always just seemed to let the winds of chance dump her wherever. But apparently her little sister had had plans for Andy all along.

"How would she know I'd let her—"

Mae just looked at Andy. Because men were predictable, maybe? Because if they thought they had you, they'd head for the nearest flat surface without a second thought? She rolled her eyes.

He looked away and shrugged. "Yeah, okay. I guess it was that." All the excitement had gone out of him. He probably needed a minute, but Mae didn't have time to let him process the crushing news that maybe he wasn't as irresistible as he'd thought.

"She stole our recipe!" Mae said, "What are we going to do? Can we prove it? Can we test it?"

Before Andy could answer, they both heard the click of heels running up the sidewalk. Sabrina was coming, as fast as her shoes would let her. As their eyes met, she called out to them. "What is it? There was something about the chicken. What's up?"

Andy put a warning hand on Mae's arm, but Mae was too upset to wait. "Amanda stole our recipe! Their chicken—it didn't used to be the same, and now it is. Andy noticed it first, but he's right. It's Mimi's seasoning on their chicken."

Sabrina stopped short. "No way." She pulled out her phone. "Say that again, Mae. Tell me again."

Andy waved his hand in front of the phone's camera. "Maybe she doesn't want to. Maybe this isn't a good idea, Mae. We should talk about it. Talk to Amanda."

There was no good explanation for this, though. None. For Amanda to give Nancy that recipe, to betray Mimi and Barbara and Mae and her entire family, she had to hate them. Not just Mae. All of them. A week ago, Mae would have confessed she didn't really care about Mimi's. She wanted it to thrive, sure, but it didn't mean much to her. After these few days back, though, after cleaning it up, after her night behind the stove, the family restaurant felt like more a part of her than she had ever realized. She could even see how the rhythm of the cooking line was her rhythm, had fed her need to have only what was necessary to the job at hand and her desire to keep things moving. That order was what Mae was looking for, as she cleaned and organized her way through life. She wanted every space to live up to the simple utility of Mimi's kitchen. Because that simplicity was beautiful. Mae had always wanted to share what made Mimi's special with people who didn't get enough authenticity in their lives.

And Amanda wanted to take all that away. Whether her plan was to shut down Mimi's, or beat them, or just steal what made Mimi's special, Mae didn't know, and she didn't care. What mattered was that she stand up for a place she finally realized she loved.

Mae looked right into Sabrina's camera. "When we tasted Frannie's chicken this morning, we were surprised—because it's our recipe. It's the same chicken. You can't copy what makes Mimi's magical just by duplicating some seasoning, especially not if you're just going to throw it on a plate with a bunch of stuff you don't even care about—but it's just so wrong to try. My sister must have taken the recipe." She wasn't going to say how. Let Sabrina put all that together if she wanted to.

Sabrina turned to Andy. "I could tell by your expression when you tasted the chicken that you were shocked. What did you think had happened?"

Mae crossed her arms. *Come through with it, Andy.* She hoped his chef's pride outweighed anything else. After what seemed like a minute, he looked at the camera.

"I could tell it was the same," he said. "For a minute, I thought I'd mixed up the plates—that I was eating my chicken. Our chicken. But it's fried differently. We just use the deep fryer for the fries; we cook the chicken in cast iron, and you can taste and usually see the difference. But the seasoning—I'd know it anywhere. And when I ate at Frannie's a few months ago, before I took the job with Mimi's, it was different. And now it's the same."

Sabrina turned off her camera and shoved the phone into her pocket. "This is incredible," she said. "We've never had anyone actually steal a recipe before. And Amanda, of all people!" She laughed. "I admit it, Mae, I thought you were the ruthless one. And you're a natural for television, of course. The camera loves you. But I figured if anyone would do something crazy to win this, it would be you, not Amanda." She shook her head. "Well, as my mother used to say, you're never safe from being surprised until you're dead."

"But what do we do?" Mae asked.

Sabrina was already turning around to head for the parking lot, practically skipping. "We confront Amanda, of course."

Confront Amanda. Amanda, with the perfect makeup and the great hair and, apparently, a mind full of schemes so hidden from Mae that it was almost as if Mae had never known her sister at all. She looked at Andy. "What if you're wrong?" she asked.

"I would really like to be wrong, actually," he said. "But I'm not."

AMANDA

As she got out of her car, Amanda was already stripping off her Frannie's shirt, which was soaked in sweat both from anxiety and from the ride home in an un-air-conditioned car thoroughly heated by the sun. The morning had basically sucked, although the chicken was fine and Nancy was fine and she hadn't actively done anything—else—to make a fool of herself. Mae looked like a tiny, adorable Dorothy, in a blue cotton print blouse with a flared skirt, bonus annoying because Amanda knew her sister hated *The Wizard of Oz* with a passion only someone who has grown up in Kansas and then tried to leave it behind could achieve. Next to her, Amanda felt, and surely looked, like a hulking, sweaty mess as she went through the motions of "sharing" their specialty with the three chefs.

Other than what was necessary for the taping, Nancy still hadn't said much to Amanda. She hadn't been unfriendly, exactly, just so wrapped up in the chicken and the show that Amanda had not felt able to push for absolution as much as she wanted to, and now she was stuck feeling like everything was still wrong but unable to point to anything she could fix.

The minute she was inside the screened-in porch, she peeled off her pants and threw both shirt and pants over the old swinging bench that hung there. Laundry, later. Right now, ice water. Shorts. T-shirt.

When she came out of her bedroom, pulling an old tank top over her head, there were cars in the tiny driveway. Mae's rental. A convertible—wait, that was Sabrina. And there was Andy, the last

person Amanda wanted on her front steps, climbing out of yet another car. Behind him was Sabrina's favorite camerawoman.

What were they doing? No one had said anything about coming
to her house, and she didn't want them here. Why were they here?
She had all of four hours before she had to be at work, and she was
done with *Food Wars* for the moment. And she was wearing a faded
tank top with a car wash logo on it. But if she ran back for something else, they'd come to the door and see inside, to the piles around
the sink and the remains of multiple days' breakfasts on the table
and the stack of recycling sliding its way past the stove. Instead,
she ran straight for the porch, opened the door, and nearly fell down
the stairs in her rush to meet the unwanted visitors on the lawn.
Once she was there, she stopped, hands on her hips. "What are you
guys doing here?"

Sabrina motioned to the camerawoman, who nodded and
aimed. No one said anything. Something about this didn't feel right.
Amanda's heart began to pound, and the sweat on her face and arms
felt cold even in the sun. Should she ask again? Say something else?
What was this? Mae glanced at Sabrina, and Amanda thought her
sister looked a little uncertain, but then Mae—still wearing her
cute skirt, of course—walked up to Amanda and faced her, arms
crossed over her chest.

"Andy tasted the chicken," Mae said. "The Frannie's chicken.
And it's Mimi's chicken. What the hell, Amanda?"

"What?" Amanda stared blankly at her sister.

"The chicken. Frannie's chicken. We know it's Mimi's recipe,
Amanda. Did you think no one would notice? Seriously?"

"What are you talking about? Of course it's not Mimi's recipe.
Nancy made that chicken same as she always makes it." Amanda
crossed her own arms over her chest, then uncrossed them. This
wasn't an argument. This was just—she didn't know what this was,
or why Sabrina was filming it.

"No, she didn't," Mae said, "It's exactly the same seasoning as Mimi's, and not the way Nancy always makes it. Frannie's chicken used to be way different. Now it's just like Mimi's, which means that you took the recipe, Amanda. You must have taken a picture of it when you were in the kitchen with Andy. It was down off the wall when I came in. It's the only way."

"That's— I— What? That doesn't even make any sense, Mae." Amanda looked at Andy, then at Sabrina, which was a mistake, because Sabrina was right in front of the camera. Andy was staring at the ground now, but he looked serious. Mae looked serious. The camera looked serious.

"There is no recipe for Frannie's chicken," Amanda said slowly. "Nancy makes it the way Frank made it and he made it the way his father made it and he made it the way Frannie made it. I don't have anything to do with it."

"Maybe you didn't before, but this time you did. You stole Mimi's recipe when you were in Mimi's, and now the chicken tastes exactly the same."

What? Amanda kept looking from one face to the other, waiting for someone to laugh. How could the chicken be the same? Was Mae making this up just to mess with her? "How would you even know what Frannie's chicken tastes like?" Amanda asked. "You've never tasted it. Until today, apparently."

"Andy's tasted it," Mae said. "Maybe you thought nobody could tell, because you don't eat chicken, but Andy tried Frannie's chicken before he even worked at Mimi's. And then right when he started. And it was different then. Really, really different." Mae looked at Andy, who was still staring at the ground, looking as if he'd rather be anywhere but here, a sentiment Amanda wholeheartedly agreed with.

He took a breath and looked at the camera, not Amanda. "It's the same recipe," he said. "Before I took the job at Mimi's, I ate fried chicken everywhere. I studied it. And Frannie's had a totally different flavor profile. Kind of a surprising one, actually. It was quite notably different. And now it's exactly like Mimi's."

That night at Mimi's, he'd taken her hand and drawn her in, and Amanda had gone. She'd felt welcome, relaxed, in a way she never had at Mimi's. It felt right, being there with him, and she had leaned lazily back, sitting there on the counter, appreciating his broad back and the way his height matched hers as he turned toward the sink, with a pleasant sense of anticipation that she hadn't felt in years. Did he really think she'd only gone in to steal a recipe? Her ears were ringing, a strange hum between her and the world, and the skin on her scalp prickled and crawled. Everything already felt wrong, and now it was tipping over into a point where she couldn't feel at all.

"I didn't— This is crazy. Why would I do that? That's not why I—" The camera was on her.

Mae stared into her face. "First you and Nancy stole our chicken. Now you took Mimi's recipe. You'll do anything to win this." She pointed to Andy. "Anything at all. You stole and you cheated and now you're lying."

"I don't lie!" Mae knew that. She knew this couldn't be true. Andy's dark eyes met hers as she spoke, and before he looked away Amanda thought she saw a hurt and betrayal that mirrored her own feelings. What right did he have to feel that way? Looking at him, at Sabrina, Amanda could see that they really believed she had done this, and while Amanda didn't know how Mae had pulled it off, she knew there wasn't anyone else who would stand up for her. She had put her whole world in the hands of something that was now spiraling wildly out of control and threatening to take everything she had with it. She had to show them that she wasn't the one who was hiding something—and there was only one thing she could say.

"You're the one who lies, Mae. You say anything you have to— Your whole life is a lie! It's all a sham, all this Mae Moore the organizer, Mae Moore 'I can help you clean it up and live a beautiful life.' You can't help anybody! You can't even help Mom, and if anybody ever needed help, it's her, and you just leave her alone in her filth and her hoarding and don't ever lift a finger."

And Barbara didn't lift a finger either. She would just let Mae ruin Amanda and Nancy if that's what Mae wanted, and Nancy was too nice to stop them. There was nobody to protect Frannie's except Amanda, and if everyone just knew, knew what she and Barbara were really like, they would never believe anything Mae or Barbara said, not about this, not about anything.

Mae hadn't moved. Amanda could tell by the look on her sister's face that she'd thought she was safe, that this was the one thing Amanda would never tell the world, but Amanda was done with pretending. She spun to face Sabrina. "Go look," she said. "Go look at my mom's house and just see. See if you can believe anything they say. They're hiding things, both of them, all of them. Andy, too." She shot an angry look at him, but he was still staring at the ground. He had to know about the house. Everybody in town knew. And everybody ought to know.

"Mom's house doesn't have anything to do with the recipe," Mae said. "It's totally"—she looked at Sabrina—"it's beside the point. It's the way she likes it. It's nothing to do with Mimi's, or me."

The camera was on Mae now.

"Is that true, Mae?" Sabrina's tone was interested, intrigued. "Your mother is a hoarder? And you've never tried to help?"

"I— This doesn't have anything to do with anything," said Mae. "I'm not even going to talk about it. It's ridiculous."

"No, you saying I took Mimi's recipe is ridiculous." Amanda was ready to talk, now that the cameras had turned. "This is just truth, Mae. You don't want it to be true. You don't want anybody to know it. But it's true."

Mae reached out to grab Amanda's arm, but Amanda yanked away. She didn't want to hear it; she was done. She turned, ready to go into the house and lock them all outside and away, and then she slowed. *Damn it.*

Frankie was in there, and just about the only thing that could make this worse was—

Frankie opened the screen door just as Amanda reached it. "Mom, what's up?"

That. Amanda frantically rearranged everything about herself, her face, her arms, what she was going to say next. Anything to get Frankie out of this.

"Everything went great this morning, Frankie," Amanda said, stepping up close to her and holding out an arm as if she could herd her daughter back into the house. "They're just— We're just recapping. Only people who were there, though." If Frankie would go inside she could use this as an excuse, follow her in, end this now.

But Frankie stood her ground. Worse, Amanda could tell by the look on Frankie's face that her daughter saw this as an opportunity. Sure enough, Frankie put her hands on her own hips and stepped down onto the step next to Amanda, staring at her aunt and suddenly also resembling her. "I can't believe you made a big deal out of the frozen biscuits, Aunt Mae. You know everybody freezes biscuit dough anyway, and we get them from a really good place, these two women outside Kansas City. They're fresh and they're homemade and they're delicious. So it's no big deal, and you made those chefs come freak my mom out about it." She spoke loudly, and as she did, she looked around, appearing satisfied with the impression she was making. Then she seemed to run out of steam. "And I don't think that was very nice."

In spite of everything, Amanda felt a burst of pride in Frankie. That couldn't have been easy. She didn't have time to admire her daughter now, though. She needed to get Frankie back in the house before anyone said another word.

"It's okay," Amanda said. "All's fair in love and *Food Wars,* right? Mae and I will work it out." She shot her sister a look that was supposed to say, *Please, just leave my kid out of this.* Couldn't Mae just give her that?

Apparently not.

"I guess what I would say to that," Mae said slowly, "is that in general, if you don't want people to know you're doing something, you shouldn't be doing it."

Frankie shrugged. "We'll tell people where they come from, then. But I still don't think you should have told everyone like that. On TV. That wasn't fair."

Amanda waited for Mae to start in on all the things Amanda shouldn't have done, but Mae just stood there, probably planning her next attack. Amanda needed to move fast. "Let's go inside, Frankie. They were just leaving." She opened the door wide and gestured. Frankie looked from Mae to Andy to the camera, as if expecting more of a reaction, but other than Sabrina, madly tapping away at her phone just out of view of the camera, everyone else was still, Mae staring at the ground, Andy glancing at Amanda, then quickly looking away. In that moment, Amanda hated them all so fiercely that she wanted to go over and kick them both in the shins, kick and kick and kick until they took it all back and then kick some more. Instead, she spoke softly, trying to keep any emotion out of her voice. "Come on," she said again to her daughter, more urgently. "Everybody needs a break."

Leaving them all behind, Amanda ushered Frankie into the house and shut the door.

MAE

It took just long enough for Mae to feel safe before Sabrina made her move.

After Amanda's announcement, a mostly quiet Sabrina, apparently lost in thought, returned Andy to Mimi's and dropped Mae at the park where she was meeting Barbara and the kids. Mae was still conducting a one-sided argument with the *Food Wars* host as they pulled up at the curb. Her mother's house had nothing to do with Mimi's, or *Food Wars,* she said. It would be unfair to capitalize on it when that had not been what Barbara agreed to; it was just a distraction.

To all of it, Sabrina kept repeating that she wasn't in charge. "You know how this works, Mae. There're higher-ups. There are producers back at the ranch. I just do the filming. I have to say, you and your sister have given us plenty to work with."

Sabrina had more clout than she was admitting, and Mae knew it. It was infuriating. Amanda was not, as Sabrina called her, "a dark horse." She was a traitor and a fool, and she was going to ruin them all, because nothing Barbara did or was could change what Amanda had done. She was just dragging them down with her.

And now Mae was stuck. No Barbara, no kids, no car. Out of habit, she opened Instagram and Facebook and closed them a dozen times, sitting on the park bench, waiting, barely knowing what she was waiting for. She itched to do something. Anything.

If Sabrina decided to put it out there, then what? Would they try to film the house? It was bad in there, surely; it had to be bad. Should she try to— No. There was no going there. Her whole adult relationship with her mother was built on not touching the past.

What would Jay do? That was the one thing she could do. She could call him. Jay knew what it was to paper over a big chunk of childhood and just go forward from there. His mother left him with his father, taking his sister instead, when he was three, and the family never lived together again, and never talked about it either. But they managed cordial if overly formal meals in his mother's Manhattan town house every month.

But while Jay knew that there were things Mae and Barbara avoided, he had no idea how much of her past Mae had edited out when she left for college, and Mae wasn't sure she could stand him knowing. How could he not see her differently if he saw how she had been raised, if he knew about the squalor and the lengths she'd gone to, to escape it?

There was so much to explain, but maybe it was time. Being here, sliding back into her old self, watching Kenneth and Patrick— she didn't know exactly what she wanted from Jay, but she wanted him to be part of this, somehow. He said they'd talk later. Maybe later should be now.

But Jay didn't answer, and Mae, frustrated, couldn't think of what to put in a text. He would see she had called.

He would call her back.

Of course he would.

Just as Mae, unable to stand waiting for one more thing, was about to abandon the bench and search for her mother and the kids, there they were. Madison was running up the sidewalk to her, Ryder, smaller and slower, trailing behind, both shouting. "Mommy, Mommy, you have to come in and see them! They're so cute! Mommy, can we have one, please, the girl one, I want to call her Elsa, she's mostly white, she's so cute!"

Ryder grabbed at his sister as he caught up. "No, the black one! Blackie!"

Wait, what? Mae looked to Barbara in confusion.

"Patches had her puppies last night."

"Patches was pregnant?"

"Of course Patches was pregnant, Mae, do you not have eyes? Did you not see how her belly was practically dragging on the ground?"

Yeah, but she just thought the dog was fat, figuring her mother was about as good at feeding dogs healthy things as she had been with her kids. "I don't know much about dogs," she said. Then, for good measure: "It's not like we had one when I was little." Should she say anything to Barbara? No. Not yet. Her mother was tired; she could see it. Madison and Ryder took a lot out of anyone. Maybe the thought of adding to Barbara's list of complaints against Amanda should have made Mae happy, but it didn't. Instead, she knelt down and hugged both Madison and Ryder hard, but neither could hold still.

"Grandma said if we lived here, we could have one. Both of us." Madison was dancing around Mae, pulling her off-balance.

"Mom!"

Barbara shrugged. "So what? They could. But you don't, kids, so that's that."

"I can't believe you said that to them." Mae turned toward the park, hoping Madison would be distracted by the swing or slide, and Barbara turned away, as if to walk back toward Mimi's and home. Mae grabbed her mother's arm. "Mom. This way. You're coming with us, remember?"

Ryder wrapped his arms around Barbara's leg. "I gone throw ball puppies," he said. "When they big like me."

"Mom!" What had her mother been saying? "We're just visiting, Ryder. We're going to go home to Daddy, and then someday we will come back and see the puppies again."

Ryder stared up at her. "I want Daddy," he said, just as Madison said, "Grandma said we could stay," and now Mae was kneeling to try to soothe Ryder and still being pulled on by Madison, and her mother was just standing there, staring off down the street, an oddly blank look on her face that made Mae want to shake her.

"You cannot tell them we could stay," she said, speaking loudly over Ryder, who was beginning to cry. "You're just—confusing them."

"You could stay," said Barbara. Her voice was distant, a little off, but then she turned and looked at Mae and blinked a little, as if focusing on her for the first time. "You could. Of course I know you won't. But you could." Then, as if it followed: "Have you talked to your sister today?"

Had she— For a minute, Mae had forgotten. Hell yeah, she'd talked to Amanda today. But this was not the moment to say any of that to Barbara, who had bent down to hug Ryder and Madison.

"You can see the puppies again tomorrow," she promised. "You'll still be here tomorrow. Maybe Amanda could drop your cousin Gus by. Or Frankie." Mae braced herself for more questions—Madison and Ryder had not seen their cousins, had not, apparently, made the connection that cousins who had never been more than lines on a Christmas card might be live, accessible beings in this wonderful town full of puppies and doughnuts, and she did not need them to make it now, when meeting those cousins wasn't going to happen until—when? How? Had Amanda even realized how much her words would put an end to? Barbara put her hands to her back, stretching, and Mae was again struck by how exhausted she looked. Probably helping Patches have puppies had been an all-night thing. This thing, Amanda, the house . . . This was not going to help.

"Can we talk about Amanda later, Mom? We talked. But about *Food Wars* stuff. Forget the park, okay? Maybe go home and rest before tonight. They're going to come back and film once more." That's where Sabrina had left it, anyway. One more night of filming, *just in case we need it.* For what, Mae couldn't think about. There was no way she could avoid telling her mother about Amanda and the recipe, but the house—if Sabrina would just leave it alone, Mae was still hoping her mother didn't have to know how far Amanda had been willing to go to hurt Mimi's, and Mae. And Barbara.

"Later. Okay." Her mother straightened, turned, and walked away, and Mae watched her go, weirdly comforted by their return to a relationship in which they did not even have to say good-bye, while Madison and Ryder ran for the swings.

Mae and Barbara, and Madison and Ryder, had gained something this week. But right now, Mae was more worried about what Barbara might be about to lose.

Gus was her mother's go-to when she needed something moved or fixed, Frankie her recipient of the gifts Barbara loved to buy, spiral notebooks bearing kitten pictures, magnifying mirrors, costume jewelry, brightly colored, slightly cracked plastic containers. Barbara had a hard time living in a world in which so much was so cheap. Mae knew this from Frankie's *#withlovefromGrandma* hashtag on Instagram, which she had at first resented on her mother's behalf and then realized was really a loving tribute from someone who—like Mae—had no intention of letting anyone but herself decide what came into her space.

Amanda's words, though, had set off something that Mae couldn't keep from crashing into all of their spaces. Frankie didn't know it yet, unless Amanda had told her, which Mae doubted. Gus didn't know. Barbara didn't know. They had all, along with Andy, been stripped bare by *Food Wars,* and what Mae felt above all was responsible. If she had said no to Barbara, if she had gone with her original gut that no good would come to Barbara from letting strangers into her private world, they would all still have each other. Instead, they were stuck in this weird limbo of a script someone else was writing, and even running away from it, as Mae was tempted to do, would be written in, would play out on this stage.

She could take it, if she had to. Andy could take it. But anything Sabrina did besides nothing was going to cost her mother something, and she didn't really believe Sabrina would do nothing. There would be something. Mae spent all afternoon trying not to imagine what.

Even so, it wasn't until she saw the Facebook post that she began to realize how much *Food Wars* could do—or how much of Barbara's world they could destroy.

×

The video, posted to the *Food Wars* Facebook page, started with a confusing image. On closer inspection, Mae saw it was a squirming pile of puppies. Then, as the camera pulled back, Patches, tongue out, looking quite content (as she should; there was a visible pile of dog treats in front of her). And then, as the camera pulled back more . . .

Shit.

Oh shit.

Oh fuck.

As the camera pulled back more, there was the inside of her mother's house. *How?* How had they gotten in, without her even knowing? The dog bed turned out to be partly on a sofa and partly on a coffee table pulled up in front of the sofa. The rest of the sofa, and the floor in front of the sofa, was piled with things, with closed boxes and open boxes with rolled paper and tool handles sticking out, stacks of magazines and more paper, clothing on hangers, in dry-cleaning bags, over the tops of boxes and the back of the sofa.

The view changed to the kitchen, to stacks of unwashed dishes next to equally filthy pans next to new sets of pans and Tupperware, still in boxes, with open cereal boxes on top of them, and on the floor, still more. As Mae stared, horrified, the camera zoomed in on the bottom of a fifty-pound bag of flour, clearly chewed through, and—*Goddamn it, how had the cameraperson gotten so lucky?*—a mouse skittered out and disappeared under a nearby pile of coats.

She read the post above the video: *Is this what you want when you go grab some fried chicken? Turns out someone in this Food War has more than a little problem. Can über-organizer Mae Moore clean up anyone's act, especially when the mess hits close to home? Find out on tomorrow's mini webisode of Season Four, Round Three of GHTV's Food Wars.*

There were comments. Hundreds already, still coming. At first, mystified—*What is this, whose house is it?*—then, of course, as people figured it out, as locals weighed in on what she'd always known was an ugly open secret in their small town, exactly the disgust you'd expect. *She runs a restaurant? Makes the pies there? Gross!*

Not everybody loved Mimi's, or at least, as she had always known, some people were happy to hit anyone who was down.

There was even an extensive thread about the dog. *How can anyone raise puppies like that? That can't be safe for the animals! Someone get those puppies out of there! I hope you called the ASPCA before you even took this video, shame on you if you didn't I will take the dog and the puppies when they are taken away please message me ASAP*

And so on.

Mae closed her phone, then, unsatisfied, opened it again, intending to turn it all the way off, to lock it in the glove compartment, to leave it behind completely, except that now there was a message, dropped down over red notifications lighting up the little gleaming icons of Facebook and Twitter and Instagram, as if to shout over them all.

Really? This is who you are now, an episode of Hoarders? You're going to exploit some poor hick's mental illness for your fame or whatever? Come on, Mae. You're better than that. Don't let them drag you down.

She had thought she'd braced herself for this, but she hadn't. The text was a punch to the gut, one Jay must have fired off before even reading the comments, because it wouldn't take more than a quick skim to realize that *Food Wars* was hardly what was dragging her down. He must have seen by now that the "poor hick" was Barbara. He would know that the Mae he had married was, at least in part, a lie, that she wasn't the solid other half she had pretended to be.

And he hadn't texted her again.

That was it, then. There was no running away now. There was nowhere—no one—to run to.

She should have stayed home. Should have listened to him, accepted the *Sparkling* verdict, found some other way forward. Of course this plan had turned on her. How could she have expected the very place she wanted to erase from her past to help her find her way? She should have trusted Jay. Jay, who, she had to admit now, really wasn't trying to ruin anything with his plan for them both to take a break. He just wanted a say in the life they were supposedly building together, and she'd been so busy building it herself that she had barely noticed when he started questioning his part. Just as surely as Sabrina had been single-mindedly setting up the story she wanted to tell, Mae had ignored the fact that some of the players on her stage weren't happy with their roles, and now someone else was directing the show.

She walked into Mimi's, where the cameras and the night's crowds had not yet arrived, unable to disguise her feelings, and as she came through the back door her mother and Andy stopped their conversation and stared at her. It was clear from their expressions that her own emotions were written all over her face.

Andy was the first one to speak. "What happened?" His voice was calm, but as he spoke, he placed a hand under Barbara's arm, as though he thought he might need to hold her up, and Mae loved him for it.

"They know," she said, and, seeing that Barbara had of course not understood, explained. "About the house, Mom. *Food Wars.*

They took a video." Suddenly she couldn't bear to tell her mother what people were saying about her home, about the dogs. "It's bad, Mom."

Barbara reached out a hand, and Mae gave her the phone, where the video was looping over the stream of comments. Andy leaned over her, his arm around his boss, watching quietly. After a moment, Barbara handed the phone back without a word and turned to the counter where she had been working. Mae felt a fury boiling up inside her, with Sabrina, yes, with Amanda, of course, but also with her mother, the person she loved most in the world or at least had loved for the longest. How could her strong, brave, smart mother, a woman who could do anything in the world she set her mind to, let this happen? How did they always end up right back here, with Barbara's mess threatening to destroy their world?

If Barbara had an answer, she wasn't offering it.

She was making salad dressing. Mae watched, waiting as long as she could, while Barbara carefully began measuring in the sugar.

"Well?" she finally said.

Barbara looked up, and with a wrenching twist to her insides, Mae saw that her mother was trying not to cry. "I take really good care of Patches," she said, setting down the jar they used to mix the dressing. "She's perfectly safe. The puppies are healthy; they're the healthiest puppies you ever saw. And I'll get her fixed, I was going to, this happened too fast, we already even had the appointment, I've told Jared Brown again and again that he can't let that big Lab of his run loose without fixing him, but he's a man, won't do it."

"But, Mom—how did they even get in there? Did you let them in?"

She shook her head. "No. I don't know."

"Aunt Aida?" That might make sense. She loved a camera.

"She would never, Mae. And no. She's been helping that woman who has the new tattoo shop, over in Bradford. I dropped her off this morning."

Andy hit a fist against the cabinet, shaking the entire kitchen, making even the pans hanging above the counter rattle and keep rattling, longer than they should have, jangling with all the energy in the tiny building. "They can't just go into your house," he said, and Mae spoke over him, glad to have an outlet for her own anger.

"It doesn't even matter; it's out there, however they got it. People have seen it. People will see it. And it's not just Patches, Mom. The flour. Do you use that to make the pies? Are you still working in there?" The dog, yes. But the restaurant. If she was cooking for Mimi's in that kitchen, and people knew it—

"That's an old bag. Of course I keep all the supplies for Mimi's safe, Mae. I'm just as careful as I ever was. I can't believe you'd even think that. I didn't make the pies this week anyway. Patrick did." Barbara was calming down, her anger carrying her past her tears.

Mae shook her head. The lines her mother somehow drew around her mess, around her problem, had always amazed her, and Barbara's outrage that anyone would think she might carry that filth out into the world could sometimes be almost funny, but not now. Even the image of Aunt Aida in a tattoo parlor wasn't helping. The puppies were not the problem. Even the pies were not the problem, although it helped that Patrick had baked this week. "It doesn't matter what I think," she said. "It's what everybody else thinks. What are we going to do?"

"Call Sabrina and tell her I take good care of Patches and that none of this has anything to do with Mimi's. None of it."

That, at least, was a call Mae was spoiling to make.

AMANDA

Nancy picked Gus and Frankie up for the night at Frannie's early, pulling into the driveway while Amanda, who had decided that hard work was the only thing to quiet her churning brain, was in her front yard, hacking away at the overgrown grass and weeds around her front steps with the vague idea of planting annuals and making it all look better, but mostly just to sweat and have something to curse out. Her small flock of chickens kept getting in the way, delighted by the soil she was flipping over, and more than once she'd nearly taken one out with the shovel, which just felt like exactly the kind of day she was having, especially now that she was frantically showering and realizing that the sweaty Frannie's shirt from this morning was still the cleanest one she had.

She was done with *Food Wars*. This had all been a terrible idea, and the best thing she could do now would be to just put her head down and ignore it. She didn't know what she would do when Nancy found out that Sabrina thought they had stolen the Mimi's recipe, or that she had told Sabrina to go look at Barbara's house. Amanda was just going to—go. And do her job. And she was never going to try to make anything happen ever again.

When she finally got to Frannie's, she found Gus and Frankie standing outside the door, very clearly waiting for her. She didn't want to talk to them, or anyone. They would know she didn't take the recipe—they would believe Nancy, if not her—but how would they feel when they knew why she'd been in Mimi's in the first place? Did they know? From the looks on their faces, she could tell something was wrong.

"Mom," Gus said, pressing his phone into her hand, "you need to watch this."

Frankie was between her and the door. "Someone told *Food Wars* about Grandma Barbara's house. It's on Facebook."

So it wasn't Mae accusing her of stealing the recipe, then. Her relief came and went in an instant. The house was on Facebook? But Barbara would never let them into the house.

She looked down at the phone in her hand. It was a video, already playing. She saw a mouse skittering out of the bottom of a bag of flour, and then the video restarted, focused on Patches, who must have had the puppies, then pulling back to show the mess around her, which wasn't that bad, considering. It had been worse. It pulled back further, showing the kitchen—okay, that was bad.

Is this what you want when you go grab some fried chicken? Turns out someone in this Food War has more than a little problem. Can über-organizer Mae Moore clean up anyone's act, especially when the mess hits close to home? Find out on tomorrow's mini webisode of Season Four, Round Three of GHTV's Food Wars.

Scrolling down, she saw that people had guessed it was Barbara—of course they had; everyone in town would know it—and boggled at all the comments about the food and the pies and the puppies.

"How did they know?" Frankie demanded. "It's none of their business."

Amanda knew the answer to that, of course, but how did they get into the house? Barbara would barricade the doors before she would let them film in there. She read the words again. *Can über-organizer Mae Moore clean up anyone's act?* Was there any chance

Mae had decided to turn this to her advantage and try to get *Food Wars* to film her cleaning? Because everyone knew that was what Mae wanted most—for the whole world to know she had her life under control and could handle everyone else's besides.

She looked more carefully at the post, scrutinizing it for signs of her sister's handiwork, knowing in her heart that there was no way Mae would reveal her mother's shame like that, both for her own sake—Mae had said all along that the one thing they didn't want *Food Wars* to do was see the house—and, if Amanda was honest, for Barbara's. In all those years of Mae fighting Barbara, trying to clean the place up, trying to change her, Amanda had never seen Mae allow anyone else to criticize her. At the faintest suggestion from a teacher or another parent that Barbara could do better, no matter how much Mae might secretly agree, she instantly rose to Barbara's defense. Mae's loyalty to Barbara never faltered.

But she had no loyalty to Amanda at all. Amanda would never have told Sabrina about the house if Mae hadn't betrayed her already, making up this stupid story about the recipe and putting Amanda right in the middle of it. Barbara probably knew what Mae had done, or if she didn't, she would soon enough, and she wouldn't care. Her mother always thought the sun shone out of Mae's ass.

They didn't deserve anything from Amanda. And was this even really that bad? Mae could help Barbara clean it up. And Mae should help Barbara clean it up. All these years, it had just been Amanda, going in every so often to try to deal with the worst of it, to make sure that her mother wasn't eating anything that could kill her, that she still had a chance of getting out if the house caught fire, with Barbara scolding her to just leave things alone. Not even wanting her there. Amanda should have left her alone a long time ago.

It was Mae's turn. Nothing that bad could happen now. She and Mae weren't little girls to be taken away. They were grown-ups. Barbara was a grown-up. It was time she faced her own mess.

Amanda turned to Frankie. Mae's apt words from earlier came to her mind. "I guess I would say that if you don't want people to know you're doing something, maybe you shouldn't be doing it."

Frankie looked at her mother, and her eyes widened. "You told, didn't you?"

Gus stared at Amanda. "Wait, you told?"

Slowly, Amanda nodded.

"But they're going to take Patches away," Frankie said. "She loves Patches. Mom, I can't believe you let them do this!"

"I didn't 'let' them do anything. I don't have any idea how they got into the house. But the mess—they needed to know. Don't you guys want to win?" Amanda asked. "I mean, this is real. Her house really looks like that. She really does make the pies there." And her famous lemonade cake with sprinkles, for every one of Gus's and Frankie's birthdays, and most of Amanda's. And the chewy oatmeal chocolate chip cookie that sold out first every time one of the kids' clubs had a bake sale. But that didn't excuse her horrific mess of a house. "It's not fair to have people judging Mimi's against Frannie's if they don't know that." Amanda felt a swell of righteousness. If they could tell lies about her, why shouldn't she tell the truth about them?

"But you had to know she would find a way to get in," Gus said angrily. "They film everything. They're everywhere."

"I'm sorry, but I had to." They didn't know why, not yet, but Amanda couldn't bear to tell them. "They were saying stuff about Nancy and me, okay? And it wasn't even true. This is." She pushed past them, knowing that once she was inside, she'd be able to count on her kids not wanting to fight in front of the cameras. They'd know eventually. Everyone would know everything eventually. But for now, couldn't she just go serve some people some fucking fried chicken?

She should have known she couldn't. As she seated customers and moved back and forth through the dining room, she felt an increasing sense of being watched. In spite of Nancy's long-standing rules about phones for staff on the floor, she saw them being passed from hand to hand, huddled around, and then shoved out of sight when she or Nancy appeared. Pinky Heckard made a joke about avoiding the "mouse-dukey pies" at Mimi's. She'd gone to school with Pinky. He ate erasers—that was how he got his nickname. Pinky's mother pressed Amanda's hand, as if in sympathy. "Your poor mother," she said. "At least she can get some help, but this must be hard." No one mentioned the recipe. No one seemed to know about the chicken. But it had to be coming.

Mary Laura made her way out of the bar in a lull to lean on Amanda's hostess station, eyeing her, keeping a lookout for the cameras. "God, girl," she said. "Was that you? Or did Mae or Barbara let something slip?"

"I didn't mean to," Amanda said. "I was defending Frannie's and it just came out. I didn't think people would go after the dog. I didn't know they'd really film it."

Like Sabrina, Mary Laura rolled her eyes. "You didn't know?" She snorted. "Of course you knew. But nobody would blame you for getting a little revenge, after all those years in that house. Won't hurt her to have to clean it up. Still, you brought a fox into the hen coop; that's for sure. But there were too many hens in here, right? We needed some stirring up."

Amanda ignored Mary Laura's claim that she knew what she was doing. She hadn't intended any of this. "That's an awful analogy, though," Amanda said. "No one needs to get eaten."

"You sure?" Mary Laura was heading back to the bar, leaving a drink for Amanda behind her. She liked to get in the last word. "I have to say, I don't really see a way out of this that leaves every chicken standing."

Amanda deeply regretted showing her friend any part of her chicken-centric *Carrie* adaptation, even if Mary Laura had loved it. If there had been fewer people waiting to eat, Amanda would have thrown the seating chart at her. She endured a few more snide comments about Mimi's, and then, just as the night's rush was really beginning, she saw Nancy, pinned in the corner by Sabrina and two cameras. She appeared to be arguing fiercely with Sabrina, although Amanda couldn't hear what she was saying over the noise of the crowded bar. As she watched, Nancy looked up, and as their eyes met, Nancy pushed roughly past Sabrina and walked toward her.

This was it. Sabrina must have asked her about the recipe and told her why she was asking. Of course Nancy would be angry. Angry that Amanda would expose them to this, that she had put them in the position of having to defend themselves when there was no easy defense, no recipe they could point to and say, "Look, this is ours." She had made the very thing that was a virtue about Frannie's into a problem, and she'd done it—this was the worst part—by betraying Frank, and their marriage, and her only real family.

Nancy reached her, trailed by cameras. She turned and addressed the camerawoman, rather than Sabrina, who was standing right there. "I would like to have a word with Amanda," she said. "Alone."

The woman behind the camera didn't answer. Instead, Sabrina smiled. "Can't do it right now, Nancy. You and Amanda are kind of at the center of things tonight, and I can't let you two out of my sight."

Nancy put her hands on her hips; Amanda could see that she was struggling to control herself. "I would think you could let us have a small private word."

Sabrina shook her head. "Nope. Not tonight."

"Fine." Nancy dropped her arms, then took off the small radio she wore so that the kitchen could buzz her at any time and handed it to Amanda. "I am going home," she said. "This has gone too far, and I am through." She turned to Sabrina. "No amount of money is worth this."

Nancy walked out the door, leaving Amanda staring after her, and the cameras staring at Amanda. Could she just—leave? Didn't they have to stay? And could they say things like that—things about *Food Wars* itself? Then, as if Nancy had passed her anger to her daughter-in-law along with the radio, Amanda found herself speaking more directly to Sabrina than she had to anyone in days. Or maybe years.

"You know it's all a lie," Amanda said. "You must know. They must know—Rideaux, Cary. And I don't know how you got into my mom's house, but even if she let you in, you know she had no clue what would happen. Putting it out there, on the Internet—you know that's wrong. It's not what I meant for you to do. None of this is what I meant to have happen."

Sabrina sighed and waved away the camera. "Oh, come on, Amanda. You knew exactly what I would do. If you didn't want this out there, you wouldn't have told me. And I don't know what the hell's up with the recipe, but it will come out. This is the way it always goes. It starts out as *Food Wars,* but it comes down to *Family Wars,* every time."

"Only because you let it," said Amanda, looking down at Sabrina, who even in heels didn't reach Amanda's height. Amanda straightened, feeling the strength of her realization through her very bones. "And you don't just let it. You push it. You've been nudging us along, haven't you?"

Sabrina leaned cozily into the hostess stand, looking perfectly comfortable with herself. "It doesn't take much," she said, lifting her eyebrows. "Everybody's so willing to call everybody else out. People don't get into this unless they have something they want out there, Amanda. I never know why, when I first read the e-mails, but you can feel it. Everybody thinks they want fame, or a hundred grand, but what they really want is to tell, to have everybody know that they're right, they're the best, their father was wrong all along, whatever. It's always something, and it makes good TV, and that's my job."

She was worse than Chef Rideaux, with his witchy pronounce-
ments, and she was so, so far off base. "That's bullshit, Sabrina,"
Amanda said. "You guys all think you're so smart because you're
not from here. You think we all fit into these little patterns, and we
don't, and that's just a sorry excuse for manipulating people."

Sabrina shook her head. "I'm not so smart," she said. "I just see
a lot of people, and they're pretty much all the same that way. I'm
just giving them a chance to do what they already want to do." She
grinned. "A lot of them do this, too, by the way—what you're doing
now. Objecting. Getting all moral. So, fine, you see through us. But
you're stuck with us all the same." She nodded toward the parking
lot. "There's your next customers," she said. "Looks like you're in
charge, kid. Good luck." She walked back into the restaurant, leaving Amanda to hold the door for a party of six, one high chair, two
kids' menus, "and could we have a table, not a booth, please?"

MAE

It took all night before she reached Sabrina, a night when, more than once, Mae had seen customers bent over their phones, heads together. She'd heard snatches of conversation, thought she caught people staring—because of course anyone in town would know that video referred to Barbara. But anyone in town had also been eating at Mimi's for years, and they weren't going to let a little thing like a messy house stop them—especially not one that most of them were already vaguely aware of. None of their business, as always. Once, that attitude had infuriated Mae. Now that she was no longer a little kid wishing someone would save her—now that she had long since saved herself—she blessed it. Pay no attention to the house behind the restaurant, folks. Move along. Nothing to see here.

Mimi's was still pretty busy. The food was all gone; the pie case (which Mae had, somewhat against Barbara's wishes, clearly labeled BAKED AT THE 1908 STANDARD FROM MIMI'S RECIPES) was empty except for the few slices of coconut cream that always lingered. Sabrina never appeared, instead sending cameras and one of her minions to take some chicken back to the chefs, which must mean that the whole stolen-recipe business was still a thing, although Mae couldn't bring herself to care anymore. They were supposed to do a "winners" announcement tomorrow, Sunday morning, but Sabrina hadn't told them what to do or where to be, and what did it matter? Nobody was winning this game.

This time, the tenth time Mae tried her, Sabrina picked up even before Mae heard her phone ring. To Mae's shock, Sabrina sounded nothing but delighted to chat. "Mae! Mae, who's about to take this show where it's never been before, are you ready?"

"What the fuck, Sabrina? I told you, this has nothing to do with the restaurant, or *Food Wars*. It's my mom's fucking house, and it's none of anyone's business."

"It is if she makes her pies in there, and you know she does—I checked. Come on, Mae, this is brilliant. Don't think I can't tell you've been angling for your own show. This is your chance, right here."

Those words—"your own show"—froze Mae mid-anxious pacing, tagging some region of her brain that had been waiting to hear exactly that and twisting all her thoughts up as if someone had pulled a knot tight. Everything else was so wrong, but that felt so right—

"I've set you up, Mae. You're going to make this happen. You clean your mom's place up, get it straightened out, and the whole world will be watching. This has everything people love. Family, a little fighting, a daughter coming through for her mother, puppies... You do your thing, then we do ours—announce the winner, call it done—and you'll be able to write your own ticket with whatever network you want. Organizing, food, country living—you've got all the pieces, and you were made for television. Everyone will want you."

Sabrina had no idea what she was asking. "I can't fix my mom," Mae said. "Don't you think I've tried? It won't work." Mae remembered what she had been planning to say. "And you guys—you snuck in! Or somebody did! Someone entered the house, and nobody let them in. My mom is going to call the police."

"Door was open, Mae. Our cameraman heard the dogs—they might have been in trouble. He's a Good Samaritan. And nobody's going to care anyway. They care about the dogs, and they'll care about the pies, and the mice. That's what the story is."

"She didn't make the pies in there," Mae said, trying a different tack. "Patrick, from the coffee shop, made the pies that were on the show."

"Details," declared Sabrina cheerfully. "You're just complicating things, and no one will pay attention. Maybe that will save you from some food inspector—although there's no way it hasn't been that way when she was making pies and you know it—but it's not going to help you on Facebook."

Mae could hear the truth in Sabrina's words. No one would care. She'd seen those comments. Mimi's had done okay tonight, probably could stagger along, but this was out there now, whether Mae wanted to accept it or not.

"Maybe we're done," she told Sabrina, hearing the weakness in her own voice. "Maybe my mom doesn't want anyone in her house. She'll just shut *Food Wars* down."

"No, she won't," Sabrina said. "She's going to have protestors trying to protect those dogs if she doesn't do something, to say nothing of the damage to Mimi's. You guys are going to have to clean it up, and you're going to have to clean it up big, so people can see it happening. If you don't, your mom loses her dogs for sure, and maybe her business, too. You don't want that, Mae, and this is what you *do*. You can make this better, and it will be a triumph!"

"It's not that simple, Sabrina." Mae wanted to grab the other woman through the phone and shake her. "It's an illness. She can't help it, and I can't help her." It was what she had been repeating to herself for years, the phrase she had made her peace around. Her mother couldn't change, and Mae couldn't do it for her.

She could practically see Sabrina rolling her eyes. "I don't care if you fix her forever, Mae. Fix her now. Clean it now. Make a pretty, sparkly place for those puppies now, and paint the whole thing over with glitter and rainbows, and it doesn't matter what it looks like in six months. You'll be gone and I'll be gone and as long as your mom doesn't kill anybody with her cooking it will all be good. This is a big opportunity, and you're going to grab it, Mae. And I'm going to film it."

Mae didn't answer her. She didn't have an answer. She couldn't even think about the show or the cameras or any of that. She looked at the phone, with Sabrina waiting inside—and the video, and Facebook and Instagram and all of it—and pressed the red button to end the call, then slowly put the thing into the back pocket of her jeans shorts. She should go to the motel, probably. Madison and Ryder had been in rare form when Jessa hauled them out of Mimi's at close, hours past their bedtime, and Mae had paid very little attention to what the cameras were capturing. Jay was right; she had brought her children out here to be a sideshow. She had made her whole life a sideshow. Maybe if she went back now, if she called him again, FaceTimed him, put the kids on—maybe there was something she could fix there, somehow.

And maybe not. Instead, she turned back toward Mimi's.

Barbara didn't want to change. The house didn't want to change. This wasn't a job for an organizer; it was a job for a psychologist, and possibly an exorcist. Barbara's problems weren't something Mae could paper over for the camera, even if she wanted to. It was fine to do that for other people. She cleaned up their messes and walked away, leaving them to enjoy their tidy counters for as long as they lasted, and herself with the illusion that once clean, their lives would stay that way. She didn't have to watch and see if it worked. It worked for *her,* and that was enough.

She probably could clean up the house, if Barbara would let her. But if she cleaned it up and walked away, the change wouldn't last, and while Sabrina might not care about that, Mae did. When Barbara's mess overtook Mae's efforts, she felt herself disappearing, like writing in the sand erased by the tide. She couldn't do it again.

But what choice did she have? No matter what Mae did next, there was one thing she couldn't change: everybody knew. Sabrina,

Jessa, Lolly, all of them. They knew where Mae had come from and how much she didn't belong with them.

And Jay. He would know that Mae's entire being was rooted in a mess she had never been able to change, that where other people had something normal and secure, she had a big, fat pile of trash sliding under her feet. And he would know that she hadn't trusted him enough to tell him.

Everything she had built for herself was already gone.

Mae found Barbara inside Mimi's, sitting quietly, doing nothing. The kitchen, the counter, the tiny dining area, all were restored to the shipshape order Mae and her team had created what felt like years ago, and it was an order that came naturally to the utilitarian space. Everything and everyone had a purpose at Mimi's, and the complications of the outside world just didn't apply. Mae stood silently next to her mother for a moment, wishing they never had to leave.

The instant they stepped out of Mimi's, the door swung shut behind them, and when Barbara put her hand back to check the latch, she found the door already locked.

"I guess we're supposed to go home," said Mae, trying to speak lightly. It was rare for more than one of them to be around when the ghost of Mimi made herself known, and somehow that made it more creepy, rather than less. Barbara put a hand on Mae's shoulder as she followed Mae down the step, and Mae was surprised to feel it shaking. She reached up and took it.

"I'm so sorry, Mom." There was no point in avoiding this any longer. They walked, still holding hands, along the path around to the back of the house. "I talked to Sabrina, but it didn't make any difference." Mae let go of her mother's hand and sank down on the familiar step, scratching the toe of her shoe around in the dirt, raising one of the smells of her childhood.

"No, I'm sorry." As she spoke, Barbara opened the door behind Mae to let Patches out, and the dog trotted into the tall grass to pee. Barbara descended heavily next to Mae, and Patches, apparently unconcerned about her puppies, returned to plant herself on the stoop as well. Barbara put one arm around the dog and the other on Mae's knee. *Three lousy mothers,* thought Mae irrelevantly.

She leaned on Barbara and shook her head. "I got you into this," she said. "You never would have done the show if I hadn't told you it was a good idea. And Amanda never would have thought of it, probably, if I hadn't done *Sparkling.*" Amanda. Thinking of her sister, Mae's anger returned, but it was muted, somehow, by all that had come since. This was all Amanda's fault. So why did it feel like Mae's fault, too, like the inevitable destination of a train she had boarded a long time ago? "I got us all into this mess."

"I think your Internet would say I got us into this mess," Barbara said.

Mae tilted her head sideways to look at her mother. There was nothing to say to that. If this was where Mae's train had always been headed, her mother had bought the tickets. But Barbara had never admitted it before.

Behind them, the house, and the mess, loomed, as bad as it had ever been and maybe worse. It was spreading over to Mimi's, and no matter what her mother said about being careful with the pies, that mouse said something different. It was lucky the pies had come from Patrick that week. But if Barbara could even acknowledge that the mess was a problem . . . the teenaged Mae had tried to talk to her mother about it. Of course she had. Why buy one more thing? Why keep it all? Why pile it up higher than Mae's head, why stack it in bathtubs until only one shower remained functional, why take every orphaned chair or abandoned magazine from the end of every driveway and bring it here to rest?

But Barbara, who was so open to Mae in every other way, shut down at every turn when it came to the house. Mae could beg, she could stand right in Barbara's face and scream herself hoarse, and

Barbara would just wait until she was finished and then walk away. Mae didn't know if Patti argued with her, didn't know if their father had ever tried to come back, didn't know if anyone else had ever tried to do a damn thing, but if they had, it hadn't helped. Barbara never alluded to the state of the house except to grow angry when challenged about it, but maybe that mouse, and Patches, meant Mae had a chance to get through to Barbara in a way she never could before. Maybe Barbara would listen. Maybe Mae could make this *Food Wars* thing go away and make things better for Barbara while she was here. And maybe Andy could keep Mimi's from being sucked under after Mae was gone, if he stuck around. But those were big maybes. As big as, if not bigger than, the one that waited for her back in Brooklyn.

They sat like that, staring out into the darkness, until Barbara broke the silence. "So, what do we have to do?"

Mae looked at her with surprise. She hadn't said they had to do anything, and she wasn't at all sure she could go through with Sabrina's plan, even though it was hard to see any other way out of this.

"For Sabrina," her mother said impatiently. "Obviously it doesn't do her any good to just trash things like this. What's she left with, then—Frannie's wins on a technicality? That's crap TV. She must want something."

"She does." Mae spoke slowly. "She wants me to help you clean it up."

"Oh."

"And not just me, like me your daughter. Mae Moore me. She means Mae Moore, organizational guru."

"She wants you to make me sparkle, then."

Mae didn't know if her mother meant to be funny, but she started to laugh, and once she started, she couldn't stop. She laughed, and she cried, and she leaned on Barbara, and Patches licked both of their faces, then bounced around them joyfully. Mae's stomach ached and her cheeks ached and she was covered in snot and tears, and the whole thing felt so bleak and hopeless that she wasn't sure why she was laughing at all. Barbara didn't laugh, but Mae could feel the lift of her chest as she smiled.

"Yeah. That's exactly it. She wants me to make you sparkle, Mom."

She could hear Aida's cane thumping toward them, and the door opened. They'd have to tell her what had happened. Mae scrambled up and dusted herself off, then extended a hand to her mother, still on the step, and after a moment Barbara took it.

Barbara's hand shook in hers, as it had before, and as Mae put another hand on her mother's elbow (because helping Barbara up wasn't easy), she realized that the tremor went back through her arm, and that her mother was somehow at once heavy and frail—and different. As she took her mother's weight, Mae's sense that something was wrong was so strong that she almost lost her grip, and although she managed to help her mother to her feet, she couldn't hide her reaction to Barbara's struggle. This was not the way Mae's mother was supposed to be. Everything was wrong already, but this was something so much bigger that it hollowed out Mae's chest, leaving her unable to breathe.

Aida, who in spite of a broken foot was nearly as strong and tough as she had always been, stepped quickly through the door to get behind Barbara, who took a visible moment to steady herself. The two older women exchanged looks, and then it was Mae who needed bracing. Something was happening to her mother, and now that she had tuned in to it, a dozen things she'd seen without registering them in the past few days dropped into place.

"What's wrong? What was that?"

Barbara let out a long breath. "You better come in and sit down, Mae. It's not that bad. It's not that great, either, but it's not that bad."

A minute before, Mae would have said the hardest thing for her to do would be to walk through the door into her mother's kitchen, but now she barely noticed the piles and boxes and ever-present faint smell of rot surrounding her. In that single instant, everything shifted. The only thing that mattered now was Barbara. Aida took a stool, and Barbara cleared a paper grocery bag off another for Mae to sit down, which she did impatiently. Mae had dozens of questions rushing through her head, each a separate and new fear—cancer, Alzheimer's—and she didn't dare ask a single one.

Barbara took her own stool and pulled a cup of cold coffee toward her, staring down into it as if reading tea leaves. "I've been having these symptoms," she said. "I get shaky. I'm stiff. I can't smell things like I used to." She stirred the coffee with the spoon that was still in it, and then just as Mae was about to snatch it away and demand that she get to the point, she did. "I've been to a doctor, and they can't say for certain, but their guess is early Parkinson's disease. Which doesn't kill you."

Aida took Mae's hand and held it between both of hers. "We looked it up," she said. "On the Internet. It might not even be terrible, Mae."

It might not even be terrible. That was her family all over. Most things were terrible, but maybe not this, not this time.

"What does it mean, then? What is it?"

Barbara reached into the grocery bag and took out one of the top papers from a huge pile, and Mae pictured the two women in the public library, printing page after page, poring over the results like rune stones. "Here's why I went to the doctor." She read aloud. "Shaking or tremor. Slowness of movement, called bradykinesia. Stiffness or rigidity of the arms, legs, or trunk. Trouble with balance and possible falls, also called postural instability." She looked up. "I have all those, a little."

"She also gets this look on her face," said Aida. "Like she's pissed off, even though she's not. Resting bitch face." Mae could tell she was proud of knowing the phrase.

"I don't know what comes next," said Barbara, looking down at the paper in her hand as though there were a script printed there. "It might not be much. Here. 'Parkinson's disease is sometimes referred to as a bespoke disease: each person experiences a different version. You cannot predict which symptoms will affect you or when and how that will happen. Some people wind up in wheelchairs; others still climb mountains. Some can't tie a scarf, while others weave scarves by hand.'"

Parkinson's disease. Disease, a disease. Not a death sentence, not one of the many horrors she'd been imagining, but the weight of her mother, her inability to help herself, and her great-aunt's immediate understanding told Mae that this was big, and not new, and not going away. She could tell her mother didn't want that to be true, so she tried to match Barbara's light tone even while the heaviness of what was happening threatened to sink her.

"Weaving and mountain climbing. Got it. That will be a change for you." *Or wheelchairs,* she thought but didn't say. Mae looked around the kitchen, trying to envision Barbara, debilitated, piloting her way through the narrow corridors among the boxes and furniture. It was hard enough to navigate this mess in perfect health. A wheelchair, a walker, even an unsteady gait—did Barbara know how much she was going to need Mae to clear the path in front of her? This would all have to go, and now Mae knew she would take her mother, hale and healthy and hoarding, over any changes that came like this.

"You can read it all. Or not." Barbara put the papers back in the bag and carefully set it down on the floor. "Anyway. It's fine. I mean, I've thought about it. I'll manage. I'll run Mimi's as long as I can. And then Andy will take over, because there's no one else." And there it was, the unsung chorus that had been playing ever since Mae first walked into Mimi's earlier that week, what she knew her mother wanted, and had wanted all along. She just hadn't known why.

"It would be easier if I lived here, wouldn't it?" Mae asked.

Her mother didn't answer, but Aida did. "Your mom doesn't want you to give up anything for her, Mae. She just wishes you *wanted* to come home, right?"

Barbara nodded, still looking away from them, and Mae realized her mother was crying. The only other time she had seen her cry was when Amanda was in the hospital with food poisoning, and the nurse, who had known Barbara for years, had been very direct about what had probably led to her sister's illness: bacteria in food that was too old, or stored wrong, probably old chicken her mother brought home from the restaurant and maybe left on the counter. That had been the last time Amanda ate chicken, Mae suddenly realized, and unwillingly her mind drifted to her sister. "Amanda doesn't know, does she?"

Her mother shook her head. "We don't—" She took another breath, a sharp one. "We don't talk a lot."

"You should," Aida said angrily. "I've always said this feud thing is ridiculous. What does it matter, a little fried chicken? It shouldn't get between families."

"Of course it gets between families," snapped Barbara. "She married Frannie's great-great-grandson! It's my job to keep Mimi's going, Aida, and that means protecting it from people who want to change it or shut it down, and the Pogociellos have been trying to do that for years. Just because you bailed on Mimi's doesn't mean I'm going to."

"Lightening up on Amanda isn't bailing on Mimi's, Barbara. It's your business. You can choose how to run it."

"Amanda—she chose her side," said Barbara, as if it hurt to say Amanda's name. "It's our business. Yours, mine, and Mae's. But it won't be for long, if we don't win this thing." She looked at Mae, then turned away. "Maybe it's time to just let it go."

"Let it go?" Sitting there in her mother's hot, overstuffed kitchen, windows closed, shades drawn, as they always were, Mae actually felt a chill like the one that sometimes came when Mimi, or

Mary Cat or Mary Margaret or whichever wicked old lady had stuck around, moved through her space. But this wasn't Mimi; this was her, Mae, hearing words her mother had never said and a possibility she had been trying to ignore. Mimi's had always been here, would always be here, because Barbara would always be here.

Barbara. Who might have Parkinson's, and who was now, uncharacteristically, dragging them toward talking about what that might mean. "But you're fine now," Mae said, a little frantic. "And you have Andy, and Mimi's is doing fine, and we're going to win. But even if we don't"—if hoarding house trumped recipe theft in some grand *Food Wars* rule book somewhere—"there are so many customers, Mom. People love Mimi's. You love Mimi's. It's part of Merinac. You can't just—why would you even say that?"

"There's a mortgage, Mae. A big mortgage. And people love Mimi's and yes there's Andy, but it's not enough. It's never quite enough. And when I die"—Mae and Aida started to protest, but Barbara kept talking, rolling right over them both, as though now that she had started, she couldn't stop—"when I go, you'll never be able to pay the death taxes. My mother was dead before she got to my age, Mae. She just dropped dead. Her mother, too. They went quick. I could go quick, and then, you don't know what it's like, Mae. When I came home and you girls were tiny, they took everything, all the cash plus money from everything I could sell, just to let me keep the place." Barbara sniffled, loud and hard, and put her hand into the bottom of an empty Kleenex box, then took a paper towel from the roll on the counter and wiped angrily at her face.

"They were always on us. Frank Pogociello wanted to buy the place and his friend owned the bank and I had to do a new mortgage, and every month it was *Can you make the payment?* It will be the same for you, Mae. I don't know how to make it not the same, I can't pay it off, and if anyone comes to inspect it for a new mortgage, the building isn't up to code, the house isn't up to code, you'll never be able to do everything that has to be done."

Aida, who must have known all this, sat quietly. Barbara turned away from both of them, pressing her hands up over her lips, staring out into the room as if she were looking at the past, while Mae felt pieces of her own past clicking into place. The scrimping and saving every week, her mother's hatred and almost fear of the Pogociellos. Even the piles of stuff that hemmed them into the increasingly tiny kitchen made more sense now. Maybe if you felt like your home could be ripped away at any minute—maybe if your whole world had already changed in an instant—maybe it made more sense to just hang on to everything.

And Barbara must have been carrying all that around with her for years, since her own mother died, since she came back and took over the house and the business and the two live old ladies, not to mention the dead one. Did Barbara feel her mother in the house the way they all felt Mimi? For Mae, the spirit of the house and Mimi's was a little sad, a little funny, occasionally a little creepy. But she had never really thought about how it felt for her mother to take on the responsibility for the whole thing when she was only in her twenties—more than a decade younger than Mae was now.

Mae knew what her mother was thinking even before she said it, because Mae was thinking it, too. "I needed this place, when we came back here, when Mom died," Barbara said. "I had to leave your father; I didn't finish school. Mimi's saved us. I was lucky to have it to come back to. But—you don't need it, Mae. And I don't think you want it."

Lucky to have it to come back to. On some level, that was what Mae had been feeling all week. What had initially felt like a trip to purgatory had come to feel like a journey to a refuge, a place where all the things that started out as fun before becoming mandatory elements of selling the Mae Moore brand didn't matter anymore. The social media posts, the pictures, the constant chatter—even with the omnipresent *Food Wars,* the noise of it all died away under the reality of running Mimi's, keeping the kids and Jessa busy, even the ongoing battle with Amanda, all very present and pressing things with surprisingly little foothold in the digital world.

When Mae saw the video of her mother's house online, the sudden re-intrusion of that chattery place with all of its rush to judgment had been as much of a shock as the revelation of this piece of her history itself. Sitting here now with Barbara and Aida, it was all gone again, or at least so distant that it didn't really matter. This was real life. She was proud of her book and the people she'd helped while she was writing it, but the rest—the whole person she had built online—was slipping away, and somehow she didn't mind much. All that was what she'd thought she wanted. Maybe she was wrong. How were you supposed to make good decisions if you didn't even know what you wanted?

"I think maybe I do need it," she said softly, then realized neither her mother nor Aida could hear her. She raised her voice. "I don't know, Mom. I don't think I'm quite ready to give up on Mimi's yet."

Her mother turned and looked straight into her eyes. "Does that mean you're giving up on something else?"

Jay. Jay was not distant. He'd been in her mind this whole time, she realized. Not the superficial Jay, the one who thought champagne would cure everything, but the underneath Jay, the one who cared enough to tell her they were toasting not her failure but her—their—ability to start again The man who missed his baseball mitt. The real Jay.

But no matter how great that real Jay was, he did not know who the real Mae was. Would he get that Mae? Barbara did. Aida did. Mimi's did. Amanda—might.

How could Amanda have not seen something was happening with Barbara, not told Mae, not been here trying to help her make things right? Yes, their mother was stubborn, and it probably wasn't entirely Amanda's fault that she and Barbara didn't talk much, but that didn't give Amanda a free pass. You didn't just walk away from someone you loved. It was time somebody reminded Amanda about that.

Mae's hand went to her phone, and Jay's message, still unanswered. Sometimes it was easier to fight with people than to fight for them. She stared up at the ceiling, blinking, and pressed her lips together until she was sure she could speak. "I'll figure it out, Mom." She sighed, then pushed herself off the barstool so hard it skidded back behind her. Enough of this. "Right now, we have cleaning to do."

AMANDA

As if everything turned on Amanda's mood, the night went downhill after Nancy left. Suddenly, no one wanted the cameras there. They avoided them, squirmed away, stopped conversations in midsentence while Sabrina and her crew persisted. "I don't want you to film the inside of my purse," Amanda overheard Mary Laura snap.

She was tired. Physically tired, but also that same tired she'd been trying to push away all that time ago when she wrote that first e-mail to *Food Wars*. Tired of every night at the hostess stand, tired of closing, tired of all the smiling and the sense that she was always on, part of so many families' traditions and yet feeling so rootless herself.

The drive home with a silent and angry Gus, Frankie scrolling through her phone, interspersing dramatic gasps and frantic typing with glares at Amanda, felt endless. She refused to touch her own phone again until they'd all gone to their separate corners of the house, and now, scanning Facebook, she wished she had left it off until morning.

Comments about the mouse and the pies and the likelihood that anyone who lived like that could run a clean restaurant should have been deeply satisfying to someone who had thought pretty much the same thing since she was ten years old, but Amanda mostly found it unsettling. There was just so much venom. How could people with nothing at stake produce so much passion?

And then, Patches.

People like this shouldn't be allowed to own a dog.

Someone get those puppies out of there!

I hope they called the Humane Society after they took this video.

Food Wars ought to be ashamed if those dogs are still in that house.

Amanda read every word, the pit in her stomach deepening. Sabrina's words stuck with her like a song you hated but just couldn't get out of your head. *You knew exactly what I would do. If you didn't want this out there, you wouldn't have told me.*

All she had wanted to do was even the playing field. Her sister had accused her of something Mae should know Amanda would never do. Why didn't Amanda get to tell about something Mae *did* do—or at least, something Mae didn't do? Mae left town years ago like her tail was on fire and barely came back, and when she did come back, she did nothing to improve conditions at Barbara's, even though it was her job to help people clean up their spaces. This was perfectly fair.

And it was true.

And she shouldn't have to feel bad.

When Amanda felt bad, she drew, and as she put the phone on the table, facedown, as though that would keep the mean comments about her mother contained, her other hand reached into her tote bag, rummaging for her sketchbook. Which wasn't there.

After a moment of panic, Amanda remembered. She'd shoved it in the junk drawer, of course. She got up to get it, already feeling the pencil between her fingers, but when she opened the drawer, the sketchbook was gone.

She yanked the drawer out of the bar, not caring that she spilled half the contents on the floor, and knelt, sticking her arm all the way back in. It must have gotten caught, stuck in the back of the drawer like sometimes happened with the piles of bills and mail she dropped into the drawer to get them out of sight, but there was nothing. Nothing in the drawer that remotely resembled a sketchbook. Nothing behind the drawer at all.

Amanda opened every drawer in the kitchen. She dumped out every basket of magazines from under the coffee table, scrutinized every cabinet, moved every pile, and then opened every drawer again. She knew where she put it, and it wasn't there anymore. It wasn't anywhere.

She gave up. Amanda took two of the Ambien left over from the prescription she'd never used up after Frank's death, added a whiskey chaser, put a pillow over her head, and went to sleep.

×

Seven hours later, she woke to a terrible taste in her mouth and a vague sense of foreboding that didn't get any better when she considered the day ahead. Her hand, as always, had gone to her phone almost before she was even awake. She had sent Nancy one text last night, asking her if they could talk, just one, although she had typed and deleted many more.

Nancy had finally replied.

I don't know what to say anymore, Amanda, I don't know how to fix this. I only know where I will be tomorrow—at your mother's, helping her get out of this mess, if she'll have me.

You'd better be there, too.

She would be, but she didn't have to like it. Angrily, Amanda dragged herself out of the bed, leaving its twisted sheets and fallen pillows strewn across the floor, pulled on a sloppy T-shirt and cutoff shorts that Frankie had somehow missed in her sweeping condemnation and purge of Amanda's wardrobe, and stomped out of the house without even bothering with coffee. It wasn't going to help.

A different Amanda would have driven her car in the opposite direction. Instead, she parked down the road and walked slowly toward everything she most wanted to avoid. By the time she reached Mimi's, half of her mother's house appeared to be out on the front lawn.

Half of the house, and half of the town. None of these people had ever lifted a finger to help when the girls were little and so caught up in Barbara's mess. None of them had done more than offer a pat on the arm and maybe a casserole when Frank died. Now, here were the Russells, and Pinky Heckard, and Crystal Kennedy, carrying bags and boxes, trotting in and out the front door as though there were no more natural thing in the world, when Amanda could barely remember that door being used over the course of her entire lifetime. As she watched, Morty Rountree's wife backed a pickup into the driveway, and Morty threw a box up into it. There they all were, cleaning out the house as though that, too, was nothing unusual. Just hauling three decades' worth of crap out of the town haunted house, you know. Like you do. This must have been Mae's doing, and Amanda didn't like it.

Nancy had to be there somewhere, but Amanda didn't see her, and wasn't sure she wanted to, anyway. Amanda walked around to the back of the house because going in through that front door would just be too weird, and found herself with a perfect view of her sister, holding court in the kitchen, surrounded by acolytes awaiting her bidding. There was a shout of laughter, and Amanda could see Mae framed in the glass of one of the windows over the sink and the camera in the other. Kenneth was on one side of her sister, Patrick on the other. All three looked delighted with themselves. Mae, laughing. The camera, fawning.

This was what Mae got? Years of letting everything pile up without lifting a polished professional finger to help her own mother and now she looked like a Disney princess, basking in the sunshine streaming through the windows amid happy laughter from the crowd? How could anyone just let Mae give the orders when Mae had been part of the problem, giving up on Barbara as soon as she herself could get away? This was total bullshit. After decades in this town, Amanda had shit to show for it. Mae was back for ten minutes, and she was running the place. No matter how hard Amanda tried, Mae seemed to come out on top.

On second thought, she would go in through the front door. Anything to avoid Mae. She went back around the house and walked straight in, and was instantly punished for her boldness. She nearly collided with Barbara, who held a box in her arms and was followed by Andy, arms fully loaded with clothes on hangers, a coatrack perched precariously on top. Barbara stopped short, and Andy, too close behind, nearly ran her down.

"Amanda!" She put down her box and put both hands on her hips, facing her daughter. "Good." Amanda faced her mother, waiting. "We're just getting started in your old room. I know a bunch of this junk is yours; now you can decide what you want to take with you." With that, she picked up the box and set it off to the side with a pile of similar boxes, then turned and marched back into the house.

That was not the reception Amanda had expected. With no one else there to turn to, Amanda shot a confused glance at Andy. Did she know Amanda had told? She couldn't. Or about the recipe? Amanda struggled to frame a question. "She doesn't—"

"Know about the recipe?" His voice was flat, as if he was being carefully neutral. "Or that you're responsible for all of this? No. Don't ask me why not, but your sister said not to tell her, and so far no one has."

That made no sense. Why wouldn't Mae tell her? It could hardly make things worse, and might even make Mae look better, so why not just go all in? Amanda shrugged and strode through the door and up the front stairs. She wasn't going to bother trying to figure out Mae now. Her old room was about the last place she wanted to go, but her feet took her there regardless, until she stood in the doorway, loath to go further.

This had been her room, shared for years with Mae until one day her sister declared herself done with sharing. Mae being Mae, she'd forcefully cleaned out the room next door, packing its contents into other rooms and closets that already seemed so stuffed that adding things was unthinkable, then dragging what she wanted into the newly empty space. Mae's move had inspired Amanda, and Mae took pity on her and helped her clear out Amanda's now-solo room.

Mae bought a lock for her own door with money earned from tips at Mimi's—which she had also fought for the right to keep—not to lock herself in but to lock their mother out. Amanda, though, had been helpless when faced with Barbara, who was soon filling the room again, adding things "just to get it out of the way" or "because I thought you could use it." Amanda had felt a little special then, like she was more part of her mother's world than Mae. After Mae moved out, Amanda thought that maybe Barbara would talk to her like she did Mae, teach her to do the cooking like Mae had, sit with her out on the patio after work. But she never asked, and Barbara took over cooking again, staying late to clean the kitchen after Amanda was done behind the counter. Amanda had never fried a piece of chicken in her life, and she never would, and at this point that was fine by her.

Barbara's increasing distance had made the welcome Frank's family offered feel even warmer. In Nancy's house, she found what she'd been missing, even when Mae was home—people who were interested, encouraging, who listened when she spoke, congratulated her successes, supported her few failures. She loved Frank, with his earnest approach to school, the sweet way he finally, after she'd nudged it near him for so long, took her hand at the movies, but oh, she had loved Nancy and Daddy Frank too, basking in their approval. When they were first married, she and Frank lived with his parents. Amanda had little room for things she'd left behind and, once she realized Barbara wasn't letting her back into the restaurant, very little desire to go back for them. Now, standing in the doorway, she surveyed the few things left from her pre-Nancy life. Old track shoes. Flip-flops. Some books, a boom box, and a stack of CDs.

Well, hell. Those old running shoes were completely cool again now. She took a deep breath and entered the room, picking up the shoes and trying not to look around or be caught by her memories. Maybe Frankie wanted the books. Or Gus could laugh at the CDs. How could they never have been in here with her? Even Frank had never come in.

Gulping back a sob, Amanda stared at the floor, trying to concentrate on a stain in the old rug. Was it any wonder she always felt like two totally different people, the before Amanda and the after Amanda? And now—she didn't feel like either, and these track shoes wouldn't help. This was pointless, and it hurt like hell, and she wasn't going to do it anymore.

Amanda rushed out of the room, nearly knocking Andy over on the stairs, blinded by the tears she wasn't able to hold back. He caught her by the shoulders, and she yanked herself away. "Sorry," he said, then, looking at her more closely: "It's okay. Sorry. Just— catch your breath."

She gulped, and snorted, an ugly great sniff that she didn't help at all by wiping her face with the arm holding the dusty sneakers, and started past him, but he stopped her, putting a quick hand on her shoulder again, then yanking it away.

"You might want to wait," he said, gesturing down the stairs. "It's—there are a lot of people down there." He smiled, a weak, dubious smile. "Um, you a runner, then?" He pointed to the sneakers, still in her hand, and it was all Amanda could do not to slap him across the face with them. Anybody downstairs was better than standing here with him. She didn't answer, just kept going, but at least she didn't feel like crying anymore. She was just pissed. Why the hell was he even trying to be friendly?

Amanda did not feel friendly. Not toward Andy, or Barbara, or Sabrina, or even Nancy. She felt tricked and ambushed and as if every single person in that house—no, in this town—was out to get her, and if they weren't yet, they would be, once they heard everything Mae and Andy were saying. Everybody was all in for Mae, back home in all her glory, and everybody was ready to toss Amanda out with these stupid shoes. Nancy, too. Nancy made her come here, and Nancy had run out on her last night at Frannie's when all Amanda had ever tried to do was help. Fuck Frannie's. Fuck Mimi's. Fuck them all.

Andy's question flashed back through Amanda's mind. Was she a runner? Not today. Today she was a fighter. *Make me look like a bitch, Sabrina, and I'll give you a bitch.*

When one of Sabrina's camerapeople met her at the bottom of the stairs, she didn't hesitate. "What do I think of it? I think it's disgusting, same as you." Out of the corner of her eye, she could see her mother coming toward her, but she didn't let that stop her. "It sucked to live here, and I left the minute I could. Wouldn't you?"

Sabrina appeared, inevitable microphone in hand. "But you live five minutes away. Haven't you tried to help?"

"My mother doesn't want my help," Amanda said. "Never did. She was as glad to see me go as I was to leave." The times Barbara had helped her, especially after Frank died, Amanda pushed out of her mind. "I'll help now because anybody would. But you all are so upset about dogs living here—think about being a kid in this." It felt so good to finally say that, to finally have someone to listen, even if everyone did seem to think this whole cleanup was some kind of goddamn picnic. "Think about what that was like. And you know, we can clean it up, but she won't change. The dogs will be lost or poisoned or something within six months. But fine, try. I won't stop you. I'll even help. But it's pointless."

Amanda marched off with her running shoes, brushing past Barbara without looking at her, and threw them on a random pile—if there was some system here, she didn't know it—then marched back in, refusing to acknowledge anyone as she passed them. She had said what needed to be said, and she was done. Who the hell cared, anyway? This would all be over soon, *Food Wars* would leave, her mother would fill the house again, Andy would find some much better job in some much better town, Mae would go back to Brooklyn, Gus would go to college, if they could just find some money, and she and Frankie would be here, working at Frannie's unless Nancy threw them out, and if she did, well, Amanda was a good hostess. She'd find work. All that other crap, drawing, writing—she'd been stupid to ever waste her time on it. This was real life, right here, and it sucked.

She made herself a machine, reciting her every move to keep her mind from doing anything else. *In, get box, out. In, get pile of clothing, out. In, figure out how to wrestle chair down the stairs, out. In, two boxes this time, try to see around them to get down the stairs.*

And then there was Mae, standing on the front porch, blocking her way. Amanda shifted the boxes up in her arms. "Move, Mae. These are heavy." Why wasn't she carrying anything, anyway? "Go get some boxes yourself if you don't believe me. You look too clean to be doing any real work."

Mae did look clean. Clean and cute, with her dark braids and her red-striped T-shirt and her freckles. And she wasn't moving. Amanda shifted her weight and tried to kick her sister in the shins. "Come on, get out of my way."

"Why don't you get out of everybody's way? Put the stupid boxes down and just go? You're just"—she glanced at the camera that had inevitably appeared when Mae did—"screwing everything up. I had

Mom feeling fine about this and you just about destroyed her, just now, with whatever you said about growing up here. She's off crying, and I don't know how to fix that, but having you here isn't going to help. So you should go."

Amanda had cooled off a little since snapping at the camera, but Mae's words lit her right back up again. Mae felt the same way, and she knew it. It wouldn't hurt Barbara to hear the truth about what it had been like to be them as kids. It wouldn't hurt anybody to hear a little truth.

"I wouldn't be here if Nancy hadn't told me to come—and you wouldn't be here, either, if you could help it. You hate this place as much as I do. More, even. You never stop running away from it. It's all you ever do—run from this mess. Mom might as well know it."

"But I don't hate her, and apparently you do. I don't know what you said, but you crushed her, and that's the last thing she needs." Again, Mae glanced at the camera, and this time she lowered her voice and hissed in Amanda's ear, grabbing her arm. "Can you not see that she's sick? And she doesn't want anyone to know?"

Amanda shook Mae off. This was total typical-Mae bullshit, designed to shut Amanda up and get her to do what Mae wanted, and Amanda wasn't buying it. "Anyone can see she's sick!" Amanda dumped the boxes, as close to Mae's feet as she could, making her sister jump back, and waved her arm around the living room. "She's obviously sick! And she's always been sick and she'll always be sick and cleaning out this shit won't change her. She'll just make it even worse, and you'll go back to Brooklyn, and eventually she'll die in her filth, and I'll be the one to find her, because I'm here and you're not. *You're* the one who should go, Mae, because you're just doing this for the cameras. Why don't you take off your clothes next? You're good at that. Just strip for the camera and keep everybody's eyes on you, where you want them."

Mae stepped over the boxes and shouted in Amanda's face. "Well, apparently you'd sleep with anybody just to win this thing.

And you're wrong, Amanda. About everything. I'm here, and I'm staying, because somebody has to really be here, and you're about as useless as a two-legged stool. So *you* get out." She grabbed Amanda and pushed her out onto the porch. "Just go draw your stupid chickens and let me do the real work."

Amanda caught her balance just as she came down the first step and yelled back into the doorway at her sister. "You don't work, Mae. You just tell everybody else to work, and you're about as likely to stay here as I am to fly. The minute there's nothing in it for you, you'll be out of here so fast we'll see dust."

"Oh, I'm not lying. And at least I don't have to cheat and steal recipes and throw myself at every man in sight trying to win a game I don't even understand." Mae stepped out onto the porch and lowered her voice to a hiss. "And Mom is really sick. I don't mean the house. But clearly you don't give a shit, and that's fine. I can take care of Mom. I don't need you, I don't want you, and she doesn't either."

There were more cameras on the porch, Amanda suddenly saw, and Sabrina, too. And—

"Mom?" Gus, standing next to Frankie, was calling to her from the yard. Nancy was hurrying toward her, too, coming up the stairs to the porch.

"Amanda," Nancy yelled, "Amanda, stop this right now. Just stop." When Nancy reached her, panting a little, she grabbed Amanda's arm. "You're embarrassing yourself."

Amanda pulled her arm away. *She* was embarrassing herself? What about Mae? And what did Mae mean, about Barbara being sick? Barbara was fine; she was exactly the same as she had always been. Mae just needed to get the last word, and fine, she could have it.

It was absolutely time to get out of here. Amanda pushed past Nancy and ran down the steps, holding back tears. Frankie grabbed at her, but she shook her head. "Just give me a minute, please, honey."

Her feet knew where to go; she had run this way so many times. She turned—for God's sake, why was there actually a crowd watching this madness—and ran into a lanky man holding Mae's kids, with straight black hair just like Ryder's, staring at Amanda like he knew her as she headed for the familiar old path, for the tree that wasn't there, for anywhere but here. She had to get away, and sit, and just think, away from the cameras and everything else.

About three steps later it clicked. *Jay*. That was Jay. And Mae had just announced that she was staying in Kansas. Not that Amanda cared anymore, but maybe things weren't so perfect for Mae after all.

MAE

Jay?

Unexpectedly, her first reaction was a rush of the same excitement that would shoot through her whenever she saw him back in their first months of dating, when the only thing she could think of was her amazement that they had found each other and that she was somehow making this work. Today, that joy was immediately quenched by dread. What was he doing here, in the yard full of three decades of hoarded trash and junk?

Sabrina was pointing to him, and one camera followed her finger while the other stayed on Mae, its gaze, like Jay's, holding her frozen. How could she possibly explain any of this—the house, the way she'd just shoved Amanda across the porch like some battling real housewife, the announcement she'd just shouted at her sister—with Sabrina and her *Food Wars* cameras hanging on every word? Jay would just shut the cameras down, but her mother needed this *Food Wars* win for Mimi's so much more than Mae had realized. Mae had to carry this off, and Jay had to go along with her. Did he even know this was her mother's house? How on earth did he get here?

From behind her, Mae heard the thud of Aida's cane. "You girls need to quit fighting and get back to work," her great-aunt called as she came through the front door. "Your mother—" She stopped short as she found herself on what amounted to a stage, and the hand that wasn't holding the cane floated up to touch her hair as she straightened and smiled. Aida knew how to play her part; that was for certain.

And Mae would play hers. *Forget the fight with Amanda, pretend that never happened, cut, new scene.* Mae rushed down the stairs and threw her arms around Jay, so tall, so thin—was he even thinner than when she'd left him? It was both exactly what she wanted to do and the scariest thing she had ever done, because what if he pulled away? What if he just held her off coldly, looking around at the mess, then recoiled and walked off? "Please, just listen," she breathed in his ear, smelling the peppermint shampoo he favored and feeling the soft bristle of that spot right in front of his ear that he never quite got shaved right. She kissed him, really meaning it, and felt him respond, lips on hers, arms softening around her just a little, then straighten. It was incredibly good to feel him in her arms again, but as he began to pull away, she felt an icy panic in her throat. If she let him react to any of what had just happened, this might be her last shot at that feeling.

Mae knew exactly what she wanted now. She wanted Jay to throw himself in with her like Patrick had with Kenneth, to take this on and dig in and make it work. But she didn't have any right to expect it of him, or even ask, at least not until she let Jay see the house and the place that had made her. And she was going to have to do that in front of the trailing cameras, which he would hate, and after she'd just shouted an ultimatum right in his face, exactly the way she would have least wanted him to hear her plans. *I'm here, and I'm staying* . . . But she had plans, and they were good plans. Jay would want this; he really would. If he would just hear her out. If they could just get that far.

Madison and Ryder shared none of these conflicting feelings. They were delighted to have both Mommy and Daddy again. Ryder, who was on Jay's hip, reached for Mae with his arms while sticking tight to Jay with his legs. Madison, apparently feeling low on the totem pole, stood on Mae's foot to reach up to them both.

Mae took Jay's hand, and Madison's, and started to walk, and to her relief, he accepted her unspoken invitation, although he didn't return the pressure of her fingers. *Pretend you expected him, pretend this is all going perfectly and maybe it somehow will.* "Let me show you what's going on," she said. "First, you remember my aunt Aida." Aunt Aida, who knew better than anyone the facade Mae had created for her life in New York, who had gracefully maneuvered Barbara around Mae and Jay's wedding. "Aida deserves even more Hollywood greatness," Mae explained, "but in light of the studio's preference for casting women forty years younger than the roles they're playing, she's decided to come home and boss us all around." Aida put one hand up to each of Jay's cheeks and kissed him firmly, and Mae knew she saw him smile as he let go of Mae's hand to give Aida a one-armed hug. No one could resist Aida.

She took his hand again, and this time, she felt him holding hers. A tiny bit of her tension slipped away, but as they moved up to the porch and through the front door. Mae saw her mother's house through Jay's eyes. Things she'd accepted since she was a kid became painfully obvious—the tottering stacks of old newspapers and bags and boxes of dollar-store crap that were still everywhere even with the helpers carting box after box away, yes, but also the faded and peeling wallpaper, the water stains where the porch and house rooflines met, the outright dirt and grime on floors and stairs that hadn't been cleaned during her lifetime. Beyond that was the smell—the combined odors of decaying food, dog shit, unwashed laundry and humans and, the grown-up Mae now knew, an unpumped septic system. She saw Jay's face as he took it in and felt in him that physical lurch she had seen in everyone who had come in for the first time that day. Madison and Ryder seemed oblivious to it, their focus on something else entirely. "You have to come see the puppies," Madison squealed, running ahead, and Ryder squirmed down from his father's arms.

"Hang on," Jay said, and something in his voice stopped both children, who looked at him uncertainly. "I'm talking to Mommy now," he said, and Mae could hear him lightening his tone at their reaction. He smiled at Madison and leaned down to scoop Ryder back into his arms, and as he did, his eyes met Mae's, unreadable. He might have reassured Madison and Ryder, who came back and leaned against his legs, but Mae had never felt more vulnerable.

She met his eyes. "This is my mother's house," she said clearly. "This is where I grew up." She wouldn't explain why that needed to be said to her husband of seven years. Let *Food Wars* deal with it. She turned, heading through the passage, knowing that with the cameras trailing them both, he would have to follow her into the kitchen and the back room, the main room. Was the disgust she thought she saw in his eyes for the house, or for her? "And if you saw the puppies on Facebook, this is where they were born, but they're outside now while we clean it up."

She thought Jay might be trying not to breathe through his nose, so she took pity on him and led him out the back door, not rushing, making sure he had time to see the kitchen, still overflowing with dishes and bags and debris, before emerging onto the porch, which once would have been a refuge from the mess but was now filled with things from the cleanup.

She wanted to look at him, but she couldn't. Instead, she pressed her lips together, taking quick breaths. She would not cry. "We're taking everything out of the house, so it's going to take a while," she said. "Mom hasn't been able to throw anything away. Ever. She's always been like this. The house has always been like this. But she's ready now, she says." This time, she turned to face him, wanting to be sure he heard her, but his face was turned away, pressed into Ryder's shirt and the scent of lavender from the sachets Mae kept in their suitcases.

Why hadn't she seen before that in Jay, messed up by his parents in a totally different way when they'd split him from his sister and raised them in two separate but equally weird households, she had found someone else who could at least understand how deep the wounds your parents left you with ran? The grown-up Mae knew it wasn't Barbara's fault, exactly, especially now that she understood more about how her mother felt about the house, about Mimi's, about her tenuous hold on the things that mattered most to her.

But that didn't mean some part of Mae didn't share Amanda's resentment, or that she didn't still wish that Barbara, so strong in so many ways, could have just gotten her act together on this one. She had spent too long keeping those feelings tucked away all neat and clean inside.

She waited until Jay looked up again, and then, as their eyes met, she let her anger from the past come through to the person she knew he was inside, once a kid like her, equally confused and betrayed by the ways of grown-ups, equally determined to do better. "She wants to make a better home for the dogs."

He got it, at least. She knew it instantly. There was the Jay she married, her Jay, right there with her. His eyes widened and she saw, at the corners of his lips, the hesitant start of a smile. She was so relieved that she smiled back, first a little, then fully, knowing she was giving him permission to express what she herself was feeling.

"Your mother is cleaning this up"—he looked around, back into the sliding door, through the kitchen windows, at the boxes and bags and piles at his feet—"for the dogs."

"For the dogs, yes." Mae kept her face straight but let her eyes speak to his, and Jay laughed, and suddenly Mae could laugh, too. This was what she had been missing, someone to share this with, someone to see what was funny on top of tragic and push her to see it, too.

Jay set Ryder down on a table someone had carried out, and Madison tugged at her father. "I want to show you the puppies," she said. "I'm getting the girl one, she has spots but she is mostly white like snow and I'm calling her Elsa."

Ryder stomped, causing the table, which was none too stable, to wobble. He grabbed at Jay, who scooped Ryder up and held him. "No," he said, pushing his hands on his father's chest and struggling to get down. "Boy ones. Blackie and Spotty and Potato Chip. I'm having five." He, too, took his father's hand and started pulling him.

Would Jay know she'd never say yes to a dog at all and certainly not without his agreeing to it? He seemed unworried by this unplanned addition to his household, but Mae was far from ready to relax. Jay got what she was saying about Barbara, but could he see how much she wanted him to get her as well?

Jay, too, didn't seem ready to walk away from this moment, but between the cameras and the kids, they were fully stymied. "Hang on," he said again to Ryder and Madison, and although neither let go of his hands, they did lessen their tugging. As if Mae had conjured her, Jessa emerged from the front of the house.

"Want to go with Jessa, guys?" Mae suggested. "Maybe get the puppies ready to see Daddy?"

Madison looked scornfully at her mother. "You can't pick them up. Only touch them. Okay, Daddy? Gentle touch."

Jessa held out her hands. "But we can go make sure Patches is taking good care of them," she said. Neither Madison nor Ryder budged, and Jessa caught Mae's eye. Mae shrugged. They could all recognize kids who weren't going to be persuaded, and there was no point in causing a scene—well, more of a scene. The echo of her shouted fight with Amanda, witnessed by Jessa and Jay and everyone in the known universe, lingered. Enough scenes, then. "Okay, Daddy will go with you. But can I give him a hug first? I missed Daddy, too."

Did Jay believe her? She still didn't know why he had appeared, or how much of a chance he was willing to give her. She stepped in close to him, close enough to smell him, and hugged him with her entire body, ignoring the cameras, letting her hips melt toward his. His lips were on her ear, but he didn't say anything, although he did hold her, briefly, before letting her go and bending down to Madison so that she could not see his face.

"So, this is your town." His eyes were still on his daughter's head, and again Mae couldn't read him. But there was only one answer.

"This is my town."

"And that's Mimi's." He pointed at the old building, freshly painted but still unprepossessing, and like the house, Mae saw it with new and disappointed eyes.

"That's Mimi's. And Amanda works at Frannie's, the other one. She has ever since she married Frank, before we met. That's part of why this makes a good Food War. You know, sisters. Fighting."

"Yeah, I got that." He let Madison and Ryder begin to pull him away.

"Wait—" she said. But she wasn't sure what to ask him, what she wanted from him now, how to say even part of what needed to be said with the cameras rolling. "What do you, um, want to do after you see the puppies? I mean, obviously I'll be here for a while."

Jay looked back at the house, looked it up and down, then turned to Mae as the kids tugged at him. She wanted a smile, a nod, anything, so badly. "It looks like you could use another set of hands," he said, and she clung to the little streak of hope in those words. "I'll hang out with the kids for a bit, and then I'll come help."

Help. She had never wanted his help more, but that wasn't really the problem, and Mae knew it. The problem was that she had never before asked for his help at all.

"I'd like that," she said softly, then more loudly as he kept walking away. "Please. Thank you."

Jay took a few steps more forward before he turned and looked over his shoulder again. "And then we'll talk," he said, and he wasn't laughing or meeting Mae's gaze.

"Yeah," she said, holding herself very still, trying to show him that she was open to whatever he could give. "Then we'll talk."

AMANDA

Snuffling wildly, Amanda walked with what she hoped looked like determination toward the path down to the river, bringing up the edge of her T-shirt to wipe her face and blow her nose. Gross, maybe, but there was no one to see, and as she came up to the fallen giant that had been her and Mae's secret tree when they were kids, she thought of the argument she and Mae had had just a few days earlier, when they were still speaking, before everything started to go so far wrong.

Maybe the tree didn't make a noise. Maybe nothing ever made a noise. Maybe nobody ever heard anything unless it was broadcast to the entire world, which meant that Amanda's whole life now amounted to about an hour of bad behavior and the failed one-night stand she didn't have with the only guy she'd even thought about since Frank, a guy who now thought she was not just needy and desperate but a liar and a thief as well.

As she stood there, breathing heavily and pressing her fist into her lips, she heard footsteps behind her, and Nancy's voice, calling.

"Amanda? Are you out here?"

Small trees and tall weeds had grown over the path in the years since it had been in regular use, and Amanda turned to see Nancy holding a particularly prickly growth out of her way, then releasing it behind her. She looked wildly out of place, her neatly pressed slacks and buttoned blouse far more mussed by pushing her tiny frame through the weeds than they had been by anything Barbara's house had to offer. Amanda's own clothes, she realized, were speckled with the seeds and burrs that clung to anything they touched, and one arm was scratched. She'd come through the brush without even noticing.

"What is wrong with you? What was that?" Nancy was breathing heavily, but her fierce energy did not appear to be depleted. She put her hands on her hips, staring intently at Amanda.

"You said it yourself," Amanda said. "You don't know what to say to me. I've gone too far. I've ruined everything."

"Amanda—" Nancy shook her head and stood there, looking at her, and Amanda looked back, her tears coming again. Nancy held her arms open, and Amanda, after a minute, took the two steps toward her mother-in-law, the best mother she had ever had, and fell into them, crying.

Nancy held her, patting, stroking her hair. "I was angry last night. I'm still angry. Maybe I don't know what to say. But it doesn't matter. I'm still here. And we will figure this out. But you have to back down, honey. You want to win. I get it. But you've gone way overboard. It's not worth destroying your relationship with your mother and your sister."

"What relationship? Mae's ruined everything. All that stuff she says—I didn't do any of it!" It was a relief to say it, even if no one would ever believe her after everything she actually *had* done.

"This isn't about Mae," Nancy said firmly. "Stop—" She held up a hand as Amanda started to protest. "This isn't who you are, Amanda. Mae's not your problem."

Furious, Amanda twisted away and kicked up the dirt and dust on the path. "Of course she is! Ever since she got here it's been all about Mae. It's the goddamn Mae show. And then—all she does is wave a hand, and the whole town shows up to clean Mom's house."

Nancy touched Amanda's arm and gently turned her back around. "That was me, not Mae," she said. "I called Kenneth and Patrick last night and asked them to post something asking for help. For your mother. And for me. And for you. It wasn't Mae at all.

But if you're looking for someone to blame here, that producer is the one pushing your buttons. And you're giving her exactly what she wants, every time."

"I know she is," Amanda said, more quietly. Nancy's refusal to respond to her anger in kind always forced her to moderate, and Nancy's refusal to enter into the *Food Wars*–fueled renewal of the old feud should have helped make Amanda more reasonable. But she really did not want to be reasonable. "I mean, I see that now. I'm not dumb. But Mae—Mae—she—"

"Marcia, Marcia, Marcia," said a familiar voice. Picking her way even more carefully through the unfamiliar foliage, Sabrina stepped over a fallen branch and was suddenly standing next to Amanda. "I've got something you need to see, Jan Brady."

Nancy put an arm around Amanda again. "There's your pusher, Amanda. That's who you're reacting to. Not Mae." She looked straight at Sabrina. "I hope you're happy."

Sabrina, wholly unchastened, grinned. "I'm always happy. Here you go, Amanda. This did not go as planned, not one bit. Which is exactly why you need to see it." She held her phone out to Amanda. "Press play."

Amanda rolled her eyes. "I seriously don't care, Sabrina," she said. There was absolutely nothing to do with *Food Wars* that she wanted. Not now. Maybe not ever, and the sight of Sabrina, perfectly made up, dark hair all neatly in place, smiling all the way up to her ridiculously big brown eyes, just made Amanda want to bite someone. And Sabrina obviously was part of the problem. Not as big a part as Mae, but still.

"Yeah, yeah, yeah. You'll care. Watch."

Amanda reluctantly took the device, which had a hot pink cover with "gorgeous" written in flowing gold script across the back. Mary Laura's face appeared first on the screen. "No way," she said, and the clip cut to Gwennie, who said, "Huh?" Faces flashed quickly by, all shaking their heads or scoffing at something: Patrick, Tony

Russell, his wife, every single waitress from Frannie's. Mary Laura returned, frowning, and you could hear Sabrina's voice saying, "The chef at Mimi's says Amanda stole their recipe to use to win *Food Wars*."

In the video, Mary Laura answered her angrily. "There is no way Amanda would do something like that. Mae, maybe. You sure you didn't make a mistake?"

Then Kenneth: "There's no way she'd take Mimi's recipe. This is a girl who once found the answers to a biology test on the teacher's desk and made me drive her to the teacher's house so she could give them to her and explain."

Even Zeus, the dishwasher at Mimi's, who had a child in Frankie's class. He looked intently at the camera. "You better be careful. That's a serious thing to say. She would never do a thing like that. She's a real good person, Amanda."

And finally there was Andy, shaking his head. "I tasted the chicken. I know it's the same. But Amanda— No, I'd never have believed it if you'd told me. I still can't—" He looked away from the camera. "Look, I'm pretty upset about this. Just go away. It's a game to you, but it's not a game to me."

Amanda hadn't realized she was holding her breath until she let it out in one long exhale. Her first thought—*They all know?*—was slowly replaced by a little warmth growing inside her.

"I could not find one person in this entire town who believed you'd steal that recipe," Sabrina said. "I couldn't even find anyone who believed you'd get a parking ticket, basically, unless your meter expired while you were rescuing a kitten from a tree. Not one, not even our hero, the hunky chef, or anyone else at Team Mimi's. So. I'll send it to you. You can watch it whenever you feel like shit."

Amanda handed the phone back to Sabrina. Her relief was like a balloon. She felt as if it could lift her right off this little trail and up into the sky. Sabrina might have believed Amanda was a thief—who knew if she believed anything? The chefs maybe. But nobody else. Or almost nobody. "Mae believes it," she said.

"Yep. And I'm still going to have to do something about it," Sabrina said. "Can't just leave it hanging out there. Simon and Cary both agreed with Andy—they were pretty embarrassed they hadn't spotted it, actually—and of course it's not like Mae's going to let it go."

It wasn't over, then. Amanda's relief evaporated as Nancy, who'd been listening to them both as if waiting for the conversation to make sense, finally spoke. "Wait. What recipe?"

"The chicken recipe," said Sabrina. "I don't know how, but you season your fried chicken exactly the way Mimi's does. Somewhere along the line, somebody ripped off the recipe, and Amanda's suspect number one, thanks to her little dalliance with Andy the other night. But nobody really thinks she'd do a thing like that. So"—she shrugged—"you be the judge."

Nancy knew that, though— No. Amanda could tell from Nancy's face that she hadn't known, and that didn't make any sense at all. But what really didn't make sense was that Nancy didn't look one bit surprised.

Instead, she laughed. "The seasoning? Seriously? That's what's going on here?" Nancy leaned forward and grabbed Amanda's hand.

"Come with me," she said, and spun them both toward Mimi's and Barbara's house. "I can clear this up."

Sabrina put her phone away and turned to them, an interested look on her face. Amanda would have sworn that her ears perked up.

"Not you," Nancy said. "I meant what I said about you. You've been pushing buttons all along, Sabrina, and you don't get to push this one."

Sabrina looked at her. "I could hold you to your contract, you know. You have to let me film if I want to, or we can void the whole thing."

"Your contract also says we don't have to reveal trade secrets," Nancy said.

Sabrina appeared a little taken aback, and Nancy laughed again. She almost seemed to be enjoying this, and now Amanda was even more confused.

"What, did you think I didn't read it?" Nancy said. "I've had enough of you, Sabrina. I think we've all had about enough. You're in too far with us, anyway. You won't leave. You'll find out soon enough, but you're not coming now." She gave Amanda's hand a little tug, then let go. "Come on. The city slicker can find her way out, I'm sure. And don't look like that. I can't help whatever else is going on with you, with Mae and Andy and all the rest, but this recipe-stealing business? That I can fix."

×

Amanda raced after Nancy and flung herself into the passenger seat of her mother-in-law's little hatchback. Nancy threw the car into reverse, turned it, and spun out of the Mimi's parking lot, driving fast, a determined expression on her face. Amanda, though, needed to slow down. She had had enough of feeling like she was on a Tilt-A-Whirl gone mad, and wherever they were going could wait. Had to wait. As they left Main Street behind, she reached out and put a hand on Nancy's arm. "Could you stop for a second?"

"I know you didn't steal the recipe," Nancy said. "I can prove it."

"But that's not the only thing that's wrong," Amanda said. "If you didn't know about this last night—why were you so angry? Where are we going? And—Andy—I need to explain."

Nancy pulled off, a little too suddenly, at a spot on the road where the shoulder widened a little, a pull-off for balers and hay wagons to head into the fields that lined either side of the road. She answered the easiest question first. "We're going to Frannie's," she said to Amanda. "And I was angry about your mother, of course.

Still am. I can't believe you'd hang her out to dry like that, no matter how she's treated you."

"Mae said I stole the recipe for the seasoning on the chicken," Amanda said. "On camera. In front of everyone. Andy said"—she hated even saying his name—"Andy said he tasted it yesterday, and now Frannie's chicken is exactly the same as Mimi's—and he says it wasn't like that before. I didn't plan to tell them about Mom. I was just so angry." Amanda prepared herself for the next question: *But how would they think you got the recipe out of Mimi's?* She would have to admit it, that she had been in there, with Andy. *Dallying,* as Sabrina put it.

But Nancy didn't ask the next question. Instead, she gripped the steering wheel and stared out into the flat Kansas sunlight. "I should have known there was more to it," she said. "You wouldn't do that without what felt like a good reason, and that part is my fault. You don't need to explain. I do. But it's easier to show you."

Amanda didn't know how to respond to that. What was there for Nancy to explain? Needing something to focus on, she flipped her phone over in her lap, and there it was, the message from Sabrina, with the video. *Watch it whenever you feel like shit,* she'd said, but it wasn't going to help the way Amanda was feeling right now.

No one was angry at her. Even Nancy, it seemed, was ready to believe Amanda was just a victim of circumstance. She had a clear path back to her job, her family—everything she had been beating herself over the head for risking for the past twenty-four hours.

But Nancy was wrong. Amanda was the one who had started all of this, and she had started it because she was already unhappy. She had been papering over so much, for so long. For that one morning, when it felt like her whole world had crumbled, she had felt miserable, yes. Crushed. Lost. Alone.

But she had also felt something else, something she hadn't even been able to sense until it was gone.

Free.

If everything was blowing up around her, she didn't have any choice. She was going to have to do something else and be someone else, somewhere else, and no one could blame her for it, not one bit.

Instead, the smoke was clearing. What she had taken for bombshells had just been fireworks, with a lot of boom and sparkle and no damage done. She turned to Nancy, who seemed to feel they'd paused long enough; she had her hands on the keys and her foot on the brake. She'd drive Amanda right back to Frannie's, unless Amanda did something about it.

Unless she blew something up herself.

"Wait," Amanda said. "I do need to explain." She reached out and took Nancy's hand, pulling it away from the keys, and then held it there between them. A wisp of cloud slid overhead, changing the light to shade and lifting, for a moment, the heat that had been growing in the stopped car. She stared out the windshield, aware that she was squeezing Nancy's hand hard, but she couldn't seem to stop. "I miss Frank." That was a terrible place to start, because now she was already gulping back tears. "I loved our life together. Working at Frannie's, with him, with you, Daddy Frank—"

Nancy squeezed her hand. "I know, honey. I know. This part—you don't have to explain. It's time for you to move on."

Amanda shook her head. "No. You're not— That's not all. This is not about Andy, I'm not talking about that, that was just—" What was it? She couldn't sort that out right now. "This is about us, about Frank, about you and me. You're my family now, Nancy. Like, really my family."

"And you're my family. I just don't want you to lose your mom and Mae."

"Don't you think I already have?" Amanda was still swallowing tears. "It's you I'm worried about, Nancy. I love my life, I am so grateful for all I have, I don't want to mess it up—but—" This was so hard, it was like standing at the edge of some terrifying cliff, but Amanda felt as though she'd been standing at the edge for too long.

"I did all this, I know," she said. "I brought *Food Wars* here, I went a little nuts trying to win—and now—I don't want this anymore. I don't know if I ever did. Even when Frank was alive, I wasn't—all in anymore. He knew it. I applied to art school in Kansas City. I was going to commute, but he didn't think it would work. We were fighting. He thought I was unhappy, and I was, but not with him." Not with him, maybe with him . . . That was the one thing that really didn't matter anymore. "We were trying to figure it out, and I want to think we would have, but I just don't know. And then he was gone . . ."

Tears started running down Amanda's cheeks, and Nancy reached for her, but Amanda gently pulled away. She wanted to find comfort in Nancy's arms, but for the first time, she knew she wanted something else more.

"I love you so much, Nancy. I don't want to lose you. If I'm not at Frannie's, if I do something else, I don't even know what, but something—would you still, I mean, how much would things change between us?"

It was too much to hope that Nancy would understand. Amanda could barely understand it herself. Because it just didn't fit together. If she loved her life, and Frannie's, and Nancy—if she'd loved Frank, and raising her kids—why would she want something else? It was what she'd been asking herself, yelling at herself, for months. Did wanting something more mean you regretted everything that led to what you'd got?

Nancy turned to her but paused before she spoke. "You don't want to work at Frannie's anymore?"

Amanda couldn't take it. She thought she was ready, but she wasn't, not really, not to really be on her own. "I do, I mean, I kind of do, it's not exactly that I don't want to—"

"No, don't take it back. You said something. You don't want to work at Frannie's anymore. You want to do something else. And you're afraid that will make me less your family." Nancy sat back in her seat, and then suddenly, with resolve, started the car again and pulled out into the road. "I can fix that too. Sometimes I think you don't even know what family is, Amanda. Of course you won't lose me if you don't work at Frannie's. There's nothing you could do to lose me, and I need you to know it—and then I need you to really know it, and to be it, with your family. Because what I'm asking myself, Amanda, and what Gus might ask, or Frankie, is—does that mean there's something I could do to lose *you*?"

"No!" Amanda was horrified. Did Nancy think she was disloyal after all?

"No? Not have a messy house, or compete against you to win something, or maybe make you jealous?" Nancy looked hard and quickly at Amanda before turning her eyes back to the road. "Not if I let you down somehow?"

"You would never let me down." Amanda understood what Nancy was saying. Kind of. But it was different. Her mother and Mae—they weren't there for her. So how could she be there for them?

"You don't know that, Amanda. You can't know that, and maybe you never learned that everyone screws up, sometimes. But we're going to Frannie's. There's something I need you to see. And then we're going to find a way for you to give your mother and Mae another chance, and for them to see what they're doing, too. Because this recipe stuff—all this stuff we're doing—this is ridiculous." She set her lips in a thin line, and the car sped up. "Ridiculous."

Amanda started to say something else, to defend herself, but Nancy waved her off. They were there, pulling into the familiar parking lot, which Amanda could already feel growing strange. She wanted to leave it behind, but she would miss it, too. Things already felt changed, no matter what Nancy said, and what Amanda felt most was uncertainty, and a deep conviction that Nancy wasn't going to let her find an easy way out of it.

Nancy got out of the car fast and walked toward Amanda. As their eyes met, Nancy spoke quickly, as though she'd been rehearsing her line.

"What makes you think I'd want to run Frannie's without you?"

She turned, and before Amanda could answer, if she'd even known what to say, Nancy was off, briskly striding over the broken-up asphalt toward the restaurant where, in Amanda's mind, she reigned. Amanda followed Nancy to the kitchen, saying hey to the cooks at the break table and to staff straightening up at the boss's appearance, trying to look like they hadn't been slacking off during the usual lull between lunch and the early-bird crowd.

Nancy marched past, through the empty kitchen toward the back wall and the old built-in cabinets, only about ten inches deep, that lined it. She opened the one that was filled with extra containers of salt and various spices and emptied a shelf at eye level, then slid her fingers behind the thin light blue painted panel behind it and pulled.

The panel came off in her hands, and from behind it, Nancy took out what looked like a card wrapped in plastic and handed it to Amanda.

It was a half sheet of lined paper, old, covered in a flowing, spidery script that gave Amanda a shock of recognition. The yellowing cellophane crackled in her hands as she took it.

Fill a large cake pan with flour up to your first knuckle, then salt well. Add pepper until mixture is well spotted, then add three large pinches nutmeg, one pinch mace, pepper again. Dredge chicken in plain flour, buttermilk, spiced flour, before frying in a good quantity of boiling lard.

The paper was oil-spotted and worn; in another hand someone had written *Crisco* underneath the recipe, and another, *mace!!!* There were measurements at the bottom, too; *3 tbsp nutmeg 1 tbsp mace to 6 c flour, ¼ c salt, 3 tbsp pepper.* But it was the original writing that transfixed Amanda. Nancy thought this was going to convince Mae that she hadn't stolen the Mimi's recipe, but it was more likely to do the opposite. How could they have this at Frannie's? And what was she going to do now?

Because what she was holding was Mimi's original recipe, in her handwriting, the same as the one that hung in the Mimi's kitchen, only scribbled on and worn and without the frame. The same, but different.

Nancy took the recipe from her hands, turned it over, and handed it back to her. "It's okay. I know. But there's no way you could have been responsible for this. Read the back."

Before she could, Amanda heard running footsteps outside the kitchen. Gus burst through the swinging doors and stared at them, as though he hadn't expected to find them there, then at the paper in Nancy's hand. He spoke quickly, as if he was a little out of breath.

"I was—I was just coming to find you, Grandma, to get the recipe. I guess—Mom told you?"

Nancy nodded. He turned to Amanda. "We didn't know what Mae said, Mom. Or I would have shown you yesterday."

Amanda looked from Gus to Nancy. "I don't understand," she said.

"I didn't know the recipe was here," Nancy said. "Gus did."

Gus smiled, a little sadly. "Grandpa showed it to me. Ages ago."

"But now—" Nancy tapped the paper in Amanda's hands. "Read the back. Gus hasn't seen that, either."

Amanda slowly turned over the page and read aloud.

Frannie, I wish you much luck with Frannie's. I do not think your man will be up to the job but I wish you much luck with him as well. Do not worry about the loan yet and do not tell him. This money and Frannie's are yours. Like all men he will want to run things but he is easily fooled. I think that it is best I leave you to it for a while, as he and I will not agree.

—Mimi

And underneath it, in a different hand,

Owe Mimi $1,400, October 29, 1889

There wasn't any more, but now Amanda knew for certain that the writing was Mimi's. And she knew something else now, too. Something that changed everything, that was impossible, but was the only answer.

"Mimi loaned Frannie money," Amanda said slowly. "She wasn't mad. And Frannie—she died, you know. Before Mimi."

"Mimi gave Frannie the recipe," Nancy said. "And you can show that to Sabrina, and that's it. You're off the hook."

Amanda stood, turning the paper over in her hands. Nothing about this made sense. "But why would it change? Why did our chicken suddenly taste like Mimi's when it didn't before?"

"Because I didn't have it," Nancy said. "When Frank—my Frank—died, there was a big mason jar of just the spices, all mixed. I didn't know what was in it. I just guessed how much to throw in with the flour each time, and then when it was gone, I didn't know how to make it. I kept trying—I did guess nutmeg at some point—but I never got it right. I kept playing with it, adding things. Cinnamon, even. Dill, which was awful. That's why it changed all the time."

That didn't answer her question. Not even close. "But where—"

"Friday, when you were talking about the chicken always being the same—right after they asked about the biscuits—and Tony Russell was complaining that it wasn't, Gus was right there. He started joking, afterward, about Tony not knowing where the recipe was hidden. I realized that Gus knew where it was."

"I never knew Grandma didn't have the recipe," Gus said. "I just assumed she did. So I showed her, and we made the chicken together for Saturday morning."

"That's why the chicken wasn't the same before, and why it was different Saturday," Nancy said. "This is the old recipe, what Frank used and everybody else used. It's been here since Frannie left it. And Frank being Frank, my Frank, he would have thought it was funny to show a little kid and never show me. He never would have thought anything might happen to him. He thought he'd live forever."

Then it was here all along. Amanda stared at the paper in her hand. "So you just made Mimi's chicken? Didn't you think someone would notice?"

"I thought the recipe was Frannie's. I didn't look at the back until we were done, and by then—no. I didn't. At a certain point, isn't fried chicken just fried chicken? I've been messing with it for years, and Tony Russell is the only one who said anything." She sighed. "They're not really here to pick the best chicken. They're here to pick us apart, and I should have seen that from the beginning. Instead—I played right into their hands, and I'm sorry."

Gus looked from one of them to the other, his excitement fading. "But we can still show this to Sabrina, right? And Aunt Mae. And everybody. Because Sabrina asked everyone about this, Mom, and no one believed her, but—this just proves it."

"I don't think it's going to be that easy," Amanda said, and she laid down the page on the counter again, more gently this time, and put a finger on the final line. *Owe Mimi $1,400, October 29, 1889*.

Gus spoke. "Do you think Frannie ever paid Mimi back?"

"I don't think so," Amanda said. "I think—that's where this all started."

Mimi had shared her recipe—probably the family recipe; after all, they were sisters—and they'd just coexisted, here in town, two chicken places with plenty of trains bringing in plenty of customers, and the coal mine, and the mill. There had been no ill will. The whole feuding-sisters story . . . it wasn't true.

Until something went wrong, and Frannie was gone, and there

wasn't anyone left to care about Mimi. Had she asked the man she had so criticized to make it right, or had she been too proud? She, too, had died young, and for generations, Frannie's grew, and Mimi's struggled, first under Mimi's daughters, the old ladies of Amanda's very early childhood, and then Barbara's grandmother, and her mother, and then Barbara, all bitter, always at least a little behind on everything, always mistrusting the bank and Merinac. When Amanda was little, when Barbara first took over Mimi's, the Pogociellos had run this town.

Nancy had seen this. Seen it before anything had really gone wrong, before the chicken tasting, before Mae accused her of stealing, before Amanda had told about Barbara, before the whole scene at the house.

Before any of it. Nancy knew—and didn't tell her. Didn't tell anyone.

"I wish I had said something," Nancy said. "I think you know how much I wish I had said something the minute I turned over that paper. But I wanted to believe it couldn't be true. That they paid it back, that all the rest of this whole feud was just Mimi's. Your mother, holding a grudge." She took a deep breath. "But I think you're right. And the truth is that Frank—my Frank, your Frank—they must have known. Or guessed."

Amanda started to speak, then swallowed her question. Nancy felt bad enough already. Sometimes people let you down—and sometimes you let yourself down. Instead, she reached out and put one arm around her mother-in-law and beckoned Gus in with the other. He looked at them both uncertainly.

"You think Grandpa—and Dad—I mean, that's not that much money now, but it was. You really think that all along they knew Frannie's started with Mimi's help, and they just never said anything?"

Nancy looked somber. "I don't want to believe it, but I do."

"We'll never know what they knew," Amanda said gently. "But

the one thing we can say for sure is that nobody is coming out of this whole *Food Wars* thing looking all that great." Except Mae, she thought, and then she remembered the look on her sister's face when she'd seen Jay standing there in Barbara's front yard, watching them battle it out on the porch. She gathered Gus and Nancy in a tight hug, then turned to Gus. "Except you, kiddo. You're the only one without any secrets."

Gus started to say something, but Nancy interrupted. "Well, I'm done with this one," she said. She picked up the recipe and handed to Amanda. "This is yours. It's up to you to decide what to do with it."

MAE

You can't clean out an entire house in a single day, especially when half the people involved have to go to work in the afternoon. To get around that, Sabrina had Mae focus on just the living room, what Mae and her mother had always called the back room, where the puppies had been born and where viewers would expect the fix to happen. While the emptying and cleaning of the rest of the house went on around them, Mae scraped together enough decent furniture to decorate, even staggering down the street holding one corner of a sofa from the Inn's coffee shop while Jay, Kenneth, and Patrick held the others, in a surreal moment that the younger versions of Kenneth and Mae must have been laughing at, cigarettes and beer in hand, from some vantage point just out of sight. They'd return the sofa later, of course, but Barbara's sofa wasn't salvageable, and Sabrina planned to Facebook Live the makeover of the room right then, that afternoon.

At Sabrina's direction, Mae gathered everything she would need, right down to the smaller details, and essentially put together the room on the lawn. Then she went in, stood in the center of the now-empty room, camera angle carefully set to avoid any of the still-remaining mess, and started directing as Frankie, Kenneth, and Andy brought things in to set up and Jay helped Jessa load Madison and Ryder into the car to head back to the motel for a swim and a nap. Mae described to the Facebook audience why things went where and how she thought Barbara, Aida, and Patches and her puppies would use the room.

"This is not some kind of designer room, obviously," she told the camera, as she put fresh issues of *People* and *Us Weekly* for Aida on the coffee table and the remote control for the TV in a flat basket beside it, "but this is Barbara's house, and Aida's, and they should have what they want and love in here, not what I would want and love, or what you would want and love." *Pause, breathe.* Good live television, like any good media, meant ending your sentences, letting the viewer take them in. "That means setting up the room for what really happens—the puppies play and get trained and socialized over here, where there's no carpet and we've got rubber mats under all the newspaper, and then my mom and great-aunt Aida do their living here, and there's room for guests to sit, and easy ways to clean up after the puppies. One reason my mom wasn't doing that very well before is that it was hard for her to manage her household—but now everything is at hand."

She smiled. This was the big ending, the part she'd been drafting in her head since she found out Sabrina wanted to do this segment. She'd learned from Lolly and *Sparkling* that hitting the close right was important, and there was something she wanted to say. Sabrina gestured—okay, right, move to the sofa, sit down, add a little visual interest. Mae did, then spoke.

"There are obviously other reasons my mom has trouble cleaning up after the puppies, and everything else," Mae said. "She's working on those. The spaces around us reflect the spaces inside us, and when those things don't go together, that's how we know we need to make a change. For my mom, she's found that as she gets older, she sees what's really important in life, and now she wants her house to feel that way too. That's going to help her make this happen."

Mae leaned forward and looked straight into the camera, imagining Jay on the other side. "Helping my mom clean up—and coming back to Mimi's and my hometown—have kind of done the same for me. If you've seen my book at all, you know I have a saying: clean space, calm mind. I guess I always figured that if I had clear counters, a clear mind would just naturally follow—and it didn't. Just like my mom needs to get her outer world in order, I need to be working on that inner stuff. Coming home is helping me figure out which few things are important, and I need to start making sure my life reflects that same simplicity and clarity I love to create in the spaces around me."

Final punch line. Mae glanced up at Sabrina, making sure she knew there was just a little more to come, and saw her nod. "So if you've been looking at my mom's space and feeling like you've got it all together, maybe take a minute to think about whether the rest of your life has that same feel. And if your physical world is a little—or a lot—messier than you'd like, then maybe you're coming at it from the other direction and getting your inside in order before you tackle the outside. Clean spaces, calm minds—they're a journey, not a destination. And wherever you are on your journey, I hope watching us build a better space for my mom and my great-aunt and for Patches and the puppies to continue theirs inspires you to work on your own spaces—inside and out."

That was it. She sat, smiling pleasantly, letting Sabrina cut it off, until she was sure the cameras had stopped. "Good?" she asked Sabrina, still holding her position.

"Perfect. We're done. Getting a little deep there, for *Food Wars,* but I loved it. We'll keep filming the rest, of course, and you need to do a reveal with Barbara, but this will be good stuff for the episode, too."

With Sabrina satisfied for the moment, Mae set out to find Jay. She needed to talk to him, but would he hear what she had to say? There was no time to linger and plan if she wanted to seize this moment when the cameras were focused on other things. She got up, then headed for the back patio. Andy, Kenneth, and Frankie were there, with Jay, who was putting his phone back in his pocket.

"You were good, Aunt Mae," said Frankie, a little begrudgingly.

"Your mom and I will work things out, Frankie," Mae said. Amanda had made Mae so angry, yes, but Amanda didn't know yet about Barbara's illness, or that as much as it mattered who came out on top in *Food Wars*, there were things that mattered more. She took Jay's arm, meeting his eyes, asking permission, and he turned to follow her. "Sorry, guys, but Jay and I need to talk."

Quickly, she led him out the back trail, the one that went down to the river and the old cottonwood tree, rushing into speech as soon as they were out of earshot. "I'm sorry. I know, I need to explain, and I couldn't, not with them filming everything. Thank you for going along with it. Seriously. Thank you."

Jay, beside her, was silent for a moment, and she loosened her grip on his arm, slid her hand down to his, willing him to take it, trying to push aside her fear that he was already halfway out the door, and the instinct to protect herself from how much it would hurt if he went. He did, and she squeezed, glad to have even the chance to tell him what she was thinking.

"You could start with why we're not in a Kansas City suburb," Jay said, giving her a sideways glance. "A very small town an hour away is not exactly a suburb."

Mae bit her lip and felt herself flush. "Well, this is it," she said. "This is home. It was hard, coming from this to New York. Or even from this to SMU. Everyone else knew what to say, and how to act, and what to wear. I had to learn to fake it. By the time we met, I had my story down. It was easier just to keep it that way."

"It didn't matter where you were from, Mae. It never would have mattered."

They had reached the path down to the fallen tree now, and Mae stopped and faced Jay at the top. "Maybe not, but it was easier to just stick with the script. I'd been telling people my mom ran a restaurant in a Kansas City suburb for a long time before I met you. In my head, all this—the chicken, my mom, the house—it felt like it was following me, all the time. It was bad enough just dealing with all the Kansas jokes—*No, we're not in Kansas anymore.* I've only heard that a thousand times."

"So you lied," Jay said. He was making his way down the path now and didn't look back at her.

"It wasn't lying," she said. "I put a good spin on things. I can see how it looks like lying. And I can see all this differently now, too. But I couldn't then. And I'm sorry. I really am."

"Yeah," he said. "I know. I guess. And your mom— I can see why you don't talk about that, although you could have, to me. My parents aren't exactly perfect either."

Mae still saw a pretty big gap between her history and Jay's, which was at least neat and clean and looked more normal from the outside, but he was right. They'd both had to be their own support as kids. She knew that, but she'd never seen how much it connected them until now.

Jay went on. "So that's it? Any other surprises? Besides our future as dog owners?" Mae cast a quick look at him, and he smiled. He was kidding about that, anyway, she could tell—probably about all of it—but there was something else she hadn't told him. Sabrina hadn't worked her stint as an exotic dancer into any questioning, but she had it. It might only be a matter of time. And she was proud of it, she reminded herself. Proud that she had found a way to support herself.

That really didn't make this any easier.

Jay was watching her, wary now, his teasing expression fading. Couldn't she just skip this and accept the olive branch he seemed ready to extend? Maybe later would be a better time—but no. Clear the counter, right? "I also might not have mentioned that I put myself through college working at a place called the Yellow Rose of Texas Gentlemen's Club."

Jay's eyes widened as the implication of the name soaked in. "Working?"

"Onstage. Dancing." Mae needed to get that clear. "Just dancing.

Nothing else, not ever." As she spoke, it all came back to her—the too-brightly lit dressing rooms, her own very neat costume bag, the other girls, some up for a little more than dancing, but most toeing the line, in it for the money, just like Mae.

Jay stood, gazing at her. Mae didn't even know what to expect. This was so long ago, before they even met, but it was— Well, if she wasn't maybe a little embarrassed by it, it would be on her résumé. She smiled weakly. "It was a long time ago."

Half of Jay's mouth turned up into a smile, and now she could see—he was trying not to laugh. For a minute, she felt a little pissed—she was telling him important things, here—but she got it, kind of. She smiled a little more herself, and then he laughed, and now they were both laughing.

"That's kind of hot, really," he said finally. "I hope you, like, remember some things."

She punched his arm, then, feeling a little bolder, took his arm and pulled him the rest of the way down the trail. They'd reached the fallen tree, and Jay found a good place to sit on its trunk.

"Amanda and I used to play down here," Mae said, taking a seat beside him.

"That would be back when you weren't pushing each other across a big reality TV stage, I expect."

Mae sighed. "We got a little worked up. Okay, a lot worked up. It's just—she did things, and I did things, and my mom really needs to win this. This part is bad. She owes money on a mortgage I didn't know about. She probably has Parkinson's. And"—Mae put her hands on her knees and stared straight down at the ground—"she's worried about what comes next. For Mimi's. For her. For me. She needs me, Jay. And I guess—I need her, and this place. That's why I said that, about staying, and I'm not sure what I meant, exactly, but I can't just run away. Again."

This was hard. Much harder than the rest of it, than the history.

They'd felt close again, just a minute ago, and now she was probably throwing all that away, but this was also it—her clearing all those internal counters. She didn't want to be keeping anything from him. No more secrets, no matter what it cost her.

And it might cost her a lot. Jay was silent—too silent, not touching her—and she didn't dare look at him. The old Mae would have told him that she didn't care what he thought or what he wanted, even if she did. The old Mae would not have given him the power to hurt her that she was extending now. But that had never worked as well as she'd liked to pretend it had.

"I miss you, Jay. I miss us, cheering each other on. And I really, really want us to find our way back to that, and I also want to give my mom the support she's going to need, and I don't know how to make it all work. I guess I don't even know if you want to, at this point. What I want to do is—" She took a deep breath and risked a glance up at him, but he was staring at the ground under his feet. "I know you've been saying you want to quit so we can spend a year traveling, but I wondered . . . I thought we could spend a year here. Or more. Maybe we could travel too, once I know what my mom's health will be like. But seriously, Jay, you could do everything you want to do here. Think, be with the kids, meditate, whatever. It's just a different way of looking at it." She gestured around, at the river, the fallen tree, the saplings already springing up to take its place. "It's peaceful. With the trees. And the river. You've got room to, uh, hear the trees falling."

Jay gave her a look that combined doubt with sarcasm at that.

"You know, like they fall, and does anyone hear them? You can hear them." Mae felt like her pitch was falling flat. What would she do if he said no? Last night, with her mom, in that house where generations of women had been let down by their men, she had let herself hope that Jay was different. Jay had never let her down. Maybe she was the one letting *him* down. Twenty-four hours ago he hadn't known Merinac existed; now she was begging him to give up his life—a life he hated, but still—and move here. For her. She must have lost her mind.

"The guy at security boarding the flight out of St. Louis looked at my driver's license and made a joke about turbans," Jay said.

"Oh." She looked up at him. He was smiling, a little. "Well, that was St. Louis. It's different here. Worse."

"Mae." Jay took her hand, pulling her, shifting her toward him. "I miss you, too. I've been missing you. For a long time. And I love your fire, and how hard you go after things, and how you pushed me to do the same. But when I started to feel like I didn't want those things, it was like you couldn't even hear me. You just kept rolling forward."

"I hear you now, though. I really do. You were right. What's here, what's in front of us—that's what matters. And what's in front of us is this—my mom, Mimi's. Not Instagram, not even *Food Wars*. We have to experience life to have anything worth sharing. It's time to get real. I get it."

Jay's eyebrows turned downward, and he squeezed her hand harder. "That's what's in front of you, Mae. Not me. You're like a steamroller, and I don't even get to help choose the direction."

This was not at all what Mae wanted to hear, and she grabbed Jay's other hand. "But you did help choose, don't you see? This is just another version of stepping back and figuring out who we are, who you are, and what we want. For ourselves, for Madison and Ryder. In a different place. I want a different kind of simple now, and it's the same kind you want. I want it with you, Jay."

Jay sighed deeply and looked around. To Mae, this spot was beautiful, with the still-new bright leaves on the saplings, the river, slow and muddy here, with tiny insects buzzing over the surface. But Jay might not see what she saw.

In the silence, a bird whistled an alarm from somewhere above them and another answered it. "I want you, Mae," he finally said. "And I want our family. But I'm not sure I want this."

Feeling like she was taking a step out onto one of the fallen tree's fragile branches, Mae spoke softly. "I'm not sure I want this either. But my mom might be really sick, and then there's my aunt, and Mimi's. I feel like I might have to decide to want it, to make it what I want. But I don't want to do it alone."

Jay was silent, looking down, his hands still in hers. Should she let go, walk away, let him think? Softly, she loosened her hold a little, and Jay loosened his, too, and just as she was about to fully let go, just as she was feeling her heart open in her chest and shift, like it couldn't hold all it was feeling, Jay tightened his fingers on hers again, and she squeezed back, and she was crying, and he pulled her into him, and there were pointy scratchy branches between them, but it didn't matter. She sat on his knees, pressed her face into his neck, and felt the stubble of his cheek on the soft skin under her ponytail.

"Can we just hold on to this and see what happens, Mae? Not have a plan, for now, not roll forward, just see?"

Mae without a plan was like Mae without breathing. She wasn't sure she could do it. "I'll try." She tilted her head back to look at him, and this time he kissed her lips, soft, nibbling kisses that became a longer, lingering one.

Jay pulled back, and this time he really was smiling. "I guess I know you'll be planning. Maybe just try not to get stuck on one plan. Make a lot of different ones. With room for me in them."

Mae couldn't speak without starting to cry even harder, and she was feeling the pressure of this stolen moment. The last thing she wanted was for Sabrina and her cameras to come thumping down this trail. She nodded, hard, then, when he didn't release her hand as she tried to pull one away, wiped her face on his shirt.

Jay laughed and let go of her, and through her tears, Mae laughed too. This wasn't an answer, not at all—she had nothing firm to cling to or plan on—but she felt as though she had found something that would hold her up just the same. They both got up and began brushing themselves off, and as they did, Mae's phone rang.

"I should just make sure that's not Jessa," she said, taking it out of her pocket and flipping it faceup to see the name on the screen: Lolly. "Huh." She started to return it to her pocket, but Jay stopped her.

"Wait," he said. "I'm curious. See what she wants."

"What, answer it? Now?"

"Yes, now." He waved his hand up, as if pushing the phone at her face. "Go on."

Mae swiped and, glancing at Jay, put the call on speaker instead of bringing the phone to her ear. "Hey, Lolly," she said. "What's up?"

"I just watched your Facebook Live, Mae. It was excellent. Just really, really good. I wanted to congratulate you. It must have been hard, with your mom and all, but you really did a great job."

Mae glanced at Jay, wanting him to see that Lolly's opinion didn't mean as much to her as it once would have. Barbara's back room was scarcely a *Sparkling* situation, and it didn't need to be, and that was the point. "Thanks, Lolly. I appreciate it." The next question hung in the air, unasked. Why bother calling about it? Mae wasn't even sure she cared.

"You really went to the heart of what that space needed, and it made me think about *Sparkling,* and how you might be able to do the same there—get below the surface, really dig into what people need from their space."

What people need from their space, Mae thought, *is not to have those needs ripped open on television.* Barbara would be okay. The people around her already knew her, and her world wouldn't change much. Plus, she had different problems to worry about now. But for most people, that kind of forced exposure would do so much more harm than good.

Lolly was still talking. "I talked to Meghan and Christine, Mae. They both agree—you're the perfect co-host for *Sparkling*. We're done experimenting with other candidates. So, what do you think? Are you interested?"

No apology, of course. No attempt at justifying the turnaround, and Mae wasn't meant to ask for one, either. She should jump at this, a chance to join the cast of an established show and make a bigger name for herself.

Mae didn't even have to look at Jay this time. "Oh, that's really nice to hear, Lolly. But I have other plans going forward." She smiled to herself. Let Lolly think those "other plans" involved the Food Channel. That must be why they'd rushed this call. That Facebook Live must be getting really good numbers. But what Lolly didn't see, and maybe Sabrina didn't see either, was that it was good because it was real, and because Mae had known it, and known she wasn't hurting anyone, or exposing anything except a deeper part of herself. It wasn't something she could take on the road, and she wasn't going to pretend that it was. She was done pretending.

But she didn't mind letting Lolly sweat a little. Lolly started to answer, to argue, probably, or persuade, but Mae cut her off. "Listen, Lolly, I'm in the middle of something. I have to go, but you take care, okay? And give my best to Christine and Meghan. Talk soon." With that, Mae tapped the red button at the bottom of the screen and tucked the phone in her pocket. Then, unable to contain herself, she beamed up at Jay.

"I must have been really good," she said cheerfully, then started up the trail. Jay reached out and caught her.

"You were good," he said. "You're a natural. Are you really saying no to them? Or is that just part of the game?"

"Really no," Mae said. "I'm sick of all of this; it's anything but real. Maybe someday. If I had something to say." She could see it still, true. Sharing a message of authenticity with a new audience . . . but not like that. A bubble of relief rolled up inside her. Like champagne bubbles. Maybe—even without knowing exactly what they were toasting—they needed some champagne. And a family pack of baseball gloves. She looked at Jay again, then hesitated. Was she reading him wrong? "But wait— Should I have asked you? I thought—"

Jay smiled. "No, that's not what I meant. It's just that I thought that's what you really wanted. To be on TV. To co-host *Sparkling*, have your own show."

"Yeah," said Mae. Their eyes met, and she leaned forward and kissed him, quickly. This was what she really wanted, and she needed to make sure he knew it. She turned and started the climb up from the riverbank in earnest this time. "So did I. But I was wrong."

AMANDA

Amanda had envisioned a dozen ways this could go, each worse than the last, almost before they were out of the driveway.

Maybe this was the wrong call. It would be easier, probably, to send Nancy and Gus to Sabrina with the recipe. Sabrina wouldn't worry about the loan business, might not even want to turn the paper over if they did it right. It's a family recipe, they're similar, oh well, case closed. *Food Wars* would zoom to a close and they could just deal with this afterward. After a winner had been declared. When Frannie's had some money, or Mimi's needed money less. Amanda had given up on predicting how *Food Wars* would bestow its largess, especially after Nancy pointed out that whoever got this windfall would be paying taxes out the wazoo.

But Mae. Telling Mae would complicate things. Amanda didn't know what would happen, and she didn't like the feeling. Maybe she was just as much of a control freak as Mae, except her way of controlling things was to try to keep anything from happening at all.

Well, she wasn't going to live that way anymore. She was blowing things up.

Still. She contemplated a big announcement and what might come after. Barbara shouting at Nancy the way Amanda and Mae had shouted at each other. Gus listening while Barbara abused his father and grandfather. People questioning whether Nancy, or even Amanda, might have known this all along, no one giving it a chance, explanations turning into excuses, and all fuel for the *Food Wars* flames. She needed help managing this, and there was only one person to get it from.

"Wait," she said, and this time she did lean forward from the back seat, putting her head between Nancy and Gus. "We need to figure out a way for me to just tell Mae first."

Nancy and Gus saw her logic immediately, but all of them struggled with how to make it happen. Amanda finally went with the simplest thing she could think of. They should look for Mae and try to distract Sabrina if they saw her, while Amanda— "What?" Gus demanded. "Hides behind the car and tries to ambush Aunt Mae?"

"Something like that," she said. "Just try, okay? You get out, send Mae this way, and keep the cameras over there."

They had no backup plan, and Amanda felt more than a little foolish as they carefully parked with the driver's side of Nancy's two-door facing the building and she crawled into the front seat, keeping her head below the windows, then slipped out the passenger side and dropped to the ground while Gus ostentatiously tried to make it appear that he was the only one getting out of the car.

"I guess Mom will come later, right, Grandma?" he said loudly. "She's probably—uh—changing her clothes." Amanda, from the ground, whacked him on the ankle.

"Too much," she hissed. "Just go."

There was no one in sight as they walked toward the house, but Amanda kept down behind the car just the same—and there was Mae, climbing up the bank from the river.

With Jay behind her. *Shit.* Oh, well.

"Mae," she called softly, then again. "Mae." Mae stopped, looking around, and Jay stopped behind her.

"Over here," Amanda said, feeling ridiculous. "But pretend you don't see me. Just—walk this way."

They strolled over, and Jay, who appeared to be taking this about as seriously as Gus was, gazed up at a nearby telephone pole, pointed at nothing, and whispered, while staring resolutely in the opposite direction, "Nice to see you, Amanda. It's been too long."

Amanda couldn't play. "Yeah. Mae, I need to talk to you." She had to convince her sister that this mattered enough to hide from the cameras Mae loved. "I have the Frannie's recipe, and you have to see it, Mae. Mimi wrote it."

"What?" Mae was looking straight down at Amanda. Anyone would know something was up. But if anyone was there, wouldn't they have already come over to see what Jay was pretending to stare at up on the telephone lines?

"You just have to see," Amanda said. "But can we try— Can I show you without Sabrina? And then we can show her. It's not a secret. It's just that I think you should see it before Mom." They'd conspired together so many times, to deceive their mother, to protect her, even occasionally to surprise her. "Please, Mae."

Mae took Jay's hand and began walking away, and just as Amanda was about to call out to her again, Mae spoke. "Oh, gosh," she said. She was a much worse actress than Amanda would have supposed. "I think I dropped my—phone. I dropped my phone, Jay. I'll just go back and look for it. You go on. And maybe"—Mae surveyed the distance between Amanda and anywhere where she couldn't be seen from Barbara's—"maybe you should move Nancy's car for her? It's really in the way, right there. Of the delivery trucks." She met Amanda's eyes and flicked hers toward Mimi's. She was right, too—it was the only place they could get to without risking someone from *Food Wars* walking out of Barbara's, seeing Amanda, and descending on them both.

"Just put it over by Mimi's," Mae said. "That's probably where I left my phone, too."

Mae walked off toward the opening in the fence that led to the Mimi's patio, and Jay approached the car, then turned back. "Keys will be in it," Mae called without turning around. "That's how we do it here."

Jay got in and started the car, rolling down the passenger-side window. "I'm guessing you're supposed to use the car for cover while I drive over there," he said. "Lots of intrigue in this town."

Amanda, now that things were going her way, could afford a smile. "More than you'd think, even without *Food Wars*," she said. She had always liked Jay, as far as she knew him. He'd never been the snotty New Yorker she had expected.

Amanda slipped through the gap in the fence and straightened up as soon as she knew she would be out of sight. Mae was waiting. Without explanation, Amanda handed her the recipe, back in its protective wrapping, faceup.

"This was at Frannie's," she said. "It's a long story, but it's been hidden, and Nancy didn't know where until yesterday when Gus showed her. But that's really not what's important."

Mae gasped, just as Amanda had known she would. "Then they stole it," she said. "Does it really matter when? They stole this, Amanda."

Amanda shook her head. "Turn it over."

Mae silently read the back while Amanda sat down at a picnic table and waited. Mae stared down at the words for a long time before she looked at Amanda.

"They owe us," she said.

"I know," said Amanda. "Mary Cat was right all along."

"And wrong," Mae replied. "Because Frannie died, right? Frannie died, and it was her husband—"

"I think so," Amanda said. "I mean, it's hard to know exactly"— she spoke quickly, so that Mae would know she wasn't defending the Pogociellos—"we can't be a hundred percent sure, but that's what I think. What Nancy thinks, too. That they never paid her back, and they knew it, or at least, the first ones knew it." But the whole story needed to be out there. "Daddy Frank, my father-in-law, Frank—they'd seen this, though. Daddy Frank showed it to Gus when Gus was little. So they might have known. Probably knew. Or they should have guessed."

"They damn well should have," said Mae angrily, and Amanda couldn't blame her. "So the feud—it wasn't Mimi and Frannie. It was Mimi and Frannie's, once Frannie was gone." Mae handed the paper back to Amanda and sat down on the bench across from her.

"If Frannie had lived," Amanda said, and then stopped. Mae could see it as well as she could. If Frannie had lived, they probably wouldn't be sitting here hiding from the *Food Wars* cameras.

They sat there for a moment, both looking at the ground. Frannie and Mimi hadn't been feuding. Or maybe they had, some of the time. Maybe Mimi was jealous of Frannie for having "her man" to help, even if it didn't sound like Mimi liked him much, and even if it seemed like Mimi might have been right. Or maybe Frannie wanted some of Mimi's independence.

It was hard not to want what your sister had.

"There's something I have to tell you," Mae finally said. Amanda looked up. An apology? An apology would be nice—she was about to offer one herself, but Mae could go first for a change. But Mae didn't look like she was apologizing. She looked like she was crying, and not just the teary eyes that had come over Amanda, too, when she thought about how things could be different. Big, gulpy sobs that made Amanda, almost without realizing she was doing it, shift quickly from her bench to Mae's and put both arms around her sister.

She knew before Mae said another word that apologies weren't what was on Mae's mind.

MAE

Damn it, she hadn't meant to cry. It wasn't that bad, at least it probably wasn't, but with Jay, too, and the whole thing. She snuffled, swallowed, wiped her arm across her face, probably leaving it gruesomely striped with dust, then took the wad of tissues Amanda had pulled out of her jeans pocket, blew her nose gratefully, and shook her head, willing the tears away.

It felt good having her there, her physical presence solid and oddly reassuring. Mae was tired of feeling as if Amanda was on the other side of some wall. Maybe that wall could be gone now. If Mimi and Frannie could still be friends, if Mimi could help Frannie—she reached out to take her sister's hand. There was no softening what she had to say, but she hoped Amanda could see that she hadn't set out to dump this on her in the middle of everything.

Mae took a deep breath, turned toward Amanda, and blurted it out. "Mom's doctor told her she may have the symptoms of early Parkinson's disease." Part of Mae was still holding out for a talk with the doctor, despite an hour on Google last night, carefully limited to only the most optimistic-sounding sites, that had mostly convinced her the doctor was right.

Amanda's eyes locked on to Mae's, and in that instant Mae got her sister back, but maybe not the sister she'd been holding in her head all these years, because while Mae saw a flash of fear in Amanda's eyes, the next thing she saw was a steel that matched her own. If Mae hadn't known it before, she knew it now—Amanda had plenty of the famous Moore fire in her. She'd just been hiding it for a long time.

Amanda pulled her hand away. "Mom has—what? Mom is sick?"

Mae nodded. "That's what I was trying to tell you," she said. "In the house." She remembered the frustration of that moment, and it crept unbidden into her next words. "But you wouldn't listen."

Amanda got up and walked away, shoving her hands in the pockets of her jeans. "I wouldn't listen because you were yelling at me, Mae. You weren't telling me something. You were telling me off."

Mae knew Amanda's reaction wasn't about her, but about Barbara, but she couldn't help herself. Amanda was still the reason she and Barbara had spent an entire day up to their elbows in cold chicken water, and the reason they were in there cleaning now. She'd been making fun of Mae ever since Mae came home, with her drinks and her enlightening Sabrina on how Mae put herself through college. She'd still broken all the rules about Mimi's. Even if they turned out to be pointless rules. Even if Mae had always thought Barbara went too far with them. Even if Barbara herself was all messed up about what Mimi's was supposed to be.

"You'd just basically told Mom you hated her." Mae stayed sitting, trying to stay calm, but she held on to the bench so hard that she could feel the grain of the wood pressing into her hands. "You made her cry, and I had to deal with her, and that's always the way it is. You just go skipping off, and I've got Mom, and it can't be that way. You can't treat her like that."

"Seriously, Mae? You haven't been here in six years. Six *years*. I'm the one that's still here. I'm the one that's coming over and cleaning out the fridge. I'm the one that sees Mom all the time."

"Maybe you think you are, but she's not telling you things, and you're not paying attention. It must have been pretty obvious something was up with Mom. She knew it. Aida knew it. So clearly you're not here. You're at Frannie's."

"Yeah, because Frannie's is normal. Everybody there is normal. In case you haven't noticed, when I *am* here, Mom alternates between criticizing me and throwing me out." Amanda crossed her arms over her chest, and Mae wanted to get up and shove her again. Wasn't she listening?

"Because she's upset. Because you went to Frannie's, and maybe it was the right thing for you, but it hurt her." Mae grabbed the recipe off the table and stood up, waving it in her sister's face. "This isn't nothing, Amanda. It never was nothing. It messed up Mom's whole life." Mae knew she was being unreasonable. The recipe, the money—not Amanda's fault, but so much of this was still on Amanda.

Amanda put her hands on her hips. "You told the whole town—the whole world—that I stole Mimi's recipe! What did you think I was going to do, smile and nod? I know it's not nothing. Why do you think I'm here? I could have waited, or just shown Sabrina to prove we had a recipe, but I'm here, right? I'm trying to—do something. Fix this."

"You can't fix this," said Mae. "I told you they were going to try to pit us against each other and crawl right into our personal lives, and they did, and you made it easy for them. You've made this week hell for Mom. Stealing her chicken, and now the house, Patches—you're the one that started this whole thing."

"You painted over my chicken!" Amanda put her hands up to her head and ran them through her short dark hair as if she couldn't contain her need to move. "You and Kenneth! You were laughing at me, and you painted over my chicken. That's what started this. Not me. You, having to win, coming here, taking over. You!"

"I didn't," Mae said, her voice rising angrily and her own hands on her hips. Behind Amanda, the back door of Mimi's swung open, but she didn't have time to go slam it shut. They were having this out, now. She stood there, staring angrily at Amanda, every emotion of the last few days, of the last six years, washing over her, everything her sister had said and done and hadn't said and hadn't done—

Thunk.

The crashing sound of wood hitting wood rolled through Mimi's and out onto the patio, and both Mae and Amanda froze. The first *thunk* was followed by a much louder one, a resounding smack, the sound of something very large falling, or swinging, or crashing, and the entire little building shook. Mae moved quickly toward the open door of Mimi's, Amanda behind her, through the kitchen, the counter, seeing nothing, but that sound—it had come from here. She hesitated, looking at Amanda in confusion now. Was someone out there, listening? A car or a person?

There was no one there. But the front door, like the back door, was open, and it was Amanda who walked out first this time, then stopped short, so that Mae careened right into her.

"Oh—" Amanda gave a little gasp, and Mae echoed her, because what had made the sound was obvious now. The sign Kenneth had hung to cover Mae's bad painting job had fallen, breaking the pot of flowers in front of it before coming to rest flat against the boards of the porch, now covered in potting soil and uprooted impatiens.

Amanda knelt in front of the sign while Mae reached up to where it had hung, embarrassed again by her paint strokes—and now by the emotion that had driven them. She put a hand on the wall where Kenneth had twisted in an eye to hold the hooks on the sign. The screw of the eye had wrenched out, leaving an ugly splintered hole in the wood, and the one on the other side looked even worse.

Amanda held up the eye itself, hook and short chain still attached to both eye and sign. "I guess." She paused, raising her eyebrows at her sister. "I guess it just got too heavy."

Mae looked at the four inches of screw in her sister's hand, and at the sign—a weight, sure, but nothing she couldn't pick up herself if she had to—and raised her own eyebrows. "Uh-huh," she said. "Too much for the old place to bear."

All the fight had gone out of her with her panicked reaction to the noise, and from Amanda, too, it looked like. Mae sat down on the edge of the porch, and Amanda left the sign, stepping down into the freshly mown grass of the tiny yard between the porch and sidewalk and sitting next to her.

"Or . . ." Amanda shrugged, and leaned gently into Mae's shoulder again.

"Or," agreed Mae. She reached out again and took her sister's hand. "I'm sorry," Mae said, at exactly the same moment that Amanda said it too. They both laughed, but Mae was the one who kept going. She didn't want to be fighting with Amanda. Not anymore. It was just so easy to go down that road with her sister. One of them said something, and the other said something, and then neither of them wanted to back down. Like a big game of chicken. Mae laughed, and Amanda looked at her, but she couldn't explain. "Kenneth was mad at me, actually," she said. "He saved me with his sign, but he was pretty pissed. I'm really sorry."

Amanda sighed and leaned against her harder. "Say that again," she said.

"I'm sorry. I'm sorry I ruined your sign." She was. But she couldn't let Amanda off too easy. "And you better be sorry too, because what you pulled next caused us a world of hurt. We had to use frozen chicken, did you know? We had to spend the whole day water-defrosting them. My hands are still chapped." Mae held them out for her sister to see, then realized they didn't look very bad and put them down. "They still feel chapped, anyway."

"Yeah." Amanda looked intently at her feet, as if she was considering her old Birkenstocks carefully, but Mae knew better. "I do feel bad about that," Amanda said. "I really do."

"I'm sorry I told them about the biscuits," Mae said. She was kind of sorry, anyway. That one still made Mae want to laugh.

"Why'd you come anyway, Mae? I told you, you didn't have to."

Mae shrugged. Did she really want to answer that? It was almost embarrassing, how big her plans had been, and how dumb, really. Amanda sat, waiting. "I came home because I thought I really wanted my own TV show," Mae finally said. "I figured I'd do this, and the Food Channel would see how great I was. I thought I wanted what Sabrina has, and you know what? She doesn't have anything."

"She doesn't have shit," Amanda agreed, picking a single long blade of grass that had escaped the mower and putting it between her lips. "Not anything anybody real would want, anyway." She tried to blow a whistle along the grass and failed dismally.

Mae picked up another blade of grass and blew a perfect tweet, then grinned, knowing she was being annoying. Just annoying enough, maybe. "Why is it so hard for us to figure out what we actually want?"

It was a rhetorical question, but Amanda stopped to consider. She gazed up at the roof of the porch above them, tilting her head back to look at the wall with the ghost of her sign still visible behind them. "Maybe because we never saw anybody want anything that worked out? Maybe because everything we ever wanted turned to trash the minute it came into the house?" Amanda tried to laugh, but Mae could see she meant what she was saying. "Maybe because everything we want dies or basically goes up in smoke? Or no, that's just me. And what do you mean, anyway? You always get what you want, Mae. Always."

Mae looked to see if Amanda was starting up their fight again, but no. She was just—saying something she thought was true. Something Mae had thought was true, too, up until just now.

"I get what I go after," she said slowly. "But that doesn't mean I go after what I want. I go after—the opposite of Mom. Just like you, I guess. Frannie's, Nancy, Frank's whole family—they were not this. For me, it was school, New York, organizing, being famous for being neat and clean"—oh God, it really was funny—"the opposite of our whole life, right? And in the end we're both still just being pushed around by Mom's mess."

Amanda sighed. "What are we going to do? About Mom, I mean."

"I don't know. I know it's big, but I don't want it to be big. I think—it's going to take both of us to deal with it." And that was exactly what she wasn't ready to talk about right now. She rushed on. "But first, we really have to figure out about Frannie's—the recipe!" Mae got up and scurried back through Mimi's, returning with the recipe in her hand. "Not something we want to lose."

"Yeah," said Amanda. "I kind of wanted to, though. At first. Just for a minute. I hate that Frank must have known."

Mae did, too. But Frank was gone, and there was no point in worrying about that. "He just did what his parents did, you know? It's one or the other. You go along with them, or you run like hell."

"What his dad did," Amanda said firmly. "Nancy didn't know. And she's trying to help now. With Mom's house."

All of the other ways in which their mom was going to need help soon sat heavy between them. Mae hoped her sister was right about Nancy. She'd like to have a Nancy to lean on.

"I guess I'm going to come home," she said, and Amanda sat up straight and turned to her.

"Seriously?"

"Seriously," Mae said. She understood why Amanda looked surprised, but wasn't that exactly what they had just been talking about? "For a while, anyway. I can still write a new book if I can sell one. I can help Mom, but it will be good for me, too. I feel like, if everybody knows you, you can't be all, *Well, I don't have any idea what I want to do with my life but at least my silverware drawer is perfect.*"

"Sure you can," said Amanda. "You just described half the parents of kids in Frankie's class."

Damn it, Amanda wasn't supposed to argue with her—wasn't this Mae telling Amanda that maybe she was right all along? "But you stayed. You're part of the town. You get to know everybody who makes your coffee and your kids got to be little here where everyone knows who they are, and you don't have to be always working so hard to make things happen. You can just live."

"That's the problem," Amanda said. "That's why I wrote *Food Wars* in the first place—nothing ever does happen. You just get up and do things, and every day is the same until it isn't, and then you're old and your kids are gone and you're still the hostess in a chicken restaurant. It's exactly what you always used to say. Which you should still be sorry for, as long as we're apologizing, because you were really mean about Frank, and about Gus. But even though I loved Frank—" Amanda paused and gulped, and Mae eyed her apprehensively, but she wasn't crying, even if she looked like she might be about to. Instead, she looked out at Main Street, ran her tongue over her lips, and went on. "Even though I loved him and I wanted Gus and Frankie, so much, it didn't exactly end up being what I thought it would be. And now there's nothing to do and nothing to hope for, and *Food Wars* turned out to be more of the same crap. Worse, even."

Mae turned Mimi's recipe, and her note for her sister, over in her hands, gently. Amanda was right. She had been mean, or at least, too blunt. A steamroller, Jay had said. But Amanda had been so young—and she had been right—

And also wrong. Especially because somehow she had thought it should be so easy for her sister to do very hard things. She'd been young too, and maybe she had thought that if Amanda did what she did, came away to college, moved heaven and earth, and, yeah, hips and boobs, to pay for it, bought into the new life Mae was creating, then it would be even more solid. When it had never been solid in the first place, whereas the life Amanda had made with Frank, especially Gus and Frankie but not just them, the whole thing, was a rock, even if it seemed like it was Amanda who was having trouble seeing it now.

"I am sorry about that," Mae said softly, and felt rather than saw Amanda's blue eyes trained on her. "I am. I wanted you with me, not with Frank, but you did okay. You guys were great. Your kids are great. Watching them, today, with Mom—you have them, you have Nancy, and even when Frank died, you had this amazing place and community around you. And you still do."

Amanda stretched her legs out, then stood up suddenly. Mae knew she was trying not to cry, but her next words were still a surprise. "It didn't really turn out to be enough."

AMANDA

Enough heart-to-heart. Amanda reached out and slid Mimi's recipe from Mae's hands, changing the subject abruptly, as you can with someone who knows when you've had all you can take.

"What are we going to do about this money thing? Because Nancy wants to make it right, and I don't know what that means, and Mom— I'm afraid Mom will take Nancy's money." She looked at Mae to make sure her sister didn't just think that was a fine idea, but Mae was still listening to her. "Nancy doesn't have any money. I know it looks like she does, or at least has more than Mom, but unless we win—"

"You're not winning," Mae said almost automatically.

Then she stuck out her tongue, and Amanda had to laugh. "Yes, we are," she said. "We're going to expand and make Frannie's the best fried chicken place in the state. Or that was the plan." Should she even say this, this next part? Might as well. She'd already said so much. "But I'm not even sure we want to anymore."

"You did all that stuff to win—and you don't want to win?" Mae was staring at her now, her face serious again.

"I still want to win. For Nancy. And Frannie's. We're still going to win. I just—I think I'm done with chicken. You said it a long time ago, and you were wrong then, but you're right now. I need to get out there and try to figure out who I am without"—she gestured around her—"any of this. Not that I know what I do want to do. And Nancy— I'm not even sure she wants it either. But we're still winning." She smiled faintly as she stood up, stretching her legs, and Mae followed. "Maybe we just want to beat the pants off you."

"No, you're not." Mae paused for a minute, and a look came across her face that Amanda recognized. Mae, thinking. Mae, about to start something. Without even realizing she was doing it, Amanda took a step back, and Mae put a hand out and grabbed her sister's arm. "What do you mean, Nancy might not want to win either?"

She had said way too much. "Oh, she wants to win. Hell yeah." Whatever Mae had in her head, it better not be that Frannie's was going to throw this thing. "It's just that she said something weird. When I told her I might be ready to—try something new." Amanda paused as Nancy's words came back to her, and she repeated them. "'What makes you think I'd want to run Frannie's without you?'"

"Huh," said Mae. "That is—weird."

"And not like she wanted me to feel guilty, either. She's not Mom. It was more like, just real. And now I don't know." Mae was looking thoughtful—and just a little too happy. "Which doesn't mean we're not winning, if that's what you're thinking, because I can tell you're thinking something."

"It's just—if she doesn't want to—what if—" Mae stopped, tapping her foot thoughtfully on the wooden boards of the porch and her fingers on one hip. Amanda waited for what seemed like forever until Mae finally looked up, eyes bright. "If she feels that way, maybe we can do something big. This is our chance. Everybody will be excited that Mimi and Frannie didn't hate each other. We'll all be trying to figure out what to do about that loan. And the thing is, we're all equal now. Anybody could win this. I think Mimi's will, you think Frannie's will, but we can all see that there are good things in both places, right?" She grabbed Amanda's arms, almost dancing with excitement.

"Sure," said Amanda. And there were. If she could have a piece of her mother's apple pie right now, she'd take it; she was starving. But other than that, she didn't see what Mae was talking about. "But I don't see how it helps."

"You will," said Mae, and she let go of Amanda's arms and

marched into Mimi's, reaching back to pull Amanda after her, grinning. They both knew what it meant for Amanda to just walk through Mimi's like it was nothing, but they had said enough.

"First, we show everybody that recipe," Mae said. "Then, we figure it out. We're going to make this work, you know?"

Amanda put an arm around her sister too, so that they wouldn't fit into the pass-through door until Mae let her go and Amanda wriggled her way into going first, which would apparently never stop mattering. To either of them. "I don't even know what you're talking about," she said over her shoulder. "But, yeah. I know we will."

She led Mae out the back door of Mimi's and through the patio, and as Barbara's house came into view, Mae held back and gestured toward it.

"Do you do that?" she asked, looking at Amanda.

"Do what?"

"Keep everything," Mae said. "I mean, you were right. Earlier. Mean, but right. Most of what I do is running from this—but really I'm just like her, underneath. It just comes out differently. And I wondered what it is for you."

"It's not this bad," Amanda said grudgingly. "Messy, but nothing like this. I just don't care about cleaning, and I guess I don't really know how."

Mae looked at her with interest. "Oh no," Amanda said. "That was not an invitation. Or a cry for help. It's not that bad. And Frankie"—she smiled—"she doesn't just look like you; she's like you. She cleaned out my closet last week and threw everything away. We're good."

"I knew I liked Frankie," Mae said, squinting her eyes into the sunlight and crinkling up exactly the same light sprinkling of freckles that Frankie had.

"I don't think it was the mess that got to me so much as just never knowing anything," Amanda said. "Like, if there would be dinner, or, if there was dinner, if it would kill me. Or even, like, if Mom would just do normal things, like go to parent-teacher night. She sent you once, remember? When you were starting junior high and I was still in fifth grade?"

"I was probably more useful," Mae pointed out. "I wrote everything down. I even signed up to bring cups or something to your holiday party. I remembered, too."

"It wasn't the same."

"I know," Mae said. "I tried. We tried. And I guess"—she gestured to the house again—"we're still trying."

"Yeah," said Amanda as they started to walk across the parking lot. "I guess." With Mimi's recipe in her hand, their whole history looked different. Even *Food Wars* looked different. If she had really been trying—if Barbara was trying, if Mae was trying—maybe they could have lived up to the real Mimi's and Frannie's legacy, instead of waiting until it got shoved in their faces. And until they had to do their real trying with cameras rolling.

She glanced at Mae, walking next to her on the familiar route between Mimi's and Barbara's house. "You sure you couldn't just show everyone this?"

"No, you should do it," Mae said. Then, with an understanding look: "Just pretend this morning didn't happen. We never fought, nothing ever went wrong. You don't even know what kind of story *Food Wars* is going to make of this, and so what? This is what matters now." She pointed to the recipe. "And you were right. It makes everything different, and at the perfect time, because believe me, nobody wants to be in the middle of this anymore." Mae gave her a little hip bump. "And you're holding our way out." She grinned, and Amanda stopped in her tracks. What was Mae up to?

"You have to tell me," she said. She couldn't do this without knowing what Mae was thinking. Mae smiled triumphantly, but before she could answer, Sabrina came around from the back of the house.

"There you two are," she said, and she didn't look pleased.

"Nancy keeps telling me you're going to clear this whole recipe question up, Amanda, and if that's the case, let's get it rolling."

Amanda took a deep breath. *Pretend it never happened.* Pretend the cameras aren't there, maybe, forget about everything else. Just focus on the really big piece of this: Mimi never hated Frannie. Frannie never feuded with Mimi. Even with Sabrina standing there impatiently, Amanda took a minute to look from the small shadow of Mimi's up at the house, thinking about the woman who had built this, who had somehow pulled together what must have been a huge sum to help her sister, who had wanted, above everything else, to make sure that her little sister, too, could take care of herself.

Impulsively, she turned and hugged Mae, hard, and then, ignoring Sabrina and her trailing cameras, walked briskly toward the patio where Nancy had gathered Barbara, Andy, Gus, and Frankie and where Jay sat, too, looking amused by Aida, who had pulled up a chair close to his. Barbara looked tired and a little more blank than usual, and Amanda saw the changes in her that her accustomed eyes had been missing, but there was no time to think about that now. Frankie and Gus each had a can of Coke in their hand and streaks of dirt and dust across their faces.

Amanda held up the letter in one hand, carefully, and waved her other arm, gathering them in.

"Okay, everybody. I have something—an announcement, I guess—just something you have to see. So, you know Andy realized the Mimi's and Frannie's chicken was the same when he tasted it at the chef competition. And he and Mae thought I stole the recipe." She saw Mae lean over and whisper something in her mother's ear and remembered—Mae hadn't told Barbara about the recipe, or any of the rest of it. Well, she had started, and the cameras were very much rolling. She would just have to go on, and they'd clear it all up later. "But they were wrong, and it turns out we were all wrong. The chicken is the same because the recipes are the same, and they've always been the same, because Mimi gave her recipe to Frannie when Frannie started her own business."

Barbara stood up abruptly, and Aida moved too, with surprising speed, to her niece's side. Amanda walked over to her mother, holding the letter so that she could see it too, but there was something she had to say first.

"I'm sorry," she said softly. Her mother might not know that she had told *Food Wars* about the house yet, but there was still plenty to apologize for. "I didn't mean it, Mom. Mae— I was mad at Mae. I'm sorry. And now—" She glanced up at her mother's face and thought she saw an opening there. "Just listen." Carefully, she showed them all the recipe on the front of the paper and described the way Gus had finally shown Nancy where it was hidden. Then she read from the back, leaving nothing out.

> *Frannie, I wish you much luck with Frannie's. I do not think your man will be up to the job but I wish you much luck with him as well. Do not worry about the loan yet and do not tell him. This money and Frannie's are yours. Like all men he will want to run things but he is easily fooled. I think that it is best I leave you to it for a while, as he and I will not agree.*
>
> *—Mimi*

And then the final line, in that different hand:

Owe Mimi $1,400, October 29, 1889

Barbara reached for the paper, and after a glance at Nancy, Amanda gave it to her. Barbara turned it gently in her hands. "You're right," she said simply. "That's Mimi's writing. That's our recipe. Your recipe."

She looked up at Amanda, then at Nancy, and gave her head a little shake before she went on. "And, I guess, an IOU."

"Which we're going to make good," said Nancy, and Amanda rushed in.

"We have to figure out how, Mom, but we know she died before she could pay it back. Or we think she did. And we know—" Amanda stopped. She didn't want to say it in front of the cameras, or really at all, but they knew at least some of the Pogociellos would have known, or could have guessed. There was good reason to be angry, but no one left to be angry with, or at least that was what Amanda hoped. She watched as her mother read the note again, and then held it, staring down as though if she looked for long enough, the scrap of paper would offer even more answers. But this one, her mother had to decide for herself. After a long, tense silence, Barbara spoke.

"It wasn't Frannie," she pronounced. "That's what matters. It wasn't Frannie, and it wasn't you, either." She handed the paper to Mae, walked over to Nancy, and stuck out her hand. When Nancy took it, Barbara pulled the other woman into an embrace. Amanda's eyes met Barbara's over Nancy's shoulder, and although no words were exchanged, Amanda felt a lightening of a load she had been carrying for so long that she was barely aware of it anymore.

When her mother and mother-in-law broke apart, they were both laughing, and Amanda nearly clapped. Nancy might not have told them about the loan right away, but Amanda knew she would have, even if Nancy had doubted herself. It was time for her mother to see who Nancy really was and why Amanda loved her—and maybe why there was room for both Barbara and Nancy in Amanda's life.

"I still don't understand," said Andy. "Why did the chicken change? Because when I first tasted it, it wasn't the same as Mimi's. Not at all."

"I didn't know we had the recipe," Nancy said. "When Frank died, I didn't even know a recipe existed. Frank Junior probably knew, but we never expected—" She trailed off, shaking her head. "Obviously no one thought they'd both die at the same time. But it turned out my Frank showed Gus, and Gus didn't know I didn't have it." Noticing the camera on her, she turned away and wiped the tears off her face before she went on.

"After I ran out of the mixture Frank had made, I started winging it. I knew it was never right, but what else could I do? When Gus realized I wasn't using the recipe just this week—it's a long story—he showed me, and we made it on Saturday morning, and I was so happy it was the right chicken again, and that's what we brought to *Food Wars*. I never dreamed it would cause such a commotion."

Sabrina stepped in front of the camera. "Well, it certainly did," she declared. "The mystery of the recipe may be solved, but the Food War still remains." She smiled and subtly pulled at Amanda's hand so that she had Amanda on one side and Mae on the other. "Our chefs report that there's much more to great fried chicken than just what spices go in the coating, and they're eager to tell you what they think, and who will ultimately win one hundred thousand dollars and the right to declare themselves the Fried Chicken Food War Champion. Will it be Frannie's, where the drinks are flowing and the regulars are happily biting into the old familiar chicken"—she gestured to Amanda—"or will it be Mimi's, where the spokespuppies have a new home and all's right in the world?" She stood, smiling, then dropped her shoulders and her smile.

"Cut. Okay, people, I'm glad you've got a happy ending to the Amanda story, but we've still got filming to do. We've decided to go back to neutral ground for the final scenes, so tomorrow morning, eight A.M., at the 1908 Standard for the big reveal." She patted Mae and Amanda on their shoulders, then called to her crew. "Pack it up, guys."

Mae looked at Sabrina in horror, then pointed to the mess around them on the lawn. "You're not going to help get all the rest of this out of here? Or film Mom in her new space?"

"Nope," said Sabrina over her shoulder as she walked toward the parking lot. "Changed my mind. We've got everything we need."

Her cameraman, moving between Jay and Gus to take down a light he'd set up there, shrugged. "We've left worse messes," he said. Then he looked around. "Well, maybe not, actually. Good luck."

Barbara disregarded the crew rolling up cords under her feet and spoke to Mae. "What's this about Amanda stealing a recipe?" She sank into a dining room chair, one of six that were strewn across the grass, and Amanda saw Nancy watching her thoughtfully.

Mae was watching Barbara, too. She flushed. "I saw Amanda in Mimi's one night. I didn't tell you. And then, when Andy tasted the chicken and it was the same, he thought—well, I thought—she took it. And I said so. To Sabrina, with the cameras . . . I'm sorry. I should have given you a chance, Amanda. I should have known you wouldn't lie."

Barbara looked up, energized for a moment. "You know your sister doesn't tell lies, Mae." She glanced at Amanda, and their eyes met. "She does a lot of things, apparently, but not that." Her voice slowed, and she paused, as if looking for words.

Amanda could see that Nancy, and probably every adult on the patio other than the self-centered Sabrina, now disappearing in the distance, had begun to realize that Barbara had more problems than just a messy house. She put a hand on Nancy's shoulder and nodded toward her mother, speaking softly so her mother wouldn't notice the exchange. "I'll tell you later," she whispered, and caught Aida's eyes on them, and Andy's. He, too, would have to know.

After much too long, Barbara went on. "I'm glad about Mimi and Frannie," she said, "but there was more to all this. Your man," she said, now looking at Nancy. "He and his father put me through a rough time. Wanted to buy the place out from under me, and they were willing to do just about anything to make it happen." She spoke very slowly, as though choosing every word. "We're a ruthless lot on all sides, I guess. Maybe it's time we stop working against each other."

"Past time," said Nancy. "And I want to say it too, Mae. I'm sorry.

When Gus showed me the recipe, I was worried about the chicken, and then when I read the back—I should have come over right then, and I didn't. Maybe I could have prevented all this."

"Maybe," said Mae, sounding more cheerful now and watching Sabrina and her crew pack into their cars. Amanda looked at her. *Are you going to tell us now?* Mae shook her head, glancing at their mother.

"And maybe it's all for the best." She clapped her hands together briskly. "Either way, we have some figuring out to do," she said, then, looking around: "And some cleaning up." She visibly assessed her troops, and her gaze landed on Gus. "You," she said. "Mom, how about launching our détente by having Gus help you prep for Mimi's tonight? That frees up Muscles here"—she gestured to Andy—"to give us a hand for another hour or so."

Barbara hesitated, and Amanda watched Mae play her trump card. She knew what her sister was trying to do—get Barbara out of the house before she had a chance to start putting things that "we might need" or "I could sell" back inside. "Of course," Mae said thoughtfully, "if you *need* Andy . . ."

Barbara got up instantly. "I'm fine, Mae," she said, and looked at Gus. "I know you're good on the baseball field," she said. "You any good in the kitchen?"

Gus nodded, with a glance at Amanda. She smiled encouragingly. "I am," he said. Barbara took his hand, and together they marched off for the restaurant.

"Nice one," said Amanda softly to her sister, and Mae laughed.

"Andy," she said, "Mom's kitchen? It's a nightmare. But the more we get out while we've got that giant dumpster thing they brought, the better."

Andy nodded. "I'll help," said Jay, and Amanda watched doubt temper Mae's resolve. Jay smiled reassuringly, and as he did, Kenneth walked up, followed by Patrick, each carrying a container of iced coffees.

"We," Kenneth said, "are in, too. Patrick will check the base-ment for the valuable antiques I am dead sure aren't in there, and I will provide Andy and Jay with additional hard labor in return for the promise of what I understand is the Mimi's-and-Frannie's fa-mous fried chicken dinner."

Mae and Amanda both looked at him, surprised.

"Ran into Sabrina on the way out, arguing with someone about how to set this up for tomorrow morning's big winner announce-ment," he said. "News travels fast."

Patrick passed out the coffees, and, for Frankie, with a flourish, "your favorite lemonade." A pump of lavender syrup, and a pump of pomegranate, Amanda knew.

"Okay," Mae said. "Jay, Andy, and Kenneth in the kitchen. Frankie and Patrick in the basement. Frankie, make sure he throws nearly everything away, okay? I don't trust him. He looks like a saver. You, on the other hand—your mom told me about you."

Frankie grabbed her lemonade and hurried off. Amanda could tell she was pleased, but still a little wary of her aunt; Amanda had a feeling Mae would win her over soon. The patio began to empty, and Mae turned to Amanda and Nancy. After a moment, she stuck out her hand at Nancy.

"Hi," she said. "I'm Mae. Let's start over."

Nancy laughed a little. It was hard to resist Mae when she wanted to be charming.

Mae pulled a chair up close to Nancy as the basement crew headed for the house, and took a sip of her coffee. "I think the three of us need a sit-down," she said, glancing at Amanda. Was Mae ac-tually asking for her help here? She waited, unsure, and Mae kept talking, a little nervously. "Amanda and I—we're just trying to fig-ure out what to do. About Mimi's, and Frannie's, and this whole—" She gestured around her.

"War," said Nancy, and she leaned back in her chair and looked at them both.

Mae looked as though she didn't know how to take that, but Amanda knew Nancy was just waiting. Nancy knew the value of listening to other people talk, even if they didn't want to. Nancy and Mae had never had a chance to get along, but maybe they could. If Mae could back off a little and let Nancy step up to be part of whatever she had in mind. Amanda jumped in, hoping to help. "Mae and I kind of figured out that we're in this together. We have a lot we can work together on, at least. No more pushing each other under the *Food Wars* bus."

Nancy shook her head. "I think that Sabrina could get anybody riled up if she tried."

Mae and Amanda both laughed. "We're trying to—end that," Mae said. "And Amanda said that you said . . . something about not running Frannie's anymore."

Wait, they were going there? Straight there? Amanda rushed in, trying to soften it, but there was no way this didn't just look like she'd been telling Mae all their business. "I didn't just tell her," she began. "I mean, we were talking—"

"It's okay," said Nancy. "You're right. I said it. You said you might want to do something else, and I just thought—I don't know what I thought. You started this, Amanda. And I know you were thinking we could grow Frannie's, and you're right, my Frank had big dreams in that direction. And I was excited. I thought I wanted that too. But then we got so busy, and there were so many more people, and I kept thinking, what if it's always like this? What if the staff is always frantic, and I've got that many more hours to work every day . . . and then to do it, not just without Frank, but without you . . ."

She trailed off, and fortunately Mae had the sense not to interrupt. "I want you to figure out what you want to do with your life, Amanda. I really do. I guess I was thinking maybe I want to figure out what to do with my life, too. I like Frannie's. I just don't know if I want to do all that alone."

Amanda wanted her to go on. They talked, they did, but never like this. Never about all this time, running somebody else's dream. Somebody—two somebodies, who were never coming back.

Mae, though, had an agenda. "Yeah, I can see that," she said, and Amanda could tell she was trying not to rush past the moment, but she just couldn't help herself. Mae would always be Mae, and Amanda watched her sister lean forward, blue eyes sparkling, to touch Nancy on the knee, hoping her mother-in-law knew that Mae meant well.

"Because it would be a ton of work alone, right? And even if Amanda stayed on, you'd know her heart wasn't in it, and that's no good either. But it's a family tradition—maybe Gus wants to run it, or Frankie—so you wouldn't want to let it go, right? And I had an idea."

Nancy looked at Mae speculatively, and Amanda had a feeling that Nancy could practically see Mae's wheels turning, in part because Nancy's own wheels turned much the same way. She had never seen it before, but Nancy and Mae were a lot alike. They were always thinking ahead and always making Amanda feel two beats behind.

Nancy was quiet a minute. Amanda expected her to brush Mae off—Nancy didn't need anyone else's ideas. But instead, Nancy looked at them both seriously. "It would be too much work alone. And I don't want Amanda to do it if she doesn't want to. I think some part of me thought that one of these days, Amanda would take over, and I'd do her job, and she would do mine. I like just managing the front of the house."

Amanda tried to keep the surprise off her face. Take over the books and the hiring and the insurance and the—the taxes, and everything?

Nancy laughed. "I know," she said. "I should have known better, right? But that was kind of my plan, and then I didn't want to mess us up, now that we both seemed to be getting to be okay. I didn't even mean for it to go on this long. I meant to talk to you about it. I meant for us both to figure out what to do with Frannie's—how to keep it going, for Gus and Frankie, if we wanted to, or even how to sell it. But it was just never the right time."

Amanda reached for Nancy's hand. "Nancy—I didn't know. I guess I never thought about you not wanting all that work. I'm sorry. I kind of did let you be the grown-up, didn't I?"

"You had the kids, and things were hard enough," Nancy said briskly, pulling her hand away and patting Amanda on the arm. "We both did what we had to do."

"But maybe now it's time to do what you want to do," said Mae. This time, Amanda was glad she was willing to rush in where others might hesitate. She still didn't know where Mae was going with this, but they needed a plan, and Mae had one, which was more than Amanda had. All Amanda had was a sinking feeling that she couldn't leave Nancy stuck with Frannie's alone—not now, and maybe not ever.

Mae, though, was beaming at them both. "Okay, here's my idea," she said. "We throw our lots in together and beat *Food Wars* at their own game. Partners, all of us, one single business. We run both restaurants, everybody does what they're good at. My mom keeps running Mimi's, Andy runs both kitchens, Nancy does the staff and the front of the house for both places, I keep track of all the details and ordering and stuff. Me, or maybe— Well, that's another idea. But it's covered."

Actually, that was kind of brilliant. Out of the corner of her eye, Amanda checked Nancy for her reaction. She looked—intrigued.

Mae kept talking. "I don't actually know if anyone wants to do this," she said. "I haven't talked to Andy. Or"—she raised her eyebrows and pressed her lips together, conveying wry doubt—"my mom. But if we could all agree—what would you think? Do you think it's possible?"

"I'd need time to think about it," said Nancy. "Maybe. I'm not saying it's a no. But it's not something we can just do overnight."

"But that's exactly what we have to do," said Mae. "Because

right now, before anybody wins—it's the only time we can do it and have everybody come in equal, no worrying about the loan or whose money is whose. If we wait, I just feel like we're going to be back at Mimi's versus Frannie's again."

Jay came out of the kitchen, followed by Kenneth, who was using his shirt to wipe his forehead.

"She's right," Jay said, pulling up a chair and planting himself firmly in the conversation. "Do you know we can hear every word you're saying in there? I don't know if you two ever brought dates out here in your misspent youth, but your mother was perfectly set up to spy on you. So—combining Mimi's and Frannie's. I'm not saying it's a good idea or a bad idea. This is your baby, not mine. But Mae's right that you have to figure this out today. You have a unique moment here."

"Look at it this way," said Kenneth. "Right now, everybody has pretty much the same shot at having a hundred thousand dollars and the *Food Wars* crown, for whatever that's worth, and in terms of promotion it's probably worth quite a bit. I know you disagree on who's going to win—"

"Frannie's," said Amanda, at the same moment Mae said, "Mimi's."

But they were just kidding now, and Amanda reached her hand out for a high five from her sister. Nancy might not go for this, or she might. But Mae was right—it was a good idea, and if Nancy didn't like it, well, maybe she wasn't as unhappy running Frannie's as she said. Maybe everything was, one way or another, going to be okay.

"Right," said Kenneth. "So, once one of you actually wins, it's different. Then it's somebody on somebody else's coattails."

"It's a classic negotiation scenario," said Jay. "You have to decide what to do before they tell you who won, because otherwise, everything changes. It's like the moment before somebody develops the bomb. The last chance to do something before the whole power differential shifts."

"That's pretty dramatic," said Nancy. "I think we could do this even after we know who wins."

"You think you could," said Jay. "But you won't."

"If Frannie's wins, Mom will think you're trying to crush Mimi's," said Mae. "She already has kind of a thing about that. And if Mimi's wins—well—I don't know what you'll think, but don't you think you might feel different?" She grinned at Amanda. "You know how this works," she said. "'The only winning move is'—"

"'Not to play,'" Amanda, Kenneth, and Jay all capped her quote in unison.

"This is our big chance," Mae said. "Plus, I think it would really piss Sabrina off."

"I'm not putting my family business into a partnership just to piss off Sabrina," Nancy protested, but she was smiling.

"And to let all of us build lives we want, instead of just kind of accepting our lots," said Mae. "It really could work, Nancy. If we each had a defined role, and if we used the hundred thousand dollars—together—to rebrand and promote ourselves based on the *Food Wars* win—which, no matter who it is, is a win for everyone's chicken, right?—we'd be the only *Food Wars* feud to ever end in a peace treaty."

"You could build a good story out of that," said Kenneth. "Between that and the history, Mimi's and Frannie's could become real destinations, at least in the Midwest."

"I believe the phrase you're looking for is 'authentic American icons,'" said Mae.

Nancy turned to Amanda, then stopped and chuckled. "I don't even have to ask you what you think, do I?"

"It does seem like a good idea to me," said Amanda, suddenly aware that she was smiling. "But it's not just that. I'm happy because—we're all here, talking about it. Not fighting. It feels good for a change. Maybe I shouldn't get a vote, though, because I'm kind of already there, in between."

"You get a vote," said Nancy. "I suppose we could always undo it, if it doesn't work. Who runs the business part of it?"

"Jay," said Mae. "That's the other part of my idea. He's been a restaurant consultant for chains and big hotels for years, and he hates it. He could wind that up—come here for a while—if he wanted to." She glanced at Jay while she was speaking, and then looked out into the distance, avoiding everyone's eyes. Amanda could see her sister's hands clenched behind her, fingers dancing in an anxious, fidgety motion. This was what she hadn't said, back in Mimi's. The part of moving home Mae hadn't talked about.

An hour ago, Amanda wouldn't have put a dollar or a doughnut on the idea of Jay moving to Merinac. But watching him with Kenneth, seeing his weird ease with this whole situation—she didn't know what to think.

"Actually, I quit last week," said Jay.

Mae snapped her gaze away from whatever she was pretending to study in the distance and stared at Jay. *She didn't know,* Amanda realized. Her sister's eyes narrowed, and for a minute Amanda thought Mae was going to stand up and resume the fight they'd been having earlier, this time with Jay as her opponent. Instead, Mae blinked a few times, quickly. "Oh," she said, and there was a long, tense pause, Kenneth on the edge of the chair behind Jay as if he didn't know whether to back him up or return to the kitchen. "You didn't tell me," Mae finally finished.

"You've had plenty of surprises for me," Jay said evenly. "You knew I wanted to quit. You just told everyone I hated it, which I did, or at least, I hated the hours and the travel. And now you seem to have lined up another job for me anyway, so it's a good thing all around." He crossed his arms over his chest and smiled. "Right?"

Amanda had a feeling Mae had not been fully ready to have her dreams granted quite so quickly. She got it, too—Amanda might not be as practical as her sister, but she knew how Mae felt about regular paychecks and health insurance and benefits. They both knew what it was like to do without.

Mae didn't answer Jay.

"You really know what you're doing, then," Nancy said to Jay. "You could do this."

"I've helped merge everything from massive chains to two tiny glamorous island hotels whose chefs hated each other, so yes. I could. If I wanted to." He looked at Mae, but she was staring down at the ground, silent.

"You're the one who says we don't have time to think about it," said Nancy. "Would you want to? Would Barbara?"

"I can't speak for Barbara, but I'm more of a leaper than a thinker," said Jay. "It's the thing Mae and I both have in common. You would think she would want to think things through, with a bunch of flow charts or something, but she doesn't, she wants to do things. And so do I. So—"

He was grinning, and although Amanda held her breath, she knew what he was going to say.

"Yeah, I don't know. Probably. I'm probably in."

Kenneth whacked Jay on the shoulder. "Come on, man," he said. "Free coffee."

"For life?"

"A year, maybe. Mae drinks a lot of coffee. She'll put us out of business."

"Let me just make Mae sweat a little, okay? Probably. You'll have to settle for that," Jay said.

"Then me, too, probably," Nancy said. "But, Mae, you've got a job ahead convincing your mother." She got up. "I hate to leave you all with that kitchen," she said, "but I need to get to Frannie's. Amanda?"

Amanda was still looking at Mae. Her sister was really upset, she could tell. Her frozen expression wasn't her thinking; it was her holding everything back. She eyed Jay. Did he know it? She couldn't tell, but she didn't want to just leave them like that. "Uh, Mae?"

"Yeah?" Mae didn't turn her head.

"Should I come with you to talk to Mom?"

At that, Mae did turn to her, but her face was still and even pale. "No," she said slowly, and took a tiny breath in, as if she was scared to do more. "I think probably not," she said. "I'll do it."

"Call me, then, after? After you all talk?"

Mae smiled a little, and Amanda felt lighter. It was just Jay quitting, but that had to be a good thing. Mae just wasn't seeing it, for whatever reason. "Everything else is fitting right into your plans, right?" She looked hard toward Jay, willing her sister to see how great this was, and saw him looking at her, and blushed. Okay, she was not subtle.

"Yeah. I guess. I'll call you." Mae stared down at the ground again, and after a minute, Amanda followed Nancy off the porch. Mae would be okay. And Barbara had to see that this would work. She just had to.

What Amanda needed now was a little time to take all this in, but Gus was standing at the edge of the yard, holding his phone, and one look at him told Amanda that he was waiting for her—and that something was wrong. When they reached him, Nancy patted him on the shoulder. "It's all going to be okay," she said. "Really. We're just figuring some stuff out."

Gus looked up at the group still sitting around outside of Barbara's house and nodded. "Yeah, okay—I mean, that's not what— Mom, can I talk to you?"

Amanda gave Nancy a worried look but nodded, and Nancy kept going, on to the car, probably, but that was fine; Amanda's car was here from this morning, which seemed like a lifetime ago. Right now, Gus's expression had her a little panicked. "What? Is it Mom? Are you guys okay?"

"It's not Grandma, Mom, she's fine, she knows where I went. It's just—I did something. And I think you're going to be mad at me."

Amanda looked at her son more closely. He looked guilty, yes, but also maybe pleased. Whatever this was, it couldn't be that bad. And compared to the last few days—

"Spill it, Gus. If it's worse than saying I stole a recipe or that we serve frozen biscuits, I'm disowning you."

Gus smiled a little. Then he eyed the phone in his hand, started to speak, and instead, handed it to her, open to an e-mail from bhen72@gmail.com.

Gus, thanks for sending me the Carleen drawings. Most people are wrong when they think I'd want to see something, but you were right. Can you tell your mom to get in touch? Best, Bill

Bill—bhen72. Amanda stared at Gus, her mouth open.

"Bill Henderson," Gus said. "You know, the guy with the kid and the penguin, the comic strip? You used to read it to me, and we have all the books?"

Why, yes, she knew. She gaped at her son, disbelieving. Bill Henderson? E-mailing him?

"The new art teacher graduated with him, and I asked him if he would— They were just in the drawer, Mom. And I was afraid you might throw them away."

Amanda could barely find words for this. "You took—my sketchbook—and someone—"

"Showed it to him. Yeah. And he wants you to get in touch. Don't be mad, Mom. It's good that he wants to talk to you, right? Really good?" He looked at her, mostly smiling, still looking a little worried. "Plus, I think he still has it. You have to at least e-mail him to get it back."

Slowly, Amanda handed Gus's phone back to him. Then she hugged him, hard.

MAE

Mae took another tiny breath, and then another. Jay had just declared that he'd quit, and now he was picking up her plan and tossing it around so casually—*I could do that, yeah. If I wanted to.*

He was enjoying himself, damn him, and very at home here, in her mother's trash-filled yard. Somewhere in the depths of the fridge he had found a can of light beer he didn't seem to consider too old to drink, and he popped its top now, grinning at her.

Mae didn't have one word to express how she felt, and it was probably a good thing. Because no matter what he had thought he was doing, he was here now.

She found, after another moment, that she could just about smile back. She nodded at the beer can. "Slumming?" Jay's usual taste ran to the craft varieties, twelve bucks a bottle at a bar and six at the corner bodega. Tough to afford with no job.

"Beer is beer when it's this hot," he said. "Another advantage of your home state, maybe. Makes all beer taste good."

Patrick came out of the kitchen and handed Kenneth another can. "No treasures," he said. "And Frankie was born to throw things away, but I think she's keeping that pink tinsel Christmas tree. I arm-wrestled her for it, and I lost." He grabbed a chair and all three men made a big production of drinking, although Mae could feel Kenneth watching her. He knew, better than anyone, how desperately she craved control, and how hard it would be for her to have it suddenly taken away.

Mae tried to focus on the beer. "Oh, come on," she said as Patrick, with a flourish, set a fourth can in front of her. Seriously, they were all boys together? And she was just supposed to be okay with this?

"I should drink this whole thing without stopping, then burp and crush the can on my head, right?" Mae took a sip. It did taste good. "Then can I join your little men's club?"

"Just belated bonding," Kenneth said, kicking his feet up on a nearby plastic container. "If we had been invited to your wedding, we would have already completed these little rituals."

Mae flushed. As embarrassed as she had been about Merinac and everything that went with it, she was now equally ashamed of having denied it, and with that shame, the anger and fear over Jay's job came crashing back. "Well, we're here now," she finally said, tightly, and there was a silence as they drank their beer until she couldn't take it any longer and turned to Jay. "So, you seriously quit your fucking job?"

"I did," Jay said. "And then I got on a plane, because it did not seem like something to text about."

Mae wanted to be cool, but she couldn't manage it. She set the beer down, hard. "Your job, Jay? I just basically lost my job, and you quit yours? What are we doing for health insurance? How are we going to pay our rent?"

Kenneth burst out laughing. "Your rent, Mae? You just announced that you were moving here, taking over the family business with Jay as your wingman. Your rent?"

Yes, that was the plan. But not without lining things up, not without getting everything organized and moving bank accounts and maybe taking vacation time or even asking his company for a sabbatical. Not without a backup plan.

"Not like that! Not just, *I quit*! What if you want to go back? What if it doesn't work out? What if one of us gets sick, or the kids—I wanted to get everything worked out first, I—" Now that she was trying to talk about this, she couldn't breathe. She had not realized how much she was relying on Jay for a stable income—which she was never, ever supposed to do—and now he had burned all their bridges. She wasn't ready to depend on nothing but Mimi's again. She took a huge breath in and out and burst into frustrated, angry tears.

Jay got up quickly, knocking his chair over, and held her by the shoulders, then pulled her into his arms. "Mae," he said, then more loudly: "Mae. It's okay, Mae. I'm sorry. I gave notice, it's true, but it's not like I stood up on a table in the cafeteria and told them all to go to hell. I could probably go back someday, if I wanted to. It's okay. And we have the rent. And I can COBRA the health insurance, and we have savings, and it's okay."

She couldn't help it. Her shoulders shook, and all she could do was pull in deep, shuddering sobs against his chest. "Okay," she said, and sobbed again. "Okay."

Part of her knew she was being ridiculous. This was her idea— but what Jay didn't seem to get is that while Mae did jump into things, she always knew where the net was. Jay had just ripped down her net.

Kenneth tapped her on the shoulder, but she couldn't face him, and instead nodded against Jay's chest. "Mae," he said, "you are not your mother. And Jay, who I do not know very well but I note is still standing here after cleaning out the most disgusting stove I have ever seen, is not your father. And you are okay for money."

Mae felt Jay nodding. "More than okay, Mae," Jay said. "I wouldn't have done this if we weren't okay. You know we're okay."

Were they okay? They had two little kids, no jobs, and nothing but Mimi's to hold on to. She took a deep breath, this time without sobbing, and wiped her face across Jay's shirt for the second time that day. It was dirtier now. "Yeah," she said. "I do know. I do."

Jay put a hand under her chin and brought her face up to his. "I thought this was what you wanted," he said.

Mae laughed, one sobbing, gulping laugh. "It is. I think. I don't know what I want, I guess."

"Then want this," Jay said. "Because you've got it. We've got it."

"Okay. I'm sorry." Another breath. Mae let a tiny smile cross her face. "And you're in, right?"

Jay crushed her back into his chest. "I'm in," he said. "I get some things I want, though. I don't know what they are yet. But you owe me."

"I owe you," she repeated, then wriggled free, holding his hand. "I'm okay now. But don't do that again. I don't like surprises."

All three men laughed, and Mae laughed too, this time without the tears.

"Okay, okay," she said. "I don't mean to surprise you, really. You just don't keep up." She shook herself. Enough, enough. Jay had definitely unnerved her, but he was right. They'd be okay. She took another deep breath.

"Time to tackle Mom." Mae looked at Patrick and Kenneth, who had produced two more beers from somewhere and were lounging in their chairs. "Well? Are you just going to let me do this by myself? Because weird as it may seem, my mother generally prefers to take anyone else's advice over mine."

Kenneth got up, followed by Patrick. "Your mother likes me," Patrick said. "Does she like Jay?"

"We haven't spent much time together," Jay said. "She will, though. I'm likable."

Mae considered her approach. Jay's logic tactics and all that stuff about unique opportunities had worked on Nancy, but for Barbara—she reached for Jay's hand. "Don't push her," she said. "Just follow my lead, okay?"

"Lead on," he said.

×

Barbara narrowed her eyes when they all trooped into the Mimi's kitchen and spoke only to Mae. "You here to work tonight?"

That was it, then? After the whole afternoon, and finding the Mimi's recipe at Frannie's, and everything? Not for the first time, Mae marveled at her mother. Nobody hid their feelings so deeply or so well. She wanted to go give her a hug, but that wasn't what Barbara wanted right now, and she knew it. If back to business was better, back to business it would be.

"Actually, Mom, I'm here because I have an idea." Mae sat down on a kitchen stool herself and tried to look casual, while Kenneth, Patrick, and Jay struggled to find a place that was out of Andy's and Barbara's way as they prepped for the night's service.

Andy raised his eyebrows. "The last Moore sister to walk in here with an idea dragged us all into *Food Wars,* and that one isn't finished yet."

"Mine's better," said Mae, and came right out with it. "We're going to win tomorrow. But I found out tonight that Frannie's doesn't even care very much. Amanda doesn't want to make Frannie's bigger, she just thought she did, and Nancy doesn't want to run Frannie's alone, or even at all, really. She just did it because Frank died. And now—they both think Frannie's owes Mimi's. So"—this was the big play—"I think we should run it."

Barbara set down the raw chicken she was holding on the cutting board with a *thunk* and turned to face her daughter. "Run—Frannie's?"

"Run it like Frannie and Mimi would. Take it back to basics, do all the food fresh. Nancy could still run the waitstaff and all the seating; we don't do that. But the food"—she raised her eyebrows at Andy—"no more frozen stuff. Just Andy's best, in both places. Partners."

Partners. That was the part her mother would get hung up on, unless—

"I don't need partners," Barbara said, turning back to the counter.

Damn. "Mom," she said, and hesitated. But there was no one to bail her out, no one who knew her mother like she did, which was kind of the point. "Mom, we get Amanda back. And Gus and Frankie. And Frannie's is part of the family. We owe her. She didn't want it to happen like this. We owe Mimi. It's our recipe, Mom. Nancy might sell Frannie's or hire someone we don't like—I just feel like we need to bring it all back together."

Barbara thunked into the chicken with her cleaver. "I don't want anyone else in my kitchen," she said.

"Hey," said Andy.

"Anyone but Andy. And you. No Pogociellos. Well—"

Mae waited.

"Maybe Gus. And Frankie."

And Mae knew it was just a matter of talking from here.

AMANDA

Amanda awoke to Mae shaking her shoulder gently. "Amanda. Amanda. Wake up. We need you."

For just a heartbeat, she was in her old bed, in her old room, a teenager again with her big sister making sure she was on time for school. Then she sat up abruptly off the hard floor of Frannie's and grabbed the sweatshirt she had been using as a pillow.

"Oh God, I'm sorry. I fell asleep."

"You fell asleep hours ago," said Mae.

While Andy and Nancy and Jay were debating the frozen stuff on the Frannie's menu. Yes. Oh man, how could anyone care so much about mozzarella sticks?

She looked around. Gus was asleep too, with his head down on a table. Mae followed her gaze. "Frankie's out in the car," she said. "We're all going to go home, get some sleep before we spring this on Sabrina." She gave a cheerful wave to the camera still running in the corner. "But first we need you. Come on."

Amanda got up—*oof*, she was too old to sleep on the floor—tossed the sweatshirt onto the bar, and followed her sister out into the warm night. Propped up on chairs in the parking lot was the sign that had replaced her drawing at Mimi's, and Amanda stopped and stared at her sister. Why would she want to see that? She didn't care if they had all made up, that still hurt, and the sight of Andy and Kenneth next to it didn't help.

Mae gave her a little push. "You're looking at the back," she said. "I know. I'm sorry. But come on. This is good."

That sign—MIMI'S, SINCE 1886—was the part that was facing down, leaning on the chairs. Reluctantly, she walked around. The front was blank, just white paint covering the boards that together formed the square.

"There," said Mae happily. "We need you to make the new sign."

Kenneth gestured to the ground, where he had spread out Sharpies, a fat pencil, black and red paint, and a few brushes, along with a pad of paper and smaller pencils. "I didn't know how you like to work," he said.

How she liked to work. Amanda looked from one face to another, all smiling at her. Andy, too. She felt a huge rush of joy. Her work. And to have them set up a place for her to do it—she could have hugged them all. Instead, she turned to the blank sign in what she hoped was a professional way, although she knew she was beaming. "What do you want on it? 'Mimi's'?" They had never talked about that. How would Nancy feel, if the Frannie's name got washed away? She wasn't even sure how she felt. Amanda knew what it was like, being the youngest. Frannie should get her due. She hesitated over the Sharpies, looking at Mae, who grinned.

"Of course not," she said. "New start, new name." She pointed to the sign. "Introducing 'The Chicken Sisters.'"

Amanda swung around to face her sister. "Mae—that's perfect."

And Mae knew it, too. "The Chicken Sisters, established 1886. Because Mimi's started it, and Frannie's kept it going." She was beaming. "We worked it all out. While you were snoring."

Amanda ignored that. *The Chicken Sisters.* She loved it, and she grabbed hold of Mae's hand and squeezed. Mae squeezed back, hard. "I know, I know," she said. "But business! Can you do it?"

Of course she could do it. She pulled her hand away, still smiling. Fine. Hugs later, if that was the way Mae wanted it. She picked up the pad. The lettering was easy, but what were they—Chicken Frannie and Chicken Mimi—what were they doing? High fiving? That would be hard at this level of detail. Wings around each other, maybe. She sat down on the ground, staring down at the blank page, and looked up to find them all watching her. She waved them away. "You can't stand here," she said. "I have to think about it. Go."

Mae and Kenneth did, but Andy lingered, and when she looked up he had his back to her, contemplating the blank sign. "I was hoping to see you draw it," he said. "I've always wished I could draw."

"Everybody says that," said Amanda. It was easier to talk to him while looking down at her pencil, and so she sketched in a beak pointing jubilantly into the air. "You probably could. Even with some talent, you still have to learn. I think anybody could learn at least enough to draw a little."

Andy, too, seemed to find it easier to talk while looking at something else. Either that or he was really interested in the way paint covered wood grain. "Maybe you could teach me."

"Oh," said Amanda quickly, "I'm crap at—" Just in time, she looked up and saw that Andy was fidgeting nervously, tapping his fingers against his leg, and caught herself. That was not the right answer. Because that was not really the question. "I mean, maybe," she said. "Or we could sit together and you could just try. For fun. Sometime."

"I'd like that," Andy said, then: "Amanda, I'm sorry about the recipe thing. I should have known you wouldn't do that. But I haven't always been a very good judge of people. I'm sorry."

Amanda put down her pencil and met his eyes. He didn't look confident or cocky at all, just like someone who really was sorry. Who wanted another chance. "Yeah," she said. "I get that. Let's just start over, okay? Plus, if that hadn't happened, we wouldn't all be here. So I can't exactly be mad."

"I'm just a tool of fate," he said. "But I wish it hadn't complicated things."

Amanda shrugged. She wasn't ready to do this now, wasn't sure if she wanted there to be anything to complicate. She had a fresh surface, good tools, chickens to draw, and she wanted to focus on that. "It's okay," she said. Then, as nicely as she could, "I'm going to concentrate on this now, if that's okay."

He hung there, shifting his weight from side to side, until she stopped, put down her pencil, and held out her hand to him. "Everything's always complicated," she offered, and he took her hand, and it was the same feeling as when he had touched the back of her neck, running all the way through her. She didn't know that she wanted that feeling, but it was there. He squeezed a little, then let go, and with a little boost of confidence, she waved him away. "Go on," she said. "I'm working."

×

A few short hours later, they were all gathered outside the front door of the Inn—Amanda, Andy, Mae and Jay, Gus and Frankie, Nancy, Barbara, even Aida. Jessa had Madison by one hand and Ryder on her hip, Madison wildly blowing kisses at them all. Kenneth ushered them grandly in, while Patrick stood just inside, soundlessly clapping. They all faced each other for a minute with a sense of suppressed laughter.

"Shhh," Mae said, as Andy let out what could best be called a giggle.

"I'm sorry," he whispered. "I can't help it."

"Come on," said Mae. "Before she sees we're all together."

Mae turned and grabbed Amanda's hand, letting Jay fade to the back, and the two of them, with Nancy and Barbara close behind, strode right into the dining room. Mae's feet were loud on the Inn's old wooden floors, and Amanda looked down and saw that she was wearing a pair of gorgeously embroidered cowboy boots.

Sabrina leapt up when they came in and rushed toward them—they were late; she must have been waiting—then stopped short, staring at them. Then, just as Mae had hoped, Sabrina gestured to a camera, which swung toward them.

"Where do you want us, Sabrina?" Mae spoke with an ease Amanda envied as much as the boots. They had agreed that Amanda would do the talking for the big reveal, and Mae had refused to allow her to write something out. "Know the three things you want to say," Mae had insisted. "Hold three fingers in your pocket if you need to. Say each one, end your sentences, then stop."

That last point, Amanda knew instantly, was exactly the piece of advice she needed to hang on to. *Say what I want to say. Then stop.* If she could have done that for the past week she would be so much better off. Although—she glanced back at Andy and found his eyes on her—her way hadn't been quite the disaster she had thought it was. This wasn't anywhere close to what she had thought she wanted when she sent that first e-mail to *Food Wars.* And yet somehow it was.

Sabrina ushered them up to the fireplace end of the room, where the three chefs were settling in behind a table. "I was thinking Mimi's here, and Frannie's here," she said, pointing, then stepping back out of the scene.

Without even a glance at any of her co-conspirators, Mae released Amanda's hand, walked to the side Sabrina had gestured to for Mimi's, put a hand on her hips, and turned. "Nah," she said. "Come on up here, everybody." The rest of them scrambled around the Inn's rearranged dining tables and joined her. "We're good all here on the same side, Sabrina," said Mae, and a wicked grin crossed her face.

Sabrina surveyed them. "You're not going to tell me what's going on, are you?"

"Nope."

Unexpectedly, then, Sabrina flipped at the waist, fluffed her hair, then grabbed a mirror from a table to the side and looked herself over critically before turning back to face them. "Okay," she said. "As long as it makes good television." She shifted, took up a central position right next to Mae and in front of the group, and then gazed into the camera, morphing, before their eyes, into the warm, friendly host of *Food Wars*.

"Hello again! We're back here today for the final moments in the Fried Chicken Food War, where two century-old institutions have been facing off in a battle for who can claim the title for the best, most authentic fried chicken the little town of Merinac, Kansas, has to offer—and maybe the best fried chicken in the state of Kansas. Little Mimi's, which started as a chicken shack serving passengers on the railroad line, still serves nothing but chicken, biscuits, salad, and French fries. Frannie's, which grew from a coal-mining hangout to a full-service restaurant, has a bigger menu, a bigger dining room, and a bigger reputation. Midway through the competition, we had a big surprise—the restaurants, which were started by a pair of sisters in the 1880s, use what amounts to the same recipe—prepared differently and served differently, but all made with the same ingredients. So it all comes down to this: who does it better?"

She stepped forward, in front of the table, and addressed a different camera. "Our chef-judges, Simon Rideaux, Cary Catlin, and James Melville, have eaten at each establishment. They've had the experience and they've tasted the chicken, and then they've gone back to each restaurant with exactly that question in mind. Fried chicken, they say, sounds simple. But execution is everything. And only one of the restaurants can win our hundred-thousand-dollar prize."

Amanda felt Mae squeeze her hand. In the doorway, behind Sabrina and the cameras, Kenneth and Jay stood ready to carry in the sign she had painted last night. The sight of it made her feel better. It was a good sign, and this was a good thing. And Sabrina couldn't ruin it.

Finished with her opening speech, Sabrina turned. This was what they'd been unable to plan for. Would she start with Mae, who would then throw it to Amanda, or come straight to Amanda?

Would she ask them to talk before the judges, or after? It varied, on previous episodes; plus it would be clear to Sabrina that something out of the ordinary was going on, so who knew what she'd try.

In the moment when Sabrina began to walk back toward Mae and Amanda, Amanda saw a challenge in her eyes and knew that Sabrina was coming straight to her, to the weak spot. There was no wink in her eyes, either, as she took up that weird stance that meant she was talking to you and to the camera at the same time.

"Amanda, you grew up with Mae at Mimi's. And then you married Nancy's son, Frank, and started work at Frannie's, where you've been ever since. Of everyone here, you know most about what goes on behind the scenes at both restaurants. What are you thinking now, when we're about to declare one the winner?"

Amanda squeezed Mae's hand back, and then, resolutely, let go. "I'm thinking we all win, Sabrina," she said, to the camera, not Sabrina, as Mae had coached her. This actually made it easier. "When we found out our recipes were the same, we found out something else. The feud between the sisters that we've built our own feud on never existed. Mimi wanted Frannie's to succeed. Frannie wanted the best for Mimi's. There was room for two chicken shacks in this one little town." She had to take a breath, and Sabrina jumped in.

"But there's no room for two winners of *Food Wars,*" she said. "One of you is going to take home a hundred thousand dollars, and the other gets Miss Congeniality. We've seen a lot of strife between you two sisters over the course of the last week. You look like you've settled things now—but are we going to see something different once the winner is revealed?"

She left her microphone hovering between them, giving Mae a chance to jump in, but Mae, as they'd agreed, didn't take it. Amanda had two points to go.

"When we say we both win, we really mean it. Times have changed since it made sense for Frannie and Mimi to each run their own place. So one of us will win, yeah, but we're going to move forward together." She glanced at Mae, who nodded. She was ready. "There's room for two chicken restaurants, and Mimi's and Frannie's aren't going anywhere, but there's only room for *one* business."

Kenneth and Jay walked in, right in front of the cameras, and set down the sign for Frankie, Gus, and Nancy to hold up, with Barbara nearby, as smoothly as though they had practiced it a dozen times. It was perfect, and although Amanda was meant to keep going, she suddenly couldn't speak. Mae must have guessed, because she sailed in to make the third point, speaking as though they had planned it exactly this way.

"Whether Mimi's or Frannie's wins today, we want to introduce everyone to the Chicken Sisters, our new joint venture. From now on, whether you eat at Frannie's or Mimi's, you'll know you're getting *Food Wars*–winning fried chicken and service as we take what we've learned from working with Sabrina and Chefs Cary, James, and Simon and apply it on both sides of town." Mae smiled out over the sign, which held Amanda's drawing of two chickens, wings around each other in perfect harmony.

Sabrina's eyes narrowed, but she beamed as though all *Food Wars* had ever wanted was to become *Food Peace*. "Still, there's a verdict coming, and a winner to declare before you all skip off into the sunset." She turned. "Judges, are you ready?"

From the chefs' table, Simon Rideaux stood and clapped his hands, drawing everyone's attention, as he no doubt meant to. "We're ready, Sabrina," he announced, and pointed to his fellow judges. This would be the infamous vote.

Sabrina struck a pose and pointed. "Cary Catlin, let's start with you. Who's the winner of this Food War?"

"Mimi's," said Cary Catlin, and Amanda froze. It didn't matter. Of course it didn't matter. She cast a glance over at Nancy and saw that she, at least, was managing to look as though it really didn't matter, although Barbara was beaming and Frankie looked so much like she would cry that it was all Amanda could do not to rush over to her.

Sabrina pointed again. "James Melville, your vote?"

"Frannie's."

The room seemed to hold its breath. Rideaux would decide it, then. *It doesn't matter, it doesn't matter,* she told herself—but her racing heart and pounding head were telling her that it did.

Rideaux smiled straight into the camera and raised his eyebrows—then turned to Amanda. "You," he said. "Does this mean chicken will be your life, then?"

Shocked, Amanda let her mouth drop open, then shut it with a quick breath. *What?* He was supposed to say who won, and instead— he was waiting, a challenge in his eyes.

Amanda met them and was surprised to feel support, not ridicule, there. But Sabrina, who followed up, had mockery in her tone. "Yes, Amanda, does this mean you've decided to stick to chicken after all?"

No, you witch, it does not. Amanda spoke to Rideaux, ignoring Sabrina. "No," she said. "I'm going back to school." She pointed to the sign, which still filled her with pride. "That's my contribution for now. Mae, Nancy, my mom, and Andy are going to run the show." With Jay as executive producer, but they had decided no one needed to know that. Why complicate things? "There will be plenty of time to sort out what happens after that." After she graduated. After she finished what she started. After she made some choices of her own.

"Excellent," he said. "Well, we've discussed it among ourselves." He glanced at his fellow judges, and they nodded. "We'd like to do something new and offer your new venture—the Chicken Sisters— our ideas for taking the best of both Frannie's and Mimi's."

Amanda didn't think he was done, but Sabrina managed to cut him off, holding up her hands as though besieged on all sides. "Hold on, hold on," she said. "This clearly means great things to come, but first, we need to declare our actual victor. Will it be Frannie's? Or will it be Mimi's? Will the sister returning from Brooklyn and bringing New York flair to her small-town roots triumph, or will it have paid to stay home and build a business and a life here in Merinac from the very beginning? Simon, your vote?"

He grinned, clearly enjoying himself. "The winner is"—big pause—"everybody. Just as Amanda said."

Sabrina stared at him, then quickly gathered her face together and turned to the camera. "More when we come back." She beamed, holding her pose for one short interval, then dropped both the hand holding the microphone and her delighted expression.

"What the fuck is this?" She turned on Amanda and Mae, then on Simon Rideaux. "This is not how we end *Food Wars,* and this is not what you signed up for. What was all that yesterday, if you're all lovey-dovey today? What the hell kind of *Food Wars* ends up in a truce? Simon, you do not abstain. You vote, and somebody wins. That's the deal."

Rideaux stepped up and put an arm around Sabrina's shoulders, and suddenly Amanda knew something she had not known before. She raised her eyebrows at Mae, who nodded confirmation. They were together, Sabrina and Simon. That didn't really explain anything, but it was somehow satisfying. No one deserved each other more.

"Now, love," he said, and Sabrina kicked him in the shin.

"Don't 'now, love' me," she said. "We can start this over, and we can do it right, because you all agreed to provide conflict, and conflict is *Food Wars'* bread and butter. I don't care what stupid shit you do on your own time. You can nail your two crappy chicken shacks together, for all I care. But this is not what the network wants, and it's not what we're giving them."

Jay stepped forward, smiling as though he wanted nothing more than to meet a famous television personality having a tantrum worthy of a three-year-old. "Sabrina, so nice to meet you." He extended his hand, and Sabrina took it as if she didn't know why she was doing it. "I'm Jay Mallick, Mae's husband. I thought you might be a little distraught that things aren't working out as you'd planned, so I went ahead and took a look at the contracts the participants signed with the network before filming. You, of course, have the right to frame the footage you record into any narrative you wish. But there's no requirement that anyone here will do anything specific in the way of continuing a conflict or not."

Sabrina turned, furious, to her head cameraman. "Is this true? Do we need to double-check this?"

"It's true, love," purred Simon, although he took a step away from Sabrina's stilettos as he spoke.

"Confirmed," agreed Gordo, remaining safely behind the camera. "They do what they do, we get to film it, you get to cut it however you want. That's the deal."

"That's the deal," said Sabrina, sticking out her perfect bottom lip and tapping her shoe thoughtfully. "From their contracts. Which I had nothing to do with. And Simon? Doesn't he have to vote? I thought he had to vote."

"I'll worry about me, love," Simon said.

"Well, then." Sabrina shook her head a little, curls bouncing, and turned back to Mae and Amanda, this time with that same old friendly smile, so perfectly brought off that Amanda nearly stepped backward in shock. "You took me by surprise, but that's fine. We'll make this work. No, we'll make it great. Why don't you all come up here together, in front of the chefs' table." She stepped back and had a look, then began arranging them as though into a family portrait, tucking Jay unobtrusively behind Mae and moving Andy between Mae and Amanda with a wink, moving Nancy over to Mae's other side and bringing Barbara to stand next to Amanda, then flanking them all with Gus and Frankie.

"Wait," she said, and turned to one of the many minions just off-stage. "There were other kids, right? Get the other kids." Amanda saw Mae glance quickly at Jay, and he shrugged as Jessa handed

Ryder to him as Madison, released from behind the cameras, ran to her mother. Sabrina surveyed the girl critically, and Mae smoothed the hair that was so like hers and placed her daughter on her hip.

"Perfect," said Sabrina. "If you're going to do it this way, we're going to make it look good. Just one minute." She stepped away, took her bag off a table, and began the now-familiar routine of freshening her lips and makeup. Mae took a lipstick from her own pocket with her free hand and did the same, then passed it to Amanda, who hesitated.

"It's just a tinted balm," Mae said. "You can't do it wrong."

Amanda smeared it over her own lips, capped it, and then—why not?—handed it to Barbara, who took it even more reluctantly than her younger daughter had.

"Go ahead, Mom," Mae urged.

Frankie took the balm, smiling. "Hold still, Grandma," she said. "It will just look nice. Brighten you up a little."

Barbara submitted, then turned back to Amanda, looking over at Sabrina. "She's not ready yet?"

"No," Amanda said. "She takes a while."

"Hmm. Not a natural beauty, then." Barbara smiled, and Amanda, a little tentative, smiled back, and, as their eyes met, laughed.

"Nope." Amanda laughed, too. She felt warmer toward Sabrina than she had in days; she might be an asshole, but she was clearly surrounded by them as well. Better her than Amanda.

"Her and Mae," said Barbara, shaking her head. "All this complication. Not like you and me."

You and me. Amanda nodded, conscious of the cameras, wanting to hug her mother but not quite sure they were ready. She put out her hand instead, and Barbara took it. But her mother was still looking at Amanda as though she wanted to say something. "What?"

Amanda rubbed her finger over her front teeth. "Did I get that stuff on me?"

"No," said Barbara. "No, not that. It's just—I was wondering if you wanted a puppy."

"Oh—" Now Amanda did hug her mother. Hard, and probably smearing lip balm, or whatever, all over her shoulder. "Yes. Yes, I do want a puppy."

Sabrina swirled back into their midst, pointing them back into their places, then went to stand between Simon and Cary. "Let's turn this into good television, people."

Sabrina held her practiced pause, bringing on that manufactured smile, but it was Mae who jumped in one last time, stepping out in front before Sabrina could even draw in a breath. With the faintest, fastest possible glance back at Amanda, Mae shot a wholly genuine grin at the camera and spoke. "And, we're back."

ACKNOWLEDGMENTS

I'm not going to lie, I thought about not having any acknowledgments. The risk, no, the probability that I will leave someone out is overwhelming. How can you thank everyone who makes it possible to do work you love? Start with the carpool and go from there, I guess.

Thank you to everyone who drove any member of my family anywhere ever, especially during NaNoWriMo 2017, when I first drafted this book, or over the next year and a half, when I was madly revising it. And thanks to those who helped mightily in that revision process, in particular my agent, Caryn Karmatz Rudy, and Jennie Nash and the Author Accelerator team. Down the road, thank you to beta readers Sarina Bowen, Lisa Belkin, and Wendi Aarons.

Thank you to Margo Lipschultz, who is proof positive that editing is alive and well and who made this whole story—as well as writing it—much more fun, and to her entire team at G. P. Putnam's Sons, whose enthusiasm for "the chicken book" brought me much joy. You're just the right number of cooks in this kitchen.

Into the writing of any book some rain must fall, and in the summer of 2019 I was diagnosed with breast cancer. There is nothing about that sentence that is not a cliché, but none of it felt like a cliché at the time. Thank you to the doctors, nurses, and radiation therapists at the Norris Cotton Cancer Center at Dartmouth-Hitchcock for being relentlessly and rightly optimistic, even when it must have been obvious that I was not entirely receptive to your good cheer, and for, we all hope, so thoroughly removing all traces of cancer that I will never again fall into your clutches. Thank you to Dwight Sperry and Kimberley Moran for providing unexpected support when I answered the question "How are you?" too honestly; to Mimi and Jason Lichtenstein (and Trevor) for striking just the right balance between understanding and distraction; to Kendall Hoyt for many much-needed walks, and to Sheryl Stotland, Nancy Davis Kho, Mary Laura Philpott, and Liz McGuire for being Team KJ in the form of cards and gifts and snark. That's my love language, crew.

Thank you, too, to our Spanish family, Eva, Miguel, Ici, and Paula, for becoming such a joyful part of our life during that strange season; to Holly and to Judi, Nick, Natalie, Kira, and Tia for putting family and friends above everything else; and to Kristyn, Greg, Lyn, and Brittney for doing a whole lot of farmwork so that I wouldn't have to.

Thank you, Mom and Dad, for never, ever not encouraging me in following this inexplicable career path, for supporting me at every turn and reading every word, although when it comes to that terrible novel draft from 2011, I really wish you wouldn't. And thank you, Mom, for resisting the urge to tell me the real story behind Chicken Annie's and Chicken Mary's. I guess it's okay now.

Thank you to Jess and Sarah. I probably could do it without you two, but I wouldn't really want to.

And thank you to the best possible husband and partner for me, Rob. I'm still sorry about your baseball glove. Finally, thank you to Sam, Lily, Rory, and Wyatt for apparently just accepting that some days, the people in my laptop would be as real to me as the ones outside it. I hope you all know there is no one more real, or more important, than you.